ADOBE MOON

Eric Wilder

Gondwana Press

Copyright © 2026 Gary Pittenger

All rights reserved

The characters and events portrayed in this book are fictitious. Any similarity to real persons, living or dead, is coincidental and not intended by the author.

No part of this book may be reproduced, or stored in a retrieval system, or transmitted in any form or by any means, electronic, mechanical, photocopying, recording, or otherwise, without express written permission of the publisher.

ISBN-13: 9781946576293
ASIN : B0FKRDQJRV

Cover design by: Gondwana Graphics
Printed in the United States of America

For Anne

PROLOG

The setting sun west of Taos cast a molten glow across the high desert, painting the sagebrush and piñon pines in shades of amber and gold. The vast expanse shimmered with heat, the air thick with the scent of dust and destiny.

Jagged silhouettes of the Sangre de Cristo Mountains rose in the distance, their peaks catching the last fiery rays, glowing like embers against the deepening indigo sky. A soft breeze stirred, carrying the faint howl of a coyote, as the desert seemed to hold its breath in the twilight's embrace.

Elena Tafoya, a Tiwa elder with silver-streaked hair woven into a tight braid, sat cross-legged on a woven blanket near the center of the base camp, her weathered hands moving through the air as if greeting the ancients. Beside her, Anna Luna, with her vivid brown eyes contrasting a cascade of chestnut hair, adjusted a powerful telescope aimed at the petroglyphs carved into a nearby basalt outcrop.

The base camp was a tidy oasis of purpose amid the wild expanse of northern New Mexico. A sturdy canvas tent stood staked against the wind, its open flap revealing rolled sleeping bags and a neatly arranged propane stove.

Anna's dust-streaked ATV sat parked next to a stack of gear: sketchbooks, a leather-bound journal, and Elena's ceremonial herbs and prayer bundles. A low fire pit crackled, smoke curling upward like an offering, while Fetch, Anna's dog, lay curled nearby, ears twitching at distant sounds.

As dusk settled, Elena hummed a low Tiwa chant, her voice blending with the desert's nocturnal rustle, while Anna sketched a spiral petroglyph, her pencil scratching softly. Elena's calloused fingers traced a spiral sun, its rays curling into a starburst—the mark of the Sky People, her grandmother had called it.

"The petroglyphs are incredible," Anna said, her voice soft with awe. "What is their meaning?"

Elena's weathered face softened. "They tell of the Sky People. Long ago, my people saw lights descend from the stars. Beings who taught us to plant corn, to read the heavens. My grandmother said they'd return when the earth needed their wisdom."

Anna's pencil stilled. "Like the stories in town—lights over Pot Mountain, the Taos Hum. You think they're connected?"

Elena's lips tightened. "The Hum's been here since I was a girl. Some call it spirits, others machines. I only know what the desert tells me." She gestured to the petroglyphs. "These are our truths, not the stories outsiders chase."

They settled on the blanket, the sand cool beneath them, and closed their eyes to meditate. Elena's voice guided Anna.

"Breathe with the earth. Listen to the stars."

The desert's silence deepened, but the Hum pulsed stronger, vibrating in Anna's chest. Her mind drifted, imagining a painting of stars spiraling into adobe shadows. A sudden flicker broke her trance.

The petroglyphs shimmered, their lines bending as if melting. Anna blinked, her vision swimming.

"Elena," she said. "Do you see that?"

Elena's eyes snapped open. The basalt outcrop flickered, its surface briefly translucent, revealing a glimpse of alien stars before snapping back to stone.

"The earth is unsteady," she said.

The air grew heavy, the Hum now a teeth-rattling buzz. Anna's sketchbook trembled, the pencil lines warping into impossible spirals. A cactus nearby twisted, its spines glinting like crystal, then reverted. Gravity tugged sideways; Anna's water bottle rolled uphill before stopping.

"Elena, what's happening?"

Anna's voice shook, her senses assaulted by a high-pitched

whine. Colors bled into the sky—violet streaks pulsing unnaturally.

Elena clutched her prayer bundle, her face pale. "The veil is thin. Something's breaking through."

Time stuttered. The fire pit flared, flames briefly turning blue. Fetch whined, fur bristling as he stared at the mesa. The air over it rippled like liquid glass. A jagged tear split the sky, leaking a pulsing blue glow.

Anna's head throbbed. Flashes hit her—memories of places she'd never been, faces unknown. A wave of longing struck, homesickness for somewhere beyond the stars.

"Elena, I feel... so strange."

Elena's eyes were distant. "Whatever's happening, it's touching your mind, pulling at your spirit. Don't let it take you."

The ground trembled, a localized quake rattling the camp. A fissure snaked through the sand, glowing faintly with iridescent minerals. The air crackled with plasma, arcs dancing over the ATV.

Then, a silver disc emerged from the tear, its surface reflecting the desert like a liquid mirror. A spotlight swept the ground, riveting their attention. Anna's skin prickled, colors too vivid, sounds too sharp. Elena's braid lifted slightly as gravity faltered.

Two figures appeared in the beam, tall and humanoid, grayish skin shimmering, eyes like onyx. They carried a glowing orb, its surface swirling with patterns that whispered. Anna felt it in her mind—a warning, images of cities crumbling, skies torn open, the desert consumed by chaos. The figures tilted their heads, then levitated into the disc, the orb vanishing with them.

The saucer's hum spiked, a sonic boom cracking as it shot skyward, the tear sealing behind it. The desert fell still, the Taos Hum fading. Anna's migraine eased, but her hands shook as she grabbed her sketchbook, sketching the orb's glow; its warning burned into her mind.

"Elena... was that the Sky People?"

Elena stared at the horizon, her face unreadable. "They must be here for a reason."

"What reason?" Anna asked.

"I don't know."

She pointed toward the petroglyphs, steadying herself. But as she knelt to touch the ground near the fissure, her fingers brushed something half-buried in the sand—a weathered leather-bound notebook, no larger than her palm, its cover etched with faint petroglyph-like symbols that pulsed once before dimming. She hadn't seen it before the tremor occurred. Maybe the Sky People had left it, she thought, or the earth had yielded it up in their passing.

Elena unwrapped the outer hide carefully, revealing pages of aged paper inscribed in ancient Navajo script—Diné bizaad—interspersed with star charts and precise diagrams of a strange device. It looked like something that Galileo had dreamed up and then sketched.

Her grandmother's warnings echoed: Some gifts from the stars must be hidden, guarded by those who remember the old ways. Heart pounding, Elena tucked the notebook deep into her prayer bundle.

"What is it?" Anna asked.

"Nothing," Elena said with a shake of her head.

"You put something in your prayer bundle," Anna said.

"Something the world isn't ready for," Elena said.

"Like what?" Anna asked.

"I don't know. Something dangerous the Sky People chose for only me to see."

"What do you intend to do with it?" Anna asked.

"A question I can't answer," Elena said. "Please, let me deal with it for now."

Anna shook her head. "Show me," she said.

Elena was hesitant but handed the leather-bound notebook to Anna. Fetch moved closer, and Elena waited as Anna examined it.

"What the hell is this?" she asked.

"Something we were chosen to see," Elena said.

"But why?"

"We aren't here randomly," Elena said. "We witnessed this phenomenon for a reason: you to sketch what you saw and me to protect this artifact."

Anna nodded as Elena stowed the notebook in her prayer bundle, and her pencil began to move furiously, capturing the orb, the figures, the tear. The stars burned brighter, but the shadows deepened. A coyote howled, and Anna felt the weight of a truth too vast to hold, the desert shouting a chaotic secret that could swallow it all.

Anna and Elena weren't the only ones in the high desert that night; a drone flew overhead, circling several times before disappearing over a distant mesa. Something else had watched the scene. High above them, a reconnaissance balloon captured video of the chaotic event.

CHAPTER 1

A gentle rain fell in lazy drops, softly pattering against the cracked sidewalks of downtown Tulsa. Late September had finally broken the summer's grip on the land, with the heat wave retreating for another year.

The air carried that wet-earth smell, mixing with the faint tang of oil from the street and the neon hum of the city waking up for the night. I splashed through shallow puddles, making my way down Boston Avenue, with my shirt collar turned up against the drizzle.

Tulsa's skyline, a jagged mix of art deco relics and glass towers, reflected the fading light. I hurried past the Philtower Building, its gothic spires cutting through the mist, and dodged a couple of hipsters in psychedelic T-shirts hustling toward some craft brewery.

Sidewalk traffic was subdued, the rain keeping the usual Friday night chaos in check. A young man with a guitar huddled under an awning, his mournful chords curling through the damp air. I tossed a crumpled five into his open case, earning a nod as I kept moving.

I was looking for a bar called The Rusty Nail, a quirky joint tucked between a vintage record store and a tattoo parlor that probably smelled faintly of regret.

The Rusty Nail's sign flickered in red neon, the "T" half-burned out, giving it a lopsided grin. I pushed through the heavy oak door, and a wave of cold air hit me, thick with the scent of whiskey, fried onions, and old wood.

The place was a surreal jumble of mismatched decor—velvet paintings of Elvis and unicorns hung beside taxidermy fish, and strings of Christmas lights draped lazily over exposed brick walls. A jukebox in the corner played some outlaw country tune, competing with the low hum of conversation and the clink of glasses—a classic dive bar right in the heart of downtown Tulsa.

When my eyes adjusted to the old bar's dim glow, I scanned the room—a Friday night destination half-full with a mix of grizzled regulars, artsy types with eccentric mustaches, and a few suits slumming it for the vibe. I saw the people I was there to meet tucked in a shadowy corner booth.

Jake Huntington, reality TV's own Cryptid Hunter, his face lit by the flicker of a candle in a mason jar. Across from him sat Colley Hornbeck, his chopper pilot, a wiry guy with graying hair that was a little too long for his age, and a grin that said he'd seen too many close calls to care.

I weaved past the bartender, shaking a cocktail as if he were auditioning for Broadway. When Jake saw me and waved, I smiled, signaling I'd seen them.

Stately gray peppered Jake's movie star haircut. He was tall and slender, his white linen blazer, light blue shirt, and khakis further imparting his aging movie star vibe. When I reached the booth, he smiled and shook my hand.

"Where's Mama Mulate?" I asked.

Mama Mulate was Jake's significant other, and they were ideally suited for each other. Both were middle-aged, attractive, and highly intelligent. Mama held a PhD in English and taught at Tulane. Since she was also an authentic voodoo mambo, she led a double life—a match made in heaven for billionaire cryptid hunter Jake Huntington.

"New Orleans," he said. "Tulane's school year is cranking up. We're apart for a while."

"Got to hand it to you, Jake. This place is a pleasant surprise. You didn't pick it just for me, did you?"

He chuckled. "Thought you'd like it. We were beginning to wonder if you were going to make it."

"Sorry about that. I came by way of old Route 66. When nature called, I stopped at an Indian casino and wound up playing a few hands of blackjack."

Colley said, "What did she look like?"

I grinned and said, "Colley, you know me too well. The dealer was a dark-haired beauty named Laura with big brown eyes and a killer smile. We have a date tomorrow night."

"Cancel it," Jake said. "You'll be nowhere near here tomorrow."

Jake nodded when I said, "You have a job for me?"

"A possible new episode of Cryptid Hunter. I want you to scout it out; see if it's a viable idea."

"Tell me what's on your mind," I said.

Outside, the storm had intensified, the lights flickering when thunder shook the walls. Two new customers came through the front door, laughing and shaking off the rain.

Jake tapped his cell phone, pulling up a news video. "Ever hear of Kirsten Louise Maldonado?"

"Can't say as I have," I said.

"Congresswoman from New Mexico. Check out a few snippets from this podcast."

Congresswoman Maldonado was a striking woman in her thirties, with dark eyes and hair that brushed against her blouse. Turquoise earrings and a squash blossom necklace complemented her style. The video had already started, and the first words I heard were "interdimensional beings." When the video ended, I looked at Jake with a confused expression.

"What the hell was that about?" I asked.

"Seems Congresswoman Maldonado believes in beings who inhabit other dimensions and is suggesting our government has proof of their existence."

"Nothing new," I said. "UFO conspiracy theories have floated around for decades."

"UFOs are old news," Jake said. "The congresswoman is talking about UAPs, unidentified anomalous phenomena. Beings that occupy the same space but in a different dimension."

"Where are you going with this?" I asked.

Jake pulled up a picture on his phone: a painting: a glowing orb, its surface swirling like a galaxy trapped in glass. The image hit me like a punch—too vivid, too strange.

"A poster from some sci-fi movie?" I said.

"An eyewitness account captured in colored pencils," Jake said. "Taos, New Mexico." His voice dropped to a conspiratorial hush. "A famous artist—think O'Keeffe with a cosmic twist—sent this to a gallery buddy who owes me favors.

"You're saying this drawing is an account of something the artist saw?" I asked.

"She saw something—a flying saucer, up close and personal. And she wasn't alone—Elena Tafoya, an Indian elder, and Tiwa medicine woman, backed up her story. This could be cryptid hunter gold or just another hoax. I want you to find out."

"You chasing Roswell now?"

The word Roswell carried weight, conjuring headlines of crashed discs and government lies. Experience had taught me to tread lightly around the unexplainable, but aliens? That was a stretch, even for Jake.

"Not just UFOs," Jake said, undeterred, his fingers dancing over his phone keyboard.

A photo flashed up—a Taos desert under starlight, petroglyphs carved into basalt, their spirals glowing faintly. He handed me the phone—a picture of a handsome American Indian woman.

"Elena Tafoya?" I said.

Jake nodded. "She was with Anna Luna ad not only saw what she saw, but also experienced the same phenomena."

"What phenomena?" I asked.

"I don't know," Jake said. "In an interview with a local TV station, Ms. Tafoya claimed to have seen and experienced things that defied reality."

"Maybe she's a crackpot," I said.

"I don't think so," Jake said. "She says what she and Anna Luna saw and experienced is tied to her people's stories—Sky People, some ancient mumbo-jumbo. Luna's sketch matches what they claim to have seen: a disc, a spotlight, and these...

things carrying that orb."

"Interesting," I said. "I presume this is all tied to my assignment?"

Jake nodded again. "Go to Taos, talk with Anna Luna and Elena Tafoya. Poke around, see if what they allege is legit."

Before I could reply, a smiling waitress with blond hair cascading down her back appeared at our table with fresh drinks for Jake and Colley. Her smile grew brighter when she saw me.

"Hi, cowboy," she said. "I'm Stormy. What's your name?"

Jake and Colley were both grinning, and I said, "Buck. You're the sweetest piece of eye candy I've seen in a while."

She was dressed in satin shorts and a sleeveless white T-shirt, like a Hooters girl with a white Stetson and cowboy boots. Before I could react, she straddled me in the booth and gave me a hug that I wouldn't forget for a long time.

"You're the sweet one, cowboy," she said.

"Stormy," I said. "You smell fantastic."

"Better tell me what you're drinking, Buck, before I get ideas."

"Coors, can, no frosted mug," I said.

"Too bad my shift just started," she said. "You'd be in trouble."

"I can wait," I said.

Jake and Colley were probably blushing, though the light was too dim to see.

"No, he can't," Jake said. "Mr. McDivit will be out of town shortly."

"Spoil sport," she said as she pranced away from the table.

Jake and Colley were both shaking their heads when I said, "Now, what were we talking about?"

"You know, Buck," Jake said. "Some race horses need to be gelded before they can reach their full potential."

By now, Jake and Colley were both laughing and exchanging high-fives. Jake pulled a hundred-dollar bill from his shirt pocket and handed it to Colley.

"You two set me up, didn't you?" I said.

"Colley bet me a hundred bucks you'd have our waitress in your lap before the night was over," Jake said. "You surprised both of us."

I crossed my arms, my boots scuffing the polished floor.

"Damn!" I said. "Some people get no respect."

"Get your panties out of a wad," Jake said. "I need you to scout Taos for me. Find out about the orb, the ETs, and the phenomena Elena claims to have experienced."

"And if they're a hoax? Or some military stunt? New Mexico's crawling with bases—Los Alamos, Sandia. Could be a drone, not ET."

Jake leaned back. "That's why I pay you the big bucks, McDivit. Sniff out the truth, but make it sexy for the cameras. Meet Anna and Elena, get their story, find me something tangible—debris, witnesses, anything. You in?"

"My dance cards open. When do I start?"

Now. I've booked you on a flight to Albuquerque at midnight. A driver will pick you up and take you to Taos. I've got you scheduled at the Palacio de Marquesa."

Jake's smile disappeared when I said, "No can do."

"Why not? You just said your dance card's open."

"I've stayed at the Palacio before," I said. "I love the place. It's truly a palace, but I'm not sure how long this assignment will take, and I want to bring my horse and dog."

Jake and Colley exchanged a glance as Jake slid out of the booth.

"I'll call Angie to see what she can line up," he said.

When Colley and I were alone, he asked, "How did your Vegas trip go?"

"Best time I ever had," I said. "Tess and me, our dogs and horses, rodeoing, gambling, and non-stop fun. I was sorry to see it end."

"Don't see a ring on your finger," he said.

"Or through my nose. Tess landed a filming gig with National Geographic. She's off to the Antarctic for six months."

"Good for her," Colley said. "That girl has talent. Jake wanted to keep her, but even his money wasn't good enough."

Stormy interrupted us with more drinks before I could reply.

"Can't believe you're leaving town just when I was getting to know you," she said.

Her smile grew wider when I said, "Plans change. I'm not leaving town until tomorrow."

She crawled into the booth again, straddling me and covering my face with kisses.

"I clock out at eleven," she said. "Don't you dare go anywhere."

When Jake returned to the booth, Colley held out his hand.

"What?" Jake asked.

"You owe me another hundred bucks."

"Was Stormy in Buck's lap again?"

"Hell, Jake, she was all over him. Would have made a blind man blush," Colley said.

Jake shook his head as he handed Colley another hundred.

"Angie's on it," he said. "Taos is crowded with tourists this time of year, but if anyone can find you, your horse, and dog a place to stay there, it's Angie."

Earlier in the summer, we'd wrapped an episode of Cryptid Hunter on pollution and a mysterious shadow in Picher, Oklahoma. It was the first time I'd worked with Jake since leading a Bigfoot expedition for him in the wilds of eastern Oklahoma.

"I never had a chance to meet Angie when we were working on the Picher episode," I said.

"She's a gem," Jake said. "Harvard MBA and works harder than any dock hand."

Angie soon joined us, peering through the bar's dimness until she saw where we were sitting. She flashed me a smile as she scooted into the booth beside me. She was nothing as I had expected, her African braids and café-au-lait complexion screaming Creole heritage. I whistled.

"Jake told me how smart you are," I said. "He didn't bother telling me that you are also drop-dead gorgeous."

Angie was smiling when she said, "That's sexist, you know?"

Jake's smile was gone. "Angie's off limits," he said. "She's engaged."

"Not anymore," Angie said. "Bradley and I are separated."

"Oh?" Jake said.

"Private story, Mr. Nosy," Angie said. "I'm free again, not white, as they say, but well over twenty-one. I don't see a ring on Buck's finger, and if he wants to flirt with me, well... it's helping my bruised ego right about now."

She nodded when I said, "You caught your boyfriend messing with another woman?"

"Red-handed," she said.

She grinned when I said, "Hate it when that happens."

Everyone at the table was smiling when Stormy appeared to take Angie's drink order—everyone except Stormy. She motioned for me to join her in a dark corner.

"You didn't tell me you have a date," she said.

"Angie? We only just met," I said. "She works for Jake."

"She's practically sitting in your lap," Stormy said.

"She's feeling insecure. Just broke up with her boyfriend," I said.

Angie was wearing low-rider jeans and a yellow sports bra. To say she stood out was an understatement.

"Bet she's a great dancer with legs like hers," Stormy said.

Stormy's smile returned when I said, "You like line-dancing?"

"My second favorite thing," she said with a wink. "Ever been to the Whiskey and Diamonds Ballroom?"

"No, though I'd love to," I said.

"Ask Angie to join us," Stormy said. "The three of us can line dance together."

"Trouble in paradise?" Colley asked when I slid into the booth.

"What's life without a few complications?" I said with a grin.

Angie's eyes rolled. "I have you booked at a boarding ranch west of Taos," she said. "The Double Moon Ranch. It features rustic charm, horse stables, log cabins with kiva fireplaces, and some eerie undertones. I've arranged for you to stay in the Starlight Cabin, a one-bedroom retreat with a wide porch overlooking the mountains. Dogs and cats are welcome."

"Love it," I said. "You sound like a tour guide."

"Just quoting from their website," she said. "Wish I were going with you. It's lonely since Brad and I split the sheets."

She smiled when I asked, "You like line dancing?"

"My second favorite thing," she said.

CHAPTER 2

Road trips are fun, especially when you have someone to share them with. My dog, Pard, was snoring softly in the back seat, and wasn't much of a companion. The endless miles along the dull interstate highway were getting tiresome.

I'd made the drive from Oklahoma City to the Texas border along I-40 more times than I could count, and the trip ranged from dull to downright mind-numbing. The only thing keeping me sane was the awesome stereo system in the lime green Jeep Gladiator Jake had given me before I left Tulsa.

There's nothing in the high desert of New Mexico except cactus, rattlesnakes, and solitude," he'd said. "The Jeep will get you there and back. You're going to need it."

Jake's prediction was ominous, though, so far, except for the boredom, it seemed like a walk in the park. The Gladiator wasn't the only thing Jake gave me. I also had a new laptop fully loaded with tons of information about Taos, New Mexico, and the surrounding area. I had peeked at the database before leaving Tulsa and found it almost as overwhelming as the trip from OKC to the Texas border.

The database was provided by Jake's gorgeous assistant, Angie, and I'd learned during our night of boot-scooting that research wasn't her only talent. She and Stormy were incredible, both beautiful and polished dancers.

That wasn't the only thing they shared. Both were emerging from broken relationships, which meant trouble. To put it mildly, I was eager to get out of Dodge. When my cell phone rang, and I saw it was Angie, I answered on speakerphone with a bit of apprehension.

"You got away without saying bye, cowboy," she said.

"Sorry about that," I said. "I had to pick up my horse and dog in Oklahoma City, and Jake was eager for me to get on the road."

"No problem," she said. "I had a wonderful time, and I wanted to thank you."

"No need to thank me," I said. "I had the time of my life."

"We both did, and so did Stormy. Thanks for introducing us."

"Our date was kind of awkward, and I'm glad everything worked out," I said.

Since breaking up with Bradley and moving from New Orleans to Tulsa, I've experienced the loneliest days of my life. Meeting Stormy has changed that."

"Wonderful," I said.

"We have so much more in common than line dancing. She's attending the University of Tulsa part-time, working on her MBA, and we work out at the same gym."

"Awesome," I said.

"That isn't the only reason I called," she said. "I did some research on the Double Moon Ranch, the place where you're staying."

"Hit me," I said.

"Randle Roberts owns the place, married to a Navajo woman named Rita. Randle is neither American Indian nor from New Mexico."

"Oh?" I said.

"He's from Michigan and has double Master's degrees in Nuclear Engineering and Radiological Sciences."

"Interesting," I said. "How did he get to New Mexico, and why is he running a tourist ranch?"

"Very interesting," she said. "There's no record of him working for the government at either Sandia or Los Alamos, either as a full-time employee or as a government contractor."

"But?" I said.

"Rumors and innuendoes, nothing concrete, tying him to Area 51," Angie said. "That's not all. His mother-in-law, Lily, is full-blooded Navajo and suffers from a malady known as moth madness."

"What does that mean?" I asked.

"Buck, she's a witch."

"A real witch?" I said.

"Don't know, but I have a feeling you're about to find out," she said.

"Thanks, Angie, I'll keep my eyes open,"

"You're welcome. I'll keep digging. And Buck..."

"Yes?"

"Stormy and I can't wait until you're back in Tulsa so we can all go boot scooting again."

I was happy for Angie and glad she wasn't mad at me for leaving Tulsa in such a rush. I was also more than eager to finish my time on I-40. When I exited the federal highway at Elk City and took TX 152-W, heading northwest toward Taos. The New Mexico sun burned like a furnace, its glare bouncing off the windshield of Jake's Jeep. Pard awoke with a start when I turned the radio to a country station and began singing off-key.

The horse trailer rattled behind me, Lady nickering now and then, her impatience matching my own after hours on the road. Pard sprawled across the passenger seat, his Australian sheepdog ears twitching at every strange sound.

Oklahoma's endless plains—miles of wheat and red dirt that stretched so wide you could see forever—were long gone. Out here, the land was wild, alive, almost defiant. The Sangre de Cristo Mountains loomed ahead, their jagged peaks clawing at a turquoise sky, snow dusting their tips even in late September.

Sagebrush and twisted piñon pines dotted the high desert, casting sharp shadows across red-dirt trails that snaked into nowhere. The air was crisp, smelling of juniper and dust, nothing like Tulsa's humid streets.

I gripped the wheel, my Stetson tilted back, taking in the raw beauty. Back home, the land's so flat you can spot trouble from a county away. Here, the desert folded into itself—mesas rising like ancient castles, arroyos cutting deep scars through the earth.

The mountains seemed to watch me, their rocky faces hiding secrets far older than humanity. Pard lifted his head, growling low, as if hearing a coyote's faint howl echoing through a canyon.

"Easy, Pard," I said, scratching his neck. "This isn't Oklahoma anymore."

The road to Taos twisted through valleys where cottonwoods blazed gold, their leaves dancing in the breeze. I passed a roadside stand with strings of dried chiles glowing like embers and an old adobe church, its bell silent but likely heavy with stories.

A low hum pulsed in my ears—the Taos Hum, Jake had called it—like the desert itself was breathing. I shook it off, blaming the long drive, but Pard's tense stare out the window told me he felt it too.

Cresting a rise, I spotted the Double Moon Ranch nestled in a valley where the desert met the foothills. A weathered sign swung at the entrance: "Double Moon Ranch: Horses, Hounds, and Home."

According to its website, the place sprawled across two hundred acres of sagebrush and juniper, with red-dirt trails winding toward cliffs carved with petroglyphs. Cedar stables stood sturdy against the wind, flanked by log rental cabins with tin roofs glinting in the sun.

Smoke curled from a kiva chimney, and the sweet scent of piñon wood drifted through the air. My first thought was that this place was caught between worlds—cozy as a campfire yet humming with something eerie, as if the land were holding its breath.

I eased the Jeep down the gravel drive, dust kicking up red in the sunlight. A tall man stepped out from the ranch office, broad shoulders filling a flannel shirt, gray hair swept back like a silver-maned lion.

Randle Roberts, I figured, meeting his piercing gray eyes as he offered a handshake that could crush walnuts.

"Buck McDivit?" His voice was gravelly, like he'd smoked his way through a few too many desert nights. "I'm Randle Roberts, and you've reached your destination, the Double Moon Ranch."

"Pleased to meet you, Mr. Roberts," I said, tipping my hat.

"Just Randle," he said. "Welcome to Double Moon."

"Happy to be here," I said. "I'm curious. Where did the name of your ranch come from?"

Randle chuckled and said, "My wife, Rita, is half Navajo. She named it. Comes from a rare lunar event the founders witnessed—a blood moon paired with a faint second halo—said to bless the land with strange energies."

"These mountains are epic, your ranch a gem," I said. "I feel as if I'm in another world, and I should have known the name had something to do with American Indian cultural mysticism."

"From your dark hair and eyes, you look as if you might be part Indian yourself," he said.

"Cherokee," I said. "It usually ends up getting me into more trouble than the other way around."

"I hear that," he said. "Heard you're here with a horse and dog."

"Yessir," I said. "This is Pard, and Lady's in the trailer. Appreciate you taking us in on such short notice."

"Our pleasure," he said. "Always happy to accommodate, and your boss's assistant, Angie, is persuasive."

"That she is," I said with a knowing grin.

Randle's gaze flicked to the trailer, then back to me, a glint in his eyes like he was sizing up more than just a cowboy.

"Long haul from Oklahoma, huh? You'll find this place... different. Let's get your girl settled."

Before I could answer, a young woman strode from the stables, her jet-black hair catching the light like a raven's wing.

"I'm Tara," she said. "You must be Buck."

She grinned when I said, "Yes, ma'am."

"Never been called ma'am before," she said. "I'm only twenty."

Twenty maybe, but Tara Roberts was every bit a woman and

moved like she could outride a twister. Her denim shirt was rolled to the elbows, her boots scuffed from hard miles, and her worn Levis were so tight I wondered how she had gotten into them. Her smile hit me like a shot of whiskey—bright enough to stop a stampede.

"You're the cowboy Angie booked," she said, her voice warm but with a teasing edge. "That your horse raising hell in there?"

"Lady has a mind of her own," I said, grinning. "Doesn't much like being cooped up."

"Smart girl," Tara shot back, already heading for the trailer. "Let's get her out before she kicks a hole in your fancy rig."

Randle was a rock, warm but guarded. Tara was a wildfire—bold, sharp, and maybe a little dangerous, her flirty edge stirring up trouble I didn't feel like dodging.

The ranch itself felt alive, its beauty concealing something more profound, possibly darker. Pard stayed close, his hackles raised as we approached the stables, his nose twitching at the piñon-scented air.

Tara swung open the trailer, cooing to Lady as she led her down the ramp. Lady snorted, her chestnut coat gleaming, and Tara ran a hand along her flank, nodding like she approved.

"She's a beauty. How much did you have to pay for her?"

"Nothing," I said. "The woman I used to work for gave her to me."

Tara's eyebrows raised. She grinned and said, "What kind of work did you do for her?"

Catching her implication, I grinned and said, "Not what you think. She was old enough to be my mother."

"Never saw that stop a horny man."

I started to reply, but stopped mid-sentence, deciding to let the comment go and change the subject instead.

Tara led us to the stables, where cedar beams and fresh hay made a warm and earthy haven. Lady's stall was next to a sleek palomino—Tara's horse, I figured, spotting the name "Starfire" on a brass plate.

Tara nodded when I said, "Your horse? She's a beauty."

"They'll be neighbors," she said, tossing me a wink. "Starfire's a barrel racer, like me. Hope Lady can keep up."

"She'll hold her own," I said, unhooking Lady's lead.

Pard sniffed the stall door, tail wagging but eyes sharp, like he sensed something beyond the hay and horses. Tara pointed across the ranch to a cluster of cabins, their log walls glowing amber in the late light.

Dad must have liked Angie because he gave you the Starlight Cabin. It's not our biggest, but it's my personal favorite. I'll show you."

Tara smiled when I asked, "Did you talk to Angie?"

"She told me to watch out for you."

Angie's comment could have meant a few different things, and as Tara led me and Pard along a path lined with sagebrush, I wondered which one she was referring to. From Tara's knowing grin, I sensed Angie wasn't asking her to check if I was okay.

The Starlight Cabin sat on a rise, its wide porch overlooking the Sangre de Cristos, their peaks turning purple in the dusk. Inside, it was cozy—hand-hewn beams, a Navajo rug, a kiva fireplace crackling with piñon logs.

"I got it going for you," she said. "It already gets cold enough at night here for a fire, though it stays fairly mild during the day."

"Just the way I like it," I said.

A bookshelf held beat-up books on UFOs and Pueblo lore, and a window framed the distant mountains bearing the petroglyphs.

"Home sweet home," Tara said, leaning against the doorframe, her smile softening. "Need anything, cowboy, you holler. Me or Daddy will be around. Supper's almost ready—Rita's frybread tacos'll ruin you for any other food. Come when you hear the dinner bell."

"Thanks, Tara," I said, dropping my duffel on the pine table. Pard curled up by the kiva, ears twitching at a coyote's yip in the distance. "This place... It's something else."

Tara's eyes lingered on me, a spark of curiosity in them.

"You'll see, Buck. Double Moon has a way of pulling you in," she said, then paused. "Oh, and watch out for Grandma Lily. Sweet as pie but... peculiar. She's full-blood Indian and mutters blessings that'll raise the hairs on your neck."

As Tara's boots crunched down the path, I stepped onto the porch, staring at the mountains. The desert air was cool now, stars punching through the sky like diamond dust.

That damn Taos Hum vibrated faintly, and Pard growled low, his eyes locked on a shed across the ranch, its tin roof glinting under the rising moon.

CHAPTER 3

At seven, a sharp clang cut through the evening—a metal triangle dinner bell swinging from the porch rafters of the main house. Pard was sprawled by the kiva, snoring like a buzzsaw, so I left him to his dreams and headed out.

The air was sharp now, the stars blazing brighter, and that Taos Hum pulsed like a heartbeat in the ground. Tara met me at the door of the two-story log cabin house, her smile catching the lantern light.

"Right on time, cowboy," she said, her voice teasing but warm.

She led me inside, and I damn near stopped in my tracks. The house was a stunner—polished log walls, a vaulted ceiling with exposed beams, and a massive stone fireplace crackling with piñon. Navajo rugs hung like tapestries, their colors glowing under wrought-iron chandeliers.

Tara guided me through a wide hallway, past a staircase carved with spiral patterns that reminded me of Anna Luna's petroglyph sketches, and into a dining room that could've hosted a governor's ball. A long oak table stretched under a chandelier made of antlers, set with plates of blue-glazed pottery.

The air smelled of roasted chiles and fresh frybread, a New Mexico feast that made my stomach growl. Randle sat at the head of the table, his gray eyes scanning me like he could read my thoughts.

"Buck, take a seat," he said, gesturing to a chair beside Tara. "Meet the family." He nodded to his wife, Rita, a Navajo woman with a warm smile but a gaze that could cut glass. Next to her was Lily, her mother, hunched but sharp-eyed, her silver hair braided tight, a strange amulet glowing faintly at her neck.

Ran, a lanky twenty-something with a wannabe-cowboy grin, gave me an eager nod, like he was ready to rope the moon if I'd show him how. Then there were the two guests—a German couple, introduced as Hans and Greta Mueller, though their stiff handshakes and mismatched body language seemed a mystery.

Hans looked like a weightlifter, with shoulders bulging beneath his shirt, a buzz cut, and hawk-like eyes; Greta had blonde hair pulled tight into a bun, a shallow smile, and seemed at least twenty years older. Vacationers, they said, but their questions were too sharp to be typical tourists.

"Randle, what can you tell us about Area 51?" Hans asked, cutting into his frybread as if he were interrogating it.

The room went quiet, forks pausing midair. Tara and Ran swapped amused glances, like they'd heard this song before.

Randle leaned back, his face unreadable. "Area 51? Just a patch of desert folks like to spin stories about. I know nothing about it."

His tone was flat, but the lie hung heavy—every soul in Taos knew something about Area 51, even if it were only whispers.

Greta pressed, her accent crisp. "But the lights in the sky, the ones locals talk about. You've seen them, yes?"

Her eyes flicked to me, then back to Randle, like she was fishing for a slip.

Randle shrugged, sipping his coffee. "Desert plays tricks. Stars, planes, maybe a drone. You see what you want to see."

The conversation veered to aliens and UFOs, Hans leaning in like a bloodhound.

"There are stories of... beings. Craft that moves without sound. Surely you've heard?"

His voice was too eager, his "vacation" story thinner than the frybread.

Tara stifled a laugh, her boot nudging mine under the table. "Folks love a good tale," she said, her eyes sparkling with mischief. "Half the valley claims they've seen little green men."

Ran piped up, grinning. "Or gray ones! With big ol' eyes!" He mimed a saucer with his hands, earning a sharp look from Rita.

Rita's voice cut through, calm but heavy. "Our people have older stories. The Sky People, who came long before planes or drones." She glanced at Lily, who nodded, her amulet catching the light. "They taught us to read the stars, to plant corn. Their marks are in the petroglyphs."

Hans's eyes lit up. "Skinwalkers, perhaps? Shape-shifters?"

He leaned forward, too hungry for answers. Lily's gaze snapped to him, her voice low and sharp.

"Yee naaldlooshii are not for outsiders to speak of."

She muttered something in Navajo, her fingers tracing the amulet, and I swear the air grew colder. Pard wasn't here, but I could almost hear his growl.

Hans backed off, but Greta's stare lingered on me. "And you, Mr. McDivit? Why are you here?"

Her tone was polite, though it felt like a trap.

"To enjoy the Taos vibe and ride my horse," I said, leaning back with a grin. "Lady and I want to see the trails and vistas, and I've heard there's nothing like a New Mexico sunset."

I kept it light, but their eyes didn't buy it. They were too curious, too focused, like they knew I was chasing the same shadows they were.

The meal was a masterpiece—frybread tacos stuffed with green chile pork, posole rich with hominy and spice, and prickly pear lemonade that cut through the heat.

But every bite came with a side of tension. Hans and Greta's questions kept circling back to UFOs, their "vacation" excuse fraying at the edges. Randle's evasions were smooth but practiced, Tara's amused glances hid a sharpness, and Rita and Lily's talk of Sky People felt like a warning wrapped in folklore. Ran's eager chatter about lights in the sky only thickened the fog of secrets.

As I left the dining room, my boots echoing on the hardwood, I couldn't shake the feeling I'd stumbled into a gold mine —or a snake pit.

The Double Moon Ranch was a puzzle, each piece sharper

than the last. Randle's Area 51 denials seemed too practiced; Hans and Greta, if that were their actual names, weren't here for the views, and that amulet around Lily's neck seemed to pulse with a light that wasn't just fireglow.

When I returned to my cabin, I found a surprise awaiting me. Pard was outside, barking happily to see me. Something felt wrong because I had left him sleeping on the bed.

As I looked around inside, I realized someone had been there. Someone had rifled through my duffel, and Jake's folder of information was gone. A knock on the door stopped me in my tracks. It was Ran Roberts, smiling when I invited him in.

Ran was a handsome young man, probably a year or two older than his sister, Tara.

"Sorry to bother you," he said. "The lady who booked you told Dad that you are a professional cowboy."

"Used to be," I said. "Not anymore."

I nodded when he said, "You rodeoed professionally for a while. Why did you stop?"

"You drink beer?" I asked.

He nodded and said, "I'm twenty-two."

"You like Coors?" I asked.

"Don't know," he said. "Never had it."

I grabbed my red ice chest and said, "Let's sit on the porch."

Navajo rugs draped over the backs of two cane rockers on the rustic porch. I tossed Ran a Coors from the ice chest and invited him to join me. The sky was bright, lit up with thousands of stars and a partial moon, while the Cristo de Sangres loomed as shadows in the distance.

"Pretty damn good," he said.

"Used to, they only sold strong Coors in Oklahoma in liquor stores," I said. "Now, you can buy a six-point tall boy at your local convenience store while you're filling your gas tank."

"Progress," he said. "Someday, they'll probably be sold in machines. No ID required."

I grinned and said, "My dream as a teenager."

"You didn't answer my question," he said. "Why did you quit

rodeoing?"

"I was pretty good, though far from the best. I loved the prize money and respect, but not the broken bones, sprained joints, and sore muscles."

"What are you doing now that you've given up the rodeo?" he asked.

"Right now, I'm working for Jake Huntington, the Cryptid Hunter. Heard of him?"

"You kidding? It's my favorite program on TV," he said. "What do you do for him?"

"Scout locations and potential episodes," I said.

"Now I get it," he said. "You're here looking for aliens and UFOs."

"Yes," I said. "Damn! It's cold. I didn't even bring a light jacket."

"You're about my size," he said. "I'll get you something to break the chill."

Ran was gone for less than five minutes, returning with a baby blue, fleece-lined long-sleeved sweatshirt featuring a flying saucer and a caption that said, "New Mexico, Saucer Sighting Capital of the World."

"That was quick," I said.

"The bunkhouse isn't far from here. It's where I live," he said.

"How many cowboys does this spread have?" I asked.

"Just me," he said. "Used to be a working ranch. Now, we only cater to guests."

"Thanks," I said, pulling the sweatshirt over my shirt. "I'll return it tomorrow."

"Keep it," he said. "A Christmas present. Too big for me and I've never worn it."

"You sure?" I asked.

"Looks good on you," he said. "Maybe you can help me out in exchange."

"Doing what?" I asked.

"I want to join the rodeo circuit. I was hoping that you could give me a few 5-pointers."

Ran had finished his beer, and I tossed him another.

"What's your favorite event?" I asked.

"Saddle bronc riding," he said.

"Tell you what," I said. "I'll go you one better than giving you a few pointers; I'll coach you while I'm here at the ranch."

Even in the dimness of the porch, I could see Ran's eyes lighting up.

"You'd do that for me?" he asked.

"Yep, but there's a catch," I said.

"What?"

"You help me with my Cryptid Hunter assignment."

Ran's smile disappeared. "Don't know. Dad doesn't like me or Tara talking about, you know… Roswell and such."

"Then hell, Ran, if you don't tell him, I sure as hell won't."

He was still hesitant and said, "Well…"

"You're twenty-two. Big enough to kick the old fart's ass if you want to," I said.

"I'm not afraid of him. I don't want him to kick me off the ranch."

"Might be the best thing to ever happen to you. Then you could get a job on a working ranch with real cowboys," I said.

"Okay," he said. "How can I help?"

"When I got back to my cabin after dinner, I found out someone had broken in and gone through my things. How many rental cabins do you have, and who's staying in them that weren't at the dinner table tonight?"

"Was something stolen?" he asked.

"Nothing that can't be replaced."

"Have you reported the break-in to Dad?"

"The only people who need to know are you and me," I said.

There are five other guest cabins besides yours. Some are larger and hold more guests than others. They are all full," he said.

"Why weren't the guests at dinner tonight?"

"Hell, Buck, we're only ten miles from Taos with some of the best restaurants in the world. They were probably off sightseeing and dining out."

"Not all of them," I said. "One of your guests was casing my cabin while I was at dinner in the big house."

"You sure?" he said. "Could have been someone from Taos."

"No one from Taos knows I'm here. I need a copy of your guest list."

"That could get me in lots of trouble," he said.

"If you're making big prize money on the rodeo circuit, you'll have an expensive truck, a fat bank account, and dozens or more rodeo groupies that won't be able to get enough of you," I said. "I'll give you your first lesson tomorrow."

"Mom and Dad turn in early, and the reception office isn't part of the big house. I'll get the list for you."

"Good man," I said. "You have part of the lesson one already mastered."

"I do? What's that?"

He grinned when I said, "You drink Coors like a world champion."

CHAPTER 4

The morning sun had barely crested the Sangre de Cristo Mountains, painting the Double Moon Ranch in hues of gold and shadow, when a sharp knock rattled the cabin door. I hadn't been up long and was still shirtless, coffee steaming in my hand. I opened the door to find Ran Roberts, his lanky frame buzzing with nervous energy.

"Ready for that lesson, coach?" Ran grinned, his cowboy hat tipped back.

I nodded, slurping my coffee. "Maybe. You have something for me?"

Ran glanced behind him to see if anyone was looking, and then handed me a folded sheet of paper.

"Names, addresses, and phone numbers," he said.

There were many names on the list. One jumped out at me. Someone named Ri Sun Young.

"You often have Asian guests?" I asked.

"Quite a few lately," he said.

I pointed to a name and said, "You know this person?"

"Sun Young," Ran said.

"You knew her?"

Ran smiled. "She made a point of introducing herself. A real looker, that one."

"American?" I asked."

Ran shook his head and said, "I don't think so."

"She was here alone?"

Ran nodded. "I wasn't the only one she made a point of introducing herself to. Mom got a little pissed when Sun Young sat in Dad's lap and came on to him."

"Does that happen often?"

"More often than you might think," Ran said. "The German woman came on to him."

He nodded again when I said, "Greta Mueller? Head out to the corral. I have a call to make, and then I'll meet you there."

After calling Angie and giving her the list of guest names, I followed Ran outside to a weathered corral where a muscular stallion thundered in circles, snorting clouds of dust. His coat gleamed like polished steel, eyes wild with untamed fire.

"Looks dangerous," I said.

"Big Lou," Ran said. "Dad hired a couple of cowboys to break him for us. They didn't come close. Never lasted more than a heartbeat on him."

I leaned against the fence, studying the beast. "He's as scared of you as you are of him, Ran. Deep down, he's just a force looking for direction."

Ran grinned and said, "If you say so, coach."

I set my mug down, boots crunching as I stepped into the corral. Big Lou reared, hooves slashing the air, but I moved slowly, hands low, my voice a steady hum, like a breeze over sagebrush.

The horse's ears flicked, then softened. He slowed, snorting, as my hand grazed his flank, calming the storm in those wild eyes.

"Feel his rhythm, Ran," I said. "He's not your enemy. He's the wind—raw, powerful, alive. You don't fight the wind. You ride it."

Big Lou allowed me to lead him into the chute. He didn't protest much, just a slight buck and a few snorts, when I saddled him.

"Okay, Ran. You ready?"

"Looks to me like you already broke him," Ran said.

I smiled, shook my head, and said, "Far from it. He knows what's coming next, and he's ready for you."

"Any advice?" he asked.

"Give him all the respect in the world. He expects you to take control, wants you to. Don't let him down," I said.

Ran swallowed hard, climbing the chute where Big Lou was now saddled, nostrils flaring. The gate swung open, and the stallion exploded, bucking like a demon loosed from hell. Ran's body twisted, arms flailing, but he clung for three seconds—then hit the dirt hard, dust billowing around him.

I was there in an instant, hauling him up, brushing off his shirt. "Not bad, kid. You felt him, didn't you? His power?"

Ran coughed, nodding. "Felt like he was gonna launch me to Roswell."

I chuckled, clapping his shoulder. "Here's the secret: Big Lou's stronger, faster, meaner than you'll ever be. You can't outmuscle him. But he can't outthink you. Tune into your inner senses."

"Mind explaining how I do that?"

"You're a quarter Indian. I don't have to teach you something that's inbred in your soul."

"I laughed when he said, "Maybe a little clue?"

"Let your mind go quiet—feel his moves before he makes them. You aren't riding a bronc, Ran. You're dancing with a storm. Be the storm."

Ran's eyes lit up, the fear giving way to something fiercer. He adjusted his hat, spitting dust.

"All right, coach. Let's dance."

I grinned, stepping back. "Climb back on, genie. Ride the damn wind."

I leaned against the fence, coffee in hand, the Taos Hum vibrating faintly underfoot. The kid had heart—maybe enough to tame Big Lou, and sufficient to help me unravel the secrets Jake Huntington was chasing. But for now, the corral was their world, and the lesson was simple: fear the storm, but become it.

"Are you going to lead him back to the stall?" Ran asked.

"You do it," I said.

Ran said, "He'll kick my head off."

If you believe that, then that's what will happen. Look him in the eyes. Let him know you're not the enemy."

"How do I do that?"

Speak to him with your thoughts. He's waiting for you. Take a deep breath and don't let him down.

Ran inhaled deeply.

The morning sun climbed higher, casting long shadows across the Double Moon Ranch's corral as Ran dusted himself off, eyes blazing with determination. Big Lou snorted, pacing the arena, still untamed but less wild after my touch. Ran adjusted his hat, walked confidently up to the stallion, and stroked his neck.

Big Lou followed Ran back to the chute and didn't buck when he mounted him. When I opened the gate, Big Lou came bounding out in a whirlwind of twisting muscles and flying hooves. This time, Ran stayed aboard till he stopped bucking. I watched as he leaned down and hugged the big horse's neck.

"Ran, you just broke your first bronc. How does it feel?" I asked.

I laughed when he said, "Like I cheated."

"You didn't cheat. You had an extra tool in your chest all along. You just needed someone to show you how to use it."

"Is that all it takes to be a champion?"

"Why hell no!" I said. "Big Al's a pussycat compared to some of the beasts you'll encounter on the circuit, but they're all God's creatures. Treat them as such."

"When's our next lesson, coach?" Ran asked.

"Let this one sink in first," I said.

"What else?" he asked.

"Fight the urge to let your dick do your thinking. Stallions have way bigger dicks than you do."

Tara had ridden up on Starfire, her palomino gleaming like molten gold. She was grinning ear to ear.

"Good advice, cowboy," she said. "Is that something you truly live by, or do you just hand it out to wide-eyed kids?"

"Maybe a little of both," I said.

"How's my brother's coaching going? You got him ready for the big leagues yet?"

I leaned against the fence, coffee mug in hand, a grin tugging at my lips. "Kid's got heart. Needs to loosen up, though. You want to show him how it's done?"

Tara laughed, sharp and wild. "I'd have broken that horse and your ego in one ride. But I have a better idea. Feel like some real fun? High desert, open trails—see if you and Lady can keep up with me and Starfire."

I raised an eyebrow, catching the challenge in her tone. "Lead the way."

We saddled up, Lady's chestnut coat gleaming as I swung into the stirrups. Tara's tight Levi's and rolled-up denim shirt made her look like she was born in the saddle, her braid swinging as Starfire pranced.

We tore out of the ranch, hooves pounding red dirt, the Sangre de Cristo Mountains looming like silent giants. The high desert stretched wide, sagebrush and juniper blurring past, the air sharp with piñon and freedom.

Tara pushed Starfire into a gallop, and I matched her, Lady's muscles rippling as they raced across the mesa. The wind roared in our ears, the Taos Hum a faint pulse beneath it. Tara glanced over, her grin daring me to push harder. I leaned low, urging Lady faster, our laughter mingling with the thunder of hooves. It was raw, electric—two forces testing each other's power, the desert our playground.

We slowed at a cliffside vista, the valley sprawling below, cottonwoods glowing gold against red rock. The horses grazed on sparse grass as Tara and I dismounted, settling on a flat boulder warmed by the sun. The view stole my breath—mesas carved by time, distant peaks dusted with snow, the sky a turquoise so vivid it hurt.

Tara pulled a canteen, taking a swig before passing it to me. Her flirty edge softened, her eyes tracing the horizon.

"Ran's always been like this, you know. All heart, no head. Wants to be a rodeo star but freezes when it counts. He's scared he'll never measure up to Dad, to me, to anyone."

I sipped from the canteen, the water cool and sweet. "He has potential. Just needs to trust himself. You're too hard on him."

She sighed, tucking a stray hair behind her ear. "Gotta be. Dad has secrets—stuff he doesn't tell us, stuff Ran's too naive to see. Like why he left Michigan, why he's so cagey about Area 51."

"I noticed last night at dinner," I said.

"Mom and Grandma Lily… they're different. Navajo magic runs deep in them. Grandma's amulet? It's not just jewelry. I've seen it glow, Buck, like it's alive. Mom sometimes chants under the stars, calls it 'balancing the world.' Ran thinks it's just stories. I know better."

I leaned back, studying her. "Sounds like you're carrying the weight of those secrets yourself."

Her eyes met mine, a spark flickering. "Maybe. But I'm tougher than Ran. Always have been. I was watching you and Ran."

"And?" I said.

"You're a horse whisperer," she said. "Wasn't Ran that broke Big Lou. It was you."

"I'm good with horses," I said.

"I can tell," she said.

Our gaze held, the air between us crackling like a storm brewing. Tara's lips parted, a half-smile teasing, when—

CRACK!

A bullet struck the boulder inches from Tara's hand, spraying rock dust. She froze, eyes wide. My instincts kicked in, yanking her down behind the boulder, my body shielding hers.

"Get down! Now!"

Tara's breath hitched. "What the hell was that?"

"Thirty-ought-six," I said, my voice low, scanning the ridge across the valley. My eyes narrowed, tracking the faint glint of sunlight on metal, already fading. I stood, dusting off my jeans, calm but alert.

Tara grabbed my arm, panic in her voice. "What are you doing? They'll kill you!"

"They're gone," I said. "If they wanted us dead, we'd be bled out by now. That was a warning shot."

Tara scrambled up, her face pale but fierce. "Who'd shoot at us? Why?"

My gaze drifted toward the ranch. "Maybe that's a question for your dad."

She gave me an electric stare, as if questioning what I meant. "What's that supposed to mean?" she asked.

I mounted Lady and rode off without answering.

The desert stretched silent around us, the Taos Hum pulsing faintly, as if the land itself knew more than it let on. As we spurred our horses, the thrill of the chase turned darker, the high desert no longer just a playground but a battlefield. Someone was watching, and I knew this was only the start of the trouble Jake Huntington had sent me to find.

As we reached the Double Moon Ranch, we saw Randle Roberts waiting for us, his frown and arms crossed tightly over his chest showing he wasn't happy. Tara didn't stop, taking her big palomino straight to its stall.

I reined in Lady in front of Randle and dismounted.

"What's up?" I asked.

"You and me," he said. "I don't want Ran rodeoing and I don't want you giving him any more lessons."

"Ran's of age," I said. "Old enough to do what he pleases."

"Not and stay on this ranch, he doesn't," Randle said.

"Fine," I said. "I'll be checking out. When I have my things packed, I'll meet you at the office and clear my tab."

"There's not another place to stay between here and Albuquerque," he said.

"Won't be the first time I've slept in my vehicle," I said.

"You're pretty hard-headed," he said.

"I don't like being pushed around." I started to walk away, but turned and said. "Someone fired a shot at Tara and me while we were riding. Wouldn't have been you, would it?"

"Now wait just a minute," he said, grabbing my shoulder.

I brushed his hand off and said, "I'm not one of your kids."

"What's that supposed to mean?" he asked.

"It means keep your damn hands off where they don't belong," I said.

Tara was waiting in my cabin when I arrived, sitting on the edge of my bed, frowning, with her arms crossed tightly over her chest.

"What was that all about?" she asked.

"You tell me," I said. "You know your old man better than I do."

"He can be a prick, but he's never hit me," she said.

"Yeah, well sometimes words hurt worse than fists," I said.

"Where do you think you're going?" she asked.

"Don't know," I said. "Angie will find me a place to stay."

"There's an abandoned ranch about ten miles from here. No one has occupied it in years."

"Oh?" I said.

"Has a well, a cabin, a barn, and a corral for Lady," she said. "I'll show you."

"Your dad will be pissed," I said.

"No, he won't," Tara said. "He's the one who told me to take you. He doesn't want to lose out on being part of Cryptid Hunter."

"Couldn't have proved it by me," I said. "What's the name of this place?"

"Shadow Ranch," she said. "Finish packing, and we'll go."

Shadow Ranch sat atop a hill overlooking the Rio Grande gorge. Tara led the way in her old truck. The barn and log cabin showcased superb craftsmanship, with both structures tightly built and protected from the high desert winds.

We settled Lady into a cozy stall and unloaded the hay Tara had brought in the back of her truck. After filling Lady's water trough from the well, she showed me the cabin.

The inside felt as if someone had just left yesterday—the bed, the sink, and the kiva stove all appeared untouched, as if abandoned only the day before. Tara had brought sheets, a blanket, piñon wood, and an ice chest filled with tacos, tamales, and open-faced enchiladas. Pard loved it and was dancing around.

Tara grinned when I asked, "How did you know about this place?"

"My ex-boyfriend and I used to come here to go parking."

She grinned again when I glanced at the bed and said, "I see."

"Dad was upset that you moved out," she said. "If this place doesn't work out for you, he'll welcome you back with open arms."

"I don't like his conditions," I said.

"He knows he can't keep Ran and me under his thumb forever," she said.

"Wouldn't know it to hear him talk," I said.

Tara stood on her tiptoes and kissed me. "Ran and I will be back tomorrow," she said. "We won't let you starve."

CHAPTER 5

I woke to the scent of piñon smoke and the soft crackle of embers in the kiva stove. The fire had burned low overnight, but it had served its purpose—my bones were warm, the chill kept at bay.

The cabin creaked around me like a familiar friend stretching in the morning light. Sitting up, I rubbed the sleep from my eyes and listened—nothing but the hush of wind through juniper and the distant call of a raven.

Pard shot past me like a bullet as I opened the door, tail high and nose twitching, already halfway to the ridge before I could blink. I stepped out, boots crunching on the frost-hardened dirt, and took in the view.

The Sangre de Cristos were waking, their peaks blushing pink under the rising sun. I smiled, remembering the wolves last night—how their howls had threaded through the canyon like a hymn. It had stirred something profound within me, something long forgotten.

Back inside, I cracked a couple of eggs into a skillet and nestled it into the belly of the kiva oven. The fire licked at the pan, and the smell of breakfast began to mingle with the last breath of smoke. I was just about to flip them when I heard the crunch of tires on gravel.

A pickup rolled into view, dust trailing behind it like a ghost. Ran climbed out, his hat low, boots thudding against the earth. He gave me a nod and slapped the side of the horse trailer.

"Brought Big Al," he said. "And some feed. Oats, hay, and a little something for the soul."

He hefted a case of Coors from the truck bed, the cans clinking like wind chimes in the breeze.

I grinned. “Exactly what this man needs.”

Ran leaned against the tailgate, eyes scanning the horizon. “Rodeo de Santa Fe’s this weekend. I entered the saddle bronc competition. Thought you might help.”

“What’s your dad think about it?” I asked.

“Haven’t told him yet.”

He nodded when I said, “Is that why you brought your stuff?”

“I was hoping I could stay here with you,” he said.

I pointed to the loft above us. “There’s a bunk up there, and no one’s using it. Is that all your stuff?”

Ran had a knapsack and a duffel. “This is it,” he said. “No one has ever called me a packrat.”

“You’ve taken minimalism to the next level,” I said.

I watched as he climbed the ladder to the cozy loft overlooking the cabin.

“Kind of nippy in here. Where’s all your wood?”

“Burned it last night,” I said. “Just enough left to cook breakfast.”

“I have an axe in the carrier. I’ll cut us some,” he said.

“Let’s eat first. I have bacon and eggs cooking,” I said.

Ran grinned. “Good deal. Had to skip breakfast because I didn’t want to face Mom and Dad.”

“There are plenty of stalls in the barn. Take care of Big Al, and I’ll finish cooking while you’re gone,” I said.

“Thanks, Buck. Be right back.”

Ran soon returned, and the bacon and eggs, along with the aroma of strong coffee, combined to whet our appetites. I glanced out the window toward the mountains, where the sky stretched vast and endless.

The idea of dust, sweat, and adrenaline under the Santa Fe sun stirred something restless in me. We’d barely finished breakfast when the sound of another truck broke the silence. It was Tara.

When she saw Ran, she said, “You’re in big trouble.”

“For what?” he asked.

"Dad found out you entered the rodeo. He's pissed."

"You told him?"

Tara shook her head, "I wouldn't do that. One of Dad's buddies from the rodeo commission called him."

"Shit!" Ran said.

"He doesn't own you," Tara said.

Ran smiled and said, "Unless I want to stay at the Double Moon. I moved out this morning before he had a chance to boot me."

"You should at least call and tell him where you're at," she said.

"He has my number. It works both ways."

Tara frowned and folded her arms. "You aren't being fair," she said.

"You're riding in the rodeo this weekend. What's the difference?"

"Barrel racing isn't as dangerous as bronc riding."

"Hogwash," he said. "How many times have you had a sling on your arm or one of your legs in a cast?"

"That's different," she said.

"It's not, and you know it," he said.

Tara looked at me and said, "You're the cause of all this."

"Whoa!" I said. "How am I the cause?"

"Ran wouldn't have had the courage to sign up for the saddle bronc competition if you hadn't goaded him," she said.

"Ran's of age, and he's right. Barrel racing is every bit as dangerous as saddle bronc riding. Why are you exempt and he's not?" When she didn't answer, I said. "Want some coffee?"

Tara reached into my ice chest and fished out a cold Coors. After popping the top, she chugged half of the can.

"Hell, I may have to move in here myself," she said.

"Plenty of room," I said.

When my cell phone rang, I pardoned myself and stepped outside. It was Angie.

"Why did you move from Double Moon Ranch?" she asked.

"How did you find out so fast?"

"Randle Roberts called me at six. Wanted me to know he had nothing to do with your moving."

"Not exactly true," I said. "Doesn't matter. The place I'm at is perfect, but Jake will need someplace like Double Moon for his crew if he decides to start filming."

"I ran the list of names you scanned for me," Angie said. "Hans and Greta are free agents who sometimes work for a German manufacturing company with ties to the military."

"They were with me when my cabin was rolled, though they could have had an accomplice. Makes sense since they were the only ones besides the Roberts family who knew I wasn't in my cabin at the time of the robbery."

By the way, they aren't married," Angie said.

"I had a feeling they weren't," I said. "They were very interested in what Randle had to say about Area 51."

"Industrial spies, maybe," Angie said. "I'll do more checking on them, but people like that have lots of loose ends that are hard to connect."

"I hear that," I said. "What else?"

"Ri Sun Young. She's Korean."

"What's an attractive single Asian woman doing alone at a dude ranch in northern New Mexico?" I asked.

"Don't know," Angie said. "You have reason to suspect her of something?"

"Ran said she came on to both him and his dad. Suspicious enough for you?"

"Sexpionage," she said.

"Pardon me?"

"Honey trap," she said. "Spy tactic to gain intel."

"We're dealing with spies here?" I asked.

"Maybe," she said.

She laughed when I asked, "Are you and Stormy spies?"

"What we were after wasn't information," she said. I let the subject drop, and so did she. "You have an appointment at two to interview Elena Tafoya. She'll be waiting for you at the gate of the Taos Pueblo."

"Thanks, Angie. I'll text you the coordinates of where I'm staying."

"Good. Jake's getting antsy and wants to fly out this weekend and scout things for himself."

"Tell him to hold his horses. I got shot at yesterday, and things aren't exactly safe."

"What the fuck!" she said. "What happened?"

"A warning from someone sporting a high-powered rifle while Randle's daughter, Tara, and I were doing a little trail riding."

"Uh-huh!" she said. "What else were you and Tara doing?"

"Nothing but scouting locations," I said. "Tara's too young for me."

"Uh-huh!" she said again. "Did you call the police?"

"Didn't bother," I said. "The sniper was only trying to warn us, not kill us,"

"Warn you of what?" she asked.

"Don't know yet. I'll find out, though."

"You be careful, Buck. You're the best line dancer I know. I don't want to lose you."

"I'm watching my ass," I said.

She laughed and said, "If I were there, I'd help you out."

Ran and Tara were still bickering when I left them to interview Elena Tafoya, though they agreed to look after Pard while I was gone. The sun was high and harsh, casting jittery shadows across the cracked adobe walls of the abandoned ranch I now called home.

Jake's lime green Jeep looked like a misplaced tropical bird in the dusty yard, but she was reliable, loud, and just quirky enough to fit me. I tossed my duster into the passenger seat and turned the ignition. The engine coughed once, then roared into life.

The road to Taos twisted through high desert scrub and ancient cottonwoods, the kind that whisper secrets if you drive slow enough. I didn't, in a hurry to reach my appointment with Tiwa elder Elena Tafoya. She'd agreed to meet me at the Pueblo gate, which meant she either didn't trust me or wanted to size me up before deciding if she should.

As I climbed toward Taos, the Sangre de Cristo Mountains around me loomed, their peaks dusted with the last stubborn snow of the season. The air thinned and cooled, scented with juniper and the faint trace of woodsmoke.

I passed roadside shrines, rusted mailboxes, and a herd of indifferent cows who watched me like I owed them something. I could have bypassed Taos, but decided to drive through and see what had changed.

The last time I'd been in New Mexico, I was a landman for an Oklahoma oil company. I'd bid on some state leases in Santa Fe and then visited Taos. The small town hadn't changed much, with adobe facades and the plaza featuring artists, musicians, and world-class chefs. It wasn't far from the plaza to the Taos Pueblo.

The Pueblo appeared like a mirage made of earth and time —multi-storied adobe dwellings stacked like clay bookshelves, their walls the color of cinnamon and memory. I pulled up near the gate, where a wooden sign warned against photography and bad manners.

A few tourists milled about, snapping photos of the iconic multi-story dwellings, their wooden vigas jutting like bones from the mud-plastered walls.

Elena was already there, standing like a sentinel in silver jewelry that caught the sun like lightning. Her hair was braided tightly, and her face bore lines that told of decades under the sun. A woven shawl of turquoise and red wrapped her shoulders, and her eyes were sharp as obsidian.

She nodded once. "Buck McDivit," she said, her voice dry as mesquite. "You're early."

"Ma'am," I tipped my hat. "I figured I'd rather wait on you than the other way around."

She studied me for a beat longer than comfort allowed, then turned and gestured for me to follow.

"Come. We'll talk where the spirits don't have to shout."

We walked through the Pueblo, past drying racks, ceremonial kivas, and children playing with sticks that might've been swords or wands. Elena's apartment was tucked into the northern edge of the complex, a modest adobe unit with a blue-painted door and chili ristras hanging like crimson sentinels.

Inside, the air was cool and smelled of sage and old stories. Her walls were lined with woven baskets, faded photographs, and shelves of books that looked like they'd been read more than once. A small clay fireplace crackled in the corner, and a pot of something fragrant simmered on the stove.

She motioned to a chair carved from pine and covered in a woven blanket. "Sit. You're here about the lights."

I sat. "Yes, ma'am. The UAPs. I've seen things out near the ranch. Things that don't make sense."

Elena poured two cups of tea from a kettle that looked older than me. "Things that don't make sense," she echoed. "That's where the truth lives."

I took the cup, grateful for the warmth. Outside, the wind had picked up, rattling the door like an impolite ghost.

"Thank you for seeing me. How did you know I would ask about the lights?"

"The Cryptid Hunter sent you to find something. What else would you be looking for?"

"You've heard of the Cryptid Hunter?" I asked.

"You kidding? It's my favorite program. I never miss it."

"Well, he needs your help. Would you consider working with us for a few weeks? The pay's pretty damn good."

"You kidding? I'd work for the Cryptid Hunter for nothing," she said.

I smiled and said, "I won't tell him you said that. Angie will have an employment contract in the mail today, but if you're amenable, consider yourself on the payroll as of this very moment."

Elena was beaming. "I'm going to be on Cryptid Hunter?"

"Not just an appearance; a major role," I said.

She stood and said, "This calls for a celebration. She disappeared briefly, returning with two glasses of a thick drink, handing me one.

"What is it?" I asked.

"Atole," she said. "The Tiwa drink it to celebrate special occasions."

She grinned when I asked, "Is it alcoholic?"

"A thick, warm, and comforting drink made from roasted blue cornmeal. Non-alcoholic. Its roots date back to the Aztecs. It's still a significant part of Pueblo culture in New Mexico today."

"Good," I said, after taking a drink.

"It grows on you," she said.

She shook her head when I said, "I usually drink mescal when I celebrate."

"You're Indian, aren't you?" she asked.

"Part Cherokee," I said.

"More than part," she said.

"Don't really know," I said. "I grew up in Indian schools."

"I'm sorry," she said.

"No problem. PTSD's no hill for a stepper."

She touched my wrist and said, "Embrace that thought. Sometimes your atole is filled with maggots, and it isn't always easy to toss it away and find something else to eat."

Elena's words were cryptic, but I perfectly understood what she was saying.

"I'll take your advice," I said.

"You have questions for me," she said.

"Jake saw a picture drawn by artist Anna Luna." I showed her a photocopy of the glowing orb. "Were you with Ms. Luna when she drew this?"

"Yes," she said.

"Jake thinks it's somehow associated with aliens and flying saucers."

"What my mother called the Sky People," Elena said.

"Did she draw the picture because of something you both saw?" I asked.

"Anna was looking for something deeper in her life and hired me as a spiritual advisor," Elena said. "We were camping in the high desert, looking at the ancient petroglyphs and studying the stars."

"That's when you saw the orb?"

Elena nodded. "Two human-like creatures were carrying the pulsating orb. A craft appeared, casting a beam that levitated the two beings into it. It disappeared in a flash, leaving Anna and me wondering if we'd really seen what we saw."

"Jake said you both experienced some other things out of the norm," I said.

"To put it mildly," she said.

"Please, I'd like to hear."

"Are you familiar with what people call the Taos Hum?" she asked.

"Yes," I said. "I've heard it."

"That night in the high desert, the Hum grew louder than usual. Much louder. At first, I didn't notice. Then, other things became noticeable."

"Such as?" I said.

"Anna and I were looking at a petroglyph. The lines of the glyph began to bend, as if it were melting."

I blinked and said, "Go on."

"The dark rock the glyph was carved into became momentarily translucent. A cactus twisted, as if alive. Gravity began to tug sideways."

"What do you mean?"

"A water bottle began rolling uphill," she said. "The colors in the sky began to bleed, and a crack of light split it."

"The sky?" I asked.

Elena nodded. "Like a tear. It was then that Anna became physically ill, her head splitting with a migraine and her stomach churning. When she began clutching her chest, I thought she was having a heart attack."

"She didn't, did she?" I asked.

"She was fine after a few minutes, after the ground stopped trembling."

Elena nodded again when I said, "An earthquake?"

"A fissure appeared in the sand, glowing as it snaked into the distance. It was then that we saw the flying saucer and the strange beings carrying glowing orbs."

Elena didn't strike me as a liar, but her description of what she witnessed strained my belief. I needed to speak with Anna Luna to see if she corroborated Elena's story.

"Are you still in contact with Ms. Luna?" I asked.

"She bought a house in Taos and lives no more than five miles from the Pueblo."

"I'd like to speak with her," I said. "I'd also like to visit the place where you saw the orb?"

"We could do it Saturday," she said.

I shook my head and said, "I already have plans for Saturday. The rodeo in Santa Fe."

"You competing?" she asked.

"Coaching," I said.

Elena flashed me a knowing smile and said, "I'll call Anna and ask if she'll talk to you. First, there's something I want to show you."

Elena disappeared momentarily into another room, returning with a leather notebook. She handed it across the table to me.

I asked, "What is this?" after scanning through the old notebook.

"Something I found in the high desert after witnessing the phenomenon I described."

"Do you recognize the language it's written in?" I asked.

Elena shook her head. "Anasazi is my guess," she said.

"Can you read it?"

Elena shook her head again. "No one can. If it ever existed, it's a dead language. Maybe as old as the glyphs."

"This looks almost like…"

"A blueprint?" she said, finishing my sentence.

"Of some device," I said. But what?"

"Something dangerous and life-changing," she said.

"Why do you say that?"

Elena indicated a glyph depicting two arrows pointing away from each other.

"The arrows in opposition represent the danger of conflict. War. Then there's the serpent glyph. This one's a rattlesnake, generally considered a symbol of danger and death."

"This glyph looks ominous," I said.

"The Thunderbird glyph," she said. "A powerful supernatural entity that often represents dangerous forces of nature."

"Thunder and lightning?"

"And earthquakes," she said.

"What else?"

"Someone other than you knows that I possess this," she said.

"How do you know?"

Because they've been watching the Pueblo since I came back from the desert with this artifact.

"How would they even know you have t?" asked. "Was there someone else in the desert the night you found this?"

"No one but the Sky People," she said. "Whoever is watching the Pueblo is human. I don't feel safe with the notebook. Will you give it to the Cryptid Hunter for me? He'll know what to do with it."

"Of course," I said.

She touched my hand and said, "Thank you. I'll call Anna."

CHAPTER 6

The sun dipped low behind the Sangre de Cristo Mountains, casting golden and crimson light across Taos's adobe walls as I parked the dusty Jeep just off the Plaza. I dragged my boots over the gravel while I climbed the stairs to the second-story cantina Elena had recommended. The Spiral Glyph exuded the aroma of roasted green chile that made my stomach growl like a coyote in winter, and I remembered I'd not eaten since breakfast.

I spotted Anna Luna right away, sitting at a wrought-iron table on the balcony, with strings of papel picado fluttering in the breeze. Her chestnut hair caught the last light like a halo, and those big brown eyes locked onto mine. Not flirtatious. Not guarded. Just... cosmic.

Her flowing skirt was the color of desert sage—soft, muted, and catching the wind as if it had somewhere to be. Her blouse was embroidered cotton, ivory with threads of turquoise and rust winding through the fabric like old canyon trails. Around her neck hung a silver pendant shaped like a crescent moon, and her wrists were stacked with thin bangles that chimed softly with each step. Her boots were scuffed yet elegant, the kind worn by someone who walks with purpose but never rushes.

There was paint on her fingers. Charcoal smudges stained her forearm. A sketchbook lay open beside her, half-filled with swirling lines and shadows that seemed drawn from dreams. She didn't smile, but her gaze held me like a note held too long—resonant, vibrating with something I couldn't name.

"Buck McDivit," I said, tipping my hat as I slid into the seat across from her. "Appreciate you meeting me."

She nodded, her fingers wrapped around a mug of something herbal and steaming. "Elena said you were different. That you'd listen."

"I've been known to do that," I said. "Especially when the story involves glowing orbs, extraterrestrials, and desert earthquakes."

Her lips curled into a smile, but her eyes remained serious. "We were out past the petroglyph wall, just before moonrise. Elena was tracing the spiral glyphs with her fingers, whispering in Tiwa, as I sketched the stars. That's when the air shifted, as if the desert was holding its breath."

Four tables overlooked the Taos plaza, all occupied, a white-smocked waiter bringing a steaming plate of green enchiladas to the table next to us. I leaned in, the busy clamor of the restaurant fading behind me.

"Go on."

"They came from the arroyo," she said.

When she paused, I said, "Who came from the arroyo?"

She sipped her herbal tea before answering. "More like what than who. Two beings, tall and thin, like shadows made of light. Their skin shimmered, not silver, not blue—something in between. They carried an orb that pulsed like a heartbeat, glowing from within."

"That's a pretty vivid description," I said. "Any idea about its purpose?"

"Only that I felt it in my chest, like it was syncing with me."

Anna reached into her satchel and pulled out a sketchpad, flipping to a page that took my breath away. There they were—two figures etched in charcoal and starlight, the orb cradled between them like a sacred flame. Behind them, a saucer-shaped craft hovered, silent and smooth, its surface rippling like water under moonlight.

"Your sketch is stunning," I said.

Apparently used to lavish praise, Anna didn't respond to mine.

"They didn't speak," she said. "But I heard them in my mind.

They were... ancient. Curious. And afraid."

"Afraid of what?" I asked.

She looked out over the Plaza, where tourists wandered and children laughed, oblivious to the mysteries just beyond the veil.

"Of what was about to happen in the high desert that night."

I sat back, the weight of her words settling into me like desert dust. I'd chased outlaws, uncovered secrets buried in old bones, and forgotten trails. This was something else. Something bigger.

The scent coming from the kitchen was downright criminal—roasted green chile, smoked carne adovada, and something sweet, maybe piñon and cinnamon. I leaned back in my chair, letting the aroma wrap around me like a warm blanket.

"You hungry?" I asked, watching her eyes flick toward the swinging kitchen doors.

She smiled, slow and radiant. "How could I not be, with these wonderful aromas engulfing us?"

"Thanks for agreeing to speak with me. Dinner's my treat," I said.

We ordered like locals—blue corn enchiladas smothered in red and green, stacked high with melted asadero. A bowl of posole arrived, steaming and fragrant, with tender pork and hominy swimming in a broth that tasted like it had been simmering since the Spanish came through. Sopapillas followed, puffed and golden, served with a side of honey so rich it could've been spun from desert sunlight.

"Elena made some pretty extraordinary claims about what you saw that night in the high desert," I said.

Responding to the disbelieving tone of my voice, she said, "Elena is a Tiwa elder. She neither lies nor exaggerates."

"I got that impression. Still..."

"Did she tell you about the high-pitched whine? It was like a tornado had passed over us. The sky bled red, then pixilated, and then changed into a multi-colored fractal pattern. There was an earthquake."

When Anna paused, I said, "I checked the U.S.G.S. website and confirmed there was an earthquake felt in northern New Mexico. You and Elena were near the epicenter. Is it possible the proximity to the quake caused the other phenomena you reported?"

Anna shook her head. "The things we saw were unexplainable."

"Elena said you became physically ill."

"My head felt as if it were splitting open."

"Do you have a history of migraines?" I asked.

"I haven't been sick since I was thirteen. It passed as soon as it manifested itself," she said.

"Do you think the alien spaceship was responsible for the strange things you witnessed?"

Anna shook her head. "I felt as if they were there because they were worried."

"Why would aliens worry about what happens on Earth?" I asked.

"I have no idea," she said.

As we ate, the sky deepened from turquoise to indigo. The Plaza below glowed with lanterns and laughter, but on the terrace, it felt like we were floating above it all—two strangers orbiting the same mystery.

Anna dipped a sopapilla into honey and held it up. "You know, there's something sacred about food like this. It's like the land is feeding you its story."

I took a bite of the enchilada, the heat from the chile making my eyes water just enough to feel alive.

"If that's true, then this land's got a hell of a tale to tell."

She laughed, and it was soft and musical, like wind through cottonwoods. "You always talk like that? Like you're narrating a Western?"

"Only when I'm trying to impress a beautiful woman," I said, and let the words hang there.

Her eyes met mine, steady and amused. "Well, it's working. But you might want to dial it back before I start sketching you with a halo and a six-shooter."

I chuckled, wiping my mouth with the corner of a cloth napkin. "Long as you get my good side."

She leaned in, her elbow brushing mine, and the air between us shifted—less mystery now, more magnetism. The stars were out, scattered like silver dust across the velvet sky, and I couldn't help but wonder if they were watching us the way we watched them.

Anna tilted her head. "You ever think maybe the aliens weren't the strangest part of that night?"

I raised a brow. "What do you mean?"

She smiled again, this time with something behind it. "Maybe the strangest part was how it felt like we were meant to see them. It was as if there was a problem, and they wanted us humans to know about it."

I didn't answer right away. I just looked at how her hair caught the starlight, how her words lingered like the last note of a song. And, I felt something stir that had nothing to do with mystery or danger. I was enjoying the moment and didn't want it to end. Anna apparently felt the same.

After dinner, we wandered down from the balcony and into the pulse of downtown Taos. The adobe walls glowed under the streetlamps, soft and golden like candlelight. Music drifted from a nearby cantina—Spanish guitar, slow and sultry—and the air carried the scent of juniper and mesquite.

Anna walked beside me, her arm brushing mine, as if the universe were nudging us closer. We passed galleries with windows full of surreal desert dreamscapes and boutiques selling turquoise jewelry that looked as if it had been mined from the very soul of the earth. She paused at a mural—an imaginative explosion of color, stars, and ancient symbols.

"Taos remembers things the rest of the world forgot," she said. "It doesn't simply sit on the land. It listens to it."

We kept walking, past the Plaza and out toward Kit Carson Park, where the lights thinned, and the trees grew tall and whispery. I knew a spot just beyond the edge of town, where the pavement gave way to dirt, and the sky opened up like a cathedral.

We climbed a short ridge, boots crunching over dry grass

and scattered stone. At the top, the world fell away. No streetlights. No noise. Just the hush of the high desert and so many stars it felt like the sky was spilling over.

Anna tilted her head, her hair catching the moonlight. "It's like standing inside a story," she said.

I watched her silhouette against the cosmos, and something inside me stirred—something old and quiet and aching to be known.

"You ever wonder," I said, "if the stars are looking back?"

She turned to me, eyes reflecting constellations. "Maybe they're waiting for us to ask the right question."

I stepped closer, close enough to feel the warmth of her breath. "And what if we already did?"

She smiled, slow and knowing. "Then maybe the answer's standing right in front of us."

The wind picked up, carrying the scent of sage and secrets. And in that moment, under a sky older than memory, I didn't care about aliens or mysteries or the strange pull of fate.

I just wanted to know her.

After our walk under the stars, Anna turned to me with that quiet spark in her eyes and said, "I want to show you something."

We cut through a narrow alley off the Plaza, past a crumbling adobe wall and a rusted gate that creaked like it had stories to tell. Her house stood just beyond—a weathered building with thick walls and a bell tower that had long since stopped ringing.

"Used to be a church," she said, brushing her fingers along the old wooden door. "A woman from back East renovated it and lived here until she passed. I found it last year, bought it on the spot, and never looked back."

Inside, the place was magic.

The ceilings soared with exposed vigas, and the plaster walls glowed with candlelight and warm tones of ochre and turquoise. Paintings—hers, I assumed—hung in clusters: desert moons, spiraling glyphs, and dreamlike landscapes that felt half real, half imagined. A fireplace crackled in the corner, its mantle lined with smooth stones and bundles of sage. The scent of cedar and linseed oil hung in the air.

Then came the sound of nails on tile and a friendly woof.

"Fritz, my baby," she said.

Fritz trotted in from the hallway, a shaggy mutt with mismatched ears and eyes full of mischief. He came right up to me, tail wagging like we'd known each other in another life.

"Well, hey there, partner," I said, crouching to scratch behind his ears. "Fritz and my dog Pard would hit it off. Same kind of soul—loyal, scrappy, and smarter than most folks I know."

Anna laughed, leaning against the archway. "He likes you. He usually barks his head off when strangers come around."

I stood, brushing fur from my jeans. "I like him too. And this place... It's something else."

She walked over, her hand grazing mine as she passed. "It's home. Finally."

We moved into the den, where a low table held a half-finished sketch and a mug of cold tea. She lit a few candles, and the shadows danced across the old stone walls like spirits waking up. I sank into a worn leather chair, Fritz curling up at my feet like we'd done this a hundred times.

Anna sat across from me, her legs tucked beneath her, eyes reflecting the flicker of the flame. Barely audible music played from hidden speakers, the melody haunting—a guitar solo performed by a talented guitarist. The music faded into the background as Anna's voice captured my attention.

"You ever think about settling down?" she asked, voice soft.

I looked at the art, the warmth, the dog, and the woman who seemed to carry starlight in her haunting eyes.

"More than I admit," I said. "But I've never found a place that felt like it could hold me."

She smiled, slow and thoughtful. "Maybe you weren't meant to be held."

I didn't say anything. I just looked at her, and for the first time in a long while, I felt like I'd arrived somewhere worth staying.

I watched Anna move through the candlelight like she belonged to it. There was something about her—something that didn't ask for attention but held it anyway. She didn't fill the room with noise or flash. She filled it with presence.

It's late, and I still have a long way to go back to where I'm staying," I said.

"Where are you staying?" she asked.

"An abandoned ranch about twenty miles from here."

She didn't ask me why I was staying at an abandoned ranch.

"Sounds intriguing," she said. "I'd love to sketch it. Can I come by on Saturday?"

"Any day other than Saturday," I said.

"Hot date?" she asked with a sly grin.

"Rodeo de Santa Fe. I'm coaching a young man who's entered in the saddle bronc competition."

"Coaching and not competing?"

"Rodeoing gets in your blood," I said. "I was good, but realized I was never going to be the best."

"Is being the best so important?" she asked.

She smiled when I said, "I think you already know the answer to that question."

I'd met plenty of people who wore mystery like a costume. Anna didn't wear hers. She was hers. The kind of woman who could say more with silence than most folks could with a sermon. And when she looked at me, really looked, it was like she saw past the dust and dents I'd picked up over the years. Not to fix me. To know me.

It scared me a little.

"I've never been to a rodeo," she said. "What's it like?"

"A heartbeat with spurs on," I said. "The sun blazing down, the crowd hollering like thunder, and some poor fool hanging on to a thousand pounds of fury for eight eternal seconds, praying the ground doesn't come up too fast."

She chuckled and said, "I'd love to see it in person. Would you mind if I joined you on Saturday?"

"I'd love it," I said.

We exchanged phone numbers and I departed, feeling

strangely empty and wondering what Tara would think. I decided not to worry about it as I walked to the Jeep.

Something else was on my mind. I couldn't get rid of the feeling that something or someone was watching me.

CHAPTER 7

The road back to the ranch was dark and dusty, and I had plenty of time alone to reflect on my meeting with Anna. There was a steadiness to her, like the desert itself. She didn't need to chase storms or stir up drama.

She just waited, rooted, and let the wind come to her. I'd been the wind for a long time. Always moving, always searching. But sitting in her old church-turned-home, with Fritz curled up at my feet and her eyes on mine, I felt something shift.

The stars, scattered like diamonds across a velvet sky, were out in full force when I pulled up to Shadow Ranch. The kind of night that makes you feel small, but not in a bad way. A bite was in the air, a crisp September chill that sneaks in after sundown and settles in your bones if you let it. Someone had lit the fire, and I was glad to see smoke curling from the chimney.

Pard met me at the door, tail wagging like he hadn't seen me in years. I knelt and scratched behind his ears, feeling the warmth of his welcome seep into me.

"Good boy," I said, and he leaned into my hand like he understood every word.

Inside, the kiva glowed with a soft orange light, shadows dancing along the adobe walls. The place smelled of piñon smoke and something else—chile, maybe. Something Tara must've cooked. I felt a pang of guilt. I hadn't meant to be gone so long.

Ran stirred in the loft, his boots thudding softly on the wooden steps as he came down, rubbing sleep from his eyes. I popped open the ice chest and tossed him a can of Coors. He caught it one-handed, cracked it open, and took a long pull before speaking.

"Tara was here," he said, settling into the worn armchair by the fire. "Waited all damn day for you. Made some enchiladas. She left maybe an hour ago. Didn't look too happy."

I sank into the old leather couch, the cold can sweating in my hand. "I didn't know she was waiting on me," I said.

Ran gave me a look, one eyebrow raised. "You two got something going?"

I hesitated, then shrugged. "We shared a kiss. Quick one. Nothing serious."

Ran chuckled. "You couldn't prove it by Tara. I think she's sweet on you."

I stared into the fire, watching the logs crackle and shift. The warmth was welcoming, but my mind had drifted to the Rodeo de Santa Fe on Saturday and the potentially tense meeting between Tara and Anna.

"Let's get some sleep," I said. "There are some things I need to go over with you before the rodeo on Saturday."

Ran nodded and started up the stairs to the loft. Outside, the wind whispered through the sagebrush, and Pard curled up at my feet. I tipped my head back and looked up through the window at the stars again. Something was moving.

It started low, like a distant engine idling beneath the earth—steady, pulsing—the Taos Hum. It was back, and more than sound. It was a feeling, as if the ground itself were holding its breath.

I burst out the door, boots crunching on the gravel, Pard scrambling after me. The sky above was clear, stars sharp as needles. But then I saw the lights. Not a saucer, or anything shaped like a craft. Just three orbs, pale and silent, drifting in a loose triangle high above the mesa.

They weren't blinking like aircraft. They weren't falling like meteors. They just… hovered. Moved. Shifted. Ran came out behind me, shirt half-buttoned, eyes squinting against the dark.

"You hear it too?" he asked.

I nodded, never taking my eyes off the sky. "Up there."

He followed my gaze and fell quiet. The lights pulsed faintly, as if breathing. One dipped lower, then shot sideways—fast, too fast for anything manmade. Then it stopped dead, as if it had never moved at all.

"Is that what I think it is?" Ran asked.

"The lights," I said. "They aren't ours."

The hum grew louder, vibrating in my chest like a tuning fork struck deep within me. Pard whined and pressed against my leg. The air felt charged, like the moment before a lightning strike, yet there wasn't a cloud in sight.

There we stood, two men and a dog, in the high desert night, watching something unexplainable. The lights stayed a little longer, then flickered out as if a switch had been flipped off. The hum faded along with them, leaving only the wind and Pard's breathing. We stayed a moment longer, staring at the empty sky.

Morning came slow and golden, the kind of light that creeps in through the cracks of old adobe and warms the chill out of your joints. I stirred to the smell of piñon smoke and coffee, Pard already nosing around the hearth like he'd been up for hours.

The kiva fire had burned low but steady through the night, and the room held that smoky hush that only comes after a good sleep. Ran was already cracking eggs into the cast-iron skillet, the sizzle waking up the room.

I poured us both coffee—black, no sugar—and pulled the foil off the dish Tara had left—green chile enchiladas, still fragrant, layered with cheese and that earthy bite of roasted Hatch. I felt a pang again, remembering she'd waited all day. I hadn't meant to leave her hanging.

We ate in silence for a while, the kind that's easy between men who've shared trail dust and long drives.

Ran finally leaned back, wiped his mouth with the back of his hand, and said, "So, you got a rodeoing lesson for me today, or are we just gonna sit around and philosophize over eggs?"

I didn't answer right away. Just reached into my duffel and pulled out the braided bronc rein I'd carried for years. It was worn smooth in places, stiff in others, the kind of leather that had seen sweat, blood, and more than a few eight-second battles. I tossed it to him.

"Show me how you hold it."

Ran gripped it like he was holding a garden hose, fingers loose, wrist limp. I winced.

"That won't cut it," I said.

I took the rein from him and showed him the grip, tight, but not clenched. Thumb locked over the top, pinky curled under, wrist angled just so.

"This is the proper way. You get comfortable with this until it becomes second nature. It's the only way you're going to stay on a bronc's back when it's trying to send you to the moon."

He nodded, tried again, and did better this time. But then he set the rein down to pick up a spoon he'd dropped.

"Hey," I said. "Keep the rein in your hand. All day. If you go to the toilet, the rein goes with you."

He looked at me like I was half-crazy. "What if I need to pick something up? Like a load of firewood?"

"You figure out how to do it with the rein in your right hand," I said. "Don't let go of the damn thing."

Ran turned the rein over in his palm, studying it as if it might bite. "Do you always carry this in your duffel?"

I nodded. "If you want to be successful on the circuit, the rein has to become a part of you. When I was riding, I practiced with it every chance I got—sitting, walking, hell—eating breakfast. It's not just about strength."

He frowned, clearly skeptical. "Seems a little obsessive."

I leaned against the wall, coffee in hand. "Bronc riding's like any other sport. It's all about muscle memory. Your hand on the rein, the way you sit in the saddle, the position of your knees. Little things. They're what make the difference between a clean ride and getting dumped in the dirt so hard your teeth rattle."

Ran didn't say anything, just gripped the rein tighter and stared into the fire. I could see it working in him, that slow churn of understanding. He wasn't just holding leather—he was holding the first thread of something bigger. Something that might change him.

My phone buzzed on the windowsill, screen lit up with Angie's name. After wiping my hands on a dish towel, I picked it up, coffee still steaming in my other hand.

"Buck," she said, brisk as ever. "Anything to report?"

"I met with Elena Tafoya and Anna Luna yesterday."

"And?"

"More than we'd hoped for," I said. "Elena found something interesting the day of the earthquake. She shared it with me."

"What?"

"An old leather notebook with notes partly written in glyphs and a language Elena believes is Anasazi, along with illustrations of a device that Galileo might have sketched."

"What's its significance?" Angie asked.

"Elena thinks the Sky People left it for her to find and that it signals great danger."

"Danger as in what?" she asked.

"The illustrations look to me like a plan for something. Maybe a bomb. Hell, I'm only guessing here."

"Can you send me pictures of the notebook?"

"I can do better than that," I said. "She gave me the notebook to give to Jake."

"Better hold on to it and give it to him in person."

"There might be a problem," I said. "Elena thinks someone has been watching the Pueblo since she returned. She didn't see anyone else. How would anyone know she has it?"

"Drones, balloons, satellites," she said. "Lots of ways to surveil these days other than with eyes and binoculars."

"We were at Elena's apartment when she gave it to me. Unless someone has installed spy cameras there, nobody knows I have it."

"Have you told anyone other than me?" Angie asked.

"Just you," I said.

"Keep it that way for now. In the meantime, I have a lead for you. Interview's set for noon. Guy's name is Kermit Sanderson."

I raised an eyebrow. "Sanderson? What's he do?"

"Builds guitars. Repairs them too. Has a little shop tucked in a back alley off Bent Street."

I stared out the window at the sun climbing over the Sangre de Cristos.

"You want me to interview a guitar builder?"

"He's not just a luthier," she said, voice tightening. "PhD in physics from Caltech. Used to work at Sandia Labs in Albuquerque. Retired early, married a local woman from Taos Pueblo, and now he spends his days carving spruce and rosewood."

I leaned against the counter, Pard nosing at my boot. "So what's the angle?"

"He was privy to some of the deepest classified work in the country—nuclear stuff. Advanced propulsion. Maybe even UAPs. He probably won't tell you anything useful, but Jake thinks he'll make a good guest for the Taos episode. Add flavor."

I snorted. "Flavor. Right."

"Just talk to him," she said. "He's eccentric. Brilliant. Might say something that gets people thinking."

"What else?" I asked.

"Jake can't stand it any longer. He's flying out tomorrow. He'll want a report," she said.

"I told you to tell him to hold his horses," I said.

"You know as well as I do that when Jake makes up his mind, nothing's going to change it. Why are you so adamant about him not coming?"

"Randle Roberts' son Ran is helping me with the investigation. He's the one who got the guest list for me. He wants to ride the rodeo. I agreed to help him," I said.

"And?"

"The Rodeo de Santa Fe starts Saturday. I had the whole day blocked out to help Ran," I said.

"Jake and Colley like the rodeo," Angie said.

"Good," I said. "Explain the situation and tell them I'll get their tickets."

I hung up and turned to Ran, who was still gripping the

bronc rein like it might bite him.

"I'm heading into Taos. Got an interview with a guitar builder who used to play with classified tech."

Ran blinked. "Sounds like a hell of a résumé."

"Yeah. We'll see if he's more than just varnish and strings."

Pard perked up at the sound of "Taos," tail wagging like he knew the road ahead. I grabbed my jacket and keys, then turned back to Ran.

"What else?" he asked.

I fished a hundred dollars out of my wallet and handed it to him. "Drive into Santa Fe and get me two tickets to the rodeo."

He laughed. "The rodeo has been sold out for weeks. Even if there were something available, you wouldn't get them for a hundred bucks."

Jake had given me a traveler's check for $5,000 before leaving Tulsa, and I gave it to Ran.

"Find me two tickets. If that's not enough, I'll have Angie wire more." I started to leave, but had a second thought and turned around. "And Ran, don't let go of the damn rein. Not for anything."

"What if I need to—"

"Nope. Toilet, firewood, doesn't matter. You figure it out. That rein stays in your hand."

He groaned, but nodded. "You always this tough on rookies?"

I gave him a half-smile. "Only the ones I think might make it."

Pard trotted ahead of me, nails clicking on the tile. I followed him out into the morning light, the air sharp and clean, the kind that makes you feel like something's about to happen.

I didn't know what we'd find in that alley shop in Taos, but I had a feeling it wouldn't be just guitars.

CHAPTER 8

Taos was a place halfway between worlds, where the desert met the mountains and the past never quite let go of the present. The past and present were braided together, whispering secrets through the sagebrush.

I parked the Jeep near the plaza, its adobe walls glowing like embers under the late afternoon sun, casting long shadows that seemed to pulse with intent.

Pard leapt out before I cut the engine, his nose twitching, tail slicing the air. His amber eyes darted toward the horizon, sensing something I couldn't yet name.

Angie's directions were scribbled on a napkin, vague as a half-remembered dream, but the alley revealed itself easily—a narrow crease between a gallery spilling with vibrant canvases and a shop glittering with turquoise jewelry. The kind of place you'd miss if you weren't looking for it.

Above a weathered door hung a hand-painted sign, 'Sanderson Strings', its faded letters curling like smoke. The wood was carved with intricate whorls, as if the sign itself held stories older than the town.

I knocked once, the sound swallowed by the thick air, then pushed the door open. A bell jangled faintly, its chime swallowed by the shop's heavy atmosphere. Inside, the air was thick with sawdust and linseed oil, laced with something deeper—pipe smoke, perhaps, or the musk of aged secrets.

The space was a controlled chaos: guitars hung like sacred relics on the walls, each one a character in its own right. Some gleamed with fresh lacquer, catching the dim light like liquid gold; others bore the scars of time, their surfaces dulled by countless hands.

A workbench anchored the back, strewn with chisels, tuning forks, and the half-carved body of a twelve-string, its curves soft as a lover's hip. Shelves sagged under jars of screws, coils of wire, and scraps of rosewood that seemed to hum with potential.

Behind the bench stood a man with silver hair tied in a low braid, wire-rimmed glasses perched on a nose sharp as a hawk's beak. He didn't look up, just kept sanding a guitar neck with slow strokes, as if coaxing a melody from the wood itself. His hands moved with the precision of a surgeon, or maybe a priest.

"You Buck?"

His voice was low, dry as the desert wind rattling the junipers outside.

"Yes, sir," I said, stepping forward.

Pard's claws clicked on the worn floorboards as he followed, his ears twitching. He set the wood down and turned. His eyes were sharp as broken glass, glinting with a hunger that had seen too much and still craved more.

"Angie said you'd be coming. Said you were curious. She sounded like a doll on the phone."

"She is, and I'm always curious," I said, leaning against the counter. "Especially when a physicist trades particle beams for rosewood."

He smiled, a flicker of amusement that didn't reach his eyes. "You think it's a downgrade?"

"I think it's a story."

He gestured to a stool near the bench, its seat worn smooth by years of visitors.

"Then sit. I'll tell you what I can. But you won't get what you came for unless you're willing to listen between the notes."

Pard settled at my feet, his fur brushing my leg, ears perked like he was tuning into something beyond my reach.

I pulled out my recorder but kept it off. This wasn't a sound-bite interview. Outside, the wind shifted, carrying the sharp bite of sage and something electric, like the air before a storm. Maybe it was the altitude. Or maybe Taos was already whispering its truths.

He nodded when I said, "Did Angie tell you I'm the advanced scout for Jake Huntington, the Cryptid Hunter?"

"It's the reason I agreed to talk to you."

"Oh? How so?"

"Don't get me wrong. I love the show. Never miss it, but no one's ever going to take anything said on it seriously," he said, his voice carrying a wry edge.

I grinned. "Not something Jake's going to want to hear."

"Then don't tell him. Still, it's the only way I'd ever get away with an interview about my former career."

"Jake's not asking you to reveal top secrets."

A slight smile cracked Sanderson's craggy face, like a fault line in the desert floor.

"Know anything about quantum physics, Buck?"

"No, sir, can't say as I do."

"Neither do most people," he said, leaning back, his fingers tracing the grain of the workbench.

"What are you getting at?" I asked, feeling the conversation tilt toward something vast and unsteady.

"I could spell out the country's darkest secret using an example from quantum physics, and most people wouldn't have a clue what I was talking about."

"Does that mean the government knows about the orbs and lights in the sky and has an explanation?"

"The short answer is no," he said, his tone clipped, like he was measuring each word.

He sighed when I pressed, "What exactly does the government know?"

"Not much. The scope of human knowledge is just a drop in the ocean. Quantum computing is our best chance of understanding what's happening around us in the universe, and it's still in its infancy."

"So the government isn't responsible for the lights in the sky and orb sightings?"

Sanderson didn't answer, instead reaching into a dented

mini fridge tucked beneath the workbench. The hinges groaned as he pulled out two cans of craft beer from a Santa Fe brewery, their labels faded but proud.

"You like beer, son?"

"Yes, sir," I said, catching the can he tossed me.

"Never spent much money on any particular thing except beer. Might say I'm a beer snob. IPA," he said, popping his own can. "Hope you like it."

I cracked the tab, the hiss sharp in the quiet shop. The IPA was crisp, bitter, with a piney bite that lingered like the desert itself.

"Tasty," I said, taking another sip.

We'd finished our third beer, the alcohol warming my veins, when Sanderson finally circled back to the heart of it. He'd been cagey, talking about a guitar he'd built to mimic a signal no one could explain. My curiosity sharpened, cutting through the buzz.

"Sounds intriguing. I'd love to hear it."

He didn't respond immediately. Instead, he turned to the workbench, his fingers grazing the fretboard of the unfinished twelve-string, then reached beneath and pulled out a case that looked older than the shop itself.

The leather was cracked, the brass latches tarnished to a dull green. He set it down with reverence, like it cradled a relic from another world.

"I built this after I started hearing the signal," he said, his voice softer now, almost confessional. "Not the Taos Hum. Something else. Higher. Cleaner. Like a sine wave wrapped in silk."

He opened the case, and the air seemed to shift, growing heavier. Inside lay a guitar unlike any I'd seen. Its matte black body drank the light, unadorned by gloss or flourish. The sound hole was elliptical, rimmed with copper wire that glinted faintly, like a portal to somewhere else.

The fret markers weren't standard dots or diamonds but tiny etched symbols—some angular, like equations; others swirling, and ancient petroglyphs scratched into canyon walls.

"I was working on a project at Sandia," he said, his fingers hovering over the strings, not quite touching them. "Deep frequency mapping. We picked up a pattern out near the Four Corners. It wasn't natural. It wasn't ours. But it repeated. Like a song."

He strummed once, and the sound was a living thing—low, resonant, with a shimmering edge that lingered like heat rising off sun-scorched asphalt. Pard whimpered, pressing closer to my leg, his warmth grounding me against the strangeness of the note.

"I spent six months tuning this to match the signal," Sanderson said, his voice barely above a whisper. "The wood, the bracing, the copper inlay—it's all calibrated. When I play certain progressions, it resonates with the frequency. I've had people say they feel it in their teeth. Others say it makes them dream in languages they don't speak."

I leaned closer, drawn to the faint hum still vibrating in the room, a sound that seemed to curl around my thoughts. "You think it's communication?"

"I think it's presence," he said, his eyes locking onto mine. "Something watching. Or waiting."

He handed me the guitar. It was heavier than it looked, warm as living flesh. I plucked a string, and the note rang out—pure, eerie, like it had traveled across galaxies to reach me. My palms grew slick, the wood seeming to pulse under my fingers, as if it were sizing me up.

Sanderson watched me, his gaze unyielding. "Play it long enough, and you'll start to hear things. Not with your ears. With your bones."

I didn't want to play it. At least not yet. The guitar felt alive, watchful, its weight pressing against something deep in my chest. But I couldn't walk away either.

"Play it for me," I said, my voice quieter than I meant.

He didn't speak, just slung the strap over his shoulder and cradled the instrument like it was an extension of himself. He didn't tune it or check the strings. He closed his eyes, and his fingers began to move.

The first chord hit me like a physical force, not loud but deep, bypassing my ears and sinking into my ribs. It was a vibration that seemed to hum from the earth itself, ancient and relentless.

Then came the progression—minor chords bent into shapes that felt wrong yet achingly beautiful, each note shimmering like a mirage. The shop dimmed, the fluorescent lights flickering to a sickly pulse. The adobe walls seemed to recede, stretching into an impossible distance, as if the room were unraveling.

Pard whimpered again, his body tense against my leg. I rested a hand on his back, feeling his heartbeat race beneath his fur.

The music layered itself— a low thrum like thunder rolling beneath the desert, a glassy tone like ice splintering on a frozen lake, and something else, something alive. A whisper, not of words but of rhythm, breath, gravity. It curled around my thoughts, tugging at memories I didn't know I had.

Sanderson's fingers danced, his face slack, eyes half-lidded, as if he were somewhere else entirely. He wasn't playing. He was channeling. The air grew thick, heavy with the scent of ozone and something metallic, like blood or rust. My teeth buzzed, my tongue tasted coppery, and my vision blurred at the edges, the world smudging like wet ink.

When he stopped playing, the silence was a wound. It wasn't just quiet—it was the absence of something vital, something the guitar had pulled into being and then hidden again. I realized I'd been holding my breath.

"You heard it, didn't you?"

Sanderson's voice was soft, but his eyes were fierce, searching.

I nodded, my throat tight. "I don't know what I heard. But it wasn't just sound."

He smiled, and it was a jagged thing, sharp with knowing. "It never is."

"Is that...?"

"The sound of the universe?" he said, finishing my thought,

his voice a low rumble.

I nodded, my pulse still uneven. "Is it?"

"Quantum mechanics tells us humans don't truly perceive the fundamental nature of reality," he said, leaning forward, his braid swaying like a pendulum. "Most of what we perceive might be described as illusion."

"Like a waking dream?"

He nodded, his eyes glinting. "Someone once said humans cavort in the playgrounds of their minds."

"What does that say about science and our systems of belief?" I asked, my voice steadier now but still hungry for answers.

"God, angels, Jesus, Buddha, maybe even ghosts—they're interdimensional beings," he said, the words landing like stones in still water.

"That's pretty heavy. What the hell does it mean?"

"A man named Edwin Abbot wrote a book called Flatland: A Romance of Many Dimensions. Published in 1884. Heard of it?"

"Can't say as I have," I said, the beer buzz making my thoughts sluggish.

"In Abbot's book, he described a two-dimensional world to explain the hierarchy of the Victorian Era. The word 'flatland' is now an important concept in quantum physics."

The words felt like they were slipping past me, too vast to hold. The IPA wasn't helping.

"You're losing me," I said, half-laughing.

Sanderson chuckled, a warm sound, and tossed me another beer. The can was cold, grounding.

"Better now?"

"Much," I said, cracking it open. "Please finish your thought."

He chugged his own beer, the empty can rattling as it hit the trash basket. "We live in a 3-D world—length, width, height. String theory suggests there are additional spatial dimensions curled up within the three we know, undetectable to us."

I blinked, the idea sparking something in my mind. "So the UAPs could be from right here on Earth, not another planet?"

He didn't answer directly, just glanced at his watch, the gesture abrupt.

"I've been away from my work too long. I must conclude our interview."

"Please," I said. "One more thing."

I handed him the weathered leather notebook, his demeanor darkening as he studied it.

"Where did you get this?" he asked.

"The high desert, near the epicenter of the recent earthquake. Any idea what the diagrams mean?"

"Doomsday device," he said.

"You sure? The language is Anasazi. How could an extinct tribal group have had the plans for a doomsday device?"

"Maybe it's the reason they're extinct," he said.

Sanderson reached under a cabinet, grabbed a bottle of mescal, and poured us each a shot. He finished his and poured another while I was still contemplating it.

"How do you know what it is?" I asked.

"Every country in the world is looking for such a weapon."

He shook his head when I asked, "Do we have one?"

"No, thank God! Not one that works."

He laughed when I said, "Maybe I should let you take possession."

My advice is to toss it into the nearest kiva and not walk away until you see the last ember. That notebook will get you killed if you're not careful.

Sanderson's words had spiraled into realms I couldn't follow, and I sensed he'd said all he would. Jake and his crew would eat this up, though. Cameras rolling, lights glinting off that eerie guitar. I stood, legs unsteady from the beer and the weight of what I'd heard.

"Thank you, sir," I said, moving toward the door.

He stopped me, his voice low, urgent. "I'll leave you with one last thought. Buck, don't show that notebook to anyone else, and don't overlook interdimensional beings."

I turned, sensing he was about to reveal something more important. “You have something else you want to tell me?”

“Sorry,” he said, shaking his head, his braid swaying. “You were such a good listener. I drank too much IPA and opened my mouth when I shouldn’t have.”

He waved me off when I started to protest.

“But…”

The door creaked shut behind me, the bell’s faint jangle swallowed by the Taos wind. Outside, the plaza was bathed in the last light of day, the adobe walls glowing like they held the sun’s secrets.

Pard trotted beside me, his ears still perked, as if the guitar’s strange song lingered in his bones too. The air crackled with something unspoken, and I knew I’d be back.

Meanwhile, that haunting melody Sanderson had played on his cosmic guitar reminded me of the music from the night before when I visited Anna’s. Her house was nearby, so I decided to pay her a visit.

CHAPTER 9

As Pard and I stepped out of the shadowed alley and back into the pulsing heart of Taos Plaza, the air felt charged, like the moment before a lightning strike. The haunting melody Sanderson had coaxed from his cosmic guitar clung to me, a ghostly echo I couldn't shake.

It wasn't just familiar—it was the same tune I'd heard the night before, drifting through hidden speakers at Anna Luna's house, its notes weaving through the smoke and laughter like a secret code. The plaza buzzed around us, vendors hawking chiles and woven blankets, but the melody looped in my head, pulling me toward answers. Anna's place wasn't far, so I decided to drop by and ask where she'd gotten that music.

The narrow street to her house was lined with adobe homes, their earthen walls glowing like sun-baked clay in the fading light. Piñon smoke curled from a chimney, its resinous scent mingling with the dust my boots kicked up.

Pard trotted beside me, his ears twitching as if he, too, sensed the town's undercurrent. When Anna opened her door, the faint creak of its hinges was drowned by the surprise in her voice.

"Buck," she said, her dark eyes narrowing. "What are you doing here?"

"I was in Taos and had a few questions, so I thought I'd drop by," I said, trying to keep my tone light.

She cracked the door only an inch, peering out like I was a stranger selling salvation. Her face was taut, her fingers gripping the frame.

"I'm sorry," she said, voice clipped. "I'm busy right now."

Behind her, Fritz's golden fur flashed as he wedged his head between her legs, tail wagging furiously when he spotted Pard. The dogs locked eyes, their excitement a sharp contrast to Anna's tension. Fritz squirmed, forcing the door wider, and Pard yipped, eager to unite.

I grabbed Fritz's collar, his warmth wriggling under my hands, and handed him back through the gap. That's when I heard it—a low voice, muffled but urgent, coming from inside.

My old law enforcement instincts kicked in, heart pounding as I imagined Anna caught in a home invasion—or worse. I pushed the door open, my shoulder brushing the rough wood.

A young woman stood in the dim hallway, her face pale, eyes wide with a sheepish glint. She was about Anna's age, her presence soft but steady, like a juniper holding fast in a storm.

Relief washed over me—Anna wasn't in danger—but the air still crackled with something unspoken. I stepped back, raising my hands.

"So sorry, Anna. I was in law enforcement for a while, and I thought you might need assistance. I'll leave you two alone."

Whispers passed between them as I turned toward the steps, the words too soft to catch but heavy with intent.

"Buck, wait," Anna called, her voice softer now, almost pleading.

"No problem," I said, glancing back. "I'll call you tomorrow."

"No, you don't understand," she said, stepping onto the porch, the door swinging wider. "Dusty's in trouble. I'm trying to help. We could use some advice. Please, come in."

Inside, Fritz and Pard collided like long-lost brothers, noses bumping, tails whipping the air into a frenzy. The living room smelled of sage and old wood, the walls adorned with Anna's paintings—swirls of ochre and turquoise that seemed to pulse in the low light.

"This is Pard," I said, patting his flank as he settled beside me.

Anna was rattled; a jittery edge had replaced her usual warmth. She didn't introduce the woman, who stepped forward, hand outstretched.

"I'm Dusty," she said, her voice steady despite the storm in her eyes.

She wore a turquoise Western shirt, faded jeans hugging her frame, and scuffed cowboy boots built for ranch work, not barroom dancing. Her face was bare of makeup, her dark hair pulled into a practical braid, and I got the sense she lived hard and honestly, like the land itself.

Anna led us to her den, a cozy room with a kiva fireplace, its embers casting a warm flicker across the woven rugs. She disappeared into the kitchen, returning with a tray of steaming tea, the scent of chamomile faint against the heavier notes of smoke and tension.

Dusty pushed her cup aside, her calloused fingers brushing the table.

"I love you to tears, sister, but right now what I need is a shot of mescal."

I'd already had three IPAs at Sanderson's, their bitterness lingering on my tongue, and tea felt like a weak apology for the weight in the room. Anna caught my glance, her lips twitching, and returned with a bottle of mescal, its amber glow catching the firelight, and three shot glasses etched with desert motifs. She poured, the liquid glinting like a promise.

After a shot and a salud, the burn settling in my chest, I said, "Okay, tell me what's the matter and how I can help."

Dusty's hands were steady, her jaw carved from years of facing down storms and heartbreak, but her eyes—wide, glassy, unblinking—betrayed a raw devastation. She stared into her empty shot glass, as if it might hold the answers she couldn't find. Anna sat beside her, one hand on Dusty's knee, the other clutching her untouched glass, her knuckles pale.

The air thickened, the dogs sensing it too. Pard lay at my feet, ears perked, his breath slow but alert. Fritz curled by the fireplace, his tail giving a single twitch before stilling. The room felt like a held breath, the kind before a confession or a scream.

Dusty inhaled, the sound jagged, like it scraped her throat. "She's been murdered," she said, her voice low but sharp enough to slice through the quiet.

I leaned forward, the mescal's heat spreading through me. "Murdered? Who?"

"My roomie," Dusty said, lips tight. "Kirsten Louise Maldonado."

I blinked, the name landing like a stone. "The congresswoman?"

Dusty nodded, her eyes glinting with unshed tears. "From New Mexico. She was more than my roommate, Buck. She was my friend. My anchor. And someone didn't just want her gone. They wanted her silenced."

Anna's gaze met mine, intense and unreadable. "We don't know who to trust. Dusty's scared. I'm scared."

"I just left Kermit Sanderson's guitar shop," I said, the memory of his music still vibrating in my bones. "He played a cosmic guitar for me. The song sounded like what you were playing last night."

"Illusional Beings," Anna said, her voice softening. "I wandered into his shop a while back and heard it playing in the background. Mr. Sanderson burned me a copy."

She smiled faintly when I said, "But he's a scientist, not a musician."

"Music is rooted in objective principles of physics, mathematics, and even human biology, which can be studied and explained scientifically," she said, her artist's eyes glinting with understanding.

"I never thought of music that way," I admitted, the mescal loosening my thoughts.

"Most people don't," Anna said. "Rhythms and pitches can be expressed mathematically, and the human body physically and emotionally reacts to music in measurable ways."

"Hell, yes!" Dusty said, her voice cutting through the haze. "Changes in heart rate and brain activity. Turn on some music and let's drink another shot."

Anna flipped a switch, and the room filled with the eerie notes of Sanderson's cosmic guitar, its melody curling around us like smoke. Dusty refilled our shot glasses, the mescal splashing faintly, while Anna's remained untouched.

"Music also involves art and emotion; its underlying structure and the way it's created, transmitted, and perceived are inherently scientific," Anna said, her voice steady despite the tension.

"You're an artist," I said. "You would know."

"Kirsten wasn't just Dusty's roomie. She was a friend of mine. And that music—Sanderson's guitar. Kirsten was obsessed with it."

The mescal's burn deepened, but it wasn't the drink quickening my pulse. It was the sense that something vast and deliberate had been set in motion, a cosmic thread tying Sanderson's shop to this moment.

Anna nodded when I asked, "Did she visit Sanderson's shop and speak with him?"

"Twice," Anna said, her voice barely above a whisper.

"All right," I said, leaning forward. "Start from the beginning. Tell me everything."

Dusty's voice cracked like dry timber. "She was on her way to meet a reporter and share some information with her. Someone ran her into the ditch. Killed her."

The mescal burned up my throat, the room going still. Even Pard's panting ceased, his eyes fixed on Dusty. "For what reason?" I asked.

Dusty didn't answer immediately, her hands covering her eyes, elbows on her knees, as if holding her skull together. Her voice came out muffled, trembling.

"Kirsten... she'd learned something important about..."

When her words faded, I said, "Interdimensional beings?"

"They killed her because she knew something they didn't want exposed," Dusty said, her words hanging like smoke in the firelight.

Anna's eyes flicked to mine, wide and searching. A cold weight settled in my gut, heavy as the guitar's hum.

"Kirsten had proof," Dusty continued, her voice raw. "She

was going to share it with the reporter. She said they weren't just watching—they were influencing. Government. Military. Maybe more."

I rubbed my jaw, the mescal's warmth warring with the chill in my spine. "And you think someone killed her to keep that quiet?"

Dusty nodded, her face pale as moonlight. "And now they're after me. I found her notes. Her recordings. Equations. Maps. Frequencies. She said they were hiding in the signal."

Anna paced, her fingers twisting the hem of her blouse, the fabric fraying under her touch.

"This is bigger than politics. Bigger than Taos. If what Dusty's saying is true..."

"It's not just true," Dusty snapped, her voice breaking. "It's my life, and I'm scared shitless."

I leaned back, thinking fast. "My boss, Jake Huntington. He has pull—media, legal, and even some federal connections. If anyone can keep you safe while we figure this out, it's him."

Dusty's red-rimmed eyes met mine. "You trust him?"

"He's the Cryptid Hunter, for God's sake. You can trust him with your life. And he'll protect the people who bring it to light."

Anna stopped pacing, her silhouette sharp against the flickering fireplace. "What if it's not just people we're dealing with?"

I didn't answer. I couldn't. The guitar, the signal, the lights over the mesa, the hum—it was all circling the same dark truth. Outside, the wind howled, rattling the windows like restless spirits. Fritz barked once, sharp and sudden. Pard growled, ears flat, his hackles rising.

I crossed to the window, the glass cool against my palm. The street was empty, the shadows too deep, too still.

"We aren't waiting till Saturday," I said, turning back. "We start digging now. Tonight."

"Dusty can't stay here," Anna said, her voice urgent. "Too many people know about our connection. It's only a matter of time before someone knocks with questions."

“They won’t look for her at the Shadow Ranch,” I said.

“Where’s that?” Dusty asked, her voice steadying.

“Not far. An abandoned ranch in the high desert. No one will find you there. Grab your stuff, and we’ll head out.”

“Didn’t have time to pack,” Dusty said, gesturing to her clothes. “All I have is what I’m wearing.”

“We’ll find you a change of clothes,” I said. “Right now, we need to get the hell out of here.”

Anna handed Dusty the mescal bottle, its weight heavy in her hands. “Take it,” she said. “It was Kirsten’s.”

“Let’s have one more before we go,” Dusty said, her voice softer now, almost reverent.

Anna nodded, silent, her eyes glistening. Dusty poured another round, her hands trembling just enough to spill a drop that gleamed like amber on the table. I raised my glass, the mescal’s scent sharp and smoky.

“To truth. Whatever the hell it turns out to be.”

Dusty and I drained our shots, the burn grounding us. She held a glass to Anna’s lips, urging her to drink. Anna coughed, wiped her mouth, and managed a faint smile, her eyes catching the firelight.

“Girl,” Dusty said, a spark of her old fire returning. “I’m going to liven you up yet.”

CHAPTER 10

The lime-green Jeep, dirty from the dusty roads, growled as it carved through the high desert, its headlights slicing the velvet darkness of the Taos night. The road to Shadow Ranch stretched ahead, a narrow ribbon of asphalt swallowed by the vastness of sagebrush and piñon, the air sharp with their mingled scents.

Overhead, the sky was a riot of stars, each pinprick of light so vivid it felt as if the universe were pressing down, whispering secrets. I gripped the wheel, the Jeep's rumble a steady counterpoint to the tension knotting my shoulders.

Pard sprawled in the back, his nose twitching at the cracked window as he caught the cool desert breeze. Dusty sat shotgun, her turquoise shirt faintly glowing in the dashboard's green light, her cowboy boots propped on the dash, one hand clutching the mescal bottle Anna had pressed into her hands.

"Twenty miles to the ranch," I said, glancing at her. "You okay with roughing it? Shadow's got charm, but it's no Hilton."

The Jeep hit a rut, jolting them, and I tightened my grip, steering through the crunch of gravel.

Dusty's lips quirked, her eyes glinting like the stars outside.

"Roughing it? Hell, Buck, I grew up sleeping in horse trailers between rodeos. A bunkhouse with a roof's a step up." She tilted the mescal bottle, the amber liquid catching the faint light. "You're staying out there with some kid, you said?"

"Ran's twenty-two; no kid," I said, the Jeep's tires humming as they left the asphalt for a dirt track, dust swirling in the beams. "He has a fire in him for saddle bronc riding. I'm coaching him for the Rodeo de Santa Fe this Saturday. He has grit, but he's green as this Jeep."

"Ran Roberts?" she said. "His daddy owns Double Moon Ranch?"

"That's him," I said.

"I know his sister, Tara. Barrel raced with her more than once. Nice little ass, that one. I didn't know she had a brother."

"His daddy doesn't want Ran riding the rodeo, so he packed up, left

Double Moon, and moved in with me," I said.

"You're not from around here," she said. "What are you doing in New Mexico?"

"Chasing shadows for Jake Huntington, the Cryptid Hunter."

"Catch any yet?" she asked.

"So far, the only thing I've caught is hell," I said.

Dusty's laugh was low, warm, cutting through the night's chill. "Saddle bronc, huh? That's a hell of a dance. I'll help you whip him into shape. Rodeo's my church."

"Had a feeling it might be," I said.

She leaned back, her braid brushing the seat, and took a sip of mescal, wincing slightly.

"State amateur barrel racing champ, by the way. Me and my mare, Sweetie Pie, have left plenty of dust clouds in our wake."

"I'll bet," I said, shooting her a grin.

The Jeep bounced over a rise, the horizon a jagged silhouette of mesas under the star-strewn sky.

"I'm going to miss Kirsten," she said. "We were close."

"Hang in there," I said. "Grief is unavoidable and only gets worse."

"I'm trying to keep my mind off of it, but I'm having no luck. She had the dreamiest eyes I've ever stared into. She was ten years older than me, but we went together like night and day."

"I'm sorry for your loss," I said.

She reached across the console, touched my knee, and said, "I know you are. Thanks for helping. Anna's a mess. Maybe worse than me. She and Kirsten had known each other since high school."

"I know," I said. "I'm so sorry for your loss."

Dusty fumbled with her keys and took out a flashdrive, which she handed to me.

"Kirsten gave this to me and told me to forget about it unless she disappears. I can't handle this right now. Will you hold on to it for me?"

I handed her my keychain. "Put it with my keys. I'll have it when you're ready to deal with whatever it is."

"Thank you," she said.

"I want to call my people in Tulsa," I said. "I'm afraid, though, that someone may be monitoring my phone."

"I left mine in the apartment," she said. "Along with everything else I own."

"I might as well toss this one out the window. I'm afraid to use it," I said.

"What if someone calls you?" she asked.

"I turned off my phone at Anna's house. Can't track it without a signal."

"Sure about that?" she asked. "We could be dealing with aliens, or some powerful government tech."

"Never know," I said. "Let's take a detour."

I veered off the road back to Shadow Ranch at the first possible intersection and drove for twenty minutes in another direction. Dusty watched with folded arms as I rolled the window down and tossed the phone into a bar ditch.

"Now what?" she asked.

"Burner phone next time I'm in town," I said. "What about Sweetie Pie?" I asked.

Dusty sniffled before answering. "I board her at a stable outside of Albuquerque. Kirsten and I had planned to buy a ranch of our own."

When she sniffled again, I handed her a tissue from the console.

"Ran and I both have horse trailers. We can drive to Albuquerque and pick up Sweetie Pie."

"I'd die if I lost Kirsten and that horse in the same week," she said.

"We won't let that happen," I said. "Ran'll be stoked to have a champ around. Maybe you can show him how to stick a landing without eating dirt."

She chuckled, but her gaze drifted out the window, where the desert seemed to hum with secrets older than the stars.

"Kirsten loved the rodeo too," she said, voice softening, the mescal bottle heavy in her lap. "She'd sit in the stands, cheering like a kid, even when she was in her fancy congresswoman suits. Said it reminded her of home."

"I know you miss her," I said. "Take a deep breath. Things will be dark for a while, but they'll lighten up."

Her fingers tightened around the bottle, knuckles pale. "I can't believe she's gone, Buck. And those notes… whatever she found, it's tied to that damn music. Sanderson's guitar."

My jaw tightened, the memory of the cosmic guitar's haunting notes still vibrating in my bones.

"We'll figure it out. You, me, Jake's crew—we'll dig until we hit truth. But tonight, you're safe at Shadow Ranch. No one's finding you out there."

The Jeep crested a hill, and the silhouette of the ranch emerged—a cluster of low adobe buildings, their sagging roofs silvered by starlight, nestled against a stand of gnarled junipers.

Dusty nodded, her eyes scanning the dark, as if expecting shadows to move. "Safe sounds good. But I'm not hiding forever. Kirsten deserves better than that." She tilted the bottle toward me. "One for the road?"

I shook my head, a faint smile tugging my lips. "Three IPAs and your mescal back at Anna's is my limit. You hold onto that for Ran. The kid might need it when we show up."

She smirked, tucking the bottle between her knees. "Fair enough. Let's get to this ranch and see if your cowboy's got what it takes to ride with the big dogs."

The Jeep rolled on, the desert's quiet roar swallowing our words, the stars above burning with questions no one could yet answer. The Jeep's engine growled to a stop as we rolled into Shadow Ranch, the lime green paint dulled by a fine layer of desert dust. The night was thick, the high desert air sharp with the scent of sage and cooling earth.

Stars burned overhead, fierce and unblinking, like they were keeping watch over the sagging adobe buildings huddled against the junipers. The ranch house loomed ahead, its weathered walls silvered by starlight, the kiva's faint ember glow seeping through the windows like a heartbeat.

I killed the ignition, and the silence rushed in, broken only by the soft crunch of Pard's paws as he leapt from the back, nose twitching toward the corral where the horses snorted faintly.

Dusty slid out, her cowboy boots scuffing the dirt, the mescal bottle glinting in her hand. Her turquoise shirt caught the dim light, and her braid swayed as she scanned the ranch, eyes sharp despite the weight of her grief.

"This place looks like it's been forgotten by time," she said, voice low, almost reverent. "Perfect spot to disappear."

"Let's hope it stays that way," I said, slinging my pack over my shoulder. "Come on, let's get inside before the night decides to spit us out."

The door creaked as I pushed it open, the air inside heavy with the smoky warmth of the kiva's dying embers and the flicker of a few candles on a scarred wooden table. Their light danced across the adobe walls, casting shadows that seemed to shift just out of sight.

The room was sparse—worn rugs, a sagging couch, a ladder leading to the loft where Ran slept. Pard's claws clicked on the floor as he padded toward the hearth, curling up with a contented huff. I set about filling his water bowl, the tinny splash grounding me as Dusty surveyed the space, her boots echoing softly.

A rustle came from above, followed by the creak of wood. Ran's bare feet hit the ladder, and he climbed down, all lanky grace and sleep-tousled hair. His jeans hung low, well-worn and frayed, his bare chest catching the candlelight, lean muscle taut from hours in the saddle. He blinked at us, rubbing his eyes, then froze when he saw Dusty, her silhouette framed by the kiva's glow.

"Ran, this is Dusty," I said, setting Pard's food bowl down. "She's crashing here tonight. Got some trouble following her, and this place is off the radar."

"Trouble?" Ran's voice was rough with sleep, but his eyes sharpened, flicking between us. "What kind?"

Dusty set the mescal bottle on the table, the glass clinking softly. "The kind that gets people killed," she said, her tone flat but heavy, like a stone dropped in still water. "My friend—Congresswoman Kirsten Maldonado—she knew something she shouldn't. Someone ran her off the road. Now they're after me."

Ran's fingers curled around the rein I'd given him earlier to fidget with, a habit when he was thinking.

"Damn. That's… heavy. You're safe with us."

"At least for now," I said, pouring water for Pard.

"Don't worry about Lady," Ran said. "She's good—fed, watered, exercised.

"Thanks for looking after her," I said.

Ran nodded, still clutching the rein. "No problem. I'm ready for Saturday." He glanced at Dusty, sizing her up. "You know Buck's coaching me for saddle bronc at Rodeo de Santa Fe?"

Dusty's lips curved, a spark of her cowgirl fire breaking through the grief. She stepped closer, her eyes roving over Ran's frame with a boldness that made him shift his weight.

"Turn around for me, cowboy," she said, twirling a finger. "Let's see what you're working with."

Ran raised an eyebrow but obliged, spinning slowly, his jeans hugging his lean hips. Dusty let out a low whistle.

"Well, damn. You got a nice cowboy butt, and not an ounce of fat on that skinny frame of yours. But Buck's right—you're green. If you're riding broncs on Saturday, you need more than tips. Squats, core work, legs, arms. You gotta be a steel spring to stay on those beasts."

Ran grinned, a mix of shy and cocky, twisting the rein in his hands.

"You know rodeo?"

"She's the state amateur barrel racing champ," I said, leaning against the wall, arms crossed. "Knows her way around a saddle. And she knows Tara."

Ran's grin widened, his eyes lighting up. "Tara? My sister. Hell of a rider. Been kicking my ass since we were kids."

"Sibling rivalry?" Dusty asked, settling onto the couch, her boots propped on a crate.

"Since the day I first laid eyes on her," Ran said, laughing, but there was a warmth in it, a pride that softened his edges.

He sat across from her, the candlelight carving shadows across his face.

I watched them, the air easing slightly despite the weight of Dusty's story.

"Ran, Dusty's here because someone's after her—maybe connected to what Kirsten found. Notes, recordings, something about signals and interdimensional beings. We're keeping her out of sight until Jake and the crew can help."

"Interdimensional what now?" Ran's brow furrowed, but he didn't push, just glanced at Dusty. "You're in deep, huh?"

"Deeper than a desert well," she said, uncorking the mescal. "You want a shot? Might take the edge off this mess."

Ran's eyes flicked to me, then back to her. "Hell, why not?"

He grabbed two tin mugs from a shelf, and Dusty poured the amber liquid, glinting like liquid fire. They clinked mugs, downed the shots, and grimaced in unison, laughing as the burn hit.

"Another?" Dusty asked, already pouring. The mescal flowed freely, and soon their laughter grew loose, their words slurring as the bottle dwindled.

Ran's cheeks flushed, his drawl thicker, while Dusty's cowgirl bravado shone through, her grief momentarily buried under the liquor's haze.

I shook my head, smiling despite myself. "You two are going to regret that in the morning. Dusty, you can take my bed. I'll make a pallet on the floor."

"Keep your bed," she said, her voice slurring but firm, a mischievous glint in her eye. She jerked her thumb toward the loft. "I'll bunk with Ran. Ain't my first time sharing a hayloft."

Ran choked on his mescal, coughing as he laughed. "You sure? I kick in my sleep."

"I've handled worse," Dusty shot back, winking. She grabbed the bottle and stood, swaying slightly, her braid swinging like a pendulum. "Come on, cowboy. Let's see if you can keep up off the bronc."

"Wait," I said. "I need to borrow your cell phone."

"Where's yours?" he asked.

"Lost it in a dry arroyo," I said.

Ran climbed the stairs and returned with his cell phone. I watched them go up the ladder. Ran's bare feet slipped once, and Dusty's laughter echoed as she steadied him.

The kiva's embers pulsed, casting a warm glow over the room, but the night outside felt alive, the stars too bright, the desert too quiet. Pard whimpered softly, sensing the same unease that gnawed at me.

Kirsten's death, Sanderson's guitar, those cryptic notes—it was all tied together, and Shadow Ranch was only a temporary hideout. Come Saturday, with Jake arriving, the rodeo would bring more than broncs and barrels.

CHAPTER 11

The New Mexico night bit at my knuckles as I pulled Ran's old flying-saucer sweatshirt over my head. The ranch house creaked behind me, its wooden bones settling in the chilly dark. I stepped onto the porch, my boots scuffing the warped planks, and dialed Angie's number on Ran's beat-up phone.

The stars above were sharp as knife points, the kind of sky that makes you feel small and exposed. Angie picked up on the fourth ring, her voice rough, as if she'd just rolled out of a dream.

"Why're you calling on a phone I don't recognize?" she asked, suspicion cutting through her grogginess.

"Long story," I said, my breath fogging in the cold.

"Give me the short version."

I leaned against the porch rail, the wood splintery under my palm, and told her about Kirsten Louise Maldonado.

"Have you heard anything about her death?"

"You kidding?" Angie said. "It's all over the news. Conspiracy nuts are already saying it's Karen Silkwood all over again."

"May not be nuts," I said, my voice low, like the desert itself was listening. "Maldonado's roommate, Dusty, is here at the ranch. She was at Anna Luna's place when I swung by earlier. Says someone ran Kirsten off the road—killed her."

Angie's tone sharpened, like a blade on a whetstone, and she asked, "How would she know?"

"She was on the phone with Kirsten when it happened. She heard the whole damn thing—some car slammed into her fender, sending her into a ditch. Dusty's half out of her mind and swears it was no accident."

"Maldonado was on her way to meet David Eastman from the BBC to show him a tape of an explosive interview."

"Who was the interview with?" I asked.

"Eastman didn't know, and there was no tape found in the car."

"Dusty has a copy," I said.

"Can you get your hands on it?" Angie asked.

"Maybe," I said. "Why was she meeting with someone from the BBC and not one of the major American networks?"

"No idea," she said. "What else did Dusty tell you?"

"Not much. She was half-drunk and a mess with grief. I'll press her for details tomorrow when she's sober."

"What's Maldonado's tie to Anna Luna?"

"Grew up together, went to high school. Anna's straitlaced, but Kirsten? She was wild, always chasing trouble."

Angie snorted. "Sounds like someone I know. Jake's antsy, says we have enough to start filming. He and Colley are headed your way tomorrow."

I rubbed my jaw, feeling the stubble scratch under my fingers. "Good or bad, I don't know, but Jake's right. The story's here. My interview with Kermit Sanderson alone could carry a whole episode. Man has secrets that'd make your skin crawl."

"Like what?"

"He said the diagrams in Elena's notebook were plans for a doomsday device."

"You showed it to him?" Angie asked.

"He seemed on the up and up," I said.

"If someone killed Congresswoman Maldanado, then who can we trust? Whose phone are you using, anyway?"

"Ran's," I said, glancing at the cracked screen in my hand.

"You need an encrypted one," Angie said. "We don't know who we're dealing with."

The weight of her words settled in my gut like a cold stone.

"You think?" I said, half-sarcastically.

"I'll overnight one to Tara. But Buck, it only works if you're calling me, Jake, or Colley."

"Got it. Anything else?"

"Don't let Dusty out of your sight," she said, her voice like a whip. "And call me with a report."

I hung up, the silence of the desert rushing in, thick with the zooming of bats and the distant yip of a coyote. The night felt heavier now, like it was pressing down on my shoulders. I stood there a moment, staring at the horizon where the mesa's shadow swallowed the starlight, wondering just how deep this mess went.

Morning came slowly, the sun crawling over the mesa as if it were in no hurry. Pard's warm tongue lapped at my hand, dangling off the bed, pulling me out of a restless sleep. The room smelled of dust and old coffee, the light slicing through the window harsh and unforgiving.

I'd overslept—way past my usual dawn wake-up. My eyes flicked to the coffee table where I'd left Ran's phone. It was gone. In its place, a folded note sat like a bad omen.

"Gone to get Dusty's horse, Sweety Pie," it read in Ran's scrawled handwriting.

"Damn!" I said, the word echoing through the quiet house.

My gut twisted, a mix of frustration and dread. Ran and Dusty, out there alone, chasing a horse while God-knows-who was hunting her. I felt as helpless as a coyote caught in a trap.

I fed Pard and the horses, the familiar routine doing little to calm the storm in my head. The crunch of tires on gravel snapped me alert. It was Tara, pulling up in her dusty Jeep, an encrypted phone in her hand.

"Where's Ran?" she asked, her boots hitting the ground with a thud.

"On his way to Albuquerque," I said.

"What the hell's in Albuquerque?"

"Come inside, and I'll tell you," I said.

Over coffee, I filled her in on Dusty's story. Tara's face darkened with every word, her fingers drumming the chipped mug.

"I've known Dusty a while," she said. "She's wilder than a

March hare."

"Starting to see that," I said, glancing out the window at the endless stretch of scrub and sky.

"Ran's never had a girlfriend," Tara said, her voice tight. "I can't believe you let him sleep with Dusty last night."

I smirked, despite the tension. "Didn't sound like much sleeping was going on."

Tara's frown deepened. "Ran and Dusty are in danger. If someone's after her, they could be watching the stable where Sweety Pie's boarded. Dad's going to be pissed."

"Lots of places to board horses around Albuquerque," I said.

The thought didn't ease the knot in my chest as Tara dialed Ran, her face paling when he answered.

"They're about thirty miles from Albuquerque on Highway 14, the Turquoise Trail, the scenic bypass. They've been stopping along the way to sightsee."

"Tell them to turn around and get back here," I said, my voice sharper than I meant.

"No can do," Tara said, her eyes wide. "Someone has them pulled over."

"Shit!" I said, grabbing the phone. "Ran, soon as they let you go, turn around and head back to the ranch. We'll get someone else to pick up Sweety Pie."

"Too late, Buck," Ran said, his voice shaky. "We already got Sweety Pie and were heading back. Took the scenic route."

"Maybe it's just a taillight out," I said, clinging to a thread of hope.

"Don't think so. They have pistols drawn, and one of them is pointing a rifle at me."

"Cops?"

"Black suits, black sedan. Not cops."

"Damn," I said, my heart pounding like a war drum. "Sounds like feds."

"What do we do?" Ran asked, panic creeping into his voice.

"Cooperate and don't get shot. I'll call Angie."

I dialed Angie, my fingers fumbling on the new encrypted

phone. She answered on the first ring, and I spilled the situation fast, my words clipped. Tara sat across from me, her face pale as the desert dust outside, both of us useless as we waited.

Angie's voice crackled through. "Jake and Colley are airborne, already over Albuquerque. I'm patching you through."

Jake's voice boomed over the line. "Buck, what's the sitrep?"

"Ran and Dusty got pulled over on the Turquoise Trail," I said, gripping the phone so hard my knuckles whitened. "Black sedan, armed suits, not cops. Pistols and rifles."

"On it," Jake said. "Colley, divert to Highway 14."

In the chopper, Colley Hornbeck, a grizzled vet with a scar across his jaw, banked hard over the desert. His eyes scanned the horizon, Afghanistan instincts kicking in.

"There," he said, pointing to an abandoned horse trailer and Ran's truck glinting in the sunlight. "They can't be far."

Jake, strapped into the co-pilot seat, spotted a black sedan speeding south, with no government plates and windows tinted as dark as night.

"That's our target," Jake said. No dot gov tags. Could be mercenaries."

Colley grinned, pulling a smoke grenade from a duffel. "Let's give them a wake-up call. You up for it?"

"Give it to me. I'll drop it right in front of them," Jake said.

Colley ducked the chopper low, its blades kicking up dust. Jake leaned out, launching the grenade. It exploded in a blinding cloud as the sedan swerved to avoid the erupting smoke. The driver lost control of the sedan, dust swirling into the air as it crashed into the ditch with a sickening thud.

Colley landed on the highway, the chopper's skids kissing asphalt. Grabbing an AK-47—his souvenir from Afghanistan—he sprayed the sedan's tires, shredding them.

Three men in black suits piled out, guns drawn. Jake had a 9 mm Glock and clipped the driver's shoulder. The man collapsed, cursing in a guttural language—Russian? Arabic? Jake didn't care.

"Cover me, Colley!" he shouted, tossing a percussion grenade over the sedan.

The blast stunned the other two suits, who slumped behind the car, disoriented. Jake sprinted forward, pistol in hand, and shot the lock off the sedan's back door. Ran and Dusty stumbled out, coughing, eyes wide with panic.

"Move!" he barked, waving them to the chopper.

As they lifted off, Colley muttered, "Hope to hell those boys aren't feds, or our asses are cooked."

Dusty, clutching Ran's arm, screamed, "We're not leaving without Sweety Pie!"

Jake groaned. "Lady, that was a warzone back there."

"She's all I have left!" Dusty said, tears streaking her face.

Colley scanned the horizon and said, "No backup yet, Bossman."

"Fine. Truck's a few miles back. Let's get it."

"Then hold on."

Colley banked the chopper, flying low and then landing beside Ran's truck. Sweety Pie, still in the trailer, snorted nervously.

Ran and Dusty piled out of the chopper, Dusty heading for the trailer to check on Sweetie Pie. She tossed something to Jake.

"The tape," she said.

"We'll run interference," Jake said. "But no one's going to miss that red pickup and horse rig of yours."

"I've lived in New Mexico all my life and know every backroad and passable trail there is. I'll take the backway. We'll be good," Ran said. "Meet you at Shadow Ranch."

Jake smiled and gave her a thumbs up as Ran climbed behind the wheel, Dusty jumping into the passenger seat beside him.

"Move it, Bossman," Colley said. "We need to plot our own alternate route."

Jake had barely shut the chopper's door when it lifted off the ground and banked north.

"Can you get us to Shadow Ranch without being followed?" Jake asks.

"Hell, Bossman, this terrain reminds me of Afghanistan. If you aren't afraid of flying under the radar, I'm not afraid of a few cactus tops."

"Sounds like fun, "Jake said. "Turn on the camera. Don't know where we'll use the footage, but I'll find a place."

Colley nodded, already plotting a path through a maze of desert canyons.

"Low and fast, under the radar. Wonder what's in those saddlebags."

"Something those goons were willing to kill to keep buried."

Colley gripped the chopper's controls, his scarred knuckles white as he dropped the bird low, the skids kissing the jagged tips of sagebrush and ocotillo.

The New Mexico desert sprawled beneath them, a maze of red-rock canyons and bone-dry arroyos, the Turquoise Trail's dust still swirling in their wake.

Jake had braced himself in the seat next to Colley, wincing and shutting his eyes as the nose of the chopper barely missed clipping the top of a giant cane cholla cactus.

"Shit!" he said. "You trying to kill us?"

Colley answered in a voice rough as gravel, his Afghanistan-honed instincts threading the needle between radar detection and pursuit.

"I got this. Hang on, Bossman,"

The chopper's blades thumped like a war drum, kicking up clouds of grit that danced like ghosts across the desert. Jake held on, clutching his pistol, his eyes scanning for the glint of a tail—mercenaries, feds, or something worse. The view stretched for miles, with nothing below but dust and an occasional frightened coyote.

Colley banked hard into a narrow canyon, the walls closing in like a trap, rotor wash rattling loose stones and flushing birds.

"I don't see a damn thing. Nothing short of a drone or another chopper could follow the God-forsaken path you're taking," Jake said.

The chopper was skimming so close to the ground that a jackrabbit bolted in panic. The engine screamed, heat shimmering off the desert floor, as they vanished into the canyon's heart.

"Nothing's catching us down here," Colley said.

"How much further?" Jake asked.

"Just ahead."

Shadow Ranch emerged from the dust, a squat cluster of adobe and tin roofs nestled against a mesa's shadow. Colley flared the chopper, dropping it fast onto a patch of hardpan, the skids grinding against gravel with a bone-jarring crunch.

Dust exploded around them, swallowing the chopper in a blinding swirl, as Jake unbuckled and leapt out, boots hitting dirt before the rotors slowed.

"Clear!" he said, sweeping his pistol across the silent ranch, the air thick with the scent of creosote and tension. Colley killed the engine, his AK-47 slung across his chest, eyes darting to the horizon for any sign of pursuit.

"Hope Ran and Dusty make it," Jake said, spitting into the dust. "If those bastards track us, we may have to evacuate to Tulsa."

"There's Buck," Colley said. "Who is that with him?"

"Randle Robert's daughter, Tara," Jake said.

"Randle Roberts?"

"Someone of extreme interest," Jake said. "Soon as we check in with Buck and Tara, we're going to look him up and pick his brain."

CHAPTER 12

Tara and I watched as Jake's chopper landed in a swirling cloud of dust. Jake smiled when I waved, and he and Colley began walking toward us—his worn saddlebags draped over his shoulders.

"Tara," I said. "This is Jake Huntington, the Cryptid Hunter, and his pilot, Colley Hornbeck."

Tara gushed, as if Jake were the first celebrity she'd ever met. Jake was used to it.

"I love your show," she said.

"Good," he said. "There's a better than decent chance that you're going to be on it."

"Really?" she said.

"Bossman never exaggerates," Colley said.

"Did you see my brother, Ran?" she asked.

"He and Dusty are on their way here," he said.

"What's in your hand?" I asked.

"Kirsten Louise Maldonado's tape."

"Good work," I said. "There's coffee in the ranch house if you need a cup."

Jake nodded. "What I need is a tall scotch. You can brief us while we wait for Ran and Dusty."

Jake was on his second scotch when Tara's head snapped up.

"You see that?" she said, pointing toward the window. A cloud of dust rose in the distance, swirling like a specter against the sky. "Could be Ran and Tara."

"Might just be," I said.

As we watched from the door, the dust cloud grew, and soon the growl of Ran's red pickup broke through the silence, the horse trailer rattling behind it. Relief hit me like a slug of whiskey, warm but fleeting.

The truck skidded to a stop, kicking up more dust that choked the air. Before the engine cut, Dusty flung open the passenger door and got out, her boots hitting the ground with a thud.

Her hair was wild, streaked with dirt, and her eyes were red-rimmed but fierce. She ran straight for Jake and Colley, throwing her arms around them in a hug that nearly knocked Colley off balance.

"You crazy sons of bitches!" she cried, her voice raw, half-laugh, half-sob. "I've seen barfights before, but never an actual shootout."

Jake grunted, patting her back awkwardly, while Colley smirked.

"Just another day in the desert, darling," he said.

Dusty turned to Tara and me, her hands shaking. "Buck, Tara, you should've seen it," she said. "Those goons had us pinned, guns drawn, ready to drag us God-knows-where. Then Jake and Colley dropped out of the sky like damn avenging angels! That smoke grenade—boom!—sent us swerving into the ditch. Colley's chopper moves were insane, skimming so low I thought he was going to clip a cactus!"

I nodded. The image of Ran and Dusty staring down rifle barrels painted in my thoughts.

"You're safe now," I said, glancing at Ran as he climbed out of the truck.

Sweety Pie snorted from the trailer, her hooves stomping as if she sensed the tension.

"Safe for now," Dusty said, her eyes flicking to the saddlebags. "And we rescued Kirsten's tape."

"A tape someone's willing to kill for," Jake said. "Unfortunately, we don't have the equipment here to listen to it."

"What, then?" I asked.

Jake pitched the tape to Colley and said, "Hate to do this to you, but you need to take it back to the studio where it'll be safe, and we can have professionals transcribe it."

"On it, Bossman," Colley said, tossing the saddlebags over his shoulder and heading for the chopper.

We watched him take off in a swirl of dust and noise.

"What now?" I asked.

"I'm starved," Jake said. "Have anything to eat?"

"I'll cook you a green chili omelette you won't soon forget," Tara said.

"Girl," he smiled and said. "I think I'm going to like you."

Ran joined us, his hands stuffed in his pockets, but his eyes were sharp, scanning the road he'd just traveled.

Tara laughed when he said, "Did I hear someone say something about food?"

She didn't answer, shaking her head as she headed toward the little ranch house. Dusty followed her.

"I'll help," she said. "Can you put Sweetie Pie in the barn with Lady and Starfire for me?"

"You bet, baby," Ran said, heading back to the horse trailer.

Tara's laughter echoed from the porch as she and Dusty disappeared into the ranch house, the screen door slapping shut behind them. The sun had shifted, painting the desert in shades of amber and rust, and the air carried that earthy scent that always seemed to settle in after a day of chaos.

I followed Jake and Ran toward the house, the weight of the day still pressing on my chest like a bruise, the cloud of dust from Ran's truck still lingering in my mind.

Inside, the kitchen was a warm pocket of normalcy. Tara was already at the stove, cracking eggs into a bowl with a flourish, her dark hair pulled back in a loose ponytail. Dusty was chopping green chiles, their tangy scent filling the air, while a couple of cold beers sweated on the counter.

Jake grabbed one, popped the cap, and handed it to me.

"Buck, you ever had Tara's green chili omelettes?" Dusty asked, her knife pausing mid-chop as she grinned. "She cooked them on the circuit once for us. Swear to God, they're so good you'll forget your own name."

"Hope so," Jake said, leaning against the counter. "I need something to remind me life isn't all smoke grenades and rifle fire."

Tara whisked the eggs with a vengeance. "Keep talking like that, Cryptid Hunter, and I'll burn yours on purpose."

"How long will it take to transcribe the tape?" I asked.

"My editors are wizards. Doesn't matter if it's encoded or written in ancient Sumerian. They'll crack it faster than you can say 'conspiracy.'"

"Encoded?" I raised an eyebrow, sipping my beer. The cold fizz cut through the dust in my throat. "You think she went that far?"

Jake's expression darkened for a second before he masked it with another grin.

"Wouldn't be the first time. People who dig into the kind of stuff Kirsten was chasing? They don't leave their secrets in plain text."

"Your editors have it covered?" I said

"We have everything—digital forensics, decryption software, the works. We'll know what's on the tape by tomorrow night."

"Tomorrow night," Ran echoed, stepping in from the barn, brushing hay off his jeans. "That's assuming Colley doesn't get jumped on his way to Tulsa."

The room went quiet for a beat, the only sound Tara's whisk scraping the bowl. Ran's words hung like a storm cloud, and I caught Dusty's eyes flicking to the window, like she half-expected to see another dust cloud rolling in. I took another swig of beer.

"Colley's fine," Jake said, his tone firm, like he was convincing himself as much as us. "He's flown through worse than this. Besides, nobody's dumb enough to take on a chopper piloted by a guy who thinks he's Han Solo."

That got a chuckle out of Dusty, and the tension eased, if only a little. Tara slid the first omelet onto a plate, the golden edges crispy, flecked with vibrant green chiles.

"All right, hotshot," she said, handing it to Jake. "Taste the magic."

Jake took a bite, his eyes widening. "Damn, woman. You weren't kidding. This is the real deal."

"Told you," Dusty said, grabbing her own beer and raising it in a mock toast. "To Tara's cooking and not getting shot today."

"Hear, hear," I said, clinking my bottle against hers. The laughter felt good, like a brief reprieve.

We were halfway through the second round of omelettes and beers when a low rumble cut through the chatter. Jake's head snapped toward the window. The sound was sharper than a truck, higher-pitched, like a souped-up engine tearing across the desert. Tara set her spatula down and gazed out the window.

"Expecting company?" Jake asked.

"Nope," I said, standing and moving to the window. A black ATV roared into view, its chrome accents gleaming in the fading light. The driver cut the engine, and a woman stepped off, her silhouette all curves and confidence.

She wore a leather jacket, dark jeans, and boots that looked like they'd seen their share of rough country. Her hair was a cascade of brown waves that matched her eyes.

"Anna," Dusty said.

"Anna Luna?" Jake asked, already halfway to the door. "The artist?"

Jake was out the door before she finished, and I followed.

Anna wasn't alone; Elena Tafoya was with her."

"Anna and Elena," I said. "I wasn't expecting you, but it's a pleasant surprise. Jake, this is Anna Luna and Elena Tafoya."

Jake stepped from behind me with a smile and extended his hand. "I'm Jake Huntington. So pleased to meet you."

Elena shook his hand and said, "Jake Huntington as in the Cryptid Hunter?"

"The same, I confess," he said.

"I love your show," she said.

"Well, the two of you are the reason I'm here. Anna's drawing of the orb drew me. I want to film an episode about it. Are you amenable?"

When Anna glanced at Elena, she nodded. "Elena is my spiritual advisor," she said. "She knows more about American Indian protocols than anyone I know. I won't do anything without her express approval."

"Understood," Jake said. "Trust me when I tell you I would never do anything to come between you and your spiritual beliefs."

"I hear the honesty in your voice," Elena said. "I trust you."

Anna smiled and said, "If Elena trusts you, then so do I."

"Please," I said. "Come into the house. Tara and Dusty cooked green chile omelets, and we just finished eating."

Tara was standing behind me and said, "I'll make more."

Elena walked over to her and touched her hand. "You're Indian, aren't you, child?"

"Yes, ma'am," Tara said. "My grandmother, Lily, is full-blood Navajo."

"What's her last name?" Elena asked.

"Harjoe," Tara said.

"I know Lily," Elena said. "I hope it doesn't offend you if I tell you your grandmother is a powerful witch."

Ran was smiling as he joined Tara. "This is my brother, Ran," she said. "We've both known for a long time that Grandma has powers."

"Don't ever cross her," Elena said with a wink.

Tara and Ran laughed, and Tara said, "No worries about that."

"Your dad is white."

Elena's words were a statement, not needing confirmation. Tara and Ran seemed to understand.

Everyone laughed when Ran said, "No one's perfect."

"Your dad is a powerful man and commands respect from both whites and Indians," Elena said.

"We brought you something," Anna said when we were all back in the house.

She handed me a CD, a copy of Sanderson's cosmic guitar

tape.

"Thank you," I said. "Wish we had something to play it on."

"I have a boombox in the pickup," Ran said.

He soon returned with the boombox and inserted the CD, and everyone fell silent as the haunting, hypnotic strains filled the room. Jake and Dusty were deeply affected, with Dusty starting to cry.

"I can't listen to it without thinking of Kirsten," she said.

Ran followed her out the door as the song continued. The music was affecting everyone, and I finally switched off the boombox.

Elena touched my wrist when I said, "Too much."

Jake glanced at his Rolex and said, "Sorry to be a killjoy, but I have to visit the Double Moon Ranch. My crew's arriving tomorrow, and I need to speak with Randle Roberts."

"Elena and I must return to Taos," Anna said. "We can drop you off, but we won't be coming back this way."

"No problem," Jake said. "I'm planning on staying there tonight in anticipation of the arrival of my crew."

"Need me to come with you?" I asked.

"I'll get with you tomorrow, and you can brief me about what you've found," Jake said. "It'll keep until then."

After watching Jake, Anna, and Elena thunder off in a cloud of dust, I walked out to the corral to check on Ran and Dusty. Her mood had elevated tremendously since leaving the ranch house. She was laughing as she watched Ran straddle an oil drum, emulating a ride on a bucking bronc.

"Is that helpful?" I asked.

"You kidding," Dusty said. "Works wonders for balance and muscle memory. Style points are the key to winning a saddle bronc competition."

Tara walked up and pinched my ass. When I turned, she was smiling, her hand on her hips.

"Ready for another ride, cowboy?"

"Yes, ma'am," I said, returning her smile and heading for the barn to saddle Lady.

CHAPTER 13

The sun was setting behind the Sangre de Cristo range, its last glow casting long shadows on the scrub and rocks. Starfire and Lady stood silently, reins loosely hung over a juniper branch, their chests rising and falling with the land's rhythm. The desert was entering its night quiet, that special silence that only happens when the heat subsides and the stars start to whisper.

Tara knelt beside a boulder etched with ancient petroglyphs—spirals, antlered figures, a handprint that looked impossibly small. She traced one with her finger, reverent. I watched her, the way the fading light caught the ebony in her hair and turned it to fire. She looked like she belonged here. Not just in the desert—but in the story it was trying to tell.

"My grandmother brought me here once," she said, voice low, like she didn't want to disturb the spirits. "Lily. She's full-blood Navajo. A witch, some say."

Tara gave me a look when I said, "Moth madness?"

She shook her head. "The term moth madness has both racist and sexist connotations," she said. "I'm sure you didn't mean either one."

"I'm an idiot sometimes, but I would never knowingly say anything to hurt you or your family. If you perceived it that way, I'm truly sorry because it isn't what I meant."

"If I thought it was, I'd be riding back to the ranch alone right now," she said.

"What did you feel when you were with Lily?" I asked.

"The desert was breathing. That's how it felt—like the land itself was alive, exhaling warmth from the sun-soaked rocks and inhaling the cool breath of twilight. I followed Grandmother Lily through the scrub, her small boots kicking up dust that shimmered in the fading light.

"She walked ahead, her long braid swinging like a pendulum, her steps sure and silent. She wore a turquoise scarf around her neck and a silver concho belt that caught the last rays of sunlight. I had always thought my grandmother looked like she belonged to the earth—like she'd been carved from the same stone as the mesas.

"We reached the petroglyphs just as the sky began to change. The sun dipped low, bleeding orange and violet across the horizon. Lily knelt beside the rock face, her fingers tracing the ancient symbols—spirals, animals, stars. She whispered something in Navajo, a prayer maybe, or a greeting. I didn't understand the words, but felt them like music in my bones.

"Then Lily stiffened. It happened fast. Her body jerked, her eyes rolled back into her head, and she collapsed against the rock. I screamed, rushing to her side. her limbs flailed, her head striking the stone scarf with a sickening thud. She was speaking—no, chanting—in a voice that didn't sound like hers. The language was foreign, ancient, like wind through canyon walls.

"I knelt beside her, crying, unsure what to do. The sky darkened unnaturally fast, stars blinking into existence like eyes opening. The moon rose, full and heavy, casting silver over Lily's still form. Her breathing slowed, then stopped altogether.

"I thought she was dead.

"Minutes passed—maybe hours. Time wasn't working right, and I don't know how to explain it.

"Then Lily's eyes fluttered open. She looked at me—not with fear, but with knowing."

"They're here," she whispered. "The Sky People."

"I turned my gaze upward. And there they were—four orbs of light, dancing across the heavens. They moved like thoughts, like dreams—zigzagging, looping, vanishing, and reappearing."

When Tara's breath caught in her throat, I squeezed her hand.

She waved me off when I said, "It's okay."

"They've always watched," Lily said. "They know who we are. I didn't speak. I couldn't. The desert was too quiet, too vast.

"Lily touched my cheek. "'You'll remember this,"' she said. "'Even when no one believes you."'

"And I did. Every detail. Every sound. Every silence."

It was the night the desert spoke. The night the stars came alive. The night her grandmother became something more than human.

I didn't know what that meant, but I didn't interrupt. Her eyes were locked on the stone, but her mind was somewhere else—ten years old, maybe, standing where we stood now, watching her grandmother unravel under a darkening sky.

"She had a seizure. Right here. Started speaking in a language I didn't know. Her arms were flying, her head hitting the rock scarf like she was trying to break through it. I thought she was dying.

"The wind picked up, brushing against us like a memory. I felt it in my chest, that ache you get when someone shares something too big for words."

Tara's voice trembled, but she didn't cry. She was stronger than that. Or maybe she'd cried all she could years ago.

After I'd kissed a tear off her cheek, she began again.

"When she came out of it, she told me about the Sky People. Said they were watching. That they'd always been watching."

Tara looked up then, and I followed her gaze. The stars were out in force, a million pinpricks in the velvet black. The moon hung low and full, casting silver over the desert floor. And then—just like she said—four orbs of light appeared. Not planes. Not satellites. They moved like thoughts—fast, erratic, impossible.

I felt her hand slip into mine. It was warm, steady. I pulled her close, and she let me. Her breath was sweet with sage and something wild. I kissed her because I couldn't not. Because the desert had opened something in both of us.

"I can't do this," I said, the words catching in my throat. "You're just a baby."

She laughed, soft and defiant. "I'm twenty. I've been sexually active since I was fifteen. I probably know more about life than you do."

I grinned, because what else could I do? She was fire and stone and sky, and I was just a man trying to keep up.

"Maybe so," I said.

The lights danced above us, chasing each other like spirits playing tag across the cosmos. The horizon lit up like a Roman candle, and for a moment, I felt like I was standing inside Lily's vision—like the desert had folded time and brought us back to that night. Coyotes began to howl, their voices rising like a chorus of ghosts. A night owl cut across the moon, silent and sure.

Tara squeezed my hand. "We need to start back."

I nodded, but I didn't move. Not yet. I wanted to hold onto this—her story, her strength, the way the desert had made everything feel ancient and new at the same time.

We mounted up, and as Starfire and Lady picked their way through the sagebrush, I looked back once more at the petroglyphs. They were just scratches in stone. But tonight, they felt like a map to something bigger. Something watching. Something waiting.

The horses moved slowly and sure beneath us, hooves crunching over dirt and dry brush. The desert had gone full dark now, the kind that swallows sound and makes you feel like you're riding through a dream. Lady's ears twitched at the distant howl of coyotes, but she didn't spook. Starfire walked beside her, head low, Tara swaying in rhythm with her gait like she'd been born to it.

I kept glancing at her, trying not to make it obvious. She was quiet now, her face turned toward the horizon, where the last shimmer of those impossible lights had faded. But I could still feel them—like they'd left something behind in the air. A charge. A question.

Tara had told me about Lily like it was a confession, but it hadn't felt like one. It was more like a gift. That kind of story doesn't come easy. You don't share it unless you trust someone to carry it right. And I was trying—trying to hold it the way you'd have a fragile thing you didn't fully understand.

I thought about Tara at ten, standing over her grandmother's body, the desert watching. I imagined the fear, the helplessness, the way the stars must've looked like eyes, and then, Lily awakening, whispering about the Sky People as if it were a prophecy. I'd seen the lights myself now. I couldn't explain them. Couldn't rationalize them away. And maybe I didn't want to. Perhaps that was the point.

Tara turned, her eyes catching the moonlight. "You believe me, don't you?"

I nodded. "I've seen them myself, now. How could I not?"

She smiled, but it wasn't smug. It was soft. Like she'd been waiting for that answer for years.

I felt something shift in me then. Not just about her—but about everything. The desert, the stories, the way time folds in on itself out here. Tara wasn't a baby. She was a woman shaped by things I couldn't see, couldn't measure. She carried history in her bones—mystery in her blood.

And me? I was beginning to understand that there's more to this world than what you can fix with your hands or explain with logic. There are stories etched in stone, passed down in seizures and starlight. And sometimes, if you're lucky, someone lets you walk beside them long enough to hear one.

We rode on, the ranch still miles away, the night owl circling back overhead like it was keeping watch. Tara left when we reached Shadow Ranch. After grooming the two horses and putting them in their stalls for the night, I returned to the little ranch house alone.

There was a chill in the air as I climbed beneath the covers, the fire in the kiva burning brightly. It was the last thing I remembered.

Until...

The CD hummed in the old player, a haunting guitar solo weaving through the stillness of the ranch house. Anna Luna had dropped it off—a cosmic guitar, built by physicist Kermit Sanderson after his people at Sandia Labs tuned to a signal they caught out near Four Corners. Not natural. Not ours. But it repeated, like a song from the stars.

The notes clawed at my mind, sharp and strange, as I drifted into sleep, the melody curling into my bones like a living thing.

I don't know when I woke up, or if I was actually awake. The room was dim, the kind of dark that feels alive, heavy with secrets. My eyes adjusted to the faint glow of moonlight slipping through the cracked blinds, painting slivers of silver across the warped floorboards.

The guitar solo was still playing, soft but insistent, looping like a heartbeat in the walls. It's stuck in my head, an earworm burrowing deeper, pulling at something I couldn't name.

Then I felt it—a presence. My skin prickled, and my heart kicked against my ribs. Someone was here. I propped myself up on my elbows, squinting into the shadows, and saw her.

She was standing at the foot of my bed, staring down at me. Not human, at least not quite. Her hair was sun-bleached, shoulder-length, like some California surfer girl who had wandered out of a dream.

But her eyes—God, her eyes—were wrong. Too big, larger than any human's, glowing vivid blue, like twin sapphires catching fire. They didn't blink or move. They just saw, right through me.

Her silver bodysuit shimmered like liquid mercury, hugging her form and her boots, which gleamed as if they'd never touched dirt. Her image flickered, like a projection on an old movie reel, with rippling edges as if she weren't fully anchored to this world. I tried to speak, but my throat was dry, and the words stuck in my throat like sand.

Finally, I managed to ask, "Who are you?"

Her head tilted, just a fraction, and her voice came—not

from her mouth, which remained still, but straight into my mind, soft and feminine as a whisper carried on a desert wind.

"I am Aeterna."

It wasn't just words. I felt her thoughts brushing against mine, like she was reading me as easily as I was reading her. My pulse hammered, but I couldn't look away. She was holding something—a glowing red orb, pulsing faintly in her hand, flat as a paper cutout but alive with light.

"What's that?" I asked, nodding at the orb.

A sensory receptor, she said, her voice-thoughts curling through me, warm and sharp at once.

"What's it for?"

"It's how we communicate."

"We?" My voice cracked, barely a whisper.

The guitar solo hummed on, weaving through the air, and I could swear it was louder now and part of her.

"Where are you from, Aeterna?"

I don't know why I asked. Maybe I needed something to ground me, something to make sense of this.

"Another world," she said.

Why are you here? This nowhere ranch house in the middle of the desert? Four Corners? Earth? I don't ask. I can't.

"Why are you here?"

My hands gripped the sheets, the rough cotton grounding me as the room started to shift. Colors bled into the air—reds, blues, purples—swirling like oil on water, dancing to the guitar's wail. The walls pulsed, alive with light.

You summoned me, she said.

"The music?"

"Yes."

Her touch sparked something between us, and it surprisingly felt warm and comforting. I reached out to grab her wrist, to touch her, to confirm she was real. But it didn't happen. She quickly and smoothly stepped back, tossing the orb into the air. It spun, flat and glowing—a crimson disc that flashed once, bright as a dying star, then disappeared. Much like the orbs Tara and I had seen in the high desert.

"I may need your help," she said.

"To do what?" I asked.

Aeterna didn't answer, her voice thoughts fading like a signal breaking up. Then she was gone—flashing out in a bolt of light that seared my eyes.

I was alone, the room dark again, the colors gone, the guitar solo fading to a faint hum. My phone glowed on the nightstand: 4:00 a.m. Still dark outside. My chest was tight, my skin clammy.

I swung my legs out of bed, shirtless, the cold floor biting at my feet, and stumbled to the ice chest in the corner, fished out a Coors, the can slick with frost.

The recliner creaked as I sank into it, the beer hissing as I cracked it open. I took a long pull, the bitter cold grounding me, but my mind was still spinning.

What the hell just happened? Was she real? Was I awake? The guitar solo looped again, faint but there, and I heard her voice in it, whispering. I stared into the dark, the beer sweating in my hand, and wondered if I was still dreaming.

CHAPTER 14

As the sun sank low in the late afternoon sky, its rays stretched across the high desert, illuminating the scrub-covered mesas and the sharp outlines of the Sangre de Cristo Mountains in the distance.

The air shimmered with heat and dust, tinged with the scent of juniper and sagebrush. The Double Moon Ranch sprawled like a mirage at the edge of reality—an eclectic fusion of adobe structures, weathered timber, and rusted metal sculptures that glinted like alien relics in the fading light.

A pair of crescent moons—one carved into the gate, the other etched into the sandstone bluff behind the main lodge—watched silently over the land, as if guarding secrets too old for language.

Wind chimes made from bones and copper tubing sang softly in the breeze, their eerie harmonics blending with the distant calls of ravens circling overhead. The chimes seemed to carry a message, a whisper of something ancient and untamed, as if the desert itself were speaking in a tongue only the initiated could understand.

Jake stepped out of Anna Luna's ATV, its chrome-plated panels catching the sun like a spacecraft freshly landed. The vehicle was a rolling gallery of cosmic graffiti—nebulae, star maps, and cryptic symbols that pulsed with iridescent paint, each swirl and line suggesting a story no one had yet deciphered.

Anna, her dark hair catching the wind, adjusted her sunglasses and surveyed the bustling scene with a mix of amusement and curiosity. Elena Tafoya, wrapped in a woven shawl the color of desert twilight, moved with quiet grace beside them, her eyes scanning the horizon as if listening for something beyond the veil.

Her silence felt heavy, not from discomfort but with the weight of knowing things Jake could only guess at, things that made the hairs on the back of his neck stand up.

The ranch was alive with motion. Semis rumbled in, kicking up clouds of ochre dust as crew members in branded Cryptid Hunter gear barked instructions and hauled equipment. Aluminum scaffolding rose like skeletal towers, framing the staging area where cameras would soon roll.

Tents bloomed across the landscape—white, red, and electric blue—like pop-up outposts on an alien world. The catering tent, striped like a circus pavilion, already exhaled the scent of roasted green chile and grilled bison sliders, drawing hungry crew like moths to flame.

Generators hummed, their low drone a counterpoint to the high-pitched buzz of drones overhead, mapping the terrain with unblinking lenses. A sound tech tested mics near a dry arroyo rumored to be a hotspot for sightings, his voice crackling through the speakers with a distorted echo that lingered too long in the air.

A production assistant chased a tumbleweed that had snagged a lighting rig, cursing under her breath as the desert seemed to mock her efforts. The whole scene pulsed with anticipation, a strange blend of Hollywood chaos and desert mysticism, as if the ranch were a stage for a performance no one fully understood.

Randle Roberts emerged from the lodge, his silver hair catching the light like moonbeams on water. He wore a faded denim shirt and turquoise bolo tie, and his handshake was firm, his smile knowing, though Jake caught a flicker of wariness in his eyes.

"Welcome to the Double Moon," he said, eyes twinkling as he shook Jake's hand. "I don't watch much TV, but the missus, my mother-in-law, and two kids love your show and think you set the moon."

Thanks, Mr. Roberts," Jake said, returning the smile. "I appreciate you going out of your way to provide my crew a base of operations."

"Randle," he said with a grin. "If I hadn't, I'd be looking at divorce papers."

Randle and Elena had already hugged, their familiarity evident in the ease of their embrace. Jake raised an eyebrow.

"You know Elena?"

"Elena and my wife, Rita, are best friends," Randle said. He turned to Anna, his expression softening. "I haven't had the pleasure of meeting this young lady."

"I'm Anna, a recent resident of Taos. Love your ranch," she said, her voice warm but carrying an edge of curiosity, as if she, too, sensed the ranch's hidden depths.

"Come into the house," Randle said. "Rita and Lily will want to see Elena and meet you."

"I have a meeting in Taos," Anna said, glancing at Elena, who nodded almost imperceptibly. "I look forward to meeting Rita and Lily on my next visit."

Jake and Randle watched as the women drove away, the ATV's cosmic paint job gleaming like a comet's tail against the dusty road. The air seemed to shift as they disappeared, the wind chimes growing momentarily louder, their notes sharper, almost insistent.

Randle's smile disappeared when Jake said, "I've already met Tara and Ran, and I look forward to meeting Rita and your mother-in-law."

"Guess that means you were at Shadow Ranch before coming here."

"Yes, sir, I was," Jake said, sensing the shift in Randle's tone. "Is there a problem?"

"Seems I have a bone to pick with you," Randle said, his voice low but firm.

"Oh? About what?" Jake asked, keeping his tone neutral.

"Buck McDivit, your advance scout."

"What did Buck do?" Jake asked.

"Encouraged my boy to join the rodeo circuit," Randle said, his jaw tightening. "Ran has stars in his eyes now, dreaming of buckles and glory. Moved off the ranch because he was afraid to talk to me about it."

"I'm sorry," Jake said, genuine regret creeping into his voice. "I heard you and Buck disagreed. My assistant, Angie, had him booked in your best guest house, and he moved to an abandoned ranch in the middle of nowhere."

Mention of Angie prompted the return of Randle's former smile, though it was tinged with something unreadable.

"Angie's a prize. You need to hang on to her."

"She's my right arm," Jake said. "Without her, I'd be in trouble."

"Well, McDivit's loss is your gain. Angie made sure you got his vacant cabin. Where's Mama Mulate?"

"The semester at Tulane has begun, and she's teaching, though she's flying in Friday night for the weekend," Jake said.

"Couldn't have picked a more festive time. The Rodeo de Santa Fe is this weekend."

"I didn't think you liked the rodeo," Jake said, tilting his head.

"Love the rodeo," Randle said, his voice softening. "Just don't like the idea of my son competing."

"Because?"

Randle patted his right thigh, the gesture deliberate. "Used to ride myself. A hard fall ended all that."

"Broke your leg?" Jake asked, his curiosity piqued.

"And my back, ribs, arms, you name it. Horse rolled over on top of me. I'm lucky I can still walk."

"I'm sorry," Jake said, his tone sincere.

"I survived," Randle said, his eyes distant for a moment, as if seeing that long-ago arena. "Just don't want my son suffering the same fate."

"Does Ran know you once rode the rodeo?" Jake asked.

"Never talked to him about it," Randle said.

"Buck and Dusty are giving him pointers. Sounds as if you could be of help in your son's development."

"Never going to happen," Randle said.

Jake could see it was time to change the conversation, though his instincts as Cryptid Hunter pushed him to dig deeper.

"Hope you don't mind me asking, but why was a Michigan graduate with a double Master's degree in Nuclear Engineering and Radiological Sciences riding in a rodeo?"

Though Randle's eyes narrowed slightly, his smile held. "As I said, I love the rodeo. I got hurt riding in the Rodeo de Santa Fe. Rita was a nurse in the hospital."

"Interesting," Jake said, sensing there was more to the story. "And you married and bought this ranch after recuperating?"

"Something like that," Randle said, his tone clipped, closing the door on further questions.

Jake pressed, unable to resist. "Angie says there's no record of you working for the government at either Sandia or Los Alamos, either as a full-time employee or as a government contractor. With your specialized degrees, you undoubtedly came to New Mexico for reasons other than riding in the rodeo. What's the story?"

Randle's expression hardened. "You aren't here to film a segment on me," he said, his voice low and edged with warning.

"There are rumors and innuendoes, nothing concrete, tying you to Area 51," Jake said, his Cryptid Hunter instincts overriding his better judgment. "That's not all. Your mother-in-law, Lily, is full-blooded Navajo and suffers from a malady known as moth madness. She's a witch. You and she are exactly the reasons I'm filming in New Mexico."

Randle's expression changed to one of indignation, his smile disappearing, replaced by a dark frown. Tara drove in the gate in her pink Avalanche as he was pointing a finger at Jake.

"Now look here, my family is no business of yours. Leave us out of your show," he said, his voice rising.

"At least let me interview Rita and Lily," Jake said, trying to salvage the moment.

By now, Randle was huffing and puffing, looking as if he were about to get into Jake's face when Tara's pickup drove through the gate. After parking and seeing what was happening, she rushed over and grabbed her dad's arm.

"What the hell's going on?" she said, her voice raised, her eyes flashing with a mix of anger and concern.

"Mr. Cryptid Hunter here is a bit nosy for my liking," Randle said, his tone sharp.

"You need to apologize to him right now," Tara said, her grip tightening on Randle's arm. "He rescued Ran today. If he hadn't intervened, he might now be dead."

Before Randle could reply, Rita and Lily came running from the ranch house, their footsteps crunching on the gravel.

"Why all the yelling out here?" Rita asked, her voice calm but firm, her dark eyes taking in the scene.

Lily spotted Jake before Randle could answer her. "Cryptid Hunter," she said, her voice carrying a lilt that was both playful and knowing.

Jake grinned and pulled her into a hug. "Miss Lily," he said. "I'm so happy to meet you."

"You know who I am?" she asked, her eyes twinkling with mischief.

"Word in Tulsa is that you're the most delightful Navajo woman in Taos County," Jake said, his charm dial turned to full.

Lily would have blushed if her complexion had allowed it. A smile lit her craggy face, and she said, "You're a liar, Cryptid Hunter, but I love it."

"And you must be Rita," Jake said, kissing her hand with a flourish that made her laugh.

When Rita and Lily quit smiling, they scowled at Randle. "Are you causing trouble again?" Rita asked, her tone half-teasing, half-serious.

Randle opened his mouth to speak. Thinking better of it, he shut it, crossed his arms, and shook his head.

"It's my fault," Jake said, stepping in to defuse the tension. "I wanted to interview all of you for the episode I'm filming here." He looked at Randle and added, "Let me apologize for getting too personal."

Randle was looking uncomfortable, shuffling his feet and glancing at the stars as Lily and Rita continued to scowl at him. He shot Rita a look that implied she'd revealed way too much when she said, "Randle can be very secretive."

"No problem," Jake said, his tone light but his mind racing. "My catering tent is up and running. Please join me for a drink. I'll do my best to watch where I'm putting my nose."

Rita and Tara grabbed Randle's arms, Lily pushing him from behind as they accepted Jake's invitation and started for the catering tent. The air was thick with the scent of roasted chiles and the hum of the crew, but Jake's attention was elsewhere.

As they walked, he noticed a faint glow near the sandstone bluff, where the etched crescent moon seemed to shimmer with an unnatural light. He blinked, and it was gone, but the sight sent a shiver down his spine.

CHAPTER 15

Inside the catering tent, the atmosphere pulsed with a warm energy, the air thick with the smoky tang of roasted green chile and the charred aroma of grilled bison sliders.

The tent's transparent walls shimmered under the soft glow of string lights, their gentle radiance reflecting the violet and indigo shades of the desert night. Shadows moved across the plastic panels, as if the desert itself was drawing closer, whispering secrets through the faint rustle of sand against the tent's edges.

Jake led the Roberts family—Randle, Rita, Tara, and Lily—toward the heart of the tent, where a makeshift bar and buffet sprawled like an oasis of indulgence. The wooden tables groaned under platters of steaming food: golden cornbread glistening with honey butter, bowls of red chile stew simmering with earthy heat, and trays of bison sliders, their juices soaking into soft brioche buns.

The clink of glasses and the low hum of laughter mingled with the distant howl of a desert wind, creating a symphony of warmth against the wild unknown outside.

"Let me introduce you to the heart of this operation," Jake said, his Cryptid Hunter charisma flaring like a beacon. His grin was all teeth and charm, his denim shirt rolled up to reveal forearms tanned from countless desert treks. He gestured to an attractive older woman behind the bar, her silver-streaked hair pulled into a tight bun, her hands moving with the precision of a maestro as she mixed a drink. "This is Norma, our bartender extraordinaire. She can whip up a margarita that'll make you see stars."

Norma's smile gleamed under the fairy lights, her eyes twinkling with mischief. She slid a tray of drinks toward them—tequila sunrises for Rita and Tara, their vibrant orange-red gradients glowing like miniature sunsets; a whiskey neat for Randle, its amber depths catching the light; and a herbal infusion for Lily, its faint green hue swirling with flecks of sage and mint.

"To a night worth remembering," Norma said.

Lily nodded approvingly, her craggy fingers curling around the glass as she inhaled its earthy aroma. "Smells like the desert after rain," she murmured, her voice low and reverent, as if the drink itself were a communion with the land.

Jake waved over a short man with a cookie-duster mustache and a white beret tilted rakishly atop his head, his smock pristine despite the frenetic pace of the kitchen.

"Meet Neil, our head chef. He's the reason this tent smells like heaven. Cost me a small fortune to hire him away from Galatoires."

Randle's eyebrows lifted, his silver hair catching the glow of the lights. "I'm impressed," he said, his tone thawing slightly. "Rita and I dined there when we visited New Orleans; the food was nothing short of fantastic."

"Try his bison slider. He's been perfecting them all day," Jake said, his enthusiasm infectious.

Neil grinned, his mustache twitching as he handed out plates with a theatrical flourish, the sliders' savory aroma drawing appreciative murmurs from the group. The meat was seared to perfection, a faint char marking the edges, and the accompanying green chile relish sparkled with flecks of cilantro, its heat promising a slow burn. Rita took a bite, her eyes widening.

"Divine," she said, her voice muffled by the mouthful. "Neil, you're a wizard."

"Flattery gets you seconds," Neil said with a wink, saluting as he returned to the buffet to oversee a fresh batch of cornbread.

Jake turned to a man with a clipboard, his white polo embroidered with the Huntington logo, his blue chinos streaked with the red dust of the desert. Rod Bloustine strode over with a smile, his weathered face creased from years under the sun, and extended a hand.

"Rod's my production supervisor," Jake said. "He's seen more cryptid hunts than I've had hot meals. Keeps us all in line."

Rod's handshake was firm, his voice a gravelly drawl that carried the weight of experience. "Pleasure, folks. Jake's charm is the only thing louder than my arthritis."

The group laughed, the sound bright against the tent's warm hum. Jake handed out the drinks, his easy laughter filling the space as he clinked glasses with Randle.

"To new friends and good stories," he toasted, his eyes gleaming with the promise of adventure.

Rita and Tara giggled, their shoulders loosening under the spell of the tequila sunrises, while Lily sipped her infusion, her gaze piercing yet amused, as if she saw beyond the tent's walls to the secrets buried in the sand.

Randle, still stiff from their earlier tension, took a cautious sip of his whiskey, the liquid sliding down like liquid fire. His frown softened, the lines around his mouth easing as the warmth spread through him. The fairy lights cast a magical glow through the transparent walls, the desert outside transforming into a sea of shadows and starlight, the horizon swallowing the last traces of dusk.

Jake leaned back in his chair, his voice dropping into the cadence of a seasoned storyteller as he regaled them with tales from past hunts —bigfoot tracks in Oregon, their massive imprints pressed deep into the mud; a chupacabra sighting in Texas, its red eyes glinting in the moonlight.

His hands danced through the air, mimicking the frantic gestures of a flustered Buck McDivit, drawing a reluctant chuckle from Randle. Rita leaned in, her dark eyes wide with fascination, while Tara laughed until tears glistened at the corners of her eyes.

Lily remained apart, her presence like a still point in the storm of revelry. After a second round of drinks, her eyes gleamed with something ancient, as if the desert itself spoke through her. The tent seemed to hum with an unseen energy, the plastic walls rippling faintly as if brushed by an invisible hand.

She leaned closer to Jake, her voice a whisper carried on a night breeze, sharp with the scent of sage and dust.

"You seek secrets, Cryptid Hunter. I'll give you one. The moths that dance around me aren't madness, they're messengers. The desert speaks through them, tales of the old ones who walked before us, hidden in the sand."

Jake's breath caught, his journalist's mind racing like a hound on a scent. "Messengers? What do they say?" he asked.

Lily's smile was cryptic, her eyes reflecting the flickering lights like stars in a desert sky.

"They warn of shadows that move when the moons align—two crescents, like ours tonight. Watch the bluff. You might see more than you bargained for."

Her words hung in the air, a shiver running through the tent as the wind chimes outside sang faintly, their notes sharp and discordant, like the cry of something ancient stirring in the dark. Randle, now relaxed with a third whiskey, clapped Jake on the shoulder, his earlier wariness dulled by the night's magic.

"You're a silver-tongued devil, I'll give you that. Maybe you're not so bad."

Rita nodded, her arm linked with Tara's, both beaming under the spell of the evening.

"This feels like a dream," Rita said softly, her voice tinged with wonder. "The desert, the lights, your stories—it's like we've stepped into one of your hunts."

Tara raised her glass, her cheeks flushed. "To more nights like this," she said, her grin infectious.

The tension had melted, replaced by a tentative camaraderie, the magical night binding them together like a thread woven through the stars.

Jake glanced at the bluff through the tent wall, where the etched crescent moon shimmered faintly in the rock face, its outline glowing under the starlight. The shadow he'd seen earlier flickered again—a fleeting shape, too deliberate to be a trick of the light. His pulse quickened, the desert's mysteries tugging at his instincts.

The feast had ended, the last of the bison sliders consumed, the air now carrying a lingering warmth spiced with the fading aroma of green chile and whiskey. The Roberts family gathered their shawls and hats, their faces softened by laughter and drink.

The plastic walls shimmered under the dimmed fairy lights, the desert night pressing in with an almost tangible weight, the sky outside ablaze with a fiery star explosion that seemed to pulse with hidden energy, as if the cosmos itself were watching.

Randle stepped forward, his silver hair catching the faint glow, his turquoise bolo tie glinting like a distant signal fire.

"Jake, you're a gracious host," he said, his voice gruff but sincere. "Didn't think I'd enjoy a night with a TV man. You've proven me wrong."

Rita nodded, her dark eyes warm as she adjusted her shawl. "This night—it's something special," she said, her voice soft with gratitude. Tara squeezed Jake's arm, her grin wide. "Thanks for the stories—and the drinks."

Lily, her craggy face serene, fixed Jake with a look that seemed to pierce through time.

"The desert approves, Cryptid Hunter. Watch the shadows," she said, her words carrying the weight of prophecy before she turned and slipped into the night, her footsteps silent on the gravel.

Norma wiped down the bar, her movements precise despite the late hour, the silver streaks in her hair glinting like moonlight. Neil adjusted his beret, his smock still pristine.

"We're heading to Taos," Norma said, her voice bright with anticipation. "Staying at that world-class hotel you booked—marble baths, a spa, the works. You never spare a dime, Jake, and I love you for it."

Neil chuckled, hefting a bag over his shoulder. "Rod's already gone ahead with the crew. We'll see you tomorrow."

They waved and disappeared into the night, leaving the tent eerily silent, the air heavy with the aftertaste of revelry.

Jake sank into a chair at the center table, the overhead lights lowered to a dim glow that cast wavering shadows across the plastic walls. Through the translucent barrier, the sky burned with a wild constellation, stars flaring like the aftermath of a cosmic detonation.

He squinted, sure he had glimpsed a fleeting shape—a winged silhouette slicing through the heavens, its edges blurred yet deliberate—before it vanished into the void. His pulse quickened, the hairs on his neck prickling as the desert's breath seemed to press against the tent, a low moan weaving through the wind chimes' eerie song.

The flap rustled, and Randle stepped back inside, his broad frame silhouetted against the starry night. He pulled up a chair, its legs scraping the dirt floor, his face etched with worry. A bottle of scotch and a bottle of whiskey sat on the table, flanked by a lone red candle whose flame flickered like a trapped spirit. Jake poured a measure of whiskey into Randle's glass, the liquid catching the light like molten gold.

"I've been worried sick since Tara told me about those people kidnapping Ran," Randle said, his voice low and strained, the candlelight deepening the lines in his face. "She said they had foreign accents. German, maybe."

"They were after Dusty, not Ran," Jake said, his tone steady but his mind racing, piecing together fragments of the day's chaos. "She was the target."

Randle nodded slowly, his fingers tightening around the glass, the whiskey trembling slightly. "Tara told me Ran's sweet on her. What's the story?"

Jake leaned back, the candlelight dancing in his eyes like a far-off fire. "Dusty was Kirsten Louise Maldonado's roommate. You know, the Congresswoman from New Mexico." Randle's nod was curt, his expression unreadable, as if he'd already braced himself for grim news. Jake continued, "I guess you heard about her death—someone ran her off the road into a ditch."

"I heard," Randle said, his voice flat, betraying nothing.

Jake met his gaze. "Someone wrecked her on purpose. She was

taking a tape of a clandestine interview to a reporter—supposedly to reveal secrets about inner-dimensional beings."

Randle's face remained impassive, as if the term "inner-dimensional beings" was as mundane as the weather.

"Murder?" he asked, his tone clipped, like a man used to cutting through nonsense.

Jake nodded, his voice steady but laced with urgency. "Dusty was on the phone with Kirsten when it happened. She fled Albuquerque, thinking whoever killed her was coming next. After today's kidnapping, I'd say her instincts proved correct."

"Tara filled me in," Randle said, swirling his whiskey, the liquid catching the candle's glow. "She also mentioned Dusty's the state barrel racing champion."

Jake grinned, a spark of admiration lighting his face. "Wild as the wind in west Texas, strong as a bronco, and could probably outarmwrestle us both without breaking a sweat. She's a force, Randle —tough as leather, with a laugh that could wake the dead. Picture a woman who can rope a steer and charm a snake, all while wearing a grin that says she knows something you don't."

Randle chuckled, the sound rough but genuine, like gravel shifting underfoot. "What's her interest in Ran?"

"Dusty's the epitome of a cowgirl," Jake said, his voice warm with respect. "She's taken Ran under her wing, teaching him the ropes—literally. She's got him practicing for the saddle bronc riding competition at the Rodeo de Santa Fe."

Randle's smile faded, his jaw tightening. "I may have something to say about that. Boy has no business risking his neck."

Jake topped up Randle's glass, the whiskey glinting like a dark promise in the candlelight. "You may be Ran's dad, but right now, Dusty's his woman. He's smitten—head over heels. If I were you, I'd let well enough alone."

Randle raised an eyebrow, a wry smile tugging at his lips. "Sounds like a tomboy from what you and Tara say. Does she even like men?"

Jake leaned in, his voice dropping to a conspiratorial whisper, his eyes glinting with humor. "Was your dad happy when you told him you were marrying a half-Navajo woman?"

Randle's smile froze, his gaze sharpening as he took a long slug of whiskey, the silence stretching taut like a bowstring. The candle flickered, casting jagged shadows across his face. Finally, he set the glass down with a clink that echoed in the quiet tent.

"Point taken," he said, his voice low, almost a growl. "But Ran's my son. I'll always worry."

Jake nodded, respecting the weight of Randle's words. "Fair enough. But Dusty's not just some fling. She's got a fire in her, and Ran's caught in it. Let him burn a little—he might just shine."

Randle's expression softened, a flicker of pride breaking through his gruff exterior. "He's a good kid," he said quietly. "Stubborn, like his old man."

"Stubborn's not so bad," Jake said, raising his glass. "Keeps you alive out here."

Randle clinked his glass against Jake's, the sound sharp in the stillness. "I got something on my chest," he said, his voice barely above a whisper, as if the desert itself might overhear. "Something I've never told another soul. Not even Rita."

Jake's interest sharpened, the candle flame reflecting in his eager eyes like a beacon. "Want to tell me now?" he asked, leaning forward, his journalist's instincts humming.

Randle shook his head, his gaze distant, lost in the shadows beyond the tent. "Not now. I want Ran and McDivit there when I spill it. It's time they know."

Randle stood, the chair scraping again, and headed for the flap, his silhouette merging with the night like a figure stepping into a dream. Alone again, Jake stared at the flickering candle, its flame dancing as if alive.

He turned his gaze to the sky through the tent's translucent wall, where the stars burned with unnatural intensity, their light pulsing like a heartbeat. The strange shape flickered once more—a winged shadow, its edges sharp against the burst of starlight, moving with a purpose that was neither bird nor beast.

Outside, the wind chimes trembled, their eerie notes rising like a warning, sharp and insistent, as if the desert itself were stirring. The air grew heavy, thick with the scent of dust and something older, something that lingered in the bones of the earth. Jake's hand tightened around his glass, his pulse thrumming in time with the desert's unseen rhythm. The secrets buried in its sands were closer than ever, and he knew the night was far from done with him.

CHAPTER 16

The morning sun spilled gold across the porch boards of the old ranch house, warming the cracked wood beneath my boots. Pard lay beside me, his ears twitching at the occasional breeze, eyes half-lidded but alert.

Beyond the scrub and cottonwoods, the Sangre de Cristo Mountains loomed like a painted backdrop—shades of purple and blue in the distance, their peaks touched by the first mountain snow of the season. The air smelled of juniper and dust, clean and dry, with that faint electric scent that always made me feel like something was about to happen.

And then she appeared.

Anna Luna's cosmic ATV kicked up a swirl of ochre dust as it rolled up the drive, shimmering like something out of a dream. She stepped out like she owned the sun—smiling, radiant, her chestnut hair catching the light like strands of burnished copper.

Sandals and shorts that made my heart skip a beat, a frilly blouse that danced with the breeze, and silver and turquoise jewelry that whispered of old stories and canyon spirits. She looked like the desert itself had dressed her.

"Santa Fe run," she said, tossing me a grin. "Art supplies. You in?"

I didn't even answer. I just whistled for Pard to watch the ranch while I was gone, then climbed in.

The drive was like slipping into a trance. The road wound through high desert country—rolling hills dotted with piñon and sage, the occasional adobe ruin crumbling into the earth as if it had grown there.

The sky was impossibly blue, the kind that makes you believe in things you'd forgotten. Anna drove with one hand on the wheel, the other resting lightly on her thigh, humming something soft and Spanish. I watched the land roll by, feeling like I was being gently pulled into another world.

Santa Fe hit me like a scent memory—chile roasting in sidewalk drums, mesquite smoke, lavender, leather, and old wood. The streets were alive with color: adobe walls in sunbaked pinks and oranges, doors painted turquoise and cobalt, strings of ristras hanging like festive sentinels.

Anna gave me the tour with the ease of someone who belonged to the place—pointing out galleries, hidden courtyards, and the best spot for green chile stew.

We parked near the plaza, and I followed her through the winding streets, past vendors selling silver rings and woven blankets, the air thick with incense and the sound of a flute playing somewhere unseen. Every shop we entered felt like a portal—cool interiors filled with pottery, paintings, hand-carved santos, and wild bursts of color.

The artists greeted Anna like an old friend, some with hugs, others with reverent nods. She spoke to them in Spanish and English, her voice warm and familiar, and I realized she wasn't just known here—she was part of the fabric.

I watched her laugh with a weaver whose hands looked like they'd shaped mountains, and I felt something shift in me. Like the desert had opened a door and let me peek through.

By the time the sun began to lean westward, casting long shadows across the plaza, Anna was sipping horchata from a clay cup, her eyes reflecting the golden light.

"You glad you came?" she asked.

I looked around—at the colors, the smells, the people, the mountains in the distance—and nodded.

"Feels like I just remembered something I didn't know I'd forgotten."

She smiled, and for a moment, the whole town seemed to share her happiness. We had explored much of downtown Santa

Fe, though we still needed to visit the artist's supply shop. It wasn't far away.

I never saw the alley until Anna turned into it. One moment we were strolling past sunlit adobe storefronts and chile ristras swaying like crimson wind chimes, and the next we were swallowed by shadow.

The narrow passage twisted between buildings like a forgotten artery, its walls close and cool, painted with faded murals and cryptic symbols. I wouldn't have found it on my own if I'd walked Santa Fe for a hundred years.

At the end of the alley stood a crooked wooden door beneath a rusted tin awning. A hand-painted sign read La Mano del Espíritu. Anna pushed it open, and bells tinkled overhead—delicate, almost mournful.

Inside, the air was thick with incense and candle smoke, the scent of copal and myrrh clinging to the walls. The shop was dim, lit only by flickering candles and shafts of light filtering through stained glass panels. Shelves overflowed with jars of pigment, bundles of dried herbs, and strange talismans carved from bone and obsidian.

A man stepped from behind a velvet curtain. "Buck, meet Hector Diaz," Anna said.

Hector was dressed head-to-toe in a black linen shirt, slacks, and polished boots that gleamed like glass. His slicked-back hair shimmered like oil, and his mustache curled at the ends, reminiscent of an old borderland legend.

Silver jewelry adorned him—rings on every finger, a heavy necklace that looked forged in moonlight, and bracelets that clinked softly as he moved. But it was the tattoo on his neck that caught my eye: a jagged symbol I'd seen before, inked on men who'd done time in prison and come out changed.

Hector caught my gaze and smiled, revealing teeth too white, too perfect.

"Curandero," Anna said, gesturing toward the altar in the back. "Hector practices Brujería."

Hector chuckled. "Not a curandero. More like brujo, amigo. A wizard. Spells for love, luck, and protection. Whatever the soul craves."

Anna began gathering supplies—brushes, canvas, jars of paint so vivid they looked alive. Hector promised delivery to her casa in Taos, no charge. I lingered near the altar, drawn to it like a moth. Candles burned low, their wax pooled like blood. Offerings lay scattered—coins, feathers, bones, and a small bowl of what looked like ash and rose petals.

"Want your fortune told?" Hector asked, voice low and velvet.

I started to decline, but Anna grinned. "Do it, Buck. Hector's amazing. It's almost scary."

Before I could protest, Hector flipped the sign on the door to Cerrado and locked it. He led us through another curtain into a room that felt like it had been carved out of time. No windows. The walls were lined with shelves of skulls, candles, and jars filled with things I didn't want to identify. A single black candle burned on an ornately carved table, its flame steady despite the lack of breeze.

A black cat slinked in, silent as smoke, weaving between our legs like it was part of the routine. Ritual drumming began —soft, rhythmic, pulsing from hidden speakers. Hector's smile faded. He draped a black cloak over his shoulders and produced a satin pouch, embroidered with silver thread. We sat around the table, the candle casting long shadows that danced like spirits. He chanted in Spanish, voice rising and falling like a tide. Then he looked me dead in the eye and spilled the bones.

They clattered across the table, some landing upright, others twisted in unnatural ways. The candle flickered, and the cat hissed once, low and sharp. Hector stared at the bones, unmoving. His face drained of color.

Anna leaned forward. "Hector, what is it?"

He didn't answer. Just stood there, gathered the bones, and walked out of the room. We followed, the cat padding silently behind us.

Back in the shop, the incense seemed heavier, the air electric.

Anna begged Hector to explain, but he refused, shaking his head like he'd seen something he wished he hadn't.

As we turned to leave, he placed a hand on my shoulder. His grip was firm, cold.

"Go with God, my friend. You're going to need him."

Then he opened the door, and the sunlight outside felt foreign—too bright, too clean.

Anna didn't speak as we walked back to the car. Neither did I. The cat watched us from the alley's mouth, eyes gleaming like twin obsidian stones.

And somewhere deep inside, I knew Hector hadn't been bluffing.

The sky over Santa Fe had turned like Anna's hair, the color of old copper, streaked with lavender and gold as we stepped out of Hector's shop. The air was cooler now, tinged with the scent of mesquite and the faint metallic tang of something unrevealed.

Anna glanced at me and said, "Hector's reading doesn't mean a thing."

I patted her hand and said, "The man's a natural-born showman. Bet he has performed the same ceremony hundreds of times."

Anna looped her arm through mine and said, "Hope you're right. I need something alcoholic. How about you?"

"I was thinking the same thing," I said.

Anna started down the sidewalk. "My favorite bar's right around the corner."

"Lead the way, pretty lady," I said.

There seemed to be more people in town than the last time I was in Santa Fe. Anna noticed it too.

"Lots of people in the Plaza," she said. "You aren't the only person in a stetson."

"The rodeo this weekend," I said. "People coming in early for a little sightseeing."

Anna nodded and said, "Of course."

"Rodeo people aren't the only ones here," I said. "Two men are following us."

Anna glanced around. "Where," she said.

"Stop at the storefront ahead and pretend you're window shopping. Don't make it obvious, but glance to your right—those two men in baseball caps."

After following my directions, Anna said, "Are you sure?"

"They've been with us since we walked out of the alley."

"What'll we do?" Anna asked.

"Go in one of these shops and see if they have a back door," I said.

"I know the owner of this shop. She'll let us use the back door. We can take the alley to the Pagan Bar without returning to the Plaza."

"Perfect," I said. "Don't make it too obvious. Maybe even take the time to buy something."

"No problem," Anna said. "Maria and I are old friends."

I followed Anna into Maria's shop, the bell above the door chiming softly as we stepped inside. The place was a kaleidoscope of color and texture—woven rugs draped over wooden racks, shelves lined with turquoise jewelry, and pottery painted in earthy reds and blues.

The air smelled of sage and cedar, with a faint undercurrent of sweet tobacco, like someone had been smoking a pipe out back. Dim light filtered through a single window, casting a warm glow over the cluttered space. Maria, an attractive woman with silver-streaked hair pulled into a loose bun, looked up from behind a counter strewn with beads and leather cords. Her eyes lit up when she saw Anna.

"Anna Luna, as I live and breathe!" Maria's voice was rough but warm, like gravel smoothed by a river. She came around the counter, arms already open. "What brings you here, mi amiga?"

Anna hugged her tight, then pulled back with a grin. "Just passing through, Maria. Needed a break from the plaza crowd. You know how it gets with the rodeo folks in town."

Maria's gaze flicked to me, sizing me up with a knowing look. "And who's this? Your cowboy bodyguard?"

She smirked, her hands settling on her hips. I tipped my hat slightly.

"Buck, ma'am. Just along for the ride."

"Uh-huh." Maria's eyes twinkled with mischief. "You watch this one, Anna. He's got trouble written all over him."

Anna laughed, the sound easing the knot in my chest. "Oh, Maria, you have no idea."

She wandered toward a display of silver earrings, her fingers brushing over the delicate designs. I stayed near the counter, keeping one eye on the door and the other on the street outside.

Through the window, I caught a glimpse of movement—two figures lingering across the way, dressed in dark jeans and loose jackets, one with a baseball cap pulled low, the other with a scarf wrapped loosely around his neck. Their movements were too deliberate, their eyes too sharp for tourists.

"Maria," Anna called softly, her voice casual but with an edge I recognized. "Mind if we slip out the back? Got a bar to hit, and the plaza's too packed."

Maria's brow arched, but she didn't miss a beat. "Back door's always open for you, chica." She jerked her head toward a curtained doorway behind the counter. "You know the way."

Anna stopped after a few steps, pretending to admire a clay pot. I took the opportunity to lean over the counter and pick up the silver earrings Anna was eyeing so lovingly."

"How much?" I asked.

"Four hundred dollars," Maria said.

I opened my wallet and counted out four hundred bucks from the retainer of cash Jake had given me.

"Want me to wrap them for you?" Maria asked.

Anna had already moved on from the clay pot, and I shook my head. "If I don't hurry, she'll leave me," I said."

Maria smiled, winked, and said, "No, she won't."

"Thanks, Maria. Nice meeting you," tipping my hat again.

She just winked, like she'd seen this kind of thing before.

Anna was waiting in the back of the little shop, her arms crossed and tapping her toe.

"What took you so long?" she asked.

When I handed her the pair of earrings, her frown quickly gave way to a smile.

"You're a doll," she said, immediately putting them on and posing for me. "How do they look?"

"Beautiful," I said.

Anna smiled and said, "Now, let's move."

We slipped through a curtain, the air growing cooler as we entered a narrow hallway cluttered with boxes and old furniture. The back door was a slab of weathered wood, reinforced with a heavy bolt.

Anna slid it open with a practiced ease, and we stepped into the alley. The light was fading fast, the sky now a deep indigo streaked with dying gold. The alley smelled of damp stone and rotting fruit, a dumpster looming at one end like a silent sentinel. I scanned both directions—clear for now, but my gut told me those two wouldn't be far behind.

"Pagan Bar's two blocks that way," Anna whispered, pointing left.

"Stick to the shadows," I said.

We moved quickly, our footsteps muffled against the cracked pavement. The alley twisted past overflowing trash cans and rusted fire escapes, the walls closing in like they were holding their breath. I kept glancing over my shoulder, half-expecting to see those two rounding the corner.

Anna's pace was steady, her shoulders squared, like she'd done this kind of dance before. Indian school had taught me to trust my instincts, and right now, they were screaming that Hector's warning wasn't just smoke and bones.

CHAPTER 17

The Pagan Bar was a quirky dive, even for Santa Fe. Dragons dangled from the ceiling, their scales glinting in the dim light. A gnarled tree sprouted behind the bar, and Louis Armstrong's portrait hung among crosses, lizards, and stained-glass dragons.

A faded sign declared, "This is the year of the dragon." The air smelled of tequila and sage, thick with the kind of mystery that clung to this town like dust.

A lone man slumped at a pink stone table, his head cradled in his arm, snoring loud enough to rattle the glasses. Anna grinned, her eyes sparking with mischief.

"My friend," she said, nudging his shoulder. "Wolf's a bit... different."

I raised an eyebrow, glancing at her. "Wolf?"

The guy looked like he'd been poured into that chair after a long night.

"You're going to love him," she said, shaking his shoulder harder. "Ahem!"

A louder snort erupted, and I chuckled. "He's down for the count."

"No way," Anna said, giving him another shake. He swatted her hand like it was a pesky fly.

A voice cut through the haze. "Hey, Chica. You wanna talk with Wolf, you know what we gotta do."

A dark-skinned woman in a bright red dress, draped low over her shoulders, stood with a hand on her hip, grinning. Anna laughed and hugged her.

"Bonita, this is Buck," Anna said, pulling back.

Bonita wrapped me in a quick hug, pinching my ass before letting go. "You gotta nice one there, cowboy," she said with a wink. "Be right back."

She vanished behind the bar and returned with a shot of tequila, setting it beside Wolf's head. He snorted awake, red-rimmed eyes blinking up at us. After downing the shot in one gulp, he tossed the glass into the adobe kiva behind him. When it shattered, he winced and massaged his temple.

"Anna," he said, voice rough but laced with a clipped British accent. "Who's this with you?"

"Buck McDivit."

I extended my hand, sizing him up as he stood, all six-six of him unfolding like a crane. His khaki shirt screamed big-game hunter, but a red stain, wine or something worse smeared across it, shattered the illusion.

"Wolf Steinhart," he said, shaking my hand with a grip that could crush walnuts. "At your service."

"Wolf's an expert in New Age philosophy," Anna said, sliding into a red lacquered chair. "May we join you?"

"Rude of me not to offer," Steinhart said, raising a finger to Bonita. "Tequila and three glasses!"

Bonita kept polishing a glass, unfazed. "Who's paying?"

I raised my hand. "My treat."

"Then make it Cuervo Gold, pretty señorita," Steinhart called, popping all five fingers on both hands like a showman.

Anna hugged him again, her earlier worry about the men tailing us fading for a moment.

"You're such a character, Wolf," she said. "I wanted Buck to meet you."

Steinhart's eyes flicked to me, sharp despite the tequila. "Sir, you've arrived at the heart of the storm, the mouth of the volcano, the eye of the needle."

"The tail of the ass," Anna teased, snickering.

Steinhart poured shots from the bottle Bonita brought. "Anna is quite correct about my knowledge of New Age Philosophy."

"Good, because I have questions," I said.

"How can I be of assistance?" he asked.

"What's the deal with all the mystics in Santa Fe?" I asked, leaning back, the chair creaking under me. "What's pulling them here?"

Steinhart tossed back a shot, his Adam's apple bobbing. "This is the hub of New Age, where everyone's karma hits the fan." He chuckled, a low rumble. "Santa Fe's got synovial fluid equalization, aura balancing, crystal healing, vibrational therapy—need I go on?"

"I'm all ears," I said, grinning despite myself.

"Connective tissue polarity therapy, colon cleansing, bio-energetic synchronization," he rattled off, ticking them off on his fingers. "Hundreds of gurus and spirit channelers flock here."

"Hell, Wolf," I said, sipping the Cuervo, its burn waking me up. "Every waiter in town's a mystic."

"But here for a reason," he said, his voice dropping. "You're part Indian, aren't you, Buck?"

I nodded, caught off guard by his question. Anna leaned in. "All these crazies come because of the Indians?"

Steinhart's eyes gleamed. "Thousands of Pueblo, Navajo, and Hopi call New Mexico home. The Pueblo believe they are here, now, and always. Their culture has been deeply ingrained in this land for 8,000 years. There are secrets we bahana—whites, not you, Buck, will never know."

"Like what?" Anna asked.

"Koshare, for one," he said, the word heavy, as a stone dropped into still water.

"Koshare?" Anna tilted her head. "The ceremonial clowns at Hopi and Pueblo dances?"

"More than that." Steinhart's voice grew quieter, and the bar's hum seemed to fade. "A secret society. Powerful. Practicing magic—white and black. They are just one reason, among many, why New Age types are drawn here. This is the center of the universe."

I felt a prickle on my neck as if the air had shifted. Anna's hand brushed mine under the table, and I caught her glance—nervous but curious.

"Someone was following us," she said. "We had to duck through Maria's shop and an alley to lose them."

Steinhart's brow furrowed. "Why are they following you?"

"We're wondering the same thing," I said, my gut tightening.

Those men in masks and baseball caps, their eyes like predators, flashed in my mind.

Steinhart poured another shot but didn't drink. "New Mexico's a magnet for shadows—human and otherwise. It started with Los Alamos, the atomic bomb. The first detonation was in our desert. That explosion changed life on Earth."

The weight of his words hit me like a punch. I'd seen grainy photos of that blast, the mushroom cloud rising over the sands like a warning. Anna's fingers tightened around mine.

"Area 51, UAPs, alien orbs?" I said, half-joking, but my voice betrayed me.

"Yes," Steinhart said, his eyes locking on mine. "New Mexico became the technological universe's center. Foreign agents prowled back then, sniffing out Los Alamos secrets. They still do."

I could still see their silhouettes in the crowd, too predatory for tourists.

"You think those men tailing us are foreign agents?" I asked.

Steinhart glanced at Anna, then back at me. "Could be. Or something else. What secrets are you hiding?"

Anna spoke up. "Kirsten Louise Maldonado, the congresswoman, died in a car accident recently. She had information, possibly about UAPs, that she intended to share with a reporter. Kirsten was a friend of mine."

"And your name is connected to the secrets she had?" Steinhart asked.

Anna nodded, her face pale. "Her roommate, Dusty, doesn't think it was an accident. She came to my house, scared that whoever killed Kirsten might come for her, thinking she knew something."

Steinhart set his glass down with a clink. "That could explain why you are being tailed. And you, Buck? How're you tangled in this?"

I took a breath, the tequila loosening my tongue. "I'm an advance scout for Cryptid Hunter, the TV show. Anna's name came up because she and Elena Tafoya saw a UAP in the high desert. Anna sketched it. My boss, Jake Huntington, saw the drawing and sent me to gather information, possibly to organize an episode. I was staying at the Double Moon Ranch when things got weird."

Steinhart blinked, tossed back another shot, and wiped his mouth, the red stain on his shirt spreading slightly.

"Randle Roberts," he said, like it explained everything.

"What about him?" Anna asked, leaning forward.

"Supposedly, he has documents—proof aliens exist.

Steinhart nodded and poured himself more Cuervo when I said, "Undeniable evidence?" My pulse kicked up. This was Cryptid Hunter territory, but realer, darker. "How'd a guy like that get classified docs?"

"Roberts is a shadow," Steinhart said, his voice barely above a whisper. "His identity's been erased—protection only the highest authority can provide."

"The US government?" I pressed, glancing at Anna. Her eyes were wide, locked on Steinhart.

"Only Roberts knows. But if anyone—foreign agents, blackops, whoever—thinks you two know his secret, you're in deep."

My stomach churned. Those tails weren't just curious—they were hunting. "What stops them from grabbing Roberts and forcing it out of him?"

"He has protection," Steinhart said. "Top-level. As long as he keeps quiet."

"And what stops them from just killing him?" I asked, the words bitter.

"I've heard it said he created a dead man's switch," Steinhart said. "A trove of information that would go public if he dies unnaturally. It would shatter science, religion—everything."

I whistled low, my mind spinning. The UAP, the tails, Kirsten's death—it's all connected, a web tightening around us.

"Maybe the Indians already know," I said, thinking of the koshare, their secrets buried in the desert's bones.

Steinhart raised his glass, his eyes haunted. "Maybe they do, Buck. And maybe that's why we're all here—chasing truths we're not ready for."

A Mexican tune played in the background as a pretty young woman entered the bar, smiling when she saw Steinhart.

"Dad," she said. "Your tour is waiting outside."

Steinhart smiled and said, "Anna and Buck, this is my daughter, Gisela, though everyone calls her Pixie."

I could see why. Gisela was tiny next to her tall father, with blond pigtails, a biergarten skirt, and a low-cut blouse that gave her a Germanic look, as Steinhart's name suggested. It made me curious about his British accent. When Anna and I introduced ourselves, Pixie stayed in character, smiling and curtsying.

After returning her attention to Steinhart, she said, "I brought you a new shirt. You can't lead a tour with taco sauce all over you and looking like you were in a food fight."

Steinhart shook his head but stripped off his shirt without commenting. After buttoning up and smoothing the fabric to his liking, he quickly downed another shot. He peered at Bonita, bending over the bar, and held up what was left in the bottle of Cuervo.

"I'll be back for this, pretty senorita." He shook my hand and then looked at Anna. "Have to go now. Don't make yourself so scarce next time."

Anna and I watched him and Pixie, the dirty shirt folded under her arm, leave the bar. Bonita joined us at the table."

"I didn't know Wolf was married," Anna said.

Bonita scoffed and said, "Wolf? What woman would put up with him?"

"His daughter, apparently, and maybe you," Anna said.

"Poof!" Bonita said with a wry smile. "You can take the Cuervo. You bought it, and Wolf don't need it."

I handed her a hundred. "Buy him another bottle and keep the change," I said. "You deserve it."

Bonita stuffed the bill in her exposed cleavage and then kissed my forehead.

"We have to go now, Bonita," Anna said. "See you next time."

"Adios, Chica," Bonita said, blowing her a kiss. "And don't forget to bring the handsome cowboy with you."

"Mind if we go out the back door?" Anna asked.

"Of course, Chica. Follow me."

Bonita led us behind the bar, through the tiny kitchen that served only snacks, and to a steel door with a sign that read "No Exit."

"Are we going to set off an alarm?" Anna asked.

Bonita flipped a switch on the wall and signaled that it was okay for us to leave. We'd been in the Pagan Bar for a while, and the daylight was fading when we stepped out into the alleyway. Anna gave me an anxious look and squeezed my hand.

"I'm frightened, Buck," she said.

"Those two goons have probably long since given up looking for us," I said. "We'll be fine."

"Hope you're right. Are you hungry?" she asked.

"You kidding? How could I not be with all the wonderful aromas wafting in the breeze," I said. "Not to mention we haven't eaten all day."

"I know a place. You'll love it. My treat."

"Can't wait," I said.

Anna didn't let go of my hand as we traversed the alleyway. The bar's eclectic hum faded, but the weight of it all pressed heavier. Whatever Roberts documents hid, we'd stumbled into something bigger than any cryptid hunt. And with eyes on us, getting out clean was starting to feel like a long shot.

CHAPTER 18

The night air in Santa Fe carried a faint chill, but the plaza was vibrant with activity, lanterns strung overhead casting a warm amber glow on the adobe buildings. Anna led the way, her boots clicking on the cobblestones as we made our way to a hidden restaurant with a hand-painted sign: La Sombra Azul.

The worn wooden door creaked as we entered, and the air inside hit me like a warm embrace—thick with the scent of roasted chiles, cumin, and fresh tortillas. The place was alive. Walls painted in deep reds and ochres vibrated with color, tables draped in woven cloths, and a small fountain in the corner trickled over turquoise stones.

A trio of musicians strummed a soft flamenco melody near the bar, their guitars weaving a spell through the hum of laughter and clinking glasses. As we stepped inside, my eyes snagged on a couple in the far corner—too stiff, too watchful for tourists enjoying a night out. Something about them felt familiar, but I couldn't place it.

The waitress greeted Anna with a hug and a teasing, "¡Hola, reina de Taos!" before leading us to a corner table by the fountain. We settled in, ordering local beers—mine a smoky amber brewed with piñon nuts, Anna's a crisp pale ale with hints of lime and coriander.

The food arrived in waves: blue corn enchiladas drowned in green chile, carne adovada that melted on the tongue, calabacitas sautéed with garlic and epazote, and a bowl of posole so fragrant it stung my eyes.

Anna was radiant, her laughter like bells ringing through

the noise of the restaurant. But as the conversation drifted, her smile faded, replaced by a shadow of worry.

"I can't stop thinking about what Hector told you," she said softly. "Three brushes with death, Buck. It's eating away at me. Kirsten's death already feels like a wound that won't heal."

I reached across the table, squeezing her hand. Her skin was warm, but her fingers trembled slightly.

"Jake called this morning," I said, hoping to shift her focus. He talked with Randle Roberts last night. Randle has a story to tell—secrets, he says. He wants me and his son to hear it."

"Secrets?" Anna's brow furrowed. "About what?"

"Maybe about who kidnapped Dusty and Ran. Could be tied to Kirsten's death, too. Jake thinks Randle knows something big —Area 51, government cover-ups, the works."

Her eyes widened. "Why didn't you tell me earlier?"

"I'm telling you now," I said.

Her lips twitched toward a smile. "Wonderful. It doesn't exactly ease my mind about Hector's prophecy."

The candle on our table flickered in her hazel eyes. "You heard what Wolf said. Santa Fe's full of channelers, witches, and every wild belief you can imagine. Hector's just one of them. Don't let it get to you."

Her smile returned, soft but playful. "You calling me cultish, Buck McDivit?"

"In the most beautiful way possible," I said, my thumb brushing her knuckles.

A faint clink of glass from the corner table pulled my attention. The couple I'd noticed earlier was still there, their heads bent together, voices low. Recognition hit me like a cold wind.

"That couple over there," I said, keeping my voice low. "I know them. They're staying at the Double Moon Ranch. Met them the night someone rifled through my stuff while I was at dinner."

Anna's eyes flicked toward them, then back to me. "You think they did it?"

"They were at dinner with me, but they could have set it

up. Angie checked them out—said they work for some German manufacturing company. Could be foreign agents, could be nothing. But seeing them here feels… off."

She stole another glance, then quickly turned around. "They saw me looking."

"Probably just a coincidence," I said, though I didn't fully believe it. "Let's enjoy the night and deal with it later."

We tried to push the unease aside, finishing with cinnamon-dusted sopapillas drizzled with honey. But Hector's warning lingered like smoke, curling through my thoughts. After paying the tab, we stepped out into the plaza, now quieter, the lanterns casting long shadows across the stones.

Anna pointed to a narrow alley between two adobe buildings, her grin returning. "Shortcut to the car," she said, her voice light but her eyes scanning the shadows. "Trust me."

I followed, my boots scuffing against the uneven pavement. The alley was tight, barely wide enough for us to walk side by side, the walls looming high with faded graffiti scrawled across them. Trash cans lined one side, their lids askew, the air thick with the smell of damp cardboard and stale beer. My skin prickled, the hairs on my neck standing up.

Halfway through the alley, a rustle broke the silence. A figure burst from the shadows—hooded, fast—hurling something at us. My heart slammed against my ribs as I caught a blur of scales and motion. Instinct took over. I lunged, hands out, and grabbed it just behind the head. A rattlesnake, big and heavy, its body writhing in my grip, scales cold and slick under my fingers. Its tail buzzed like a chainsaw, the sound echoing off the walls.

"Anna, sidewalk!" I shouted.

She bolted, her heels clacking as she reached the open street. I crouched, releasing the snake near the trash cans, watching it slither into the dark, its rattle fading like a warning swallowed by the night. My pulse hammered, my hands still tingling from the snake's weight.

I joined Anna on the sidewalk. Her face was pale, eyes wide, breath shallow. "That's one," I said, forcing my voice to stay calm.

She stared at me as if I'd just wrestled a mountain lion. "The man—he was German," she said, her voice shaking.

"How do you know?" I asked, scanning the alley's exit.

"He ran around the corner to the street. A car screeched to a stop, and someone yelled, 'Mach schnell!' before the door slammed and they sped off." The moonlight caught her face, highlighting the sharp fear in her eyes.

"Why would Germans be after you?" she asked.

"They're not trying to kill me," I said, though my gut wasn't so sure. "If they wanted me dead, a bullet would've been easier than a snake at point-blank range. That was a warning."

Anna's voice was sharp now, edged with frustration.

"A warning about what?"

"Don't know yet."

She grabbed my hand, pulling me toward her ATV. "I'm taking you home."

"I don't like you going back to Taos alone," I said. "Not after this. Spend the night at Shadow Ranch. You take the bed; I'll crash on the couch."

Anna shook her head, her jaw set. "Fritz has been alone all day. I need to check on him."

"Fine," I said, meeting her stubbornness with my own. "We'll go to Taos first, pick up Fritz, and then head to the ranch. Pard loves him—they'll have a blast together. Besides, Randle's coming tomorrow to talk secrets with me, Jake, and Ran. You'll want to be there."

Her eyes searched mine, the moonlight catching the worry still lingering in them. "You think it's safe?"

"Safer than staying here," I said. "Whoever's behind this, they're watching. Let's not give them another shot tonight."

She exhaled, her shoulders relaxing just a fraction. "Okay. Let's get Fritz and go. But if anything else tries to kill us, I'm holding you responsible."

I grinned, despite the knot in my chest. "Deal. Let's move."

The short drive was quiet, the desert stretching out under a moonlit sky, stars winking like they knew something we didn't. Anna's hands gripped the wheel, her knuckles pale.

I wanted to say something to ease her nerves, but my own thoughts were tangled—Hector's prophecy, the German couple, the snake. It was all connected, but the pieces wouldn't snap into place.

When we pulled up to Anna's house, the street was too still, the kind of quiet that feels like it's holding its breath. Her front door was ajar, just a crack, but enough to make my stomach lurch. Inside, Fritz's barks rang out, sharp and frantic, cutting through the silence.

"Fritz!" Anna called, shoving the door open and rushing in.

I scanned the shadows as Fritz, a wiry mutt with a graying muzzle, practically leapt into Anna's arms, licking her face as she knelt to hold him.

"Easy, boy," I said, stepping past them to check the house.

The place was a wreck. Drawers hung open, their contents dumped across the floor. Papers were scattered like confetti, and the closet doors stood ajar, clothes spilling out. The kitchen was worse—cans and boxes strewn across the counter, the fridge door open. In the bedroom, the mattress was flipped, the bedding slashed open.

"Buck…" Anna's voice trembled as she clutched Fritz, her eyes darting from the overturned furniture to the chaos of her home. "What the hell happened here?"

My boots crunched on broken glass asI returned to clutch her hand.

"They were looking for something. "My guess? Kirsten's documents."

Anna's face went white, her arms tightening around Fritz. "Kirsten's research… They think I have it?"

"Don't know." I put a hand on her shoulder, feeling her shake beneath my touch. "Hey, look at me. You're okay. Fritz is okay. We're getting out of here."

She nodded, swallowing hard. "Let me grab a bag."

While Anna packed, I stood by the door, keeping watch. My

mind raced. The German couple, the snake, now this break-in—it wasn't random. Someone was closing in, and Kirsten's documents were the key.

Anna emerged with a duffel bag slung over her shoulder, Fritz trotting at her heels.

"Let's go," she said, her voice steadier now, though her eyes still held that haunted look.

The drive to Shadow Ranch was long, the desert glowing silver under the moon. Fritz curled up, his head on Anna's lap as she stroked his fur. I kept my eyes on the road, but my thoughts were elsewhere.

"So," Anna said, breaking the silence, "you really think Kirsten's documents are what they're after?"

"Maybe," I said.

"Her research was dangerous enough to get her killed?" she asked. "What the hell did she know?"

"Don't know, but someone tore your place apart looking for the answer."

"I don't have anything," she said.

"Dusty did, and she was at your house," I said.

Anna sighed, leaning her head against the window. "This is insane, Buck. Snakes, break-ins, Area 51? I'm a painter, not a spy."

I chuckled, though it came out hollow. "Yeah, well, the desert's got a way of pulling people into its mysteries. Stick with me, and we'll figure it out."

She gave me a sidelong glance, a faint smile tugging at her lips. "You're awfully calm for someone who just caught a rattlesnake with his bare hands."

"Practice," I said, winking. "You should see me wrestle a coyote."

That got a laugh out of her, and for a moment, the tension eased.

We reached Shadow Ranch well past midnight. The old house loomed against the starry sky, its weathered walls blending into the desert. Pard bounded out to greet us, his tail wagging like a metronome. He and Fritz sniffed each other, then tore off, chasing shadows across the yard like old friends.

Inside, I showed Anna to the bedroom. "Take the bed," I said, grabbing a blanket and pillow from the closet. "I'm good on the couch."

"You sure?" she asked, hesitating in the doorway, Fritz at her side.

"Positive. Get some rest. Tomorrow's going to be a long day."

She nodded, her eyes softening. "Thanks, Buck. For... everything."

I waved her off, settling onto the couch as she closed the bedroom door. The house was quiet, save for the faint creak of the wind. I lay back, staring at the ceiling, my mind replaying the night's events: the snake, the break-in, Randle's secrets.

Sometime during the night, I woke with a start. The air felt charged, like the moment before a storm. My skin prickled, and there she was—Aeterna, standing at the foot of the couch, her silver bodysuit shimmering in the dim light, her too-large blue eyes glowing like twin beacons. She was flat, two-dimensional, her edges rippling as if she were a projection struggling to hold form.

I sat up. "Aeterna, what are you doing here?"

She didn't speak—not with words. Her presence brushed against my mind, warm and electric, like a current humming through my thoughts. Her smile was a faint curve of her lips, and she reached out, her flat, shimmering hand touching mine. A jolt shot up my arm, a glowing pulse of light that felt alive, like it was carrying a message I couldn't yet decode.

My skin tingled and pulse quickened as colors—reds, blues, purples—moved faintly in the air around her. Suddenly, she vanished in a flash of light, leaving me blinking in the darkness. I remained seated, my hand still warm from her touch, as the room returned to silence.

As I sat there, my mind drifted to the petroglyphs I'd seen near the ranch—a spiral carved into a boulder, its edges worn but sharp, as if it were waiting for something. I'd caught Lily staring at it once, when I'd visited with Tara and Ran.

Her eyes had lingered, her lips moving silently, like she was praying or remembering something she wouldn't share. As a full-blooded Navajo, Lily knew things—stories of star people, maybe, or secrets tied to the desert's bones. If those carvings had anything to do with Aeterna, with her glowing orb and electric pulse, Lily might hold the key.

Getting her to talk, especially to an outsider like me, would be like prying open a locked kiva. Tomorrow, when Randle came, I'd have to ask about the petroglyphs—and hope Lily was ready to trust me with whatever she was hiding about the space people.

CHAPTER 19

A chill breeze blew down from the Sangre de Cristo Mountains, rustling the sagebrush and carrying the sharp scent of piñon and earth. Early fall had settled over Shadow Ranch, painting the sky a crisp blue, the kind that makes you feel like the world's holding its breath.

I stood on the porch, coffee mug warm in my hands, watching the horizon where the sun was cresting, gilding the desert in gold. Pard and Fritz chased each other across the yard, their yips echoing off the adobe walls of the ranch house. It was a glorious morning, but the knot in my gut told me it was about to get complicated.

The rumble of tires on gravel snapped me out of my thoughts. Randle Roberts' truck rolled into view, dust trailing like a ghost. I could make out Tara's silhouette in the passenger seat, her cowboy hat tilted at a defiant angle, sitting beside him.

Behind them was a semi loaded with production equipment necessary for the filming of an episode of Cryptid Hunter. Jake and his production supervisor, Rod Bloustine, followed in a black Range Rover, and the bus behind them transported Jake's film crew.

Randle was here to spill his secrets—about Area 51, Kirsten's death, maybe even the Sky People. He blamed me for his son Ran ditching the Double Moon Ranch to chase rodeo glory. And Tara? Her crush on me was a spark in a dry field, especially with Anna still asleep in my bedroom.

The truck doors slammed, and Randle climbed out, his weathered face set in a scowl, arms crossed tight over his chest. His Stetson shaded his eyes, but I could feel the heat of his glare from across the yard. Tara hopped down, her boots kicking up dust, her dark braid swinging as she scanned the ranch house.

Jake and his crew followed, and soon the old ranch was humming with activity, cameras filming footage of the mysterious Shadow Ranch and the Sangre de Cristo Mountains in the background.

Tara's eyes locked on me, and for a split second, her smile was all fire. Jake strode up with a grin, clapping me on the shoulder. His crew was behind him, already filming with Rod Bloustine barking orders.

"Morning, Buck," he said. "Randle has a lot to say today and has agreed to let us film it. I thought, what better place than Shadow Ranch? Where's Ran?"

I blinked, wondering what kind of magic Jake used to get Randle to agree to an interview, much less on camera.

"Inside, with Dusty," I said, nodding toward the house. "They're grabbing breakfast."

Randle grunted, his arms still crossed, his limp more pronounced as he stepped onto the porch.

"You and my boy have some explaining to do," he said, his voice low and edged with resentment. "Running off to rodeo like it's some damn game. You know what it cost me, Buck."

I met his gaze, keeping my tone steady. "Ran's his own man. I didn't push him into anything."

Before he could fire back, the screen door creaked, and Ran stepped out, Dusty at his side. Ran's lanky frame mirrored his father's, but his easy grin was all his own.

Dusty had a wild energy about her, her hair pulled back under a battered hat, her eyes sharp with the kind of fear that comes from running from whoever killed her friend. She froze when she saw Randle, her face lighting up like she'd just won the lottery.

"Damn, Ran!" she said, her voice rising. "You never told me your dad is Randle Roberts."

Ran blinked, confused. "You know my dad?"

"You kidding me?" Dusty practically bounced forward,

throwing her arms around Randle in a hug that made him stiffen, then soften, his scowl melting into a surprised half-smile. "One of the greatest saddle bronc riders of all time! I had your poster in my bedroom when I was growing up. I can't believe I'm actually meeting you!"

Randle's ego flared like a struck match, his chest puffing out as he patted Dusty's back.

"Well, now, darling, that's mighty kind," he said, his voice warming for the first time since he'd arrived. "Didn't know I had fans out here."

Ran laughed, shaking his head. "She's been dodging trouble, Pop, not chasing your old glory days."

Dusty finally let go, her cheeks flushed. "Trouble or not, I'm not passing up a chance to talk rodeo with Randle Roberts."

The moment was cut short by the creak of the bedroom door. Anna stepped out, yawning, her hair mussed from sleep, wearing one of my old flannel shirts over her jeans. She looked soft in the morning light, her hazel eyes blinking against the brightness.

"Morning, everyone," she said, her voice still thick with sleep as she slid an arm around mine, her touch warm and familiar.

The air shifted like a storm rolling in. Tara's posture went rigid, her foot tapping a furious rhythm on the porch, her arms clasped tight across her chest.

Tara's eyes—dark and sharp like her grandmother Lily's—shot sparks, zeroing in on Anna's hand on my arm. I felt the heat of her jealousy like a brand, though the others seemed oblivious, caught up in Dusty's chatter and Randle's newfound grin.

Tara's lips pressed into a thin line, her fingers digging into her biceps as she turned away, pretending to study the corral. I eased my arm from Anna's grip, trying to defuse the tension before it exploded.

"Coffee's inside," I said, keeping my voice light. "Let's get settled, and Randle can tell us what he came to say."

But Dusty had other plans. "Hold up," she said, grabbing Randle's arm. "Mr. Roberts, you have to come down to the corral.

I've been working on my riding, but I'm rusty. You could give me some pointers, right? And Ran, too—he's got your talent, you know."

Randle's eyes lit up, the last of his scowl vanishing. "Well, hell, why not? Let's see what you two got."

Tara's foot stopped tapping, but her glare didn't soften as she followed the group toward the corral, her boots stomping harder than necessary. Anna raised an eyebrow at me, sensing the shift but not quite placing it. I shook my head slightly, hoping she wouldn't ask. Tara's crush was a live wire, and I wasn't about to touch it with Anna standing so close.

The corral was a wide circle of packed earth, ringed by a weathered wooden fence, the mountains looming like silent judges in the distance. The morning breeze carried a nip that made the horses' breath steam, their hooves kicking up dust as Ran and Dusty saddled up.

Randle leaned against the fence, his limp forgotten as he barked instructions, his voice carrying the old authority of a rodeo legend, Jake's crew filming the scene.

"Keep your weight centered, Dusty," he called, his eyes sharp. "You're leaning too far forward—broncs'll throw you like a rag doll. Ran, loosen your grip on the reins. Let the horse feel you, not fight you."

Dusty whooped as she urged her mare into a tight turn, her form sloppy but fierce. Ran followed, his movements smoother, his body in sync with the horse like he'd inherited his father's instincts.

The rest of us watched—Jake with a grin, Anna leaning against the fence, me trying to ignore Tara's burning stare. Every time Anna laughed, brushed my arm, or stole a peck on my cheek, Tara's posture tightened, her fingers flexing like she was itching to throw a punch.

Randle's voice softened as he coached, his pride in Ran shining through despite his earlier anger. After a while, he waved them down and pulled Ran aside, his hand on his son's shoulder. I caught a snippet of their conversation, Randle's voice low but clear.

"Having you compete in the rodeo scares the bejesus out of me, son," he said. "But I'm proud of you. I'll be there Saturday with bells on to cheer you on."

Ran's grin was brighter than the morning sun, and for a moment, the tension in the air eased. But Tara's eyes were still on me, her jealousy a smoldering fuse, and I knew Randle's secrets —whatever they were—were about to light it all up again.

The corral dust settled as we trudged to the ranch house, the morning sun climbing higher, its light cutting through the chill breeze like a blade.

Ran and Dusty were still buzzing from Randle's pointers, their laughter trailing behind them, but the air between Tara and Anna crackled with unspoken heat. Tara's boots stomped harder than necessary, her eyes darting to Anna every time she moved closer to me.

Anna, oblivious at first, was starting to catch the edge in Tara's stare, her own smile tightening as we crossed the porch. Pard and Fritz bounded ahead, oblivious to the human drama, their tails wagging like they were the only ones having a good time.

Inside, the ranch house smelled of coffee and old wood, the kind of scent that grounds you even when your nerves are frayed. The living room table—a massive slab of weathered oak, scarred from years of ranch life—dominated the space, surrounded by mismatched chairs that creaked under our weight. Jake's crew began setting up equipment.

I took a seat at the head, hoping to steer the conversation, but the tension followed us in like a shadow. Randle settled across from me, his face a mix of pride from the corral and the old grudge he still carried. Dusty plopped down beside him, her hand resting on his shoulder, her eyes still shining with hero worship.

"Mr. Roberts," she said, her voice bright, "I'm serious, those tips you gave me out there? Pure gold. I'm gonna kill it at the next rodeo, thanks to you."

Randle chuckled, his ego still stoked, the lines around his eyes softening. "Call me Randle, darling. And you keep that fire, you'll outride half the circuit."

Ran grinned, leaning back in his chair, but Tara sat stiffly, her arms crossed, her foot tapping a restless rhythm under the table. Her eyes were daggers, slicing toward Anna, who sat close enough to me that our knees brushed.

Anna's fingers grazed my arm, a casual touch that sent sparks through me—and, judging by Tara's glare, through her too. I shifted in my seat, trying to put space between us without making it obvious.

Anna's brow furrowed, her gaze flicking from Tara to me, like she was finally piecing together the storm brewing across the table. Jake, sensing the room's edge, stood and clapped his hands, his grin as wide as the canyon.

Cameras rolled as he said, "All right, folks, let's loosen up. We have serious business to discuss, but no reason we can't do it over drinks."

Someone from Jake's film crew produced scotch and whiskey. He poured generous shots into chipped glasses, sliding them across the table like a dealer in a poker game.

"To secrets," he said, raising his glass, his eyes glinting with something I couldn't quite read. "And to finding out what the hell's going on around here."

We clinked glasses, the whiskey burning a path down my throat, warming the knot in my gut. Tara barely sipped hers, her stare locked on Anna, who took a slow drink, her eyes narrowing as she caught Tara's look.

Dusty, oblivious, leaned closer to Randle, her hand still on his shoulder, her voice bubbling.

"Randle, you ever think about coaching? You could start a school or something."

Randle laughed, a rare sound that softened the room, but his gaze flicked to me, sharp and guarded, like he was remembering why he was here. I set my glass down, leaning forward.

Jake held up a hand, his grin turning sly. "My crew has been working overtime, processing Kirsten's tape."

The room went still, the air heavy with the mention of Kirsten's name. Dusty's hand slipped from Randle's shoulder, her face paling.

Ran leaned forward, his jaw tight. "What'd they find?" he asked.

"Don't know yet but from Kirsten's earlier press conference, I'd say it's something big."

My pulse kicked up, Aeterna's glowing eyes flashing in my mind, her electric touch still lingering in my bones. I kept my face neutral, but Tara's head snapped toward me, her jealousy momentarily eclipsed by curiosity.

Jake pressed on. "Point is, Kirsten's tape is a potential goldmine. Colley's flying in Friday night with the processed footage."

He winked, sipping his scotch, but his secrecy was like a match to dry grass.

Randle grunted, his arms crossing again. "You're going to keep us in the dark, Huntington?"

Jake's grin didn't waver, but his eyes turned serious. "Hell, Randle! I'm as curious as you are, but it could be something big —bigger than Area 51, maybe. Congresswoman Maldonado was chasing something world-crossing, and it has folks nervous."

Dusty's breath hitched, her eyes wide. "You think it's tied to whoever's after me?"

"Yes," Jake said, his voice low. "That's why we're here. Randle has his piece of the puzzle, and Friday night, we'll put it all together."

The room pulsed with tension, every glance a loaded gun. Tara's eyes bored into Anna, who was now watching her with a mix of defiance and unease.

Dusty's hand was back on Randle's shoulder, her hero worship a bright spot in the gloom, but Randle's face was hard again, his gaze flicking between me and Ran.

I felt the weight of Aeterna's presence, her orb and her touch, hovering in the back of my mind, and I knew whatever Randle was about to say was just the spark to light this powder keg.

CHAPTER 20

The air in the Shadow Ranch den was thick enough to choke on, a heavy mix of dust, whiskey, and unspoken secrets that buzzed like a live wire stretched to its limit.

We crowded around the scarred oak table, its gouges catching the flicker of a single hanging bulb, casting jagged shadows that danced across the walls like restless ghosts.

Empty whiskey and scotch glasses littered the tabletop, glinting like spent shells after a firefight. The early fall breeze slithered through a cracked window, carrying the sharp tang of sage and piñon, cooling the sweat beading on my neck but doing nothing to ease the tension coiling in my gut.

Jake's crew was filming, their cameras humming softly, the lighting dim and conspiratorial, just the way he liked it for Cryptid Hunter. The glow of their equipment painted the room in shades of amber and shadow, turning the familiar into something otherworldly.

Jake, sprawled at the head of the table like a king holding court, swirled his scotch, his half-cocked grin hinting he knew more than he let on. He set the scene for his audience with the cadence of a seasoned showman.

"We're here at Shadow Ranch, nestled in the high desert of northern New Mexico, at the foot of the Sangre de Cristo Mountains, where the air hums with secrets older than the mesa itself. Tonight, we're listening to Randle Roberts, a man who claims to hold truths that could unravel reality. This old ranch, not far from Taos with its art, its history, its whispers of the unknown, is the perfect stage for what's to come."

Randle sat at the table's far end, his Stetson resting on a

gnarled hat rack like a sentinel. His weathered face was a map of secrets, etched deep with lines that spoke of battles fought in shadows.

But the way he leaned back, arms crossed, his jaw tight as a bear trap, told me he was still holding the reins, even now, measuring every word like a man walking a tightrope over an abyss.

Tara's glare cut through the haze of liquor, her foot tapping a relentless rhythm against the floorboards, each tap a silent accusation. Her eyes flicked toward Anna every time she shifted closer to me, her jealousy a palpable heat that singed the air between them.

Anna, her hands folded in her lap, kept her whiskey untouched since Tara's last venomous stare, but her gaze darted to mine, searching, her fingers trembling faintly as if she sensed something lurking just beyond the room's edges.

Dusty perched beside Randle, her hand resting on his shoulder again, her hero worship undimmed despite the scotch flushing her cheeks a feverish red. Ran leaned forward, his eyes locked on his father, hungry for answers, his knuckles white around his glass. Pard and Fritz dozed by the fireplace, their soft snores a faint counterpoint to the storm brewing among us, oblivious to the weight of what was about to spill.

Jake cleared his throat, his voice cutting through the haze. "Randle, you promised us secrets. Area 51, Kirsten, whatever's got Dusty jumping at shadows. We're all here, cameras rolling. Time to spill."

Randle's eyes met mine, sharp and guarded, like a man who'd stared down too many nightmares to flinch. He took a long pull of whiskey, the glass clinking against the table as he set it down, the sound echoing like a gunshot in the quiet.

Outside, the wind picked up, rattling the windowpane, and for a moment, I swore I heard a low hum, like the desert itself was listening.

"All right," Randle said, his voice low and gravelly, rough as the mesa's edge. "But don't say I didn't warn you. This isn't the kind of truth you sleep easy with. It's the kind that follows you into the dark."

The room went still, the only sound the faint whir of Jake's cameras and the creak of the old ranch house settling under the weight of its own secrets. Randle leaned forward, his hands splayed on the table, his fingers tracing the scars in the wood as if they held the answers he was about to give. When he spoke, his words tumbled out like a river breaking a dam, each one heavy with the weight of years.

"I was a shadow figure," he said. "Not on any payroll, not in any record. The government called me Vector. No one used my name, not even in whispers. I had open rein over Los Alamos, Sandia, places where the air tastes like metal, and the walls hum with things you're not supposed to know. I walked through vaults holding blueprints for weapons that could erase continents—nuclear warheads, energy beams, tech you can't even dream up. But that was just the surface."

Dusty's eyes widened, her hand tightening on his shoulder, her nails digging into his denim shirt. "You're saying you were, what, a spy?"

Randle's laugh was a bitter rasp, like dry leaves skittering across stone. "Hell, darling, spies have names. I was a ghost. They flew me to Area 51 in '86. President Reagan was there, holed up in a bunker, his face pale as ash, sweat beading on his brow like he'd seen the devil himself.

"I sat in on secret congressional meetings—black ops briefings, projects so dark they didn't have names, just numbers. I was the guy in the corner, no title, no record, just eyes and ears. They trusted me because I didn't exist."

Jake snorted, tipping his glass, the scotch catching the light like liquid fire. "You're telling me you rubbed elbows with Reagan at Area 51? Come on, Randle. That's a stretch."

Randle's gaze didn't waver, his eyes like chipped flint. "Reagan called me 'the ghost in the room.' Believe what you want, Huntington. I was there. And I saw things that don't belong on this Earth." He paused, his stare drifting to the window, where the desert night pressed against the glass, black and endless.

"We flew in a saucer. Reverse-engineered from the wreck near Groom Lake. Chuck Yeager was the pilot, steady as ever. But his copilot... it wasn't human."

My pulse kicked up, Aeterna's glowing eyes flashing in my mind, unbidden, like a warning. The air in the room seemed to thicken, the shadows stretching longer, as if the ranch itself was leaning in to listen.

"What'd it look like?" I asked, my voice barely above a whisper, rough with the whiskey and something else—apprehension, maybe.

Randle's hands clenched, his knuckles white against the table's dark wood. "Like nothing you've ever seen. Tall, seven feet at least, but thin as a fence post, with skin like polished obsidian, shimmering with flecks of silver, like stars trapped under glass.

Its eyes were slits, glowing green, not like ours—more like a cat's, but deeper, as if they saw through time itself. No mouth, just a smooth plane where a face should be, but when it moved, you felt it thinking, pressing on your mind like a weight.

And its fingers—long, jointed things that bent backward when they touched the controls, moving like they were playing an instrument no human could hear. It didn't speak English. It sang in low frequencies, like a hymn from a dead world. Yeager understood it, said it was like flying with a tuning fork from another star."

Tara's foot stopped tapping, her jealousy forgotten as she leaned forward, her voice slurred but sharp with fascination.

"You're saying you flew in a flying saucer with an alien copilot? For real?"

Randle nodded, his eyes haunted, like he was seeing it all again. "We went to the moon, Tara. Not some Apollo mission bullshit—straight up, around it, and back in hours. The stars... they weren't just lights. They sang, a music that pulls at your soul, makes you feel like you're part of something vast and terrible. I've never felt so small."

Anna's hand brushed mine under the table, her fingers ice-cold, trembling. She was staring at Randle, her face pale, the whiskey finally hitting her, or maybe it was the weight of his words.

"Ethereal music," she said in a whisper, her eyes flicking to me, wide and searching, as if she'd heard that song in her dreams.

"Exactly," Randle said, his voice softening, like he was confessing a sin. "Then other countries got involved. They passed me around like a cursed coin. Cosmonaut Yuri Gagarin and I went into a dimensional rift outside Novosibirsk, a place where the air shimmered like heat off asphalt."

"Impossible," Jake cut in, folding his arms, his grin gone. "Gagarin died in '68. Plane crash. Everyone knows that."

Randle's lips twitched, a ghost of a smile. "Not his brain. He was too valuable to lose. The Russians transferred it to another body—some tech I still don't understand. His eyes were the same, though. Haunted, like he'd seen way too much."

Jake snickered, shaking his head, his skepticism a shield against the madness of it all. "You're spinning a hell of a yarn, Randle."

Randle didn't flinch, his gaze steady. "Yuri and I walked through a mirror, a rift where everything shimmered—colors that don't exist here, buildings made of light, air that tasted like copper and regret.

"He told me later his boys tried to wipe my mind with neural tech, but it didn't take. I came back with fragments, like dreams you can't shake, pieces of a puzzle I'll never solve."

Jake stared at Randle in disbelief. "You kept in contact with Yuri Gagarin?"

"Still do. He's still alive and kicking."

Dusty's voice was soft, almost reverent, but trembling. "What you describe sounds... emotionally shattering. Like you left part of yourself behind."

Randle's eyes softened as he looked at her, but his voice was raw. "More than you can imagine, darling. I came back changed. Broken. Too many secrets, too many worlds. I had a nervous breakdown, and I couldn't tell what was real anymore. The stars, the music, that thing in the saucer—it all bled together."

The room fell silent, the weight of his words pressing down like a storm cloud rolling in from the mesa. Jake's grin was gone, his glass frozen halfway to his lips. Tara's eyes were wide, her anger with me forgotten, her whiskey glass trembling in her hand. Outside, the wind howled, and the window rattled again, harder this time, like something was trying to get in.

Jake cleared his throat, prompting. "Go on, Randle. What happened next?"

"Black Ops decommissioned me," Randle said, draining his glass, his hands shaking now, the clink of the glass against the table like a tolling bell. "Not fired. Not retired. Erased.

"They tried to scrub me from existence, but I'd hidden a compilation of their darkest secrets—files, recordings, proof of things no government wants out. I don't even know where it is now. Someone I trust buried it deep. If I turn up dead, that cache goes public. It has kept me alive all these years, kept the hounds at bay."

"How'd you pull yourself back together?" I asked, my voice thick, the whiskey and the madness swirling in my head.

Randle's eyes flicked to the window, where the desert night seemed to pulse with an unnatural glow.

"Magic. Indian magic."

He didn't elaborate.

The silence that followed was heavy, suffocating, broken only by the distant howl of a coyote, sharp and mournful, like it knew what Randle had seen. I leaned back, my head swimming, the room tilting slightly as the whiskey and his words tangled together.

"You're telling us you flew to the moon with Brigadier General Chuck Yeager at the helm with an alien as his copilot, walked through another dimension with Yuri Gagarin's brain transplanted in a bionic body, and now you're a ghost hiding from every government on Earth?"

Randle met my gaze, his eyes hollow, like twin wells to nowhere. "Wild and crazy doesn't mean it isn't true."

Jake broke the spell, his voice sharp. "That's a wrap."

His crew moved like clockwork, dismantling equipment with practiced ease, their footsteps loud in the sudden quiet as they headed for the staging area by the semi. Rod Bloustine hurried over, shaking Randle's hand, his grin wide but uneasy.

"You did great, partner," Rod said, clapping Randle on the back. "No one's going to believe a word of it, but the Cryptid Hunter audience will eat it up."

"Hell, Rod, I don't believe it myself," Jake said, his laugh forced, his eyes still on Randle, searching for a crack in the story.

Jake tapped his scotch glass with a spoon, the sharp clink pulling everyone's attention. "Wonderful job, folks. As a reward, Cryptid Hunter Productions is throwing a bash, an old ranch-style barbecue, and you're all invited."

Dusty's face lit up, her flush deepening. "How fun! When?"

"Tonight," Jake said, his grin returning, sly and knowing. "My chef and his team have been working since dawn. Expect a feast—brisket, ribs, the works—along with a dance floor, plenty of booze, and a Texas swing band straight from Amarillo. Sleep off your buzzes and come back ready to raise hell. Starts at dark."

When Jake rested his hand on my shoulder, I said, "Kind of early in the shoot for a party, isn't it?"

"There's method in my madness," he replied, his eyes glinting. "What better place to film than a haunted ranch under a New Mexico sky? Maybe we'll catch some orbs, or something totally unexpected, floating out there in the dark."

"Are Rita and Lily invited?" Randle asked, his voice softer now, almost wistful.

"You bet," Jake said. "This party's for you, Randle. Bring 'em along."

"It's been years since Rita and Lily didn't have to cook," Randle said, a faint smile breaking through. "Even longer since we danced under the stars. We'll be back at dark with bells on."

Randle and Tara started for the door, Tara throwing a final glare at me over her shoulder, her eyes promising a reckoning. Anna's hand tightened on my arm, her touch grounding me as the room spun faintly.

Jake's grin widened when I said, "Sounds like a hell of a production."

"Colley is flying in today. He's bringing Angie and stopping at Taos Pueblo to pick up Elena Tafoya and some of her kin. Can't have a party without a crowd."

"Angie?" I said.

"This story is developing rapidly, and Angie has a better handle on things than anyone else. I thought it might be a good idea to have her here. She's bringing the tape."

"She has seen them?" I asked.

"So far, the only one who has seen them. She's briefing me tomorrow."

"Did she give you any hints about what's on the tape?"

"She hasn't watched it yet," he said.

"Because," I said.

Jake grinned. "Because I want to be first to see it."

Anna touched my shoulder, reminding me she was still near and listening to Jake's every word.

"Let's hope it leads us to Kirsten's killer," she said.

"Me too," Jake said. "So sorry for your loss."

"Her loss is everyone's loss," she said, forcing a smile. "Your party sounds like just what we all need," she said. "I need a nap to shake this whiskey off."

She kissed my cheek, her lips soft but her touch electric, then headed for the bedroom, her steps unsteady. The air seemed to shift in her wake, cooler, heavier, like the ranch was holding its breath.

"She's a good one. New romance?" Jake asked, his eyebrow raised.

"More like trouble," I said, rubbing my temple.

I nodded when he said, "Randle's daughter?"

As the room emptied, the wind outside howled louder, carrying that strange hum again, faint but persistent, like a signal from somewhere far beyond the mesa. I glanced at the window, half-expecting to see glowing green eyes staring back from the dark.

The desert was watching, and I couldn't shake the feeling that Randle's secrets had stirred something out there, something that wasn't ready to let go.

CHAPTER 21

The high desert night wrapped Shadow Ranch in a velvet shroud, the darkness so deep it felt like the sky was pressing in on me, the stars sharp as pinpricks in a canvas stretched taut.

Miles from Taos, the world was free of the city's hum—no light pollution to dull the Milky Way's glow, no noise to drown out the eerie howl of the wind curling through the sagebrush.

Tiki torches flickered at the edges of the wooden dance floor, their flames licking the air with a soft hiss, casting pools of amber that danced across the mesa. Understated lanterns hung from poles, their glow barely touching the shadows that clung to the ranch's adobe walls, as if the desert itself was watching, wary of intrusion.

Members of a Texas swing band, the "High Country Drifters," were dressed in colorful cowboy shirts, bolo ties, and scuffed leather boots, their catchy music filling the night with twangy riffs and a rhythm that beat like a heart.

Bess, the lead singer, radiated in calico and a fringed buckskin skirt, topped with a perfectly tilted Stetson, had a voice as smooth as twenty-year-old whiskey but with enough edge to cut through the chatter.

The bandstand's lighting was sparse, just enough to catch the glint of Bess's silver belt buckle as she swayed, with the natural acoustics of the desert amplifying every pluck of the steel guitar and every thump of the upright bass. The music wove into the night, blending with the distant yip of a coyote, as if the desert was singing along.

Guests sprawled around wooden tables brought in for the

night, their laughter and clinking glasses blending with the smell of smoked brisket and chili from the serving line. Open bars flanked the dance floor, bottles of tequila and bourbon shining under the torchlight as bartenders poured drinks with flair for Jake's crew, Randle and Rita, some of the Two Moon guests, and a few locals who had wandered in from nearby ranches.

Some of the partiers were already two-stepping on the dance floor, boots scuffing the wood, their shadows stretching long and thin, like specters caught in the flicker of the flames. I leaned against a table, a cold beer sweating in my hand, my best denim shirt tucked in, boots polished to a shine.

I'd been dodging Tara and Anna all evening, weaving through the crowd like a man sidestepping quicksand. So far, I'd managed to keep the two apart. Things were about to change.

The band kicked into a lively rendition of "Take Me Back to Tulsa," Bess's voice soaring, and I caught sight of Randle and Rita swaying on the dance floor, his arm around her waist, her smile soft in the torchlight.

The band shifted to "San Antonio Rose," as the roar of a helicopter, a beast of light and dust descending nearby, cut through the music. Its landing lights flashed red and white, stirring the sagebrush into a frenzy, and the crowd's chatter dulled to a hum, all eyes on the spectacle.

The chopper's blades slowed, the dust settling like a curtain parting. Out came Angie, her café au lait skin glowing under the torches, her satin shorts and sleeveless white T-shirt hugging her curves like a second skin. Her white Stetson tilted rakishly, and her cowboy boots clicked as she stepped onto the mesa, every inch the Harvard MBA who could outsmart anyone and never lost her edge.

Colley followed, his shoulders squared, his army-honed instincts still sharp from his days dodging RPGs in Afghanistan. He scanned the crowd, his eyes locking on mine for a brief nod, a silent acknowledgment of old battles we'd fought together.

My heart kicked up, a warning drumbeat. They didn't know about Tara or Anna—yet—but Angie's gaze lingered, her lips curving in a way that said she suspected I was never far from a mess.

Elena Tafoya emerged next, her traditional Pueblo garb a tapestry of earth tones and intricate beadwork, her presence calm but commanding, like the desert itself. Her brother, sister, and mother followed, all dressed in vibrant party clothes, their laughter carrying a warmth that cut through the night's chill.

My eyes flicked to Angie, who was weaving through the crowd toward me, her boots kicking up dust.

"Buck," Angie said, her voice smooth. "You didn't think you could hide from me out here, did you?"

She laughed when I said, "Hide? Me?"

Her smile was all mischief, scanning the crowd, missing nothing.

"Looks like a hell of a party," she said, her contrived drawl thick as she tipped her Stetson.

"Jake said he wanted to be the first to view Maldonado's tape," I said. "You didn't take a peek, did you?"

"I'm as curious as you are, but I would never cross Jake," she said.

"My curiosity is definitely piqued," I said.

"Viewing the tape is definitely on the agenda. Jake has a plan. Right now, that swing band and the dance floor are calling. Let's do some two-stepping."

Before I could reply, Tara's voice interrupted from behind.

"Mind if I join you?"

I spun around, utterly surprised by Tara's words as she awaited an answer. The band kept playing, the stars above burning brighter, and the faint hum from the desert grew louder. Angie broke the spell.

"You must be Tara," she said. "Buck told me how beautiful you are."

Tara quickly succumbed to Angie's charm. She was probably blushing, though it was hard to tell in the dim light. She glanced at me with a smile.

"He didn't say that, did he?"

"He most certainly did," Angie said. "Let's hit the dancefloor."

Before I could process the situation, Tara and Angie grabbed my hand, pulling me toward the sound of the Texas swing band, the floor alive, boots stomping in unison, the crowd swelling. Colley moved with surprising grace, his arm around a laughing local girl. The music pulsed, the desert's hum weaving through it, and for a moment, I was caught in the rhythm.

We danced until the song ended, breathless, the crowd whooping, and then found a table. Anna joined us, and the conversation turned to her art—her bold, haunting canvases of desert spirits and starlit mesas.

"Your work's unreal," Angie said, her eyes bright. "That piece with the coyote under the blood moon? Gave me chills."

Anna flushed, smiling. "Thanks. It's... personal. The desert's always talking, if you listen."

Then Tara spoke, surprising both Angie and me. "She's right. Your art is both visceral and beautiful, exactly like the high desert."

"Thank you," Anna said.

At first, I thought Tara's jealousy had abated. It had shifted to Angie.

"You and Buck are so comfortable with each other," she said.

Angie leaned forward, winking at me. "Buck and I met a few days ago. We realized we had a lot in common and went line dancing. You like him, don't you?"

Tara smiled. "He can ride a bucking bronc, two-step with the best of them."

"And a nice ass filling out his Levis," Anna said.

"Trouble is, he's like mountain smoke—good luck catching him," Tara said.

Angie grinned and said, "Are we making you uncomfortable?"

"Like a slab of meat hanging from a hook in a butcher's shop," I said. "There'll be lots of cowboys at the rodeo on Saturday. Sorry, I'm the only one here tonight."

Angie laughed, nudging Tara. "You'll do until then."

Anna and Tara were also laughing. Tara grabbed my hand, pulling me toward the dance floor and the Western music of the swing band. Angie and Anna followed.

"Long as he can keep up," Tara said.

We danced the night away, and I wasn't the first one to cry, uncle. Tipsy and swaying, I excused myself to hit the facilities, the desert air cool against my flushed skin. The torches were burning low, the band now playing a soft "Waltz Across Texas." Most of the crowd had thinned, and though the party was near an end, my night had just begun.

In the shadows beyond the dance floor, I spotted Lily, Tara's Navajo grandmother, sitting alone on a wooden bench, her silver hair glowing faintly under the stars. Her eyes, clouded with what Tara called moth madness, seemed to see beyond the mesa, beyond time itself.

A witch, they said. I felt drawn to her, my half-Cherokee blood stirring, memories of Indian schools and a childhood without roots flooding back. I sat beside her, the bench creaking.

"Evening, Lily," I said. "Mind some company?"

She turned, her gaze piercing despite the haze in her eyes, and squeezed my hand, her grip strong, warm.

"Buck, you carry a heavy past," she said, her voice like wind over stone. "The shadows you run from—they don't own you."

I swallowed hard and said, "I've learned to hide them."

She smiled, faint and wise. "The desert tells me you're one of us. You listen to the stars."

Before I could answer, Tara appeared from the darkness, her boots silent on the sandy earth. Her smile was soft, her eyes warm in the starlight.

"You trying to steal Buck from me, too, Grandmother?" she teased.

"Just borrowing him," Lily said, her voice a low hum, matching the desert's faint pulse.

"I heard you say that Buck listens to the stars. What do you mean?"

"He has a special talent?"

"Like what?" Tara asked.

"In Diné culture, there are those with special abilities to understand and react to the human condition and spiritual energies. Buck is dééshgizh."

"What the hell is that, Grandmother?"

Lily chuckled. "A person able to look at stars and use spiritual vision to identify the source of a problem. The condition is rare."

Tara glanced at me and said, "I knew you were special."

"More than special, baby," Lily said.

"A 'sensitive'," Tara said. "But Buck isn't Navajo."

"To me, he is," Lily said.

Tara looked at me and said, "You are full of surprises. Did you know that you are dééshgizh?"

"No clue," I said.

Tara leaned back, her gaze on the sky. "I liked them—Anna, Angie. They're good people. We're staying in touch. Anna took Elena and her kin back to the Taos Pueblo in her ATV, Fritz riding shotgun. She's staying there, safe till those bastards who ransacked her house are caught."

I nodded, relieved. "What about Angie?"

"You're alone again," Tara said, laughing. "Colley flew Jake and Angie to some fancy Santa Fe hotel."

Lily's eyes glinted, prophetic, as she squeezed my hand again.

"You like Buck, I see it, but he's a tumbleweed, baby. Enjoy him, treasure him for now, because he won't stay forever."

"I know, Grandmother," Tara said.

A shooting star streaked across the sky, its light flaring bright, then gone, the desert's hum swelling for a moment, like a sigh.

I squeezed Lily's hand and said, "You're here for a reason, aren't you?"

Lily's gaze turned distant, her voice dropping to a whisper.

"To confess," she said.

"Confess what, Grandmother?" Tara said.

"That it was my magic that saved your father from the brink," she said.

The night had gone quiet with only the sound of a night bird and the howls of a distant coyote.

"Tell us, Grandmother," Tara said.

"Your father was broken, lost in those alien worlds he spoke of. Never told Rita, his own wife, the truth about his past. It was a night like this, stars burning, when he spilled his story to me. I performed a Navajo ceremony, sang the old songs, and burned sage to pull the madness from his soul. And it was I who told him to hide his trove of secrets."

My breath caught, the air suddenly heavier. Tara leaned forward, her eyes wide.

"Where are they, Grandmother?"

Lily's smile was a secret in itself. "Chaco Canyon, deep in the reserve. Hidden in an ancient cliff dwelling."

"How will we find it?" I asked.

"You'll know it by a petroglyph."

When she paused, Tara said, "There are many petroglyphs. How will we know which one?"

Tara and I watched as she drew a glyph in the sand with a stick.

"This glyph is one that no white man has seen—a carving of the first meeting between our ancients and the Sky People, their eyes like green fire, their ships like stars fallen to earth. The trove's there, hidden in stone."

"Why are you telling us?" Tara asked.

"I'm old, and my time's short. You two are the only humans alive I trust to carry this burden."

The desert seemed to still, the hum fading, the stars above pulsing brighter, as if the Sky People themselves were listening.

Tara's hand found mine, her grip tight, and I felt the weight of Lily's words settle into me, a new burden, a new purpose, tying the Indians and the aliens in a knot I couldn't yet unravel.

Randle appeared through the darkness as Lily's words died away.

"Time to go," he said.

Lily touched Tara's hand, nodded at me, and walked toward

Randle's voice.

"You coming, Tara?" Randle called.

"I have my truck and don't need a ride," she said.

"You be careful, you hear?" he said.

Too busy unbuttoning my shirt, Tara didn't answer.

CHAPTER 22

I stumbled back alone to the ranch house, the last notes of the High Country Drifters fading into the desert night. The bartenders had packed up, and the crowd had scattered—Anna to Taos with Elena Tafoya, Angie to Santa Fe with Jake, and Colley.

Tara was also gone, though the scent of her perfume and the memory of her touch lingered like the wispy fingers of smoke from a quickly dying flame. I was alone, with the desert sky faintly glowing and the Taos Hum a steady beat in my ears. No chaos, no drama, though it wasn't the quiet I'd hoped for.

Inside, the house was dark, and Pard curled up in front of the kiva like a shadow. My cell phone rang. It was Angie.

"With all the women circling you tonight, I was worried about you," she said.

"It's possible to have too much of a good thing," I said.

"That's a fact," she said.

"After our night in Tulsa, I wasn't sure how you were going to react. Thanks for helping me diffuse the situation. It's late," I said, glancing at the clock. "Why're you still up?"

"Jake and I are viewing Maldonado's tape tomorrow morning. He wants you to be there," she said.

"No problem," I said.

"I'll text you the time and location. And Buck, there's something else I wanted to talk to you about."

"I'm listening," I said.

"Bradley and I are back together."

"Oh? As I recall, you said you were done with the big lout. Wait a minute. You didn't use me to make him jealous, did you?"

"Something like that," she said.

"Jeez, Angie!"

"It'll be okay. He's in New Orleans, and you're not."

"He's an ex-linebacker for the Saints and big enough to be a professional wrestler," I said. "Did you tell him about Stormy?"

"Not exactly," she said. "Bradley's so straitlaced, I don't think he could handle knowing I participated in a threesome with a handsome cowboy and sexy cocktail waitress. You won't tell him, will you?"

"My lips are sealed," I said. "Just don't ask me to go two-stepping with you two."

Angie laughed. "Bradley is too clumsy to dance," she said.

"Uh huh!" I said.

"He has other redeeming qualities. See you tomorrow. And Buck, you didn't tell Jake or Colley, did you?"

"Don't know about Stormy, but your secret's safe with me," I said.

"Thank you," she said before hanging up.

I headed to my bedroom, the first time I'd slept there in a while. The sheets were rumpled, carrying Anna's scent—jasmine and something softer, like sun-warmed cotton. It hit me like a wave, pulling me under as I lay down.

I was drifting, caught in that hazy twilight between sleep and waking, Anna's perfume still lingering in my mind like a half-remembered song. The scent was sweet, grounding, but then a voice sliced through the fog—soft, melodic, achingly familiar, yet alien enough to jolt my heart. "Buck McDivit," it called. My eyes snapped open, but the room felt wrong, like reality had slipped a gear.

Moonlight poured through the window, bathing my bedroom in a silvery glow that shimmered like liquid metal. The air was too still, too heavy, as if the world had forgotten how to breathe.

Out here in the high desert, the wind was a constant companion, rattling the windows and whispering secrets through the sagebrush. But now? Nothing. The wind hadn't just died—it was gone, like someone had snatched it from existence. My skin prickled, and I sat up, heart pounding. Was I dreaming? Or was something bigger at play?

Then I saw her.

Aeterna stood at the foot of my bed, her form shimmering like heat waves over asphalt. Her eyes glowed faintly, not with light but with something more profound, as if the universe itself were staring back at me.

"I need you," she said, her voice vibrating in my bones.

"For what?" I said, my throat dry as the desert outside.

"No time for questions. Will you help?"

I didn't know what the hell she was talking about, but those eyes—God, those eyes—held me captive. I swung my legs out of bed, still in my undershirt and boxer shorts, too caught up in the moment to bother with pants or boots. My bare feet hit the cold floor, and I followed her through the house, my pulse hammering like a war drum.

The night was alive with an eerie glow. A beam of blinding white light stabbed down from the sky, painting the front of the ranch house in stark relief. I craned my neck, and my jaw dropped. A saucer-shaped craft hovered above, silent as a ghost, its edges pulsing with a faint hum. Aeterna stepped into the beam, and in a blink, she was gone, sucked upward into the craft like a leaf in a storm.

Her voice echoed in my head. "Step into the beam."

My body felt numb, like I'd been slipped a cosmic sedative. Maybe I was still dreaming, or perhaps I'd finally lost my mind. Either way, I didn't argue. I stepped into the light, and the world dissolved around me. The beam didn't just lift me—it yanked me, my stomach lurching as the ground fell away.

I was floating, weightless, the desert sprawling beneath me like a patchwork quilt under the moon's silver gaze. Stars burned brighter than I'd ever seen, each one a pinprick of fire in a velvet sky. I could've sworn they were whispering my name.

The beam carried me over the high desert, past jagged ridges and endless dunes, until we reached a familiar outcrop of dark basalt. I recognized it instantly—the same place Elena and Anna had described, where they'd seen the saucer, the lights, the aliens.

A petroglyph carved into the rock glowed faintly, its ancient lines pulsing like a heartbeat. My gut twisted as the beam lowered me toward a jagged fissure in the earth below. It wasn't just a crack—it was a wound, a tear in reality itself, glowing with an unnatural red light. I braced myself, expecting to crash, but the beam guided me straight into the fissure's maw.

The world warped. Colors bled into shapes that didn't make sense, and my mind screamed as I passed through the crack. It wasn't just a portal—it was a rupture, a doorway to somewhere that shouldn't exist. When I emerged on the other side, my breath caught in my throat, and my brain short-circuited.

The desert was gone. In its place, rivers of amber light snaked across a violet sky, streaked with colors I couldn't name—colors that moved, alive and restless, like oil dancing on water. Fractals twisted into symbols that teased at meaning, only to slip away when I tried to focus. For a split second, I saw my own face reflected in a polished surface just out of reach, screaming infinitely, each reflection more distorted than the last. My stomach lurched, and I stumbled, my bare feet scraping against a ground that felt like polished glass.

I wasn't alone. Hundreds of figures surrounded the fissure, their eyes locked on me. They weren't human—not quite. Their forms flickered, broken into fractal patterns, like Picasso paintings come to life. They were different. When I glanced at my hand, I realized that so was I.

One of them stepped forward, his body shimmering with edges that didn't align. He raised a hand in what looked like a salute, though it could've been a threat.

"I'm Watly," he said, his voice stretching and warping, like sound pulled through a taffy machine. "Come with me."

"I'm Buck," I said, my voice shaking. "What the hell's going on?"

"We've been waiting for you," he said, and the weight of

those words hit me like a punch.

The crowd of fractal soldiers parted, their gazes heavy with expectation, as Watly led me to a hovering vehicle. It had no wheels, no controls—just a silver platform that floated inches above the ground. I climbed aboard, my heart racing, and we shot forward at a speed that stole my breath. The wind roared in my ears, but the vehicle was silent, like it was being steered by Watly's thoughts alone. I shouted over the wind.

"Where are we going?"

"To Chronos and the Palace of the Shifting Spire," he said.

"Chronos? Where's that?"

"Not far. It's the capital of Horatia. I'm Horatian."

The vehicle had no roof, and I felt like I was riding a magic carpet straight out of a fever dream. The sky above was electric, the colors so vivid I could taste them—sharp and tangy, like biting into a live wire.

Puffy clouds hung low, their edges shimmering with an ozone-heavy mist. I reached out, half-expecting to grab one, but they dissolved into sparks at my touch. My senses were razor-sharp, every detail burning into my brain. If this was a dream, it was the most real thing I'd ever felt.

Then I saw it. Chronos rose from the horizon like a mirage made real, a walled city that glowed gold against the violet sky. It floated, suspended among the clouds, its spires twisting and shifting like liquid metal.

Hovercrafts darted around it, their lights weaving patterns that made my head spin. As we slowed, I peered over the edge and saw a sprawling metropolis below, its streets pulsing with life. At the city's heart stood a walled complex, grander than anything I'd ever seen, its towers piercing the clouds like spears.

"That's the palace," Watly said, his voice cutting through my awe. "You go alone from here."

I stepped off the hovercraft, my bare feet tingling against the warm ground. A royal guard, clad in armor that shimmered like oil slicks, met me and led me through a crowd of thousands. Horatians lined the path, their fractal faces glowing with excitement, their cheers a deafening roar that vibrated in my chest. I raised a hand, half in greeting, half in shock, and the crowd erupted louder. What the hell were they cheering for? Me?

The guard ushered me into a grand hall, its walls lined with jewels that pulsed with inner light. The floor creaked under my feet, releasing scents of wet cedar, burnt sugar, and rain-soaked earth. The air was thick, syrupy, making every breath a struggle.

At the far end, on a throne of diamonds, emeralds, and solid gold, sat a figure who radiated power. Her cloak shimmered with colors I couldn't name, and her presence hit me like a shockwave, heavy and electric, like standing too close to a lightning strike.

"I am Chrona," she said, her voice humming behind my eyes, tasting of starlight and saltwater. "Queen of Hyperia, and this is my court."

The crowd—hundreds of regally dressed Horatians—watched in silence, their eyes boring into me. Chrona's gaze was a weight I couldn't shake.

"Why am I here?" I asked, my voice sounding distant, like it belonged to someone else.

"You are not lost," she said. "You are here because we need your help."

"To do what?" I said, my heart pounding so hard I thought it might burst.

"Save us, and yourself," she said.

I blinked, my mind racing. "You'd better explain."

"We are from different dimensions," she said. "You from the third, I from the fourth. Time is a temporal dimension, but length, width, and height are spatial in your world. In mine, there's a fourth. We call it depth, although not in the way you understand it."

"I'm not the same, either," I said.

"Normality is a matter of perception," she said. "Right now, our problem crosses dimensions and is also your problem."

"Please explain," I said.

"A fracture has formed between our worlds, leaking plasma.

If it isn't stopped, both our universes will collapse in a chaotic chain reaction. The end is unthinkable."

I swallowed hard. "I came through that fracture. How?"

"It's a spatial singularity—a portal between dimensions. That's the problem. It needs to be sealed."

"What can I do?" I asked, my voice cracking.

"Heal the fracture before it's too late," she said.

I laughed, a desperate sound. "I'm not a physicist. I don't even know where to start."

"Aeterna believes you can do it," she said. "Perhaps the only one who can."

"You know Aeterna?" I asked, my mind reeling.

"One of the Sky People," she said. "They sent you here."

"Then why don't they fix it? Their tech's light-years ahead of ours."

"Someone from your world caused this," she said. "A Chaotic Resonator tore the boundaries between our dimensions. If your people have the technology to break it, you have the means to fix it."

I shook my head, overwhelmed. "I don't even know what a Chaotic Resonator is."

"But you know someone who does," she said. "Vector. He'll know how to awaken what sleeps beneath the lattice of time. Will you help us?"

The crowd held its breath, the weight of their hope crushing me. I raised my hand in the Horatian salute, my voice steady despite the fear clawing at my chest.

"I'll do my best."

"You must do better," Chrona said, her voice like a blade. "Your life, and every life in both our worlds, depends on it."

I nodded and said, "I can do it."

The hall erupted in cheers, the sound shaking the walls as the guards led me out. The crowd outside roared, thousands of Horatians lining the path back to the hovercraft, their fractal faces alight with hope. Watly was waiting, his expression unreadable but warm.

"Thank you," he said.

He piloted us back to the fissure, now glowing a violent red, the soldiers around it tense and murmuring. I saluted Watly, and he returned the gesture, his face breaking into what I hoped was a smile. I stepped into the singularity, and the world went dark.

CHAPTER 23

I woke up in a sweat, alone in my bed, with Chrona's diamond throne and the red-glowing fracture fading as I opened my eyes. I knew it was a dream, but my heart kept racing as I felt the pull of that beam again, the way it yanked me off my feet. I don't know how long I lay there—maybe minutes, maybe an hour—before the air shifted.

It was more of a feeling than a sound as the room grew heavier, as if someone had turned up the gravity dial a notch or two. The faint piñon smoke from the dying embers thickened, turned sweet, almost like burnt sugar, and my skin began to prickle from scalp to soles.

Aeterna was standing at the foot of the bed, moonlight pouring over her golden body like liquid silver. It didn't touch her the way it should have. Her hair was that same sun-bleached gold, the silver bodysuit hugging her like a second skin. And those eyes—too large, glowing vivid blue—locked onto mine and didn't blink.

"Aeterna, you're not real, are you?" I said.

Her voice wasn't exactly human, more melodic and similar to the sweet tones of Kermit Sanderson's cosmic guitar. The room was dark, only the light of the moon and stars shining through the window and the glow of her eyes.

"Very real," she said.

"Show me," I said.

She smiled and said, "Have you ever seen a naked alien?"

I sat up in bed and said, "No, but I'd like to."

She smiled, slow and knowing, as her fingers found the edge of the silver bodysuit. With a fluid motion that seemed to defy gravity, she peeled the material away from her golden skin.

The moonlight traced every curve—full, heavy breasts that rose and fell with her breathing, the generous swell of her hips, and the smooth lines of her thighs. Her body was lush in a way that felt almost otherworldly, soft and strong at once, like warm velvet stretched over living starlight.

Aeterna pulled the covers back and slid into bed beside me, the heat of her skin radiating against mine before she even touched me. When her hand finally settled on my chest, her fingers were impossibly warm and tactile—each one stroking with feather-light pressure that sent ripples of sensation straight through me.

She traced slow patterns across my nipples, her touch both gentle and commanding, as if she were mapping every inch of me with quiet fascination. Her voluptuous form pressed close, the soft weight of her breasts brushing my arm, her thigh draping lightly over mine.

Every contact point hummed with electricity—her palm gliding lower, teasing the edge of my abdomen, while her breath, sweet and warm like the piñon smoke, ghosted across my neck.

I reached for her, my hand finding the silky curve of her waist, then sliding up to cup the generous fullness of her breast. Her skin was impossibly smooth, yielding softly under my fingers, and a melodic hum escaped her throat as I explored. She arched slightly into my touch, her glowing blue eyes half-lidded, never breaking contact with mine.

The air between us thickened with unspoken promise, every slow caress building a delicious tension that made my pulse thunder in my ears. She was real—achingly, intoxicatingly real—and for tonight, she was entirely mine to discover.

An hour passed—maybe two. I didn't know; I didn't care. Making love to an alien was perhaps the strangest, most erotic thing I'd ever done. It didn't matter. When she finally spoke, she had my full attention.

"Do you believe me now?" she asked.

"I've heard stories of alien abductions," I said. "I never imagined anything like this. You aren't…"

"Reptilian?"

It was my turn to laugh. "Anything but," I said. "You're so warm and soft, I never want to stop touching you."

"Our bodies are similar to human bodies," she said.

"I'm curious. Where are your people from if not from Earth?" I asked.

"Ophir," she said. "Our planet was dying, so some of us migrated here. The Anazasis were colonized by former inhabitants of Ophir."

"The Anazasis were primitive. You have flying saucers."

"Many Ophirians assimilated," she said.

"Because?"

"No other option. Too many people and insufficient resources. Ophirian refugees survived by blending in with the native inhabitants. All the Indians in this area have Ophirian ancestors."

She smiled when I said, "Not all of your ancestors assimilated. Did some of your people return to Ophir?"

"Ophir did not survive. We colonized a planet in another galaxy, but we continue to monitor our descendants here on Earth. We maintain a base on the dark side of the moon and in the depths of the oceans."

"You know about Area 51?" I asked.

"Yes," she said.

"Does my government know about the Ophirians?"

"Of course. How could they not?"

"The alien spacecraft pilot Randle Roberts described sounded far less human than you," I said.

"The Ophirians aren't the only aliens to have visited Earth. There are as many stories as there are lips to tell them. Area 51 is a testament to just a few of those stories."

She shook her head when I said, "Why do they keep it so secret?"

"Everyone has secrets. You included."

"What secrets am I keeping?"

"You're the lead scout for a TV show investigating alien activity, yet you've told no one about me," she said.

"Because I didn't believe you were real until now."

"Jake Huntington, the Cryptid Hunter, would have believed you. You didn't tell him,"

I opened my mouth to defend myself, but the words didn't come out.

"Do you believe me now?" she said.

"If you're a dream, I never want to wake up."

She kissed me, touching my forehead with her tactile fingers.

"Vector's stories disturbed you, didn't they?"

"Yes."

"Because of who you are," she said.

"Who am I?" I asked.

A 'sensitive,' a person with great strength, compassion, and resolve for the truth."

"That's what Lily said. She called it dééshgizh."

"Lily is wise. You are dééshgizh. It's why you were chosen."

"Chosen?" I asked.

"To save Earth from a disaster like the one that befell Ophir."

"I may well be a stargazer, but I'm the last person on this planet who can pull off such a feat."

"No," she said. "At this moment, you are the only person who can. You have the knowledge and the power. Will you help?"

"I'd go to hell and back for you, but those magic fingers of yours touching me right now make me think of things other than disaster."

"Then it's time for me to leave," she said, her kiss warm on my neck before getting out of bed.

Not bothering to dress, she stood naked at the foot of the bed, backdropped by desert starlight drifting in through the open window. I couldn't avert my gaze.

"Where do I start?" I asked.

The cosmic tones of Kermit Sanderson's mysterious guitar began resonating through the room.

"The former Sandia engineer who builds guitars," she said.

"What will I tell him?"

A soft crimson orb materialized between us, no bigger than an apple, pulsing with slow inner light.

"Tell him nothing," she said. "Give him this. He'll know what it means and what to do."

The pulsating orb inexplicably triggered the same dread I felt as a boy when the nuns read the Book of Revelation to us. Aeterna could see the look in my eyes,

"It frightens you, doesn't it?" she asked.

"Yes," I said, "and I don't know why.

"You're a 'sensitive,' and your senses are heightened."

"Damn, girl! How could they not be?"

She smiled and said, "You are the first human I have ever coupled with. I was worried that you wouldn't respond."

She smiled again when I said, "That's an item you can cross off your worry list."

"You heard Vector's stories. Did you believe them?"

"I do now, though I didn't then," I said.

"Why not?"

"Nothing he described sounded real. If it were, why would he reveal his secrets now to a massive TV audience when he's kept them hidden for so many years? Guess he thinks that no one will believe him."

"He's kept his secrets because his memory of those events was erased," she said.

"Erased? That doesn't make a lick of sense," I said.

"Someone restored his memory, extracted his knowledge of the Chaotic Resonator, and then rewiped it."

"You're blowing my mind," I said. "I think I need some more persuading."

"Sorry," she said. You've worn me out,"

"If Vector's memories are wiped, then his stories about Chuck Yeager and Yuri Gagarin are just fiction," I said.

Aeterna's head moved almost imperceptibly. "They didn't perform a total wipe. He still has memories, just not all of them. The ones he told you are true."

"Hard to believe," I said.

"I need you to believe them," she said.

"How do you even wipe a brain, or restore erased memories?" I asked.

"The brain is an organic hard drive. Someone has the technology to restore lost data, just like on a computer."

"Who?" I asked.

"The Germans, maybe."

"Surely you don't mean Hans and Greta?" I said with a snicker.

"Yes. Or maybe the people who tried to kidnap Ran and Dusty," Aeterna said.

"Angie did a background check on Hans and Greta. They work for a German industrial firm."

"A front. They are BND agents. At least they were."

"BND?"

The German equivalent of the CIA. The Resonator is vastly more powerful than the strongest nuclear weapon. The German government doesn't possess it. A political faction turned Hans and Greta. They know about the Resonator and have been attempting to acquire it.

"A German political faction?" I said.

"The Iron Order, a neo-Nazi group."

"How do you know so much about this splinter faction?" I asked.

"Governments can't survive without intelligence. We Ophirians have our own intelligence agency, and I am a part of it."

"You're a spy?"

"An intelligence agent," she said.

She laughed when I said, "So, I'm an insect lured in by your honey trap?"

"You liked it, didn't you?"

"Of course I did. That's not the point. You're trying to use me to gain some political advantage."

"We have the same political objective," she said. "Not so the Iron Order or the North Koreans."

“I’m not into conspiracy theories,” I said.

“The Iron Order is no conspiracy. They are real, and they have the plans for the Chaotic Resonator.”

“Plans, Hell!” I said. “If Chronos is real, someone already has a working doomsday machine.”

“Yes,” she said.

“And they’re using it to rip apart the dimensional worlds and are testing it, right here in the desert,” I said.

“Yes. Plasma is bleeding both ways as we speak. Your world —our world—feels it already. The Taos Hum grows louder, the lights dance more often, and gravity stutters in small places. Soon, the bleed will become a flood. When that happens, nothing survives.”

“Ophirian technology is so much more advanced than ours. Why don’t you heal the rift?”

“If we could, we would. The technology to heal the rift exists. We don’t have it or know who does,” she said.

“And you think I can find out?” I said.

“Give the Sandia engineer the orb and see where it goes. Angie and the Cryptid Hunter will help you.

“You know Angie?” I asked.

I know she’s an incredibly intelligent and motivated person, though not a ‘sensitive’ like you.

She smiled when I pulled the covers off of me, held them open, and said, “I’m hep, girl, but I could use a little more honey.”

CHAPTER 24

I left Shadow Ranch just after dawn, with the lime-green Jeep Gladiator speeding down the gravel driveway. The high desert air was crisp and clear, carrying that familiar bite of juniper and cold piñon smoke.

In the rearview mirror, the old ranch faded away, its adobe walls catching the first pink rays of sunrise. The Sangre de Cristo Mountains loomed ahead like jagged guards, their peaks already dusted with early snow.

My mind kept drifting back to last night—Aeterna's warm skin against mine, the impossible glow in her too-large blue eyes, and the way her voice had slid straight into my thoughts like a song I couldn't forget. Part of me still wondered if I'd dreamed the whole damn thing.

The other part knew better. The weight of her words sat heavy in my chest: a fracture between worlds, a Chaotic Resonator ripping reality apart, and me—Buck McDivit, washed-up rodeo cowboy and part-time cryptid scout—somehow supposed to help fix it.

I shook my head and focused on the road. Jake and Angie were waiting in Santa Fe, and whatever was on Kirsten Maldonado's tape had them both salivating. I needed to keep my head straight.

The miles passed easily, the high desert gradually softening into gentler hills, chamisa and rabbitbrush giving way to clusters of cottonwoods turning gold along the arroyos. As I crested the last rise, Santa Fe unfolded below me like a painting someone had leaned against the mountains: low adobe buildings glowing warm terracotta and ochre in the morning sun, flat roofs and rounded parapets blending seamlessly into the land.

The air already carried hints of roasting green chile and fresh coffee drifting up from the streets. I navigated the narrow roads near the plaza, passing galleries and turquoise shops, tourists bundled against the chill, locals sipping from paper cups.

The historic hotel Jake selected was one of the old gems tucked just off the plaza—an elegant adobe building with thick walls and heavy wooden vigas that had witnessed centuries pass. A discreet valet station sat beneath a portico draped in wisteria. I pulled up, shut off the engine, and handed over the keys.

Stepping into the lobby felt like entering another era, wrapped in quiet luxury. Thick Navajo rugs covered the saltillo tile floors. Massive vigas crossed the high ceiling, and a large kiva fireplace crackled in the corner, filling the air with the sweet scent of piñon.

Sunlight poured through tall windows overlooking a courtyard garden where aspens shimmered gold against the bright blue sky. A massive antler chandelier hung overhead, catching the light on turquoise and silver accents scattered throughout the space. An older man behind the carved wooden reception desk looked up with a polite smile.

"Mr. McDivit?" he asked. "Mr. Huntington is expecting you in La Fonda Suite on the third floor. The private meeting room is adjacent—an impressive space with a full wall of windows overlooking the mountains. Breakfast has been arranged."

I thanked him and climbed the wide staircase, the banister smooth under my hand from generations of use. The hallway on the third floor was decorated with original art—desert landscapes, swirling petroglyph abstracts, and portraits of Pueblo elders whose eyes seemed to follow me. I reached the double doors of the meeting room, took a breath, and pushed them open.

The room welcomed me with warmth and light. High ceilings with exposed vigas, warm adobe walls decorated with woven tapestries, and a massive stone fireplace at one end. But the real jaw-dropping feature was the wall of tall windows framing a stunning view of the Sangre de Cristo Mountains, with their snow-dusted peaks sharp and radiant against the morning sky. Jake turned from the window, flashing that movie-star grin as he crossed the room in three long strides.

"Buck! Glad you made it. Come in—Angie has everything set up."

Angie glanced up from her laptop, her café-au-lait skin glowing in the sunlight, braids tied back with a colorful scarf, and gave me a knowing smile.

"Morning, cowboy. Hope you're hungry. Jake spared no expense, as usual."

An oak table was laid out with classic Santa Fe breakfast fare: huevos rancheros smothered in green chile, warm blue-corn muffins, fresh fruit, and pitchers of orange juice and prickly-pear lemonade. The smells alone made my stomach growl.

Jake poured himself a generous scotch from a crystal decanter on the sideboard—his usual working drink, even at breakfast—and raised the glass in a mock toast.

"To Kirsten's tape and whatever fresh hell it's about to drop on us. Sit. We'll eat while we talk."

I took a seat, helping myself to a plate of huevos rancheros, the rich green chile scent rising around me. As we ate, Jake took another sip of scotch, his eyes sharp.

"Hell, Jake! Let's watch the tape. We can eat while we watch," I said.

"Why not?" he said, setting the glass down. "You ready, Angie?"

"Been ready," she said.

Angie leaned forward, expression serious but steady. The room felt charged, the weight of whatever we were about to see hanging thick in the air as the mountains stood eternal and unmoved beyond the windows. I took another bite.

The tension crackled like static electricity as we settled into our chairs. The lights dimmed automatically, plunging the space into near darkness except for the large screen on the wall. My heart was already beating a little faster than usual. I glanced at

Jake and Angie—they both looked as uneasy as I felt.

The screen flickered to life, and there she was: Congresswoman Kirsten Maldonado. She sat alone in what looked like a plain office or studio, wearing a sharp black skirt and a crisp white blouse, which contrasted with her long black hair.

She was in her thirties, attractive in that no-nonsense way, with dark eyes that seemed to pierce right through the camera. When she began to speak, her voice was strong and assertive, the kind that demanded you listen even if you didn't want to.

"My name is Congresswoman Kirsten Maldonado, representing New Mexico. I chair the House Oversight Subcommittee on UAP Transparency and lead the Task Force on the Declassification of Federal Secrets.

"For months now, I've been pushing hard for real accountability from the Department of Defense on unidentified aerial phenomena—UAPs—and making sure legitimate whistleblowers from the intelligence and military communities can come forward without getting destroyed."

She paused for a moment, her eyes fixed on the lens, then continued.

"Most of you probably saw my recent press conference. The networks, press, and social media tore it apart—calling it showboating, empty grandstanding, just me trying to boost my own profile. They weren't entirely wrong about how it appeared. But what they didn't realize is that the press conference actually served a purpose. It brought out a genuine whistleblower who contacted my office directly. His story is, well… earth-shattering."

I leaned in, elbows on the table, my eyes glued to the screen. Kirsten shifted forward in her chair, her voice dropping.

"My source wishes to remain anonymous for reasons you'll soon understand."

Kirsten was probably filming the video on her phone mounted on a tripod, as she vanished when the camera focused on a person in a chair. A black robe cloaked the person's body, and a festive Mardi Gras mask concealed their face.

"Please," she said. "Who do you work for?"

"The White House, in D.C.," a man's voice said.

"Are you an elected official?"

"I'm not, but I work there, and know all the players."

"And something has happened out of the norm?" Kirsten asked.

The man laughed. "Not much that goes on in the White House could be construed as normal."

"What exactly is out of the norm?"

"Someone in the White House is selling State secrets," he said.

Kirsten paused and then asked, "How do you know?"

"I overheard a snippet of a phone call. At first, I thought I was mistaken. Then, I started to notice things that were so obvious I couldn't ignore them."

"Like what?" Maldonado asked.

"Top secret documents just sitting in clerks' inboxes. Classified information being openly discussed among the wrong people. Hell! I found a top secret document in a toilet stall."

"Other people know?" Kirsten asked.

The man's laugh was dry. "Everyone knows."

"Then why didn't someone come forward? Why didn't you come forward? Are you afraid of reprisal?"

"I have told other people…important people," he said.

"What did they say?" Kirsten asked.

"They said there was nothing anyone could do about it and I should shut my fucking mouth and keep it shut."

"Or what?"

"Lose my job, my reputation, and my livelihood," the man said.

"Why did you finally decide to share the problem with someone who might actually take action on it?" Kirsten asked.

"Most of the information being shared was bureaucratic bullshit of little intellectual value. At least that's what I told myself to justify keeping my job and reputation. Then, something so big and dangerous fell into the wrong hands that I could no longer ignore the situation."

"How dangerous?"

"World-shattering, literally."

"Why did you come to me with this information?"

"You're a congresswoman with a net worth of much less than a million dollars."

"What does that supposed to mean?" Kirsten asked.

"You're not on the take."

"And other members of Congress are?"

"I'm not pointing fingers, and that's not the only reason I came to you. You chair the House Oversight Subcommittee on UAP Transparency and lead the Task Force on the Declassification of Federal Secrets."

After my press conference, many people believe I'm a crackpot," Kirsten said.

The man snickered. "You were targeted and tarred by the power group's disinformation brush. Another reason I trust you. They don't want anyone to take you seriously."

"Please tell me what is so world-shattering that you decided to risk your job and reputation, and who is this person you're accusing."

Kirsten's question was left unanswered because the video flickered briefly and then went black.

"What happened?" Jake asked.

"Don't know," Angie said, fumbling with the controls. She worked feverishly, finally flipping on the lights and turning to Jake. "That's it...that's all there is."

"You have to fucking be kidding me!" he said.

"I wish I were," she said, dialing someone on her phone.

"Who are you calling?" he asked.

"Sam," she said.

"Who's Sam?" I asked.

"Sam Presnel," he said. "Head of our video editing department."

Angie hung up after a fevered conversation, and Jake said, "What did he say?"

"Someone must have tampered with the video because it was complete when it left Tulsa."

"Do we have a copy in Tulsa?" Jake asked.

"You told Sam not to make one," she said.

Jake banged his forehead with his palm, tossed his set of heavy keys against the window pane, and said, "Shit! My bad! What a royal fuck up!. Now what?"

It made me think of my own keychain.

"I have something," I said, unlatching Dusty's flash drive from my keychain and handing it to Angie.

"What is it?" she asked.

"Don't know," I said. "Kirsten gave it to Dusty and told her to put it in a safe place and only look at the file on it if she disappeared. Dusty didn't want to think about it and gave it to me to keep. I forgot I had it."

Angie plugged the flash drive into her laptop and opened the file.

"Oh, shit!" she said,

"What?" Jake said.

"There's a video file," Angie said, dimming the lights.

The screen flickered, and Kirsten appeared, dressed casually, as if she were at home.

"Dusty, baby, if you're watching this video," she said, her tone steady but carrying real weight, "it's probably because I'm dead."

A chill ran straight down my spine. I quickly glanced at Jake and Angie. Jake's jaw was clenched tight, his usual laid-back attitude entirely gone, replaced by a deep scowl. Angie sat with her hands clasped so tightly in her lap that her knuckles had turned white. Both of them looked worried as hell—apprehensive, like they already knew this was going to get bad. Kirsten didn't flinch. She kept going.

"You are in grave danger, and I'm so sorry I put you in this position. Let me explain what happened, and I hope you'll someday find a way to forgive me."

"This whistleblower promised to bring me documents, recordings, and firsthand testimony that could completely change how the public understands UAPs, government secrecy, and what certain parts of our national security apparatus have been hiding for decades. What he brought me was an unbelievable story I disregarded. Until he accidentally fell out of a ten-story window."

She let that sink in, her dark eyes seeming to stare straight at me through the screen.

"I've spent weeks verifying what I could on my own. What I've seen is disturbing enough that I decided to record this video. If I'm no longer alive when you're watching this, it's because someone didn't want this information getting out to the American people, and you're not going to believe who that person is."

My stomach tightened into a hard knot. I glanced again at Jake—he'd gone pale. Angie's eyes were wide, fixed on Kirsten like she was afraid to blink. Kirsten's expression turned steely with determination.

Then she leaned in closer to the camera, ready to dive into the heart of the revelations, and my chest tightened with a mix of dread and adrenaline.

"Someone in our government sold a State secret to a foreign entity. Plans for a device more powerful than any weapon ever devised, a weapon capable of destroying our planet. That person is the President of the United States."

CHAPTER 25

The words hung in the air like a live grenade that had just lost its pin. For a frozen second, nobody breathed. The snow-dusted Sangre de Cristo Mountains beyond the tall windows stood indifferent, their peaks glowing sharp and cold in the morning light, while inside La Fonda Suite, the temperature seemed to drop ten degrees.

Jake's scotch glass hovered halfway to his lips, forgotten. His movie-star jaw had gone slack, then clenched so tight a muscle jumped in his cheek. Angie sat bolt upright, her café-au-lait hands still clasped white-knuckled in her lap, eyes wide as saucers. I felt my own stomach twist into a knot the size of a rodeo bucking barrel.

The President of the United States. Selling plans for a doomsday device capable of ripping apart reality itself. I'd been withholding information from Jake and Angie and decided it was time to share it with them.

"Any Black Jack in this joint's minibar?" I asked.

"If there's not, I'll call downstairs and have a bottle sent up," Jake said. "I thought you were a Coors man."

"I have a confession, and a shot of Jack will make it easier for me to make," I said.

We were soon sitting on the couch. Jake's shoulders had tightened, a pained expression on his face as he poured whiskey into my shot glass.

Angie drew a smile from him when she said, "Better make it two."

I killed my shot and had him pour me another.

"How serious is this going to be?" he asked. "Are we going to need another bottle?"

"Hope not," I said.

Jake snickered nervously. "If Colley were here, I bet he'd say you're about to tell us you had sex with an alien."

"Colley knows me pretty well."

Angie held out her shot glass and said, "Hit me. I think I'm about to need it."

Jake refilled our shot glasses and one for himself.

"Bottoms up," he said. "And then, whatever you think you need to confess, spill it."

"I did have sex with an alien," I said. "Her name is Aeterna."

The bottle of Jack was half empty, and I was half drunk when I finished my story. So was Angie. Jake kept drinking. He finally set his glass down with a soft clink that sounded deafening, his eyes locking onto me like twin rifle scopes.

"Quite a story," he said. "I'm not mad at you."

Angie's head snapped toward me, braids swinging. "Well, I am. You knew something this big and never said a damn word?"

I exhaled, feeling the weight of every secret I'd been carrying. The room felt smaller.

"I didn't know how to tell you," I said. "Hell, I have trouble believing it myself. But yeah… I saw lights. Not planes, not drones. Orbs. They pulled me into a beam. Took me through a fracture—some kind of tear between worlds. I ended up… somewhere else. Chronos. A city that shouldn't exist. Floating. Shifting. And there was a woman. Aeterna."

"Let's get back to the reason we're here," Jake said. "I'm still thinking about Congresswoman Maldonado's videos. Hearing that the President is selling apocalypse tech to God-knows-who."

"Everything is connected here, even Buck's cosmic squeeze. We just need to decide where to go from here."

"Lots of players here," I said. "Germans, North Koreans, the Chinese."

"The president's Chaotic Resonator is already tearing holes between dimensions," Jake said. "That's where we need to concentrate, and I can't think of anyone other than Randle Roberts to help us."

"Not if his memories are wiped," Angie said.

"If it's possible to wipe a brain clean like a computer hard drive," I said, "maybe it's possible to unwipe it."

"Sounds great, but who knows how to do that?" Jake asked.

"Kermit Sanderson, maybe," Angie said.

Jake gave her a quizzical look. "You're keeping secrets from me, too? Who is Kermit Sanderson?"

"A lead," she said. "A former Sandia engineer."

"Former?" Jake said. "What does he do now?"

"Builds and repairs guitars. Has a shop right here in Santa Fe. Buck interviewed him."

"And, how might a guitar builder help us?" Jake asked.

"He made a cosmic instrument that's tuned to the pulse of the universe. You have to hear it to know what I'm talking about."

"And?"

He knows things... He wouldn't tell me much, but if we can get him to talk, he might be of help to us. He's the person Aeterna told me to consult."

"Why would he talk to us now if he wouldn't before?" Jake asked.

"Aeterna gave me a calling card. I think it might just get his attention."

"What the hell are you talking about?" he said.

"A crimson orb," I said. "The strange light that Anna and Elena saw the night of the earthquake in the desert. The same red orb in Anna's drawing that got you here in the first place."

"And Aeterna thinks the orb will convince Sanderson to help us?" Angie asked.

"Yes. If anyone understands weird frequencies and dimensional bleed, it's Sanderson."

"Where's the orb now?" Jake asked.

"In the Jeep."

"Let's get it and then go see Sanderson," he said.

Jake drained the last of his scotch and set the glass down

with a decisive clink. Angie nodded, already closing her laptop.

I headed down to the valet station, the crisp Santa Fe morning air cutting through the whiskey haze still lingering in my head. The lime-green Jeep Gladiator sat gleaming under the portico, looking ridiculously out of place among the luxury sedans.

I popped the center console, and there it was—the crimson orb Aeterna had pressed into my hand was there where I'd left it, smaller than I remembered, no bigger than a baseball, its surface smooth and warm like living skin.

Faint veins of silver light pulsed lazily beneath the translucent shell, as if it had its own slow heartbeat. I wrapped it carefully in a spare bandana and slipped it into my jacket pocket, feeling its subtle weight like a promise I wasn't sure I wanted to keep. Angie and Jake were waiting in front of the hotel.

"Got it," I said, patting the pocket of my jacket.

"Good," Jake said. "We don't need problems."

"Like those two in baseball caps across the street?"

"Probably tourists," Jake said.

"Two Oriental men built like power lifters?" Angie said. "They look like trouble to me."

"Then we mingle with the crowd in the Plaza and shake them," Jake said.

The Plaza was crowded with tourists and rodeo fans arriving early for Saturday's big event, and we had no trouble losing our Oriental tails, who didn't even try to hide the fact that they were following us.

We reached Sanderson's shop, still tucked in a quiet alley just off Canyon Road, the kind of place tourists might miss unless they were hunting for something off the beaten path. The weathered sign still read "Sanderson Strings" in faded, curling letters, the wood carved with those same intricate whorls that seemed to shift if you stared too long. We pushed open the door, the faint jangle of the bell swallowed almost instantly by the thick, fragrant air inside.

The controlled chaos hadn't changed. Guitars hung like sacred relics along the adobe walls—some gleaming with fresh lacquer that caught the slanted light like liquid amber, others bearing the honest scars of years under working hands. The workbench dominated the back of the room, cluttered with chisels, tuning forks, and the half-carved body of a twelve-string whose curves reminded me of a woman's hip.

Shelves sagged under jars of tiny screws, coils of phosphor-bronze wire, and scraps of rosewood and spruce that seemed to hum with latent music. The scent was pure workshop poetry: sweet sawdust, sharp linseed oil, faint pipe smoke, and underneath it all, something electric—like ozone after a lightning strike.

Kermit Sanderson stood behind the bench, silver hair pulled into its familiar low braid, wire-rimmed glasses perched on that hawk-sharp nose. He didn't look up at first, just kept sanding a guitar neck with deliberate strokes, his hands moving with the quiet precision of a man who coaxed secrets from exotic wood. When he finally turned, his eyes—sharp as broken glass and glinting with that same bottomless hunger—locked onto us. They widened a fraction when they landed on me.

"Buck McDivit," he said, voice dry as desert wind. "Didn't expect to see you again so soon. And you brought friends."

"Angie and Jake," I said.

"Oh, my God!" Sanderson said, grasping his heart. "I can't believe I'm actually face-to-face with the Cryptid Hunter. I'm honored."

"It's me who is honored, Mr. Sanderson," Jake said. "I'm the face of the program, though Angie here is its beating heart."

"Kermit," he said.

Sanderson smiled and shook Angie's hand. "You're the friendly young woman with the melodious voice who arranged my interview with Mr. McDivit."

"I confess," she said with a smile. "Hope he didn't overload your angst level."

Sanderson continued holding her hand. "Not at all. The young man likes Santa Fe IPA almost as much as I do. Would you like to try a bottle?"

"Normally, my answer would be yes, but we've had a rough morning and started on the strong stuff early."

"I understand," he said. "Beer on whiskey, mighty risky. No problem. I have an unopened bottle of mescal in the back."

Angie started to protest, but Jake stopped her when he said, "I like mescal."

We were soon slugging shots of mescal, Jake and Sanderson chasing theirs with locally brewed IPA.

"Buck brought something that might interest you," Jake said.

"Oh? What you got?"

"You tell me," I said, pulling the orb from my jacket and unwrapping the bandana. The crimson sphere caught the shop's dim light and seemed to drink it in, its inner silver veins brightening like a living circuit.

"Oh, my God!" Sanderson said. "Two life-changing surprises on the same day. Is that what I think it is?"

"Yes, sir. An alien communication device. Aeterna said it would get your attention."

"Aeterna?"

Angie rolled her eyes when I said, "A beautiful blue-eyed alien."

Jake interrupted me, thankfully changing the subject from Aeterna.

"Right now," he said, "we have bigger problems than orbs and guitars—a Chaotic Resonator tearing holes between worlds, and apparently, our very own President's mixed up in selling the plans. We need your help, Kermit."

"Never trusted that bastard," he said.

He smiled when Jake said, "I thought government employees were non-political."

"Yeah! Right," Sanderson said.

Sanderson's craggy face tightened. He reached for the orb but stopped short, fingers hovering as if afraid it might burn him. For a long moment, the only sound was the slow-moving overhead fan and the faint creak of the old building settling.

Then he exhaled, a low rumble. "That damn thing… I hoped

I'd never see another one."

He finally took it, and the silver veins inside flared brighter to his touch. Sanderson set the crimson orb down on his workbench, as if it might bite him. The silver veins inside pulsed once, brighter, then settled. He rubbed a hand over his braid and exhaled, the sound rough as sandpaper.

"Does this have something to do with the recent rash of earthquakes?" he asked.

"Yes," I said.

"And it was an alien who warned you?"

"No," I said. "I visited Chronos, an interdimensional world, through a crevice created by a Chaotic Resonator."

My words didn't get the reaction I'd expected, Sanderson staring at me as if I'd told him about finding the Holy Grail.

"What…was it like?" he asked.

CHAPTER 26

The question hung in the air like a tuning fork struck against eternity itself. Sanderson's eyes—those hungry shards of glass behind his wire-rims—didn't blink. They drank me in the way the crimson orb had drunk the light from the room.

Jake and Angie exchanged a quick glance, but neither of them jumped in to steer the conversation back to the President or the Resonator. They could feel it too: this was the real hook. The thing Sanderson had been chasing his whole life through wood and wire and forbidden frequencies.

I leaned back against the workbench, the mescal still burning a slow trail down my throat, and let the memory rise up without fighting it.

"It wasn't like stepping through a door, Kermit. There wasn't a 'before' and 'after' the way we understand it. One second I was falling through that fracture in the desert night—air ripping like wet silk, colors I don't have names for streaking past—and the next… I was standing on nothing that still held me up.

"Chronos doesn't float the way a city in the sky would in some kid's drawing. It shifts. The ground—call it ground—was made of light folded into geometry that kept changing angles. One moment, it felt like polished obsidian under my boots, cool and absolute. Next, it was warm, almost soft, like the hide of some living thing, breathing in rhythm with my own pulse.

"Buildings rose and fell in deliberate waves, not collapsing, but recomposing themselves. Spires of crystal and something that looked like frozen mercury twisted upward, then braided into arches, then dissolved into lattices of pure mathematics before reforming somewhere else. Nothing stayed put, yet nothing felt chaotic. It was... orchestrated. Like the whole place was a single instrument playing a song too vast for human ears."

I paused, rubbing the back of my neck. The shop's familiar smells—sawdust, linseed, old pipe smoke—suddenly felt thin and two-dimensional compared to what I was remembering.

"Time didn't run straight there. I'd look at my watch, and the hands would be spinning backward, then freeze, then melt into liquid silver that dripped upward. But I never felt lost. There was this... presence. Not voices exactly, more like knowing. You'd think a question and the answer would already be inside your head, shaped like a memory you just hadn't lived yet. Aeterna told me later it was the Chronos Mind—the collective resonance of every being who'd ever passed through or been born there.

"They don't 'speak' the way we do. Their language is frequency and emotion braided together. When the queen talked to me, it felt like someone had reached inside my chest and played my heartstrings like a twelve-string guitar."

Sanderson's hand had gone completely still on the workbench. His fingers trembled just slightly, the way a man's might when he's holding the neck of a guitar that's finally in perfect tune after years of trying.

"Describe the beings," he said, voice hoarse.

I closed my eyes for a second, pulling the sensory details back from wherever memories of other worlds hide.

"They weren't 'people' wearing weird costumes. Some of them looked like living light—tall, shifting columns of cobalt and violet that moved through the structures without touching them. Others were more... solid, but only sometimes.

"I saw what I thought was a woman made of flowing mercury, her form rippling like water in zero gravity, but when she turned toward me, her face became a mirror reflecting every version of myself I could have been. It wasn't scary. It was intimate in a way that made my skin prickle and my soul feel naked.

"The air itself had weight and taste. It smelled like ozone and petrichor and something sweet—almost like mescal aged in rosewood barrels, but cleaner. When I breathed it, colors bloomed behind my eyes even when they were open.

"Sounds weren't just heard; they were felt in the bones. There was constant music, but not from instruments. It came from the movement of the city, from the beings passing through each other, from the way light bent around corners that shouldn't exist. Resonant tones that vibrated in my sternum, high crystalline chimes that made the hairs on my arms stand up. At one point, I realized I was humming along without meaning to, and the city hummed back in harmony."

I opened my eyes again. Sanderson looked like a man who'd just been shown the blueprint of God's guitar.

"And how did it feel?" he said, leaning forward. "Not just seeing. Feeling. Inside."

I let out a slow breath.

"Like waking up from a lifelong fever you didn't know you had. For the first time, my body didn't feel like a cage. Every cell remembered it belonged to something bigger. There was no fear, even when the ground dissolved beneath me and I fell upward through layers of reality.

"No loneliness. The loneliness we carry around every day—the little ache that never quite goes away—it was gone. Replaced by this… absolute belonging. Like I was a note that had finally found the chord it was meant to be part of.

"It wasn't all bliss. There was a cost. When I returned through the fracture, everything here felt… muted. Flat. Like someone had turned down the saturation on the whole world.

"Colors were duller. Sounds thinner. Even the whiskey we drank earlier tasted like a cheap imitation of itself. I think that's why some people who brush against these places come back changed. Or broken. Your brain tries to cram infinity back into a three-pound skull, and it never quite fits the same way again."

Sanderson reached out and touched the crimson orb. The silver veins inside flared in response, brighter this time, casting faint red shadows across the half-finished guitar on his bench.

"And Aeterna?" he asked softly. "What was she like… up

close?"

I smiled despite myself, the memory warming something deep in my chest.

"She was blue. Not painted—blue, like the deepest part of a twilight sky given living form. Skin that shimmered with inner starlight. Eyes like polished sapphires that saw straight through every lie I'd ever told myself. When she touched me..." I trailed off, feeling heat rise in my face. "Let's just say physics worked differently.

"Gravity, time, pleasure—everything becomes negotiable. She didn't just make love to my body. She made love to the idea of me. To every possible version of Buck McDivit scattered across the multiverse. It lasted a heartbeat and a thousand years at the same time."

Jake cleared his throat, shifting uncomfortably. Angie raised an eyebrow but said nothing, a knowing smile playing at the corner of her mouth.

Sanderson didn't laugh or scoff. He just nodded slowly, reverently, the way a luthier might when he finally hears the perfect tone emerge from a piece of wood he's been coaxing for months.

"Thank you, Buck," he said quietly. "I've spent forty years trying to tune instruments to catch echoes of places like that. Chasing frequencies that shouldn't exist. Building resonators that could maybe, just maybe, brush against the veil. And you... You walked right through it."

He picked up the orb again, holding it between both palms like a sacred relic.

"This changes things," he said. "The Chaotic Resonator, the President's peddling... It's not just a weapon. It's a sledgehammer taken to the strings of creation. If they keep ripping holes like that, the bleed will get worse. Chronos might not stay 'over there' much longer. And what leaks through won't all be as friendly as your Aeterna."

He looked up at the three of us, eyes burning with something between terror and ecstasy.

"I'll help you. But we're not just stopping a madman selling blueprints. We're trying to keep reality from untuning itself. And for that... we're going to need more than guns and politics. We're going to need music. The right kind. The kind that can stitch worlds back together."

Sanderson set the orb down gently and reached for the half-carved twelve-string on his bench, running his fingers along its curves with new purpose.

"Now," he said, voice steady for the first time since we'd walked in, "tell me everything you remember about how Chronos sounded. Because if we're going to fight this, I need to build something that can sing in the same key as eternity."

The afternoon light slanted through the dusty windows of Sanderson Strings, catching on the floating motes of sawdust like tiny stars. Outside, Santa Fe carried on with its ordinary rhythm—tourists laughing, distant mariachi music, the low rumble of pickup trucks.

But inside that little workshop, four people sat around a glowing crimson orb and a half-finished guitar, listening as one man tried to describe a song no human throat was ever meant to sing.

Sanderson's fingers paused on the half-carved twelve-string, the sanding block forgotten in his palm. He stared at the crimson orb for a long beat, its silver veins pulsing in hypnotic rhythm like a second heartbeat in the quiet shop.

The mescal had loosened something in all of us, but the weight of what I'd just described—Chronos, Aeterna, the untuned symphony of another reality—had sobered the room faster than any hangover ever could.

"I'll help you," he said again, voice low and rough, "but I can't do it alone. Not with the kind of bleed we're talking about. The Chaotic Resonator isn't just punching holes. It's fraying the strings that hold the multiverse in tune. To even get close to countering it, or to understand what our President is really selling, we need someone who's been deeper into the black programs than I ever was. Someone who helped build the devices that make memory itself negotiable."

“Who?” Jake asked.

“The one person who can shut down a Chaotic Resonator once it’s fully spun up,” he said.

“Randle Roberts?” Jake said.

Sanderson nodded. “Codename Vector back in the day. He designed the damn thing’s counter-frequency.”

“But…”

“They wiped his brain clean after he tried to walk away. Memory extraction protocol. Leaves the hardware intact, scrubs the software.”

Jake leaned forward, scotch long forgotten. “Wiped how?”

“Neural lattice purge.”

“So we’re fucked, then,” Jake said.

“Nope,” Sanderson said. “Brutal, but reversible—if you have the right rig. There’s a device at Groom Lake that can pull the data back out. Non-invasive quantum resonance scanner. Reads the ghost patterns left in the hippocampal folds. Only one in existence, far as I know.”

Sanderson grinned when Jake said, “I think I need more mescal.”

Sanderson drained the bottle and then set the sanding block down with deliberate care, as if the wood might shatter under the gravity of his next words.

“Vector. Randle Roberts—though most of us who knew him just called him Vector. Old colleague from Sandia. Brilliant mind. The kind that could look at a waveform and see how it wanted to bend spacetime instead of just oscillating. He was the one who first theorized how to map interdimensional bleed onto physical instruments. Guitars were my side project; Vector’s work was… official. Until it wasn’t.”

Jake leaned forward, elbows on his knees, the Cryptid Hunter mask slipping away to reveal the sharp focus underneath.

“Memories can be erased?”

Sanderson nodded, his silver braid catching the slanted light. “Wiped clean. Not the gentle kind of forgetting that comes with age or too much whiskey. This was surgical. Industrial. The kind of wipe that leaves a man knowing how to tie his shoes and brew coffee, but nothing about the equations that once let him whisper to the fabric of reality."

"He told us stories about Yuri Gagarin and flying around the moon in a spacecraft piloted by an alien," Jake said.

"Colorful stories that most reasonable people will consider hyperbole," Sanderson said. "He doesn't remember his work with interdimensional beings. Hell, I suspect that he barely remembers me, and we shared a lab for eight years."

Angie's eyes narrowed. "Who did it?"

"The ones who keep the real toys locked away," Sanderson said.

"Something that can restore memories?" Jake asked.

"Yes," Sanderson said.

"Where?"

"Like I said, Groom Lake—Area 51 proper, or the deeper black sites tied to it. We've had the tech for decades. Not some sci-fi ray gun that flashes and poof, you're tabula rasa. No, this is elegant. They call it the Echo Chamber, at least in the whispers I still catch from old contacts who haven't been... adjusted."

CHAPTER 27

Sanderson reached under the workbench and pulled out a battered notebook, its cover stained with coffee rings and what looked suspiciously like guitar lacquer.

He flipped it open to a page covered in frantic sketches: waveforms that twisted into Möbius strips, neural maps overlaid with fractal patterns, and something that looked uncomfortably like a human brain cross-sectioned with glowing nodes connected by threads of light.

"Echo Chamber?" Jake said.

"A system, and not a single device," Sanderson said. "Started as offshoots of old MKUltra wet dreams—drugs, hypnosis, electromagnetic pulses—but they refined it. Took it underground at S-4, the real heart under the dry lake bed."

"Explain," Jake said

"A combination of targeted transcranial magnetic fields and a proprietary waveform they dubbed the 'Null Harmonic.' It resonates at frequencies that interfere with the brain's own quantum microtubule vibrations—the tiny structures where some wilder theorists think consciousness and memory actually live, not just in synapses but deeper, where reality itself might be probabilistic."

Sanderson smiled when Jake asked, "How do you still know so much?"

"Why wasn't I wiped? Is that what you're asking?"

"Just saying," Jake said.

"Because I designed the damn machine and knew how to avoid the damage it's capable of."

Sanderson nodded when I said, "You had an accomplice?"

"She still works there. That's all I can tell you," he said.

"I understand," Jake said. "How does this brain toy work?"

"You sit in a chair that looks like a fancy dentist's rig. Helmet with superconducting coils. They play the Null Harmonic through it—inaudible to the ear, but it sings straight into the skull. It doesn't destroy memories; it untunes them. Makes the neural pathways that hold specific experiences fall out of phase with the rest of the brain."

"And it doesn't kill you?" Jake asked. "Sounds radical."

"The subject wakes up feeling fine, just... empty in certain rooms of their mind. Vector knew too much about how the Resonator prototypes interacted with interdimensional fractures. So they detuned him. Erased the parts that could have weaponized that knowledge against them—or worse, shared it with the wrong people. Or the right ones, depending on which side of the veil you're on."

Jake's jaw tightened. "And you think we can reverse it?"

Sanderson tapped the notebook. "Not easily. The Echo Chamber leaves a signature—a kind of harmonic scar in the brain's field. If we can get Vector back here, I might be able to employ a counter-resonator. Something tuned to the same key."

"You have such a device?" Jake asked.

"My guitar. It already flirts with those edges. With the orb as a stabilizer... maybe we could reintroduce the lost frequencies gently. Like restringing an instrument that's been cut and left to slack."

"Restore all of Vector's memories, not just the frivolous ones?" Jake asked.

"It won't be perfect. Some notes might stay lost. But the core melodies? The ones that let him see the bleed and the fractures? Those we might bring back."

I remembered Aeterna's words when I felt the crimson orb warm in my pocket, almost as if it were listening, and the reason we were in Sanderson's little shop. The yowl of a cat in the alleyway outside the door broke the silence.

"Aeterna pointed me to you for a reason, Kermit. If Vector's the key, we'll get him. But this Echo Chamber sounds like exactly the kind of thing the President's buyers would kill to keep exclusive."

Sanderson's laugh was dry, bitter. "Kill? Son, they've done worse. They've erased men who built the damn thing. Tried to erase me and thought they had succeeded. Vector wasn't the first. Won't be the last if the Resonator keeps tearing holes. Every new fracture risks more bleed—entities slipping through that make your orbs look like children's toys. Some friendly. Most... not."

He closed the notebook and looked at each of us in turn, the hunger in his eyes now tempered with something heavier: resolve.

"So what do you need from us?" Jake asked.

"Convince Vector without triggering whatever failsafes they might have left in his head that coming to Santa Fe is worth the risk."

Jake gave me a glance. "Can we do it?" he asked.

"If Ran and Tara help, he will," I said.

"We'll get him here," Jake said. "I'm relying on you to do the rest. Can you handle it?"

"No guarantees, but the orb gives me a true anchor. Something actually tuned to the other side. With it, and with Buck's sensory map of Chronos, I'll make it work. Assuming we can get in and out of Groom Lake without getting locked up in a Federal penitentiary."

Sanderson nodded when Jake said, "A tuning fork for the soul."

"Exactly," he said.

Jake drained the last of his mescal and set the glass down. "Angie's got the research chops. Buck's got... whatever cosmic juice Aeterna left in him. You build whatever mad guitar or resonator you need. Just make sure it works before the next big rip opens under all of us."

Sanderson nodded, already reaching for a fresh sheet of paper and a pencil. His hand moved with new urgency, sketching curves that looked suspiciously like the shifting architecture I'd described from Chronos.

"One more thing," he said without looking up. "Don't push too hard on Vector's memories at first. Ask him about music instead. Old Sandia lab parties. The way certain frequencies were used to make the equipment sing."

"For what reason?" Jake asked.

"The brain remembers in harmonics, even when the words are gone. Start there. Let the strings find their way back into tune."

The shop fell into a focused quiet, broken only by the faint creak of the overhead fan and the soft scratch of Sanderson's pencil. Outside, Santa Fe carried on—ordinary, oblivious. Inside, four unlikely allies sat surrounded by half-built instruments and the faint red glow of an alien calling card, plotting to steal back a man's stolen universe from the black heart of Area 51's deepest secrets.

Angie's eyes narrowed. "You keep talking about Groom Lake. Area 51."

Jake barked a laugh. "Area 51 is a myth for tourists and tinfoil-hat podcasts, isn't it?"

Sanderson's smile was thin and sharp. "It's real. Dry lakebed facility, Nevada Test and Training Range. About eight hours from here if you push it—north on 285 out of Santa Fe, then west through the Four Corners, hit I-40 to Flagstaff, then 93 north past Vegas and onto the Extraterrestrial Highway. State Route 375. Look for the black mailbox. Turn onto Groom Lake Road after that. You'll know when you're close. The sky gets too quiet."

He reached into a locked drawer beneath the bench and pulled out a worn laminate badge—faded photo of a younger Kermit, hair still dark, eyes harder. The holographic seal shimmered under the shop lights.

"I still have clearance. Retired doesn't always mean erased. If I go with you, I can get us through the gate. Without me, you'll be turned around—or worse. Your call."

"When do we leave?" Jake asked.

"Soon as I make a call," Sanderson said. "Not you and Angie. Just Buck and me."

The lime-green Jeep Gladiator ate miles like it was born for bad decisions, Sanderson riding shotgun, like a silver-haired oracle who smelled faintly of linseed oil and old secrets. Pard occupied the backseat, his head out the window, enjoying the breeze in his face.

The high desert unspooled around us—piñon and juniper giving way to endless sagebrush, red rock mesas rising like broken teeth against a sky so blue it felt judgmental.

By late afternoon, we'd crossed into Nevada. The land flattened and emptied, becoming something raw and watchful. Joshua trees stood like sentinels, their twisted arms pointing nowhere.

We hit the Extraterrestrial Highway as the sun bled orange across the basin, the two-lane blacktop arrowing straight into infinity. No billboards, no towns, just the occasional cow and the low hum of tires on asphalt that sounded suspiciously like the note Sanderson had pulled from his cosmic guitar. I finally broke the long silence, my hands loose on the wheel.

"I'm a cowboy, Kermit, not a damn commando. We can't just roll up to Area 51 with six-guns blazing like we're shooting up a saloon. Even if we can get in, how the hell are we gonna get out with the device? That place eats people. Spits out ghosts."

Sanderson stared out the windshield, the dying light carving deep lines into his face. For a long time, he said nothing. Then he reached into the glove box, pulled out a half-empty bottle of mescal, and took a slow pull before offering it to me.

"Janelle," he said.

I glanced over. "She's the accomplice you mentioned back at the shop?"

Sanderson nodded once, eyes fixed on the empty road ahead. "Janelle Delgado. She's still inside. And she's the only reason I walked out of that place with my mind still intact."

The engine's steady growl filled the cab for another mile. I waited, sensing the story needed room to breathe.

"I was sixty-three when they scheduled me for retirement," Sanderson began, voice low and rough as the desert gravel. "Margaret had been gone almost a year. Cancer took her fast—left me rattling around our old house in Albuquerque like a loose bolt. The brass called me in, said it was time. Mandatory protocol. Sit in the chair, let the Echo Chamber sing me a lullaby, wake up remembering nothing but sunsets and guitar strings. Clean slate. Safer for everyone."

His laugh was humorless. "I designed the damn thing. I knew exactly what it would take from me. Every classified project I'd touched—every fracture I'd helped map, every night we'd spent trying to keep the bleed from swallowing the world. They wanted all of it gone."

My knuckles tightened on the wheel, but I remained quiet.

"Then there was Janelle. Forty-four. Beautiful in that way that doesn't announce itself—dark auburn hair she kept twisted up like she was always one strong wind from letting it loose, hazel-green eyes that could read a circuit diagram or a man's soul with the same quiet precision. She grew up in Española, daughter of a physics teacher and a Navajo weaver. Smarter than half the PhDs in the building, and twice as grounded.

"She was my lead technician on the final iterations of the Resonator. Assigned to me because no one else could keep up."

Sanderson took another pull from the bottle, slower this time.

"We started with coffee at 2 a.m. in the secure break room. Talking waveforms. Talking ethics. Talking about how terrified we both were of what we were building. One night, we ended up on the hood of my old Bronco in the empty parking lot, staring up at a sky so thick with stars it felt like the universe was eavesdropping. I told her the machine scared me more than anything I'd ever touched. She told me she was afraid she'd wake up one day and realize she'd never really lived."

His voice softened, the desert wind whistling faintly through the cracked window.

"She was married. Good man, Mark. Liked him, even. Two kids in college. But there was no fire there anymore—just comfortable embers. With me... it was different. I didn't chase her. Didn't flirt. I just listened. Really listened. And she saw me—the widower who carried too many ghosts, the engineer who knew he was helping build a cage for other people's minds. She wasn't looking for a younger body or a rebellion. She was looking for someone who treated her mind like it mattered. Someone who looked at her and didn't see a technician, but a partner in something vast and dangerous."

I nodded, eyes on the road, the orange light painting everything in melancholy gold.

"We carried it on as carefully as hell. Long 'field tests' out in the Jemez canyons or the empty stretches north of Los Alamos, where the cell service died, and the sky belonged only to us. We kept a little casita under a false name—paid cash from what I made building guitars on the side. She'd tell Mark she was at a seminar in Denver. I'd tell the lab we were calibrating remote sensors. We were meticulous. Scientists, after all."

A faint smile touched Sanderson's lips, but it carried pain.

"Four years, Buck. Four years of stolen nights where we didn't just talk about the machine—we talked about what it meant to choose, remembering when the world wanted you to forget. She never said 'I love you' the ordinary way. She'd look at me under that adobe roof and say, 'If they ever wipe me, make sure you remember this sky.' I'd answer, 'I built the machine that erases people, but you're the only thing I want burned into my cortex forever.'"

Sanderson's voice cracked just slightly on the last words. He cleared his throat, but the desert had already heard it.

"When retirement came, she risked everything. Spent weeks reverse-engineering the fail-safes on a burner laptop in that casita. Wrote the patch that let me walk out whole. She handed it to me the night before, hands shaking, and said, 'They can have the rest of the world's secrets. But not yours. Not ours.'"

I swallowed hard, my eyes glistening in the dashboard light.

I didn't wipe them. Just let the road blur for a second.

"So no, we're not going in with six-guns. We're going in with the only thing stronger than their machine—someone who once chose memory over safety, love over erasure. And since she said yes... we might just walk out with our souls intact."

CHAPTER 28

Pard kept his head out the window, ears flapping, but even he went still when the black mailbox appeared on the right—beat-up, covered in stickers and cryptic messages left by pilgrims. We turned onto Groom Lake Road. The pavement ended.

Gravel and dust boiled behind us in a rooster tail that glowed gold in the dying light. Warning signs flashed past: restricted area, photography prohibited, use of deadly force authorized. The air grew thinner, electric.

The gate materialized out of the heat haze just as full dark settled: a simple boom barrier across the road, chain-link fence stretching into the desert on either side, orange posts glowing faintly under security lights. Two white pickup trucks idled nearby—camo dudes in desert fatigues, faces impassive. One stepped forward, flashlight sweeping the Jeep.

Sanderson leaned out the window and held up his badge. The guard scanned it with a handheld reader. The device beeped once. The man's eyes flicked over the rest of us, lingered on Pard, then back to Sanderson.

"We've been expecting you, sir."

"This is my assistant," Sanderson said, voice flat. "We need access to Sublevel Three, Neuro Recovery Lab. Priority Theta clearance."

"Sorry, sir," the man in camos said. "Only you have permission to proceed. Your assistant can go no further unless you want to wait for us to do a security clearance on him."

Sanderson shook his head. "I can't do this without him, and we don't have time for a security check, so I've arranged to have him wiped before we leave. Neuro Recovery will confirm. Call them."

Sanderson and I waited as the guard got on his horn, the radio crackling at his shoulder. Finally, he nodded, handed Sanderson a scanner card, and the boom lifted with a hydraulic whine.

"Use this card and return it when you pass back through. Stay on the marked road. No deviations."

Sanderson nodded when I said, "Janelle?"

We rolled ahead, the base unfolding in the darkness like a sleeping beast—long, low hangars hulking against the dry lakebed, their roofs painted to match the desert from above. Runways stretched out like pale scars.

Security cameras tracked us from every angle, red indicator lights winking like distant stars. The main complex sat tucked against low hills: windowless concrete buildings, humming generators, and the faint ozone scent of high-voltage fencing.

Sanderson directed me to a nondescript side entrance, half-buried in the slope. We parked in a floodlit lot. Armed security met us at the door—polite but stone-faced. Badges were scanned again. Retinal checks were run on Sanderson. Janelle must have had some pull because they didn't ask questions; they just waved us through after a silent nod.

Inside, the air was cool and sterile, fluorescent lights buzzing overhead. Corridors branched like veins—gray walls, heavy doors with biometric locks, the occasional distant echo of machinery. We descended via a freight elevator that smelled of hydraulic fluid and old secrets. Sublevel Three opened into a quieter wing: softer lighting, thicker carpet to muffle footsteps, and the faint whine of cooling fans.

The Neuro Recovery Lab sat at the end of a short hallway behind a door marked only with a numerical code. When Sanderson swiped the card the guard had given him, the lock clicked.

The room beyond was smaller than I expected—clinical, almost intimate. Banks of monitors glowed with scrolling waveforms. In the center stood a padded chair, surrounded by a halo of delicate copper filaments and glowing blue sensor nodes that looked as if they'd been grown rather than built.

Instruments hummed faintly, the same low resonance I'd felt in Sanderson's shop. An attractive woman was waiting for us, arms folded.

The door hissed shut behind us with a soft pneumatic sigh, sealing the sterile hush of Sublevel Three. The Neuro Recovery Lab felt more like a confessional than a black-site chamber—smaller than I'd imagined, lit by the soft glow of monitors scrolling endless waveforms and the faint blue pulse of sensor nodes that hummed like distant stars. In the center sat the chair, that padded dentist's nightmare ringed by copper filaments, looking deceptively gentle for something built to steal souls.

Janelle Delgado stood waiting, arms loosely folded, exactly as Sanderson had described her in the long desert miles. Older now, mid-fifties maybe, but the years had only refined her—still that lean, sun-browned frame from weekend hikes on the Sandia Crest, dark auburn hair threaded with silver and twisted into a loose knot at her nape, a few rebellious strands framing high cheekbones and those hazel-green eyes that seemed to hold both desert light and quiet storms. She was still beautiful in the way that hits you sideways, not screaming for attention but impossible to look away from once you did.

Pard, who'd been riding shotgun with his head out the window for most of the drive, let out a soft woof and trotted straight to her. Janelle's face broke into a warm, unguarded smile—the kind that reaches the eyes and softens everything else. She knelt gracefully, turquoise studs catching the blue light, and scratched behind his ears with both hands.

"What a beautiful dog," she said, voice low and melodic, the faint Española lilt still there after all these years. "Look at you. Bet you steal everyone's heart."

Pard leaned into her touch, tail thumping the carpet, and for a moment, the whole room felt less like a government vault and more like home.

Sanderson stood just inside the door, badge still in hand, and the air between them shifted—thick, electric, like the moment before a guitar string is plucked. No grand embrace, no tears in front of me. Just two people who had once risked everything looking at each other across a decade of careful silence.

Janelle rose slowly, brushing dog hair from her slacks, and stepped toward him. She took both his hands in hers—simple, steady, fingers lacing with the ease of muscle memory. No one else would have seen the depth in that touch, but I did. It was everything they weren't showing.

"Kermit," she said softly, her thumbs brushing the backs of his hands. "I thought I'd never see you again. Not like this. Not here."

He squeezed back, voice rough but gentle, the same voice that had told me their story under that bleeding Nevada sky.

"I wouldn't have made it through the gate without you pulling strings, Janelle. You look… God, you look exactly like the woman who saved my mind."

A faint smile touched her lips, poignant and private. "The kids are grown now. Married, with little ones of their own running around. And Mark… we divorced more than a year ago. Amicable. He's happy. I'm… figuring out what comes next. Contemplating early retirement, but I keep putting in the paperwork and then tearing it up."

Sanderson's eyes searched hers, understanding flickering there like one of those neural maps on the monitors. "You're afraid of the erasure."

"Not afraid," she said, that quiet strength I'd heard about flashing through her gaze. She gave his hands another gentle press. "There are memories I can't bear to lose. My time here—the work that scared us both. Our time together. The casita. The nights we talked about what it meant to remember when the world wanted forgetting. If they wipe me, those go too. And I'm not ready to let them go."

The room felt smaller, the hum of the machines fading into background static. I stood there like a damn statue, Pard leaning warm against my leg, and even I could feel the current running between them—deep, unbroken, forged in secrets and starlight.

It wasn't flashy. It was the kind of love that survives black budgets, broken marriages, and time itself. Buck the cowboy, I thought, swallowing hard. You've seen sunsets and stampedes, but this… this is what men write songs about when they're too choked up to sing.

Sanderson nodded, voice dropping lower. "The President's buyers are circling, Janelle. Self-serving bastards who think they can own the fractures, control the bleed. I need the Echo Chamber to stop them from erasing anyone who knows too much about what's really leaking through."

Janelle held up a hand and said, "There'll be questions, and that's all I need to know."

"You can't imagine how happy I am to see you," he said.

"Yes, I am," she said.

"We'd better dismantle the device and go. I don't won't to put you at any more risk than necessary."

"My assistant's off today—no awkward explanations. And we've been working on something better. A prototype, portable. Smaller than the old beast, more precise. No one else knows it exists. Not even the oversight logs. Harmonic tuning refined, failsafes I built with you in mind. It'll do what you need and leave less of a trace."

They stood like that a moment longer, hands linked, the weight of years pressing gently but heavily. Then she released him, turning to a wall panel with quiet efficiency. A biometric scan, a soft click, and she retrieved a compact case—matte black, no bigger than a large toolbox, humming faintly with contained power, and handed it to Sanderson, their fingers brushing one last time.

As we prepared to move, Sanderson pulled a simple business card from his pocket—his Santa Fe guitar shop address on the front. He flipped it over, scribbled something quickly with a pen from the desk, and pressed it into her palm.

"There's a message on the back," he said, voice thick with everything he wasn't saying aloud. "Put it somewhere you'll find it when the time comes. Come see me when you retire, Janelle. I'll restore your memories. I promise."

She took the card, eyes glistening but steady, and slipped it into her pocket like it was the most precious classified document on base.

"I'll hold you to that, Kermit. Go. Be careful out there."

The parting was quiet—no dramatic kiss, just that lingering look between them, two souls who had chosen remembering against every protocol the world could throw at them. I felt it in my chest like a gut punch from the desert wind. Then we were moving, Pard at my heels, the case tucked under Sanderson's arm as Janelle guided us through a service corridor only she seemed to know.

We backtracked through the base like ghosts—elevator up, side entrance out, the Jeep waiting under the floodlights. The night air hit cool and sharp, the distant hum of generators masking our footsteps. Sanderson rode shotgun again, the prototype secure between his boots. I gunned the engine low, tires whispering over gravel as we approached the checkpoint. The same camo guard stepped forward, flashlight up.

"Sir, step out, please—both of you."

"Oh, shit!" Sanderson said beneath his breath.

Before I could even kill the ignition, the night fractured.

Lights flashed high overhead—silent, brilliant, a sudden shower of glowing orbs streaking across the black sky like living comets. The ground rumbled beneath us, low at first, then building into something primal.

The Taos Hum slammed into my ears, earsplitting, vibrating through bone and steel until it felt like the desert itself was screaming. A rift tore open—not far, maybe a hundred yards beyond the fence—a jagged wound in reality spilling unearthly light and the faint scent of juniper and ozone.

Chaos erupted. Guards shouted, radios crackling with static-laced panic. Floodlights swung wildly. Someone yelled about intruders, another about atmospheric anomalies. In the strobe of orb-light and rift-glow, no one was watching the Jeep anymore.

"Aeterna," I said, my heart hammering with that old cosmic juice still singing in my veins.

No time to question it. I slammed the accelerator. The Jeep roared forward, crashing through the opening rift like a green thunderbolt. Metal screamed as I battered the bumper against the chain-link, twisting fence posts and ripping a hole wide enough to charge through.

Sparks flew. Alarms wailed behind us. We burst into the open desert, tires chewing sand and sagebrush, the prototype case rattling but holding.

"They'll never let us escape," Sanderson said tightly, gripping the dashboard as the Jeep bucked over uneven ground. "Not with this. Not after that."

I wasn't listening, my foot to the floor, the engine and gears of the Jeep screaming as the speedometer eclipsed the hundred miles per hour mark. I kept my foot to the floor until a crevasse appeared in our path, too wide and too deep to jump. When I slammed on the brakes, the vehicle began to slide, out of control. After a resounding crash, we ended up in the crevasse, the Jeep on its side.

"You okay?" I asked.

"Alive, if that's what you mean."

We climbed out of the Jeep, shaken up but otherwise unscathed. Then I heard it: Jake's chopper dropping fast into the clearing ahead, rotors whipping the air into frenzy. The side door was already sliding open, Angie waving us forward like a mad angel.

"They'll trace the Jeep," Sanderson said.

"Hell, Kermit, we're already made or thay would wouldn't have stopped us at the gate," I said.

We sprinted toward the chopper—Sanderson with the case, me behind Pard—sprinting for the bird as Colley held it steady. The moment the chopper lifted off, banking hard back toward the overturned Jeep. Jake opened the door and tossed something out.

Below us, a fireball bloomed—our lime-green Gladiator

erupting in a roaring ball of flame, lighting the desert like a second sun. Secondary explosions followed, probably the fuel and whatever else was packed into the explosives. We watched it burn as Colley turned the chopper toward Shadow Ranch.

As the flames receded into the dark, I leaned back in my seat, Pard's head in my lap, the prototype humming softly at Sanderson's feet. The old engineer stared out the window, one hand absently tracing the edge of the case, his thoughts clearly miles—and years—away with a woman who had just risked everything again for memories she refused to lose.

I swallowed the lump in my throat, the desert wind still whistling in my ears from the open door. Tender one minute, thunder the next. That was the bleed for you—beauty and bedlam, love and rifts, all tangled tighter than a lasso around a runaway steer.

Whatever came next, we had the machine. And somewhere back in that sleeping beast of a base, Janelle Delgado was tucking a business card into a safe place, holding onto the promise of a sky she wasn't ready to forget.

CHAPTER 29

There were lights on in the ranchhouse when we touched down on the outskirts of Shadow Ranch. Kermit Sanderson, the memory-wiping device resting in his lap, didn't move as Jake opened the chopper's door.

"We're here," Jake said.

"You aren't taking me to Santa Fe?" Sanderson asked.

"Complications," Jake said.

Concern crossed Sanderson's face. "What kind of complications?"

"Your shop is compromised," Jake said. "You'll have to stay here, at least for the night."

"I can't perform Vector's restoration without the orb and my special guitar. They are in my shop."

"I'm working on it," Jake said. "We can discuss our options in the ranchhouse."

Ran and Dusty were waiting when we piled out of the chopper.

"We've been worried sick," Dusty said. Where have you been?"

"Long story," I said. "We'll tell you in the house."

We were all soon sitting around the table in the kitchen, drinking mescal. Sanderson and I told our story, and then Jake launched into his.

"The shop in Santa Fe is compromised," he said.

"What exactly does that mean?" Sanderson asked.

"It's being closely watched. After your escapade at Area 51, you and Buck are at the top of the most wanted list."

He laughed when Sanderson said, "F.B.I?"

"Hardly," he said. "Black ops. Mercenaries. Probably working for the country that bought the Chaotic Resonator technology from the President."

"So," Sanderson said. "Buck and I are burned."

"That's about the size of it," Jake said.

"What now?" Sanderson asked.

"I have lots of friends in Washington, good people on both sides of the aisle. Everyone except the general public knows what the President is doing. Both sides are looking for a solution before this powder keg blows sky-high. Angie's working the phones as we speak."

"What about Janelle?" Sanderson asked.

Jake didn't answer immediately. When he did, he was looking at his toes.

"She's been wiped. I'm so sorry."

"Good God Almighty!" Sanderson said. "What the hell have I done?"

Jake touched his shoulder. "Colley and I have to go, but we'll be back tomorrow. Try to get some sleep."

When Jake and Colley were gone, Kermit and I explained the memory device to Dusty and Ran.

"I worked with your dad for years at Sandia," Sanderson said. "His code name was Vector, and he knew more about the Chaotic Resonator than anyone. When he was 'retired,' his classified memories were physically removed."

"Surgically?" Dusty said.

"Not with a scalpel but with a device such as this," he said, pointing at the Echo Chamber at his feet. "Buck and I 'borrowed' this one from Area 51. Now, someone is pissed and wants it back."

"You intend to use it to restore my dad's memories?"

"That was the plan," Sanderson said. "Problem is, I can't do it without my guitar and the orb Buck provided. Both are in my shop in Santa Fe."

"Can't you just go to the police?" Dusty asked.

"No more than you can," I said. "For the moment, we're on

the wrong side of the law."

"What's to stop us from shooting our way in?" Ran asked.

"It may come to that," I said. "Right now, we wait and see what plan Jake has."

"If you don't mind, I'm going to take Jake's advice and get some sleep," Sanderson said.

"Take the bedroom," I said. "I'm not ready to go to sleep. When I am, I'll do it on the couch."

The ranch house had gone quiet, the kind of desert quiet that presses in like a held breath. An hour earlier, Kermit Sanderson had disappeared into the bedroom, the door clicking shut with the finality of a man carrying too many ghosts.

Ran and Dusty had slipped up to the loft together, their low voices and occasional laughter drifting down like distant thunder—young, alive, trying to pretend the world wasn't cracking open beneath their boots.

I sat alone at the scarred oak table, a half-empty bottle of mescal in my hands, the faint red glow of the orb still pulsing softly inside my jacket pocket like a second heartbeat. Pard lay curled at my feet, ears twitching at every creak of the old timbers. The kiva fire had burned low, casting long, flickering shadows across the adobe walls.

When the front door creaked open, I didn't reach for a gun. I knew the sound of her footsteps—the soft, deliberate pad of bare feet on cool tile, the faint rustle of fabric that smelled faintly of starlight and warm skin. Aeterna stepped inside, the moonlight from the open doorway outlining her silver bodysuit like liquid mercury poured over living gold.

Her too-large blue eyes caught the dying firelight and held it, glowing with that impossible inner fire. She wasn't alone.

A tall figure moved behind her—male, humanoid, but not quite human.

His skin was a deep gunmetal gray that shimmered with faint iridescent undertones, like oil on water under starlight. His eyes were larger than hers, onyx-black and reflective, set in an elegantly angular face, almost regal. He wore a form-fitting matte-black garment that seemed to drink the light rather than reflect it, accentuating broad shoulders and a lean frame.

A subtle pattern of glowing silver glyphs pulsed faintly along his forearms and collar, shifting like living constellations. He moved with the same fluid grace as Aeterna, but there was a coiled readiness to him—shoulders squared, head slightly tilted, the way a predator studies new territory without fear.

Aeterna crossed the room without a sound, her bare feet silent on the floor. She stopped in front of me, close enough that I could feel the warmth radiating from her body, the same impossible heat that had burned against me the night before.

"Buck," she said, her voice sliding into my mind like velvet over steel. "This is Zephyrion."

The name resonated in my skull with a harmonic tone, like a bass string plucked deep in a canyon.

Zephyrion inclined his head slightly, a gesture both formal and wary. When he spoke, his voice was deeper than hers, layered with subtle overtones that made the air itself feel charged.

"Greetings, Buck McDivit. I am Zephyrion of the Ophirian Intelligence Directorate. Aeterna has spoken of you with... considerable regard."

He extended a hand—long, graceful fingers with an extra joint that flexed in a way that should have looked wrong but somehow didn't. I shook it. His grip was firm, cool at first, then warming to match mine, as if his body was adjusting to the contact.

"Pleasure," I said, my voice rough from the mescal and the sheer strangeness of the night. "You two make quite the pair. CIA of the stars?"

Aeterna's lips curved in that knowing smile. "Something like that. Our agency is the closest equivalent. Counter-intelligence, infiltration, and retrieval operations. Zephyrion is one of our most capable field operatives—trained in martial disciplines from a dozen worlds, advanced surveillance, and... persuasion when necessary."

Zephyrion's black eyes flicked toward the loft, then back to me.

"We've been monitoring the situation. The fracture is widening. The Iron Order and their proxies are closing in on the Resonator technology. Your President's transaction has accelerated the timeline beyond our projections."

Aeterna placed a hand on my shoulder, her touch sending that familiar electric warmth through me.

"We cannot retrieve the guitar and orb from Sanderson's shop in Santa Fe without drawing immediate attention. The black ops teams have the location under heavy surveillance—South African mercenaries, contracted through Qatari intermediaries. They're expecting a frontal assault or a technical breach. They are not expecting an approach from above."

Zephyrion's voice resonated again in my mind. "We can go there undetected. The entry is through a trapdoor that the defenders have overlooked. The place is well guarded on the ground, but the roof remains vulnerable."

I stared at them, my mescal haze burning off under the weight of their words.

"You want me to break into Sanderson's shop with an alien commando as backup?"

Aeterna's fingers tightened gently on my shoulder. "Zephyrion is trained for this. After you retrieve the guitar and the orb, we extract. Simple. Dangerous, but simple."

Zephyrion inclined his head again. "The mercenaries are South African ex-special forces. Competent, but operating on human assumptions. They do not anticipate infiltration from an orbital insertion or a being who can move through shadows as if they were doors. The Qatari buyers are the ones who acquired the Resonator schematics from your President. They are impatient. Time is not on our side."

I exhaled slowly, rubbing a hand over my face. The orb in my pocket pulsed once, warmer now, as if agreeing with them.

"All right," I said. "Let's go steal a guitar from the devil's workshop."

Aeterna's smile was real. "Good. The saucer is waiting."

The transport was silent and impossibly fast. One moment, we stood in the ranch house; the next, a soft blue beam enveloped us. I felt the familiar lurch in my stomach, the world blurring into streaks of starlight and desert darkness. Zephyrion stood beside me, utterly calm, his black eyes reflecting the glow of the craft above.

We were deposited on the flat roof of Sanderson's shop in Santa Fe without so much as a whisper of wind or scrape of boots. The night air was cool, carrying the faint scent of piñon from distant chimneys. Below us, the alley was dark, but I could see the shapes of vehicles—two black SUVs and a reinforced van parked at the mouth, figures moving in the shadows with military precision.

Zephyrion crouched, his form seeming to blend with the roof's shadows, and pointed.

"Ground teams here... and here," he communicated directly into my mind. "Thermal signatures indicate six on the perimeter, two inside the front. They are watching the doors and windows. The roof trapdoor is unsecured. They do not expect anyone to descend from above."

I nodded, my heart hammering but my hands steady. The trapdoor was old wood, weathered but solid. Zephyrion produced a small device from his suit—sleek, matte black—and passed it over the latch. There was a faint click, and the door lifted silently on hidden hinges.

We dropped into the darkness of the shop.

The interior smelled exactly as I remembered: sawdust, linseed oil, old wood, and secrets. Moonlight slanted through the high windows, painting the hanging guitars in a silver glow. Zephyrion moved like a liquid shadow, clearing the space with efficient sweeps. I headed straight for Sanderson's workbench.

The cosmic guitar was there, still in its battered case. I slung it over my shoulder. The crimson orb I'd left with Sanderson was resting in a small velvet pouch beside it. I tucked both securely against my body.

"Got them," I said.

Zephyrion's voice sounded in my head. "Movement below. They heard something. We must leave now."

We were halfway back to the trapdoor when the first shout came from the front of the shop. Boots pounded on the floorboards. A flashlight beam sliced through the darkness, sweeping wildly.

Zephyrion moved faster than I could track. One moment, he was beside me; the next, a South African mercenary was crumpling silently to the floor, his rifle clattering uselessly.

Another appeared in the doorway—Zephyrion flowed around him like smoke, a precise strike to the neck dropping the man without a sound."

Roof. Now," he said.

We climbed. I was hauling myself through the trapdoor when the first gunshot cracked below—wild, panicked. Shouts erupted. More boots. The mercenaries had finally realized the threat wasn't coming from the street.

Zephyrion was right behind me, shoving me toward the center of the roof as the beam from the saucer lanced down again, brilliant and silent. I felt the familiar lift, the stomach-dropping pull as we rose into the night.

Below us, the shop's roof erupted in gunfire—tracers streaking uselessly into the sky, men shouting in Afrikaans and broken English. The black SUVs roared to life, but it was too late. We were already gone, swallowed by the darkness and the waiting craft above.

The saucer deposited us back at Shadow Ranch just as the first gray light of false dawn touched the Sangre de Cristos. Zephyrion stepped out of the beam with me, his form still shimmering faintly at the edges.

"You did well," he said. "For a human."

I managed a tired grin, the guitar case heavy on my shoulder, the orb warm against my chest.

"You weren't so bad yourself, space ninja."

Aeterna appeared beside him, her blue eyes soft with something that looked almost like pride.

"The guitar and orb are secure. The next step is yours, Buck. Use them wisely. The fracture is widening. We do not have much time."

Zephyrion gave me a final nod—respectful, almost brotherly—before both of them stepped back into the beam and vanished upward in a silent rush of light.

CHAPTER 30

Morning light filtered through the ranch house windows like a promise it wasn't sure it could keep. I woke slowly, in a half-dream haze, where the desert still felt like it was breathing through the walls. The Taos Hum was there, low and steady, vibrating in my chest like a warning I couldn't quite shake.

My body ached in places I didn't remember bruising—last night's rooftop run with an alien commando had left its mark—but the real weight was the cosmic guitar case leaning against the wall and the crimson orb tucked safe in my jacket pocket. Both of them hummed with their own quiet power, like they were waiting for me to do something stupid with them.

Wonderful aromas drifted from the kitchen—bacon frying crisp, green chile roasting, fresh coffee strong enough to wake the dead. My stomach growled before my brain caught up. I pulled on a shirt and boots, Pard lifting his head from the rug long enough to thump his tail once before deciding the floor was still more interesting.

Dusty and Ran were already at it in the kitchen, moving like they'd been up for hours. Ran was flipping eggs in a cast-iron skillet, his lanky frame loose but focused, while Dusty stirred a pot of posole that smelled like heaven and home.

They both looked fresh-scrubbed and wired, the kind of energy that came from burning off nerves before the sun even cleared the Sangres.

"Morning, sleepyhead," Dusty said without turning around. "We've been up since before first light. Ran needed saddle time. I put him through a full set of drills—balance work, core, leg strength. Kid's gonna stick that bronc Saturday, or I'll eat my hat."

Ran grinned over his shoulder, sweat still beading on his forehead from whatever they'd been doing out in the corral.

"She's tougher than Dad ever was. Made me ride the oil drum till my thighs felt like they were on fire."

"Muscle memory," she said. "You're getting there."

I poured coffee, the steam rising hot and black. "You two training for the rodeo while I was stealing from the devil?"

I smiled and nodded when she said, "You have Sanderson's guitar?"

I didn't answer when Ran said, "How?"

Dusty laughed, but there was an edge to it—the same edge that had been there since Kirsten's tape dropped the President into the middle of our nightmare.

"Gotta keep moving. Sitting still just gives the bad guys time to catch up."

The bedroom door creaked open, and Kermit Sanderson stepped out, looking like he hadn't slept much. His silver braid was mussed, eyes sharp behind his wire-rims, but the weight of the night sat heavy on his shoulders. He froze when his gaze landed on the guitar case I'd set on the table.

"Is that...?"

I opened the case, revealing the matte-black twelve-string with its elliptical soundhole and those strange etched symbols. Beside it, I set the small velvet pouch and let the crimson orb roll gently into my palm. Its silver veins pulsed once, slow and deliberate, as if it recognized the room. Sanderson's breath caught.

He crossed the kitchen in three strides and took the guitar, running his fingers over the fretboard with the reverence of a man touching something holy. Then he picked up the orb, holding it between both hands as if it might vanish.

"Where the hell did you get these?"

I kept it simple. No need to drag him through the full cosmic rodeo just yet.

"Aeterna helped," I said. "She and an alien James Bond got me in and out clean. Roof entry. South African mercs on the ground, Qatari money pulling the strings. They weren't expecting anyone to drop in from above."

Sanderson stared at me for a long beat, searching my face like he was reading sheet music for lies. Whatever he saw there—maybe the exhaustion, maybe the faint afterglow of whatever Aeterna had left in my blood—he didn't push. He just nodded once, tight and grateful.

"That woman... she's something else. All right. Eat first. Then I'll see what I can make of this."

We sat down to breakfast like people pretending the world wasn't tearing at the seams. Eggs, bacon, posole, fresh tortillas—Dusty and Ran had outdone themselves. For a few minutes, the only sounds were the scrape of forks on plates and the low hum of the desert outside. But the stakes pressed in anyway. Every bite tasted like it might be the last normal meal we'd have if that fracture kept widening.

After the plates were cleared, Sanderson carried the guitar and orb to the far end of the table. He laid them out carefully, then pulled the prototype device from the black case Janelle had given us—the portable Echo Chamber, humming faintly with restrained power.

His hands moved with quiet precision, connecting thin filaments, adjusting nodes, murmuring to himself about harmonic anchors and memory lattices. The orb's silver veins brightened in response, syncing with the device like it already knew the song.

"I'll see if I can make sense of what Janelle gave me," he said without looking up. "Integrate it with the guitar's tuning and the orb's signal. If I'm right, this should act as a counter-resonator. Pull Vector's lost frequencies back into phase. Gently. Like restringing an instrument that's been cut and left to slack."

He worked for the better part of an hour while the rest of us cleaned up and tried not to hover. The tension in the room thickened with every passing minute, the Taos Hum seeming louder now, pressing against the windows like it wanted in. Dusty paced. Ran kept checking his phone, waiting for word from Tara. I just watched Sanderson's hands, willing them to work miracles.

Finally, he sat back, wiping sweat from his brow. The device sat assembled on the table—compact, humming, the crimson orb locked into a cradle at its center like a beating heart. The guitar rested beside it, strings already tuned to some invisible key only Sanderson could hear.

He looked up, eyes tired but steady. "It's ready," he said. "The mind-wipe reversal. I've cross-referenced everything Janelle helped us smuggle out. This should restore the core memories—the ones tied to the Resonator, the fractures, the bleed. It won't be perfect. Some fragments may stay lost. But the big ones? The ones that matter? They'll come back."

I met his gaze, the stakes suddenly razor-sharp in the quiet kitchen.

"You sure?"

Sanderson didn't blink. "It'll work. Now all we need is Vector."

The words had barely left his mouth when the sound of tires crunching on gravel cut through the morning stillness. A truck door slammed outside. Then another.

Ran's head snapped up. "That'll be Tara. I called her. Told her we needed Dad here—now. Explained enough to get her moving without spooking him too bad."

We all moved to the window. Tara was climbing out of her truck, her braid swinging, her face tight with the determination that came from knowing the ground was shifting under everyone's feet. Randle—Vector—stepped out of his own truck more slowly, limping slightly, his silver hair catching the sun. He looked every inch the rancher, but I could see the ghost of the man who'd once flown to the moon in a reverse-engineered saucer.

They came inside, boots thudding as Randle's eyes swept the room—Dusty, Ran, me—before landing on Sanderson. His brow furrowed, the way it does when someone knows they should recognize a face but the memory won't quite surface.

"Do I know you?" Randle asked, voice gruff but cautious.

Sanderson stood slowly, the weight of years pressing on him. "We worked together once, Vector. A long time ago. Sandia. The deep projects."

Randle's face hardened. "Name's Randle Roberts. And I don't remember you."

The room went still. The stakes hung there, heavy as a noose: a fractured world, a President selling apocalypse blueprints, a device that could either save us or break the last good man standing between us and the dark. I stepped forward, heart hammering, knowing every word I said next had to land perfectly.

"Randle," I said, keeping my voice steady, "we need you to trust us. What they took from you—what they erased—is the only thing that can stop what's coming. The Resonator. The fractures. The bleed that's already ripping the earth. Kermit built the machine to bring those memories back. But it only works if you let it."

Randle's eyes narrowed, suspicion and old ghosts warring across his face. Tara stood at his side, one hand on his arm, her own gaze flicking between Sanderson and me like she was ready to fight the whole damn desert if it came to that.

Randle said, nodding toward the device. "Let a man I don't know wipe something into my head?"

I held his stare, the weight of Aeterna's warning, Chrona's fractured city, and the widening rift pressing down on my shoulders like the whole sky.

"Yeah," I said. "Because if we don't get your memories back, the world's gonna tear itself apart. And you're the only one who can stop it."

Randle Roberts stood like a man carved from the same red rock as the Sangre de Cristos—shoulders squared, jaw set, eyes narrowed against the morning light slanting through the ranch house windows. The Echo Chamber sat on the table between us, its faint hum threading through the air like a warning no one wanted to hear. The crimson orb pulsed softly in its cradle, silver veins brightening and dimming in time with the relentless Taos Hum pressing against the walls.

"No," he said, the single word dropping like a stone into still water. "I'm not sitting in that damn chair. I don't know you, Sanderson. I don't remember any lab, and I'm sure as hell not letting you poke around inside my head on the word of a bunch of kids and a TV cowboy chasing ghosts."

The silence that followed was thick enough to choke on. Dusty's hand tightened on Ran's arm as he looked like he'd been slapped. Jake and Colley had arrived only minutes earlier, the chopper's dust still settling outside, and now they stood near the door, faces grim.

Jake stepped forward first, voice low and urgent, the Cryptid Hunter charm stripped away to raw necessity.

"Randle, listen to me. This isn't some rodeo grudge or family squabble. The fracture is widening. We've got confirmed reports—plasma bleed showing up in seismic data, lights over the desert that aren't ours, gravity glitches that are starting to affect instruments at Los Alamos."

"Bullshit!" Randle said,

"The Iron Order already has people on the ground. South African mercs. Qatari money. They bought the Resonator schematics from the President himself, and they're not waiting around. If that thing spins up fully, it won't just punch a few holes. It'll unravel the seams holding both our worlds together."

"I'm not buying your Cryptid Hunter drivel," Randle said.

"Then you aren't hearing me," Jake said. "Billions of lives. Yours. Tara's. Ran's. Mine. We have to do something to stop it."

Randle didn't flinch. "I've heard stories like that my whole life. Men in black suits, little green men, government boogeymen. I walked away from that world once. I'm not strolling back in."

Sanderson moved closer, his silver braid catching the light, voice softer but no less desperate.

"Vector… Randle. We worked side by side for years. You trusted me with things you never told another soul. We sat in that lab at 3 a.m. arguing about everything. You saved my life more than once when the early tests went sideways. I owe you. And right now, the only way I can repay that is by giving you back what they stole."

"I don't know you," Randle said.

"Yes, you do. The Echo Chamber won't hurt you. It'll just... retune what's missing. But without those memories, we're blind. We don't know how to shut down the Resonator. We don't know how to seal the fracture. And every hour we waste, the bleed gets worse."

Randle's eyes flicked to Sanderson, a glimmer of something—recognition? Suspicion?—crossing his face before the wall slammed back down.

"As I said, I don't remember you. And even if I did, I'm not risking what little peace I've got left on a machine built by the same people who broke me in the first place."

Tara stepped in, voice cracking with frustration and fear. "Dad, please. This isn't about the past. It's about right now. Ran and I—we're scared. The whole damn desert feels wrong."

"You starting in on me now?" he said, pointedly,

"The Hum is louder every night. If Buck and Kermit are telling the truth, we're all standing on the edge of something that could swallow everything. You raised us to face hard things. Don't turn away from this one."

Ran nodded, stepping up beside his sister. "Tara and I brought you here because I trust you, Dad. But I'm trusting them too. Dusty lost her best friend because of this. We almost lost our lives on that road. If there's even a chance this brings back what you need to stop it... You owe it to us. To Mom. To Grandma Lily."

CHAPTER 31

Randle's jaw worked, but he shook his head again, slower this time, the refusal settling like concrete.

"I said no. I've spent years rebuilding a life after they tried to erase me. I'm not handing them another shot at my mind. Not for stories about aliens and fractures and presidents selling the end of the world."

The tension in the room ratcheted tighter, the stakes sharpening with every heartbeat. Outside, the desert wind howled low across the sagebrush, carrying that relentless Hum as if the planet itself were screaming a countdown.

Every second we wasted was another second the fracture could widen, another second the Iron Order could move their pieces, another second closer to a bleed that wouldn't stop at New Mexico—it would swallow cities, skies, realities. I caught Tara's eye across the table. Her face was pale, but her gaze burned with desperate clarity. She jerked her head toward the door. I followed her out onto the porch, the morning sun already hot on the weathered wood.

"Buck," she said, voice low and urgent, grabbing my arm. "He won't budge. Not for us. Not for Kermit. Not even for Jake. But Lily… Grandma will know how to reach him. She's the only one who's ever been able to pull him back from the edge. If anyone can convince him this is worth the risk, it's her."

I glanced back through the window. Randle stood rigid, arms crossed, the weight of old scars and fresh fear locking him in place. The Echo Chamber sat on the table like a loaded gun no one wanted to fire.

Sanderson looked exhausted. Dusty and Ran looked terrified. The stakes weren't just high anymore—they were existential. If Randle walked away, we lost our best—maybe our only—shot at stopping the Resonator before the bleed tore both worlds apart.

I squeezed Tara's hand, my own pulse hammering. "Go," I said. "Find Lily. Bring her here as fast as you can."

Tara nodded, fierce and determined, then spun on her heel and ran for her truck. Dust kicked up behind her as she tore out of the yard, racing against a clock none of us could see but all of us could feel ticking down in the bones of the earth.

I stood on the porch a moment longer, the Taos Hum rising louder in my ears, the crimson orb warm and insistent like a living warning. Inside, voices rose again—pleading, arguing, the sound of desperate people staring into the abyss.

Dust boiled up behind the truck as Tara tore out of the yard, heading for the Double Moon Ranch and the only person on God's green earth who might still reach the man her father had become.

Inside, the tension crackled like dry lightning. Randle was already turning toward the door, his limp more pronounced with anger, his boots thudding heavily on the floorboards.

"I've heard enough," he said with a growl.

Jake put a hand up. "Wait," he said.

"Wait, hell! You people can chase your ghosts, your fractures, and your damn alien fairy tales. I'm going home."

"Randle, wait," I said.

Dusty moved faster, sliding between us as smooth as a barrel racer cutting a cloverleaf, her turquoise shirt brushing Randle's arm as she squeezed it with both hands. Her smile was bright, almost reverent, the kind that could charm a bronc mid-buck.

"You can't leave yet," she said, voice warm and low, the hero-worship thick as mescal. "Not before I get to tell you how much your riding meant to a little girl growing up in a horse trailer. I had your poster on the wall, right next to my saddle. That ride in '82 at the Rodeo de Santa Fe? The one where you stayed on that big black devil for the full eight when everybody else was eating dirt? I watched the tape so many times I wore it out. You were magic out there. Pure magic."

Randle paused, one hand still on the doorframe. A flicker of the old pride crossed his face, softening the hard lines around his mouth. Dusty didn't let the moment slip. She reached for the bottle of mescal on the table, poured two healthy shots, and pressed one into his hand, her fingers lingering just long enough to make it feel like a shared secret.

"Come on," she coaxed, clinking her glass against his. "One for the old days. Then you can go if you still want to. But I gotta hear you tell it yourself. What was it like, staring down that bronc when the whole arena was holding its breath?"

Randle hesitated, then tossed the shot back. The mescal burned down, and something in his shoulders eased a fraction. Dusty poured another before he could set the glass down, her laugh light and easy, pulling him back toward the table like a lasso made of nostalgia and liquor.

Ran caught on quick, dragging a chair over while Dusty kept the conversation moving—stories of Randle's legendary rides, the way he'd once stared down death in the arena the same way he was staring it down now.

Shot after shot went down, Dusty never letting his glass stay empty, her voice weaving admiration and gentle pressure until Randle was smiling again, then laughing, then singing along in a half-drunk baritone when Dusty started an old rodeo drinking song she'd learned on the circuit.

"Whiskey for my men, and beer for my horses..."

Randle's voice joined hers, off-key but full-throated, the anger bleeding out of him with every chorus. The room filled with their voices and the clink of glasses, the Taos Hum outside rising in eerie counterpoint, as if the desert itself were singing along.

We kept him there that way—laughing, drinking, singing—until the sound of tires on gravel cut through the noise. Tara's truck skidded to a stop outside. The door opened, and Lily stepped in.

She was dressed in full ceremonial regalia, the kind that made the air itself feel heavier. A long buckskin dress fringed with tiny silver conchos and dyed porcupine quills swayed around her ankles.

A heavy turquoise-and-silver squash-blossom necklace rested against her chest, catching the light like captured stars. Her silver hair was braided with eagle feathers and red yarn, and across her shoulders lay a woven shawl patterned with ancient spirals and thunderbirds that seemed to move when the light hit them just right.

In her hands, she carried a small bundle of sage and a leather pouch that smelled of sweetgrass and something older, something that made the skin prickle.

Lily didn't speak at first. She simply walked to the center of the room, her presence pulling every eye like a magnet. The Hum outside grew louder, pressing against the windows as if the land itself approved.

Without a word, she tossed Ran a small tom-tom drum. He caught it, surprised, but didn't question. Tara moved quickly, turning on the boombox. The opening strains of Sanderson's cosmic guitar filled the room—haunting, resonant, the same eerie notes that had once pulled Aeterna from the stars.

Tara and Dusty moved as one, closing curtains, killing lights, lighting ceremonial candles that flickered with blue-white flames. Shadows danced across the walls, turning the ranch house into something ancient and sacred. Lily began to move.

She danced with the deliberate grace of someone who had walked between worlds before. Her feet traced patterns on the floorboards that mirrored the petroglyphs carved into desert stone—spirals, thunderbirds, the jagged lines of a fracture between realities.

Her voice rose in a low Diné chant, words that rolled like distant thunder and tasted of sage smoke and starlight. The tom-tom joined in, Ran's hands finding the rhythm instinctively, the cosmic guitar weaving through it all like a living thread.

Randle stood frozen at first, confusion clouding his face. Then anger flared hot and sharp.

"What the hell is this? Some kind of Navajo voodoo? I told you I'm not—"

But the words died as the ceremony deepened. Lily's chant grew richer, layered with harmonics that seemed to answer the guitar's strange melody. The candles flickered in time with the drum, casting long shadows that moved like living things across the walls.

The air grew thick, charged, the Taos Hum now a physical presence that vibrated in the bones. Randle's anger faltered. His shoulders sagged. His eyes, once hard with refusal, began to glaze, drawn into the hypnotic swirl of sound and movement and ancient power.

Lily's dance intensified, her regalia whispering with every step, the eagle feathers trembling as if stirred by an unseen wind. Her chant rose and fell, pulling something deep from Randle's buried past—memories locked behind walls the Echo Chamber had built. He swayed now, eyes half-lidded, the fight draining out of him like water from a cracked vessel.

Finally, Lily slowed. She turned toward Sanderson, her dark eyes gleaming with otherworldly certainty. One hand lifted, motioning him forward. The gesture was simple, commanding, impossible to refuse.

Sanderson moved without hesitation. He lifted the portable Echo Chamber, its filaments glowing softly, and stepped toward Randle. The old rancher didn't protest. He simply sat in the chair, head bowed, as if the ceremony had already unlocked the door he'd been guarding for years.

The room held its breath. The cosmic guitar played on, the drum pulsed, the candles burned low, and outside the desert waited—its fractures widening, its secrets stirring, the fate of two worlds balanced on the edge of one man's restored memory.

Lily's voice dropped to a final note as Sanderson placed the helmet on Randle's head. The unwiping began. The room had become a temple of trembling light and sound. Candles flickered with blue-white flames that seemed to breathe in time with Lily's chant. The cosmic guitar poured its otherworldly melody through the boombox, its notes bending and stretching like light through a fractured lens.

Ran's hands moved steadily over the tom-tom, the drum's heartbeat ancient and insistent. Shadows danced across the adobe walls in patterns that looked too deliberate to be random—spirals, thunderbirds, and jagged lines that mirrored the widening fracture tearing at the edges of reality itself.

Randle sat in the chair, the portable Echo Chamber resting on the table beside him like a sleeping predator. Its copper filaments glowed, humming in harmony with the guitar. The crimson orb pulsed, silver veins brightening and dimming like an alien heart.

Everyone watched in tense silence as Sanderson worked. His fingers moved with surgical precision over the dials and nodes, adjusting frequencies only he could hear. His face told the story no one wanted to hear: a slight frown at first, then a deeper crease between his brows. He shook his head once, almost imperceptibly, and adjusted another setting. The guitar's notes seemed to strain, as if fighting to hold the correct key against an unseen opposing force.

My stomach tightened. Dusty's hand found Ran's and squeezed hard. Tara stood rigid beside Lily, her eyes never leaving her father. Jake and Colley remained near the door, faces grim, the weight of two worlds pressing down on the small ranch house.

Sanderson's shoulders tensed as he made another micro-adjustment. The orb flared brighter for a moment, then dimmed. He shook his head again, muttering something under his breath that sounded like a prayer and a curse at the same time.

Then, his expression changed. The frown softened. His eyes widened slightly. A relieved smile tugged at the corner of his mouth as he looked up at the anxious faces surrounding him and gave a decisive thumbs-up. The room exhaled as one.

Randle's eyes rolled back for a moment, then fluttered. He sagged in the chair, groggy, as if waking from a disorienting dream. His head lolled, then steadied. When his gaze finally focused and landed on Sanderson, something shifted deep behind his eyes—recognition, memory, decades of buried truth rushing back like a dam breaking.

A genuine grin spread across Randle's weathered face, cracking years of guarded distance.

"Kermit, you old dog," he said, voice thick but warm with astonishment. "I never thought I'd ever see you again."

Sanderson let out a shaky laugh, relief flooding his features. "Same here, Vector. Same here."

The room erupted in smiles and quiet cheers. Tension that had coiled like a rattlesnake finally released. Ran, Tara, and Dusty rushed to Lily, wrapping her in tight hugs.

"You did it, Grandma," Tara whispered fiercely, tears glistening in her eyes. "You were remarkable. I've never seen anything like that."

Ran nodded, still holding the tom-tom. "That chant... the way you moved. It was like the desert itself was listening."

Dusty squeezed Lily's hand. "You brought him back. You really brought him back."

Lily accepted the praise with quiet dignity, her eagle feathers trembling as she nodded.

"The old ways still have power when the need is great enough."

Jake stepped forward, eyes bright, the Cryptid Hunter grin returning in full force. He reached for the bottle of mescal on the table and poured generous celebratory shots into waiting glasses, the liquid catching the candlelight like liquid gold.

"To Lily, to old friends, and to whatever the hell we just pulled off."

Randle took a glass, still groggy but clearly coming back to himself, confusion and wonder warring across his face.

"What the hell just happened?" he asked, staring at the glass, then at the strange device beside him, then at Sanderson.

Jake clinked his own glass gently against Randle's and raised it.

"Drink up," he said, voice warm but edged with the gravity of what lay ahead. "Then I'll explain everything. Because, my friend, you just stepped back into a war that's bigger than any of us realized—and we're going to need every memory you've got to win it."

Randle took a slow sip, the mescal burning down as the cosmic guitar continued its haunting strains in the background. The candles flickered as the Taos Hum pressed against the windows like an impatient god.

CHAPTER 32

I waited in the back of the room, the weight of everything pressing down on my chest like a saddle cinched too tight. Jake was finishing his explanation, his voice steady yet edged with urgency that comes when the stakes aren't just lives but entire worlds.

The cosmic guitar had gone quiet, but its echo still lingered in the air, mixing with the low pulse of the Taos Hum that never really left us. Randle was still groggy from the procedure, but his eyes were clearing fast. The old fire was coming back.

He listened without interrupting, his face hardening as Jake laid out the fracture, the bleed, the Iron Order, and the President's betrayal. When Jake finally stopped, Randle let out a long breath and rubbed his jaw.

"I understand," he said quietly. His voice was rough, but steel was in it now. "I remember enough. More than enough. The Resonator… the way it tears holes between what should and shouldn't be. I designed the countermeasures. I hid everything I knew—every blueprint, every frequency map, every warning about what happens if the bleed gets too wide, and entrusted the whole trove to Lily. She's the only one who knows where it is."

The room went still. All eyes turned toward Lily.

She was still standing in the center of the space, her ceremonial regalia glowing softly in the candlelight, eagle feathers trembling faintly. For a moment, she looked every bit the powerful medicine woman who had just pulled Randle back from the edge of forgetting. Then her hand rose slowly to her chest. Her eyes closed. Her breathing hitched once, sharp and ragged.

"Grandma?" Tara said.

Lily's knees buckled and she crumpled forward with a soft gasp, clutching at her heart. The tom-tom slipped from Ran's hands and hit the floor with a dull thud.

Chaos erupted.

"Lily!" Tara cried, rushing forward.

Dusty was already on her knees beside the fallen woman, checking for a pulse. Ran dropped down next to them, his face pale with terror. Sanderson froze, one hand still on the Echo Chamber. Jake's voice cut through the panic like a whip.

"Colley! Fire up the chopper—now! We need to get her to a hospital!"

I moved without thinking, pushing through the sudden knot of bodies to reach Tara. She was crying openly now, tears cutting tracks down her cheeks as she cradled her grandmother's head in her lap. Lily's face was ashen, her breathing shallow and labored. I knelt beside Tara and wrapped an arm around her shoulders, pulling her close. She trembled against me, her usual fire momentarily drowned in raw fear.

"She's strong," I said. "She just pulled your dad back from the brink. She'll fight this, too."

Tara's hand found mine and squeezed hard enough to hurt.

"She has to," she choked out. "She can't leave us like this. Not now."

I looked up at Jake. "I know where the stash is," I said, the words coming out faster than I could weigh them.

"Lily told Tara and me. It's in Chaco Canyon, hidden in an old cliff dwelling marked by a specific petroglyph—the first meeting between the ancients and the Sky People. If someone will lend me keys, I'll go right now. We need those plans before the fracture gets any worse."

Tara lifted her head, tears streaming, but her jaw setting with sudden resolve. She looked at her brother.

"Ran, you stay with her. Take care of Grandma. Buck and I are going to Chaco Canyon."

Ran's eyes widened in disbelief. "What if she dies before you get back?"

Tara's voice cracked like a whip, fierce and unyielding even through the tears. "Don't lay that guilt on me, Ran Roberts. This is exactly what she would have wanted me to do. You stay here and fight for her. Don't you dare let her die without me having a chance to say goodbye."

The room felt like it was holding its breath, Lily's shallow breathing the only sound breaking the heavy silence. Jake nodded.

"Go," he said. "We'll get Lily stabilized and meet you when we can. Bring back whatever's in that trove. Everything depends on it now."

I helped Tara to her feet. Her hand stayed locked in mine as we moved toward the door, the weight of two fractured worlds riding on our shoulders. Behind us, Colley's chopper was already spinning up outside, its rotors whipping the desert air into a frenzy. Ran knelt beside his grandmother, whispering urgent words while Dusty kept pressure on her chest. Sanderson stood ready with the Echo Chamber, as if it might somehow help.

Tara and I stepped out into the cold morning light. The Sangre de Cristos loomed in the distance, snow-capped and indifferent. I squeezed her hand.

"Let's ride," I said.

The highway stretched out ahead of us like a gray ribbon unspooled across the desert, empty for miles in every direction. Tara's old truck rattled and growled under us, the engine working hard as we pushed north toward Chaco Canyon.

The Sangre de Cristos had fallen behind us hours ago, and now there was nothing but sagebrush, red rock, and a sky so blue it hurt to look at. My heart was still hammering from the ranch house, from watching Lily clutch her chest and drop, from the look on Tara's face when she said we were going anyway.

Tara's hands were white-knuckled on the wheel. She hadn't said much since we left, but every now and then her eyes flicked to the rearview mirror like she expected the devil himself to be back there.

Then two black SUVs appeared behind us, coming out of

nowhere, cresting a gentle rise in the road like sharks cresting a wave. Tinted windows, no plates. They closed the distance quickly.

"Buck," Tara said.

"I see them."

She punched the gas. The old Ford surged forward, but it was like whipping a tired horse—the truck had heart, but it didn't have legs for this. The SUVs matched our speed without even trying. One pulled up on our left, the other stayed tight on our tail.

The passenger window of the lead SUV slid down. Sunlight glinted off the barrel of a rifle.

"Down!" I said.

Bullets punched through the rear window with sharp cracks. Glass exploded inward, showering the cab like shrapnel. Tara screamed, but kept her foot nailed to the floor. More rounds stitched across the tailgate, pinging off metal and tearing through the bed. Tara's voice was raw.

"This old truck's for work and not a racehorse!"

"Keep your foot on the gas!" I said. "Don't let off for anything!"

I reached up and yanked the shotgun free from the window rack, my hands steady even as my pulse jackhammered in my ears.

"Glove box—shells!" Tara said.

She fumbled one-handed, popped the latch, and shoved a box of 00 buckshot into my lap. I racked a round, leaned out the shattered passenger window, and braced against the door frame.

Wind whipped my face, stinging with grit and speed. The trailing SUV was right there, maybe thirty yards back, its driver grinning behind the wheel like this was sport.

I aimed low and squeezed the trigger. The shotgun roared, the recoil slamming into my shoulder like a mule kick. The SUV's front tire disintegrated in a spray of rubber and sparks. The vehicle fishtailed wildly, then flipped hard, rolling end over end in a screaming cloud of dust and metal. It slammed into the ditch and burst into flames with a deep whump.

One down.

The second SUV was already pulling alongside us on the left, its passenger leaning out with an automatic rifle. Bullets hammered the driver's side door. More glass exploded. Tara ducked, swearing, but never lifted her foot. A round punched through the windshield between us, leaving a spiderweb crack the size of my fist.

I racked another shell, swung the barrel left, and fired again. This time, the shot caught the front fender and blew out the tire. The SUV swerved violently but kept coming, limping on the rim, sparks flying like a Fourth of July sparkler from hell.

Up ahead, the road was no longer empty. Three more black SUVs sat nose-to-nose, blocking both lanes like a steel wall. Men in tactical gear stood behind them, rifles raised.

"Oh, shit!" Tara said.

Instead of slowing down, she yanked the wheel hard right, sending us bouncing off the pavement and into the open desert. The truck slammed through sagebrush and over rocks, the suspension bottoming out with bone-jarring crashes. I grabbed the oh-shit handle with one hand and the shotgun with the other, trying to keep from being thrown through the roof.

We zigzagged wildly, Tara driving like a woman possessed, dodging arroyos and boulders, the truck fishtailing in the loose sand. Bullets zipped past us, kicking up dirt geysers. One round punched through the rear cab, missing my head by inches. Another shattered the side mirror in a spray of plastic and glass.

Tara was crying and shouting at the same time. "Hang on, Buck! Just hang on!"

The truck hit a deep wash and went airborne for a sickening second. We slammed down hard, the frame groaning as if it were about to snap in half. She fought the wheel, tires spinning, and for one terrifying moment, we were sliding sideways, completely out of control.

Then we spun out and slammed to a stop in a cloud of dust and grit, the motor coughing to a rattle. Silence—except for our ragged breathing and the roar of rapidly approaching engines.

Tara's hand found mine across the console and squeezed hard enough to bruise. Her eyes were wide, terrified, but fierce. I racked another round into the shotgun, the metallic clack loud in the sudden quiet.

More black SUVs were closing in from three directions now, kicking up rooster tails of dust. Men poured out, rifles up, moving in tight formation. We were surrounded. Out of road. Out of time.

Tara's voice cracked. "Buck..."

I chambered the shell and raised the shotgun, heart slamming against my ribs.

"Stay low. When they get close enough, we make them pay for every step."

This was it. The end of the line. I could already see the mercs tightening the noose, moving in for the kill.

Then the sky lit up and a searing laser beam lanced down from above—silent, impossibly precise. It struck the lead SUV dead center. The vehicle erupted in a fireball that rolled across the desert floor like a miniature sun.

Before the echo of the explosion faded, another beam took out the second SUV, then the third. One by one, the black vehicles became blazing wrecks, metal twisting and popping as the lasers carved through them with surgical fury.

I lowered the shotgun, staring upward through the shattered windshield. A faint silver disc hovered high above us, almost invisible against the bright sky except for the occasional glint of reflected sunlight.

I let out a shaky breath and felt a grin tug at my lips despite everything.

"Aeterna and Zephyrion," I said, voice rough with relief and gratitude. "Thank you."

The saucer hung there for a moment longer, then vanished upward in a streak of silent light, leaving only the burning hulks and the smell of scorched metal on the desert wind.

Tara looked at me, tears still wet on her cheeks, but a fierce smile breaking through.

"We're alive," she said.

I squeezed her hand. "Yeah," I said. "And still have a canyon to reach."

The engine coughed once, then turned over. We were moving again—battered, shot full of holes, but still breathing.

CHAPTER 33

We rolled into the outskirts of Chaco Canyon long after the sun had bled out behind the western mesas. The sky was a deep indigo, punctured by so many stars it looked like someone had taken a handful of diamonds and scattered them across black velvet.

The truck's headlights cut weak yellow tunnels through the dust, but even they felt swallowed by the vastness of the place. Chaco wasn't just land—it was memory, older than any of us, older than the Hum that still throbbed in my bones like a second heartbeat.

Tara killed the engine when the dirt road finally turned into nothing but rocks and arroyos. The silence that rushed in was heavier than it should have been. No crickets. No wind, like the canyon itself was breathing through stone.

"Looks like we walk the rest of the way," she said.

"We were running on fumes," I said.

She grinned and said, "With all the holes and broken glass, I'm surprised the old girl's running at all."

"Please tell me you have a spare can of gas in the truckbed," I said.

"I do, and it's damn lucky a stray bullet didn't hit it."

"Amen to that. Where is everybody?" I asked.

"They closed most of the park to tourists years ago," Tara said as she unbuckled her seatbelt. "Too many people disrespecting the ruins. Rangers patrol the main roads at night."

She reached behind the seat and pulled out two worn day packs, handing me one. Inside were canteens, a couple of protein bars, a flashlight, and a small first-aid kit. She gave me a half-smile that didn't quite reach her eyes.

"Never know when you're going to get stranded miles from nowhere."

I slung the pack over my shoulder, feeling the weight of the shotgun still riding across my back, and started walking. The ancient paths were faint, worn into the desert floor by feet that had passed this way a thousand years before Columbus ever set sail. Starlight and the thin sliver of a crescent moon were the only lights we had.

Tara moved ahead of me with the sure-footed grace of someone who'd walked these trails in her dreams. I kept close, my boots crunching softly on sand and broken pottery shards that glinted like tiny bones under the stars.

"You know where you're going?" I asked after a while, my voice sounding too loud in the stillness.

Tara didn't turn around. "Grandmother's spirit will guide us."

Her words should have sounded comforting. Instead, they sent a shiver down my spine. We walked deeper into the canyon, and the walls where thousands of people once lived rose around us like the ribs of some enormous creature. The air grew cooler, heavier, carrying the faint scent of sage and something sweeter—sweetgrass, maybe, or the ghost of old fires.

The Hum grew louder, no longer just in my head but in the ground itself, vibrating up through my boots until my teeth ached. Then the coyotes started. At first, it was just one, far off, a lonely howl that rose and fell like a question. Another answered. Then another. Their voices layered together until the night felt alive with them—close, then far, then right beside us.

I caught movement out of the corner of my eye: sleek gray shapes slipping between boulders, eyes reflecting starlight like tiny moons. They weren't hunting us. They were watching. Guiding. Or warning.

Night birds joined in—owls mostly, their calls soft and hollow, like whispers from another room. But the longer we walked, the stranger the sounds became. The coyote howls stretched and warped, turning into something almost human—low chants, distant laughter, the murmur of voices speaking in languages I didn't know but somehow understood in my bones. Ancestral tongues. Old prayers. More warnings.

Tara slowed. Her breathing had grown shallow. "Buck... do you hear that?"

I did. The voices were clearer now, swirling around us like smoke and speaking of sky people and broken stars, of a great wound in the earth that bled light and shadow.

I saw movement again—not coyotes this time, but taller shapes, translucent figures walking the rim of the canyon above us. Warriors in feather headdresses. Women carrying glowing orbs. Children laughing silently as they ran along paths that no longer existed.

Mirages. Had to be.

I blinked hard and looked down at my canteen. My throat was raw. I unscrewed the cap and took a long pull.

Dirt. Thick, dry, choking dirt filled my mouth. I spat it out, coughing, wiping my lips with the back of my hand. The canteen slipped from my fingers and hit the ground, spilling nothing but sand across the stones. Tara screamed.

A scorpion—fat, black, and glistening—crawled up her arm, its tail arched high and ready. She flailed, slapping at it wildly. The creature flew off into the darkness, but Tara kept slapping at her skin, eyes wide with terror.

"It was on me—it was on me!"

I grabbed her shoulders, pulling her close. "It's gone. Breathe. It's gone."

She was shaking. So was I. The voices were louder now, circling us, laughing softly. The canyon walls seemed to breathe, expanding and contracting in time with the Hum.

Stars wheeled overhead in impossible patterns, forming faces I almost recognized—Elena, Lily, Aeterna—before dissolving back into cold pinpricks of light.

I looked at Tara. Her eyes were huge, pupils blown wide.

"Are we losing our minds?" she said.

"I don't know," I said, my voice cracking.

"This place is haunted," she said.

She managed a grin when I said, "What was your first clue?"

We kept walking, hand in hand now, the ancient paths pulling us deeper into the canyon's heart. The voices followed. So did the scorpions. And the dirt in our canteens. And the growing certainty that we might never find our way back out.

The trail up the canyon wall felt like it had been waiting for us since the first footsteps carved it into the rock a thousand years ago. Each worn step pulled at my boots like it knew exactly where we needed to go, and the higher we climbed, the more the world below shrank into a painting nobody would believe—red mesas, piñon scrub, and that endless sky that made you feel small in the best and worst ways.

Tara moved ahead of me, sure-footed as a mountain goat, her braid swinging like a pendulum counting down to something we couldn't name yet.

Petroglyphs started showing up on the rock faces—spirals, handprints, figures that looked half-human and half-star. Signs of old habitation too: broken pottery shards glinting in the sun, faint outlines of rooms tucked into the cliff.

Then we rounded a bend and there it was, the first Great House, perched like it had grown straight out of the canyon wall. Massive, multi-storied, the kind of place that made you wonder how many voices had once echoed inside it.

Tara stopped, breathing a little hard, and pointed. "That's what they lived in. Ancestral Puebloans. Grandma always called them that. Used to be called Anasazi, but… same people, different name."

I nodded, wiping sweat from my eyes. "Same people, different name. Sounds about right for everything out here lately."

We kept climbing. The trail narrowed, the rock got steeper, and darkness draped us like it had a personal grudge. When the path finally dead-ended at a blank cliff face, I planted my hands on my hips and looked up.

"Where the hell do we go from here?"

Tara didn't answer right away. She just scanned the stone, then pointed higher up.

"There. That's the petroglyph Grandma described."

I followed her finger and saw it—a spiral carved deep into the rock, the lines still sharp after all this time. It looked alive, like it was turning slow under the moonlight.

The wooden ladders that once reached it were long gone, rotted to nothing but splinters and memory. Only hand and toeholds remained—small, precise notches cut into the stone, worn smooth by countless feet and hands.

Tara went first, moving like she'd done this a hundred times in her dreams. I followed, fingers finding the grooves, boots scraping for purchase. My heart hammered harder with every foot we rose. One slip and we'd be part of the canyon floor forever.

We crawled through the narrow entrance at the top, scraping elbows and knees on the rock. Inside, the air was cooler, musty, thick with the smell of ancient dust and something alive—bat guano, sharp and earthy. Tara clicked on her flashlight.

The beam cut through the dark and lit up a space bigger than I expected: a cave-like dwelling with smooth walls and, deeper in, a perfectly preserved kiva, its circular fire pit still blackened from fires lit centuries ago.

"Damn," she said. "It's exactly like Grandma said."

We proceeded slowly, careful not to disturb anything that didn't want disturbing. Bones lay scattered in the corners—small animal, maybe some human—and the floor crunched under our boots with years of dried guano.

We searched every dark cranny, every shadowed ledge, flashlights sweeping like we were looking for ghosts that might actually answer back. Tara found it first. A large pack, heavy and weathered, tucked deep in a crevice behind a fallen stone.

She dragged it out, dust puffing up around her like a sigh from the earth itself. She unzipped it, pawed through old papers and what looked like diagrams, and her face lit up in the flashlight beam.

"Found it," she said, voice hushed with awe. "Dad's documents."

I knelt beside her, my heart still pounding from the climb and the thumps in my chest. The papers were yellowed, covered in tight handwriting, with sketches of strange machines, star charts, and symbols that looked a lot like the petroglyphs outside.

Whatever this was, it felt heavy—important in a way that made the hair on my arms stand up. Before either of us could say another word, the air changed. Not just cooler—thicker.

A spectral light bloomed from the center of the kiva, pale blue-white at first, then deepening to a warm gold. It filled the whole chamber like dawn breaking underground, chasing every shadow into the corners until there was nowhere left to hide.

A figure took shape inside the light. He was tall, broad-shouldered, dressed in what looked like layered robes of woven fiber and hide, the kind you see in old pueblo drawings.

His skin was the color of sun-baked clay, his hair long and black, streaked with silver, braided with feathers and bits of turquoise. His eyes were dark and knowing, the kind that had seen empires rise and fall and still had room for two lost cowpokes crawling around in his ancestors' house.

He looked straight at us—at me, at Tara—and I felt it like a hand on my shoulder. He knew us. Not our names, maybe, but who we were, why we were here, what we carried. His voice didn't come from his mouth. It came from everywhere at once, inside my head and inside the stone, calm and deep as the canyon itself.

"You carry the weight of two worlds now," he said. The words weren't English, but I understood them anyway. "The fracture grows. The machine that tears the sky will tear the earth if it is not silenced."

"Who are you?" Tara asked.

"Hototo," the spirit said. "Your father holds the song that can mend the tear, but only if he remembers the notes. Take what you have found. Guard it with your lives. The Sky People watch, but they cannot mend what your people have broken. That burden is yours."

He lifted one hand, palm out, and the light around him pulsed once, bright enough that I had to squint.

Hototo nodded when Tara said, "You know my father?"

"And you. We are all connected," he said. "The bleed has begun. If the machine sings again, the song will become a scream, and the scream will become silence. Go now. The canyon remembers kindness… but it also remembers those who fail."

The light held for another heartbeat, then folded in on itself, shrinking back into the kiva until only the faint glow of the flashlight remained.

The chamber felt emptier than before, like something vital had just stepped out the back door. Tara's hand found mine in the dark. Her fingers were cold and steady.

"Did you…?" she started.

"Yeah," I said, my voice rough. "I saw him."

We looked at each other for a long second, the weight of the pack between us heavier than it had been a minute ago.

"Now what?" she asked.

"Get the hell out of here before the canyon decides we've overstayed our welcome."

CHAPTER 34

I shouldered the pack as we crawled back out through the entrance, the handholds growing colder on the way down, the desert wind waiting for us like an old friend who'd been listening the whole time.

The climb back to the trail seemed longer. The petroglyphs watched us pass. The Great House stood silent behind us. And somewhere far above, the stars kept turning, waiting to see if we'd be the ones to break the silence… or mend it. I didn't know which way it would go.

The climb down the canyon wall felt twice as long as the climb up, every handhold and toehold slick with the sweat of relief and the weight of what we'd just carried out of that cave.

The pack with Vector's documents rode heavily on my shoulder, like it knew it was more trouble than it was worth. Tara moved ahead of me, quiet now, the kind of quiet that comes after you've looked something ancient in the eye and it looked right back.

We hit the bottom trail and followed it out to where we'd left her old Ford truck. The moon and stars seemed to have dipped lower, painting the canyon walls in faded reds and golds, and the air still carried that electric hum that never quite left this place.

I was already thinking about gas, about rangers, about how the hell we were going to explain any of this without sounding like we'd lost our minds. Then we saw the truck and Tara stopped dead.

"What the hell?" I said.

The spare gas can we'd left in the bed was overturned, lid off, lying on its side like it had been kicked. A dark stain spread across the dirt beneath it, the sharp smell of evaporated gasoline still hanging in the air. Every last drop was gone. Tara walked over and kicked the empty can. It rolled once and stopped.

"What now?" she said.

I ran a hand through my hair and let out a long breath. "Sleep in the truck and wait for the park rangers to find us. Maybe we can talk them into giving us some gas to get back to Shadow Ranch instead of hauling us to jail."

She looked at me like I'd suggested we roast marshmallows over a fire built from the documents. But she didn't argue. We climbed into the cab, the doors creaking like old bones. The truck smelled of dust, sweat, and the faint trace of her perfume. I leaned the seat back as far as it would go and tried to get comfortable.

Tara sat there for a long minute, staring out at the darkening canyon. Then she turned toward me, her fingers finding the top button of her blouse and slipping it open, slow and deliberate.

Another button followed, the fabric parting just enough to show the smooth curve of her skin and the edge of a simple white bra. She took my hand—warm, a little callused from the climb—and guided it underneath, pressing my palm against the soft swell of her breast. Her heart was beating fast.

"I used to love to go truck parking with my boyfriend," she said, voice low and husky, a half-smile playing on her lips. "No use letting our time here go to waste."

"Boyfriend, huh?" I said, my own voice rougher than I meant it to be.

She leaned in, her breath warm against my neck.

"Shut up and kiss me, cowboy."

The rest of the world—the documents, the spirit's warning, the rangers, the whole damn fracture in reality—faded for a little while. There was just the cab of the truck, the desert night pressing in around us, and Tara's hands and mouth and the way she moved like she was trying to outrun every fear we'd carried out of that cave.

Later—how much later I couldn't say—we were tangled together in the cramped space, half-dressed and breathing hard, her head on my chest and my arm around her. The stars had come out thick overhead, and the only sound was the soft tick of our slowing heartbeats. Sleep pulled at me like a strong current. I let it take me.

When a jolt hit the truck like something had slammed into the frame, I snapped awake, heart hammering. Tara bolted upright beside me, eyes wide.

"What the hell!" she said, already yanking her jeans up and fumbling with the buttons of her blouse.

I was doing the same, shirt half-on, boots still somewhere on the floorboard. The cab was filled with a brilliant white light pouring down from above, so bright it washed out the stars and painted everything in glowing edges.

"The beam," I said. "Aeterna's ship has us."

Tara froze for half a second, blouse still open, staring up through the shattered windshield. The light grew stronger, the familiar weightless pull already starting in my stomach.

The beam lifted us—truck and all—smooth and silent, the desert dropping away beneath us like a painting someone had rolled up and put away. One moment, we were parked in the middle of nowhere; the next, we were rising fast, the canyon walls shrinking to nothing, the whole high desert spreading out below us like a map nobody was meant to see.

Tara's fingers stayed locked in mine the whole way up. Neither of us said a word. There was nothing left to say as the saucer swallowed us whole.

When the light finally faded and the beam set us down again, we were back at Shadow Ranch. The truck sat crooked in the yard, still dented and shot full of holes, but whole. The ranch house lights were on, warm and ordinary against the night. Pard was barking somewhere inside, excited and confused at once.

Tara looked over at me, blouse still half-buttoned, hair a mess, eyes shining with something between terror and wonder.

"Next time we go parking," she said, voice shaky but trying

for a smile, "let's pick somewhere without aliens."

I laughed once, short and raw, and pulled her in for a quick kiss.

"Deal," I said.

We climbed out of the truck together, the pack with Vector's documents still slung over my shoulder, the weight of two worlds still riding with us. We pushed through the door of the ranch house, the pack with Vector's documents slung heavy over my shoulder like it carried the weight of every bad decision we'd made since leaving Tulsa.

Tara was right behind me, still buttoning the last couple of buttons on her blouse, her hair a wild mess from the ride and everything that followed. The place smelled of coffee, mescal, and too many worried men who swarmed us the second we stepped inside. Jake was first, grabbing my arm as if I might disappear.

"Thank Christ. We were about to send out a search party."

Colley was right behind him, eyes wide. Vector—Randle—stood at the table, face pale but steady. Sanderson hovered nearby, and then I saw him: Yuri Gagarin, sitting calm as you please in one of the wooden chairs, wearing a plain gray shirt and looking exactly like the old photos, except alive and breathing and staring right at us with those famous haunted eyes.

They all started talking at once.

"Did you get them?" Jake asked. "The documents—did you find the stash?"

Vector cut in, voice rough. Sanderson was already reaching for the pack.

"Let me see."

I didn't waste time, swinging the pack onto the table and dumping its contents in a messy pile—yellowed papers, folded diagrams, and notebooks filled with tight handwriting and strange sketches of machines that looked like they belonged on another planet.

Yuri, Vector, and Sanderson descended on it like starving coyotes on fresh meat. Their hands moved fast, sorting, scanning, muttering to each other in low voices.

Sanderson's eyes lit up when he found a particular schematic. Vector's face went tight with recognition. Jake stepped back from the frenzy and clapped a hand on my shoulder, then Tara's. His usual movie-star grin was there, but it was tired around the edges.

"I was worried about you two," he said. "Real worried. Glad you made it back in one piece."

I gave a short laugh. "We had a little help."

Tara shot me a quick look, but she didn't elaborate. Neither did I. Some things were still too fresh to put into words.

Colley, though, had zero chill left. He was staring at Yuri like a kid who'd just met his hero at the county fair. He stepped forward, practically vibrating, and stuck out his hand.

"Colley Hornbeck," he said, voice cracking a little. "I can't believe I'm standing here shaking hands with Yuri Gagarin. The first man in space. The guy who orbited the Earth while the rest of us were still figuring out how to get a satellite up there."

Yuri smiled, shook Colley's hand, and said, "Pleased," in a Dr. Zhivago accent.

Colley continued. "Your flight in Vostok 1—April 12, 1961—you changed everything. And then the stories about the moon mission, the dimensional stuff… hell, I've read every declassified scrap I could find."

Yuri kept shaking Colley's hand with an almost regal smile. His accent was thick, rolling, the kind that made every word sound like it had weight.

"Still classified," he said simply.

Colley let out a delighted laugh, as if he'd just won the lottery. He rattled off more exploits—Gagarin's training, the flight details, the way the whole world held its breath—while Yuri listened with that quiet half-smile.

I couldn't help but grin. Colley was a grown man, a battle-hardened pilot, and right now he sounded like a starstruck teenager. I caught Yuri's eye and couldn't resist.

"So… did you really fly to the moon with an alien pilot?"

Yuri's smile widened just a fraction. He gave the same answer, same accent, same calm delivery.

"Vector's a born liar. Don't believe a word he says."

Jake cleared his throat, pulling us back to the moment. He looked at Tara, his expression softening.

"Your grandmother's stable," he said. "She's going to survive. They've got her in a hospital in Santa Fe. Heart episode, but the doctors say she's tough as nails. She's resting now."

Tara let out a shaky breath, some of the tension draining from her shoulders.

"I need gas for my truck. I have to get to the hospital. I have to see her."

Jake nodded. "That's where we're heading. You can come with us in the chopper. Colley's about to start warming it up."

Tara turned to me. For a second, everything else fell away—the documents, the aliens, the fracture tearing at the edges of the world. She rose up on her toes and gave me a quick peck on the cheek, her lips warm against my skin.

"Be careful," she said.

Then she was gone, following Jake and Colley out the door. The chopper's rotors started their low thump outside, and in a few moments the sound faded into the night sky.

That left me alone in the ranch house with Vector, Sanderson, and Yuri Gagarin. Vector rubbed the back of his neck, looking irritated and exhausted.

"Rita's going to kill me if I don't get to the hospital soon. She's already texting me every five minutes."

Yuri gave a knowing chuckle. "Wives have a way of doing that. Even in zero gravity."

Before anyone could answer, the air in the room shifted again. That familiar electric prickle ran up my spine. Aeterna and Zephyrion appeared without fanfare, stepping out of a soft blue shimmer that folded in on itself and vanished.

No beam this time—just them, standing in the middle of the kitchen like they'd been invited to Sunday supper. Vector, Sanderson, and Yuri didn't look surprised. Not even a little. They simply made room at the table, and the five of them—three humans who'd once touched the impossible, and two beings who lived there—started talking in urgent voices.

Diagrams were unrolled. The orb was placed in the center. Frequencies were discussed. Plans were sketched on napkins. It was like watching two worlds finally sit down at the same table and get to work.

Aeterna eventually broke away from the group and crossed to me, her silver bodysuit catching the low lamplight, her too-large blue eyes soft yet serious. She took my hand and led me down the short hallway to the bedroom, where she helped me out of my shirt, then my boots, then the rest, her touch gentle and efficient.

When I was down to nothing, she guided me under the covers and tucked the blanket around me like I was a kid who'd had a long day. She didn't climb in beside me.

"I have work to do," she said quietly, "and you need sleep."

She leaned down, her lips brushing my forehead. Then she blew a soft breath across my face—something sweet and calming that smelled faintly of desert night and starlight. It went straight up my nose and into my blood like the gentlest drug in the universe.

The last thing I remember was her voice, soft as a lullaby, whispering, "Rest, Buck. The stars will still be there when you wake."

Then the world folded in on itself, warm and dark and safe, and I fell deeply, completely asleep.

CHAPTER 35

I awoke from the kind of sleep that felt earned after too many nights running on empty. My body didn't ache the way it should have after everything I'd been through—the climb, the shootout, the saucer ride, the whole damn cosmic mess.

Instead, I felt rested, clear-headed, almost revived. I lay there a minute staring at the ceiling beams, wondering what the hell had been in that cool breath Aeterna blew up my nose last night. Whatever it was, it worked better than any whiskey I'd ever had. I rolled out of bed and padded over to the window.

The morning was beautiful, the kind of high-desert dawn that makes you forget the world was trying to tear itself apart. The Sangre de Cristo Mountains stood sharp and proud against a sky so blue it hurt, their peaks already catching the first gold of sunrise.

A light breeze stirred the piñon and sagebrush, and for a second, everything felt almost normal. Almost. A hot shower washed the last of the desert dust and alien weirdness from my skin. Fresh jeans, a clean shirt, and boots polished enough to pass muster.

When I opened the bedroom door, the smell hit me like a warm hug—biscuits baking, grits simmering, the savory pull of gravy. My stomach growled. Pard was already there, tail thumping softly as Jake slipped him scraps from his plate.

Colley sat across from Jake, forking up his own breakfast and working on a glass of scotch like it was orange juice. Jake had one too, of course. They both glanced up when I walked in.

"Well, look who finally decided to join the living," Jake said, grinning around a mouthful of biscuit.

"You sleep all day or what?" Colley asked with a chuckle. "Still early, but damn, Buck, we were starting to think you'd joined the Sky People permanently."

I rubbed the back of my neck, still a little foggy. "The best sleep I've had in years. Something I could get used to."

Angie was at the stove, stirring a pot and flipping biscuits in a cast-iron skillet. She glanced over her shoulder with that easy smile of hers, a lacy blue apron tied over her clothes like she'd been cooking in this kitchen her whole life.

"Sorry, it's not Santa Fe fancy," she said. "No green chile or anything exotic. Just simple southern fare—grits and gravy, buttermilk biscuits. It's what I was raised on."

I pulled out a chair and dropped into it, the smell alone making my mouth water.

"Tell you a little secret," I said. "So was I, and I love it."

Angie's smile widened. "Good," she said.

She plated up a generous helping—creamy grits swimming in peppered gravy, two fat biscuits split and buttered—and set it in front of me.

"Where is everybody else?" I asked, already reaching for a fork.

Angie wiped her hands on the apron. "Relax. After breakfast, we'll fill you in."

I nodded, dug in, and for a few minutes the only sounds were forks on plates, Pard's happy little grunts under the table, and the low clink of Jake and Colley's glasses. Angie finally finished cleaning up the kitchen and joined us.

"Love your southern cooking," I said.

"It has been so long since I cooked, I was afraid I'd forgotten how," she said.

"Cross that one off your worry list. Jake said you've been busy working the phones. Any luck?"

"Not much. The President is a will-o'-the-wisp. Seems he can say or do just about anything, no matter how heinous or repulsive, and it doesn't matter."

He may be a crook, but he's the people's crook," Jake said. "His base loves him, and he can do no wrong."

"He's like a modern-day Robin Hood, stealing from the rich and giving to the poor," Angie said. "At least that's the perception he's trying to convey."

"And he's pretty damn successful at it," Jake said. "If someone says something he doesn't like, he calls it a lie created by his enemies to harm him."

Angie laughed. "If we'd done half of what he's gotten away with, we'd be serving twenty years to life in a maximum security prison."

"Then how the hell do you stop a person like that?" I asked.

"You don't," Angie said. "The President is bulletproof."

"What, then?" I asked.

"There's no cure for this particular disease, but we can control the symptoms," Jake said.

"Nullify the effects of the Chaotic Resonator, stop the bleed, and repair the damage," Angie said.

"And put a system of safeguards in place to counteract the next global disaster," Jake said.

"How exactly do we stop the bleed?" I asked. "Is that even doable?"

"The contents of the knapsack you and Tara found were a trove of valuable information," Angie said. "Specifications for a device, Codename Harmony Generator, created specifically to counteract the effects of the Chaotic Resonator."

"Wonderful," I said. "How long will it take to build one and put it to use?"

"Too long," Jake said. "But one already exists. The Harmony Generator prototype is at Area 51. Right where Vector left it."

"Good luck trying to get it out of there," I said. "The place is locked down tighter than Fort Knox."

"Maybe," Jake said. "Zephyrion thinks it's possible. Yuri, Kermit, and Vector are with him and Aeterna."

Jake nodded when I said, "In the saucer?"

I whistled and said, "What an episode of Cryptid Hunter that would make, set inside an alien spacecraft with actual aliens as tour guides."

Jake and Colley laughed. "Like that was ever going to happen," he said.

"Why are Vector, Kermit, and Yuri there?" I asked,

"Because everything they need to counteract the Chaotic Resonator is on that saucer," Jake said.

"Everything except the Harmony Generator," I said.

"And that's where you come in," Angie said.

"Oh? And how's that?" I asked.

"Zephyrion has asked for your help," Jake said.

"To do what?"

"Retrieve the Harmony Generator from Area 51," she said.

"Zephyrion is an agent in the Ophirian Intelligence Directorate, trained in counter-intelligence, infiltration, and martial arts. I'm just a washed-up rodeo cowboy," I said. "How am I supposed to help?"

"A cowboy with many talents," Jake said. "Zephyrion thinks you're the perfect person to help him."

"He does, does he?" I said.

"If you can infiltrate like you two-step, then you're a natural," Angie said with a wink.

"Okay," I said. "When do we begin this little caper?"

"Now," Jake said. "They're waiting to beam you up."

I blinked awake to a world that wasn't mine, and for a second I thought the mescal from last night had finally done me in. But this wasn't a dream haze or a desert mirage. The air buzzed with a living vibration, as if the Taos Hum had followed me into an alien flying saucer and decided to settle in my bones for good.

I was lying on something that felt like warm glass—smooth under my back, faintly pulsing with inner light. No sheets, no pillow, just that gentle give that made me think of a horse's flank after a long ride.

The walls curved into a perfect dome, not metal or plastic but something that looked carved from starlight itself—deep indigo shot through with veins of silver and faint gold that drifted like slow rivers.

The light emanated from everywhere and nowhere, soft and golden, casting no shadows but painting everything in a warm glow. It felt alive, as if everything were breathing with me.

I sat up slowly, my bare feet touching the floor. It was cool at first, then warmed to match my skin, as if it were saying hello.

The lab—if that's what you call a place like this—spread out in a wide circle. Consoles of crystal and light hovered without wires, their surfaces alive with shifting glyphs that looked a lot like the petroglyphs back in Chaco Canyon, only these moved, rearranging themselves in patterns too beautiful to be random.

In the center stood a long table of the same glowing material, covered with tools and devices I couldn't name—some humming softly, others projecting faint holographic maps that turned slowly in the air.

Vector—Randle—stood at one end of the table, his silver hair catching the ship's light like moonlight on water. Yuri paced beside him, the old cosmonaut's face calm but focused, his hands gesturing over a floating schematic that showed the Earth as a fragile blue marble wrapped in fractures of red light.

Kermit hunched over a smaller console, his fingers dancing across symbols that responded like old friends, the cosmic guitar case open beside him, the instrument itself humming in quiet harmony with the ship.

They were deep in it, voices low and urgent, already working the problem like men who'd been waiting their whole lives for this moment.

The Chaos Resonator was tearing holes in the world, and they were here to stitch them shut—once we brought back the one thing that could balance the scales.

Aeterna and Zephyrion waited for me near the far curve of the wall. Aeterna's silver bodysuit caught the ship's glow the way moonlight loves water, her too-large blue eyes steady on mine.

Zephyrion stood beside her, tall and regal in his matte-black suit, the silver glyphs on his forearms pulsing faintly like distant stars. They didn't speak at first. They just let me take it in—the ship, the lab, the weight of what we were about to do.

Then, Aeterna stepped closer, her hand brushing my arm, her touch warm and electric. The same comforting spark I remembered from the ranch house.

"This place is fascinating," I said. "Any chance for me to get a tour of the rest of the ship?"

"Less than zero," she said, her voice sliding soft into my mind. "This is the only part of our vessel you need to see."

"Fascinating," I said. "What's the plan?"

"Vector, Yuri, and Kermit will remain here and prepare the counter-harmonics. The Harmony Generator is the only device that can silence the Resonator, and you and Zephyrion must retrieve it."

"Angie says it's at Area 51."

"In a secure vault deep underground, guarded by layers of security."

"Sounds daunting," I said. "What's the plan?"

Zephyrion's onyx eyes met mine, calm and steady. "We go in from above. The ship will mask our approach. The rest... is up to us."

"Another secret entrance like the one on Sanderson's guitar shop?" I asked.

"Maybe," he said.

I looked past Aeterna and Zephyrion to the three men at the table—old warriors from two different worlds, already deep in their work. The lab's light wrapped around them like a blessing, the hum of the ship rising and falling like a heartbeat.

For the first time since this whole mess started, I felt something solid under my feet. Not hope exactly, but purpose. The kind that a cowboy feels when he knows the trail ahead is long, dangerous, and the only way home.

I rolled my shoulders, felt the weight of the mission settle on them, and gave Aeterna and Zephyrion a slow nod.

Zephyrion placed a hand on my shoulder. "Can I count on you?" he asked.

If he were capable of that facial expression, he would have

smiled when I said, "Hell, Zeph, let's climb on that bucking bronc and see if we can manage to hold on for eight seconds."

CHAPTER 36

The beam dropped us onto the roof like we'd been spat out by the desert itself. One second, I was standing in the saucer's glowing lab with Vector, Yuri, and Sanderson hunched over their consoles like old men trying to fix the end of the world. Next, my boots hit cold concrete under a black Nevada sky, and the wind slapped me hard enough to remind me I was still human.

Zephyrion landed beside me without a sound, his matte-black suit drinking in the starlight. The rooftop was flat, wide, and ugly—vent pipes, satellite dishes, and a single steel access door set into a low concrete blockhouse.

No lights. No cameras I could see. But I knew they were there. This was the single most secure building in Area 51, buried under layers of black-budget lies. If the rest of the base was a fortress, this place was the vault inside the vault.

"Uniforms," Zephyrion said, his voice sliding straight into my head the way Aeterna's did.

He opened a small silver case that hadn't been in his hands a second ago. Inside lay two crisp dark-blue guard uniforms, complete with patches, belts, and sidearms that looked a hell of a lot more advanced than anything the Air Force issued.

"Ophirian Intelligence Directorate issue. They will pass every visual and biometric scan."

I stripped down fast, the night air biting my skin, and pulled on the uniform. It fit like it had been tailored by someone who knew my measurements better than I did. The fabric was strange—light, flexible, and warm in all the right places.

The sidearm settled heavy on my hip. Zephyrion dressed in

one fluid motion, then handed me a flat black keycard and a palm-sized device that looked like a ruggedized phone.

"What is it?"

"The security key," he said. "And the navigator. Everything in this facility is clocked and computer-controlled. Think of it as a video game with real bullets."

He nodded when I said, "Video game?"

"We must check in at each waypoint within the allotted window, or the system flags us. Miss by thirty seconds and the alarms start. Miss by two minutes, and we fight our way out."

I turned the navigator over in my hand. Its screen glowed to life, showing a glowing 3D map of tunnels, elevators, and checkpoints. A green dot pulsed at our position on the roof. A red dot deep underground marked the vault.

"Seven minutes from the moment we secure the Harmony Generator," Zephyrion said. "That is the hard window. After that, every guard in the complex converges. No second chances."

"Seven minutes," I said, tasting the number like bad coffee. "Hell of a rodeo."

We moved to the access door. Zephyrion swiped the keycard. The lock clicked green. No alarms. We stepped into a dimly lit stairwell that smelled of ozone and cold metal.

Two flights down and we hit the first checkpoint—a small security desk manned by two guards in the same dark-blue uniforms we now wore. One was flipping through a tablet. The other was sipping coffee from a paper cup.

"Won't your appearance get us caught? I asked,

Zephyrion didn't hesitate. "Trust me when I tell you I'm not the only alien in the building."

He must not have been because he walked straight up like he owned the place and slid two falsified clearance cards across the desk—Ophirian Intelligence Directorate markings, complete with our photos and holographic seals that shimmered under the overhead lights.

"Routine maintenance sweep on sublevel four," he said, voice flat and official. "Priority Theta override."

The guard with the coffee barely glanced up. "IDs?"

We handed them over. The second guard ran them through a scanner. It beeped twice—green. He nodded and slid the navigator across the desk.

"Keep it on. System logs every check-in. You miss a waypoint by more than thirty seconds, and you're red-flagged."

I almost laughed. Thirty seconds. We were already living on borrowed time.

We took the elevator down. The doors closed with a soft hiss, and the car dropped fast enough to make my stomach float. Zephyrion's voice was calm in my head.

"First checkpoint in ninety seconds. Second in four minutes. We stay on schedule, or we die here."

The elevator opened onto a long corridor lit by recessed blue strips. Cameras tracked us from every angle. I kept my face neutral, shoulders squared, trying to look like a man who belonged. Zephyrion moved as if he were part of the architecture itself.

We hit the first waypoint—a small alcove with a wall-mounted scanner. I swiped the keycard. The navigator chimed once. Green. One minute forty seconds used.

"On pace," Zephyrion said in my head. "Next elevator in two minutes and thirty. Stay tight."

My pulse was hammering now. Every step felt like it was being counted by some cold machine buried under the desert. We passed two more guards who barely nodded. Zephyrion was right—Ophirians weren't the only non-humans working down here.

One guard had eyes that reflected light like a cat's. Another moved with an unnatural smoothness that screamed something not born on Earth. Nobody looked twice at me.

We reached the second elevator. Swipe. Navigator chime. Three minutes twelve seconds elapsed.

"Cutting it close," Zephyrion said. "Vault access is three levels down. One final checkpoint before the vault door. After that, we have exactly seven minutes to extract."

The elevator dropped again. When the doors opened, the

corridor was narrower, the lighting harsher. A single guard sat at a reinforced desk in front of a heavy blast door. Behind him, a wall of monitors showed every tunnel and elevator in the complex.

Zephyrion stepped forward with the same calm authority.

"Priority Theta maintenance on the Harmony Generator housing. Override code Delta-Nine-Zulu."

The guard scanned our cards. The machine beeped once—then paused. A yellow warning light flashed on the screen.

"Hold," the guard said, voice flat. "System shows a two-second lag on your last waypoint. Explain."

My heart tried to climb out of my throat. Zephyrion didn't miss a beat.

"Minor power fluctuation on sublevel two. We logged it. Check the maintenance queue."

The guard stared at the screen for what felt like forever. Then he grunted and waved us through.

"Make it quick. Vault is hot right now."

The blast door hissed open. We stepped into a short tunnel that ended at another reinforced door—this one thicker, heavier, with a biometric scanner and a physical key slot. Zephyrion swiped the card, pressed his palm to the plate, and the door slid aside with a deep mechanical thunk.

Inside was the vault. Small, brightly lit, and dead silent. In the center sat the Harmony Generator—smaller than I expected, a sleek silver cylinder about the size of a large duffel bag, covered in faint glowing glyphs that matched the ones on Zephyrion's suit. It hummed softly, a clean tone that cut straight through the Chaos Resonator's ugly vibration still echoing in my bones.

"Secure it," Zephyrion said.

I grabbed the handles. It was heavier than it looked, but manageable. Zephyrion sealed the case around it with a quick motion, then checked the navigator.

"Six minutes fifty-eight seconds remaining. We move."

We stepped back into the corridor, and the blast door closed behind us with a heavy thud. That's when everything went to hell. Alarms screamed to life. Red lights strobed down the corridor. A mechanical voice boomed from hidden speakers:

"Unauthorized access detected. All personnel to defensive stations. Lethal force authorized."

Zephyrion's voice snapped in my head. "They found the lag. We run."

We ran. The first guards appeared at the far end of the corridor, rifles up. Zephyrion moved like liquid shadow—smoke grenade in one hand, sidearm in the other. After he'd tossed the grenade, thick white smoke billowed out, cutting visibility to zero. I heard shouts, then the sharp crack of suppressed shots. Two guards dropped. We sprinted through the smoke, boots pounding.

Elevator. Swipe. Navigator screaming a thirty-second warning. We piled in, and the car shot upward. When the doors opened on the next level, three more guards were waiting. Zephyrion took the first down with a precise strike to the throat. I clubbed the second with the butt of my borrowed sidearm. The third got off a shot that burned past my ear like a hornet before Zephyrion put him down.

"Four minutes twelve seconds," Zephyrion said. "Stairwell. Now."

We hit the stairs running. Alarms howled. Boots thundered below us. I could hear the guards shouting coordinates, calling for backup, the mechanical voice repeating the same lethal warning on a loop.

Another checkpoint. Swipe. Navigator flashing red—fifteen seconds overdue. The door at the top of the stairs slammed shut and locked with a hydraulic hiss.

"We're fucked!" I said.

Zephyrion didn't reply to my distressed comment. Instead, he slapped a small silver disc onto the lock. It flared white-hot, and the door blew open with a muffled thump. We burst onto the roof, the night air cold and clean on our faces. The saucer was already hovering silently above the concrete, its beam reaching down like a lifeline.

"Fifty-three seconds," Zephyrion said.

Guards poured out of the stairwell behind us, weapons raised, shouting for us to freeze. I heard the click of safeties disengaging. The beam caught us, lifting us and the case off the roof just as the first shots cracked the air.

Bullets whined past, one clipping the case with a metallic ping. The saucer rose fast, the rooftop shrinking beneath us, the guards' shouts fading into the wind.

We'd made it, the beam depositing us back inside the saucer's lab, where Vector, Yuri, and Sanderson were waiting, their faces tight with tension. Aeterna and Zephyrion stepped out of the light beside me. I set the case down with shaking hands.

Zephyrion glanced at the timer on the navigator. It read zero plus 15. He allowed himself the slightest smile.

"We missed our mark," he said. "Want to try again?"

I grinned and said, "Hell, Zeph, get after it. As for me, I don't like video games with live bullets."

I let out a shaky breath and looked at the Harmony Generator resting on the deck between us. One down. One world left to save. The saucer hummed around us, already turning toward whatever came next. I glanced at Aeterna. She met my gaze, and for the first time since this whole thing started, I felt we might actually have a chance.

"Next stop," I said, voice rough but steady, "is wherever the hell we stop that Resonator from tearing the sky apart."

Zephyrion placed a hand on the case.

"Agreed," he said.

CHAPTER 37

Santa Fe smelled of victory and hot grease on the day of the rodeo. The high-desert sun beat down on the old adobe town as if trying to cook the whole place golden, and every street, plaza, and alley was packed shoulder to shoulder with people who'd come for blood, dust, and glory.

Cowboys in starched Wranglers and bright shirts swaggered past tourists in flip-flops and rodeo T-shirts. Kids waved foam fingers and spun around on their fathers' shoulders while country music blasted from every bar and food truck.

The air was thick with the smell of green chile roasting, frybread, mesquite smoke, and horse sweat. Flags snapped in the breeze, and the distant roar of the grandstand crowd rolled over the rooftops like thunder that hadn't quite decided to break.

I stood near the chutes with Dusty, both of us trying to look calm while Ran paced in a tight circle, his saddle bronc number pinned crooked on his back. The horse he'd drawn—Big Lou's meaner cousin, they called Diablo—was already slamming the chute rails hard enough to rattle the whole row.

Ran's face was pale under the brim of his hat. He kept flexing his riding hand like it might betray him.

Dusty leaned in close, voice low and steady. "Eyes on the horizon, babe. You feel him before he moves. Let your body remember the drills. You got this."

I clapped a hand on Ran's shoulder. "She's right. You're not riding that horse—you're dancing with him. Just like we practiced."

But Ran's eyes were wide, breath coming too fast. He looked at the chute where Diablo was throwing his head and snorting fire, and I could see the doubt creeping in. Dusty and I exchanged a quick glance. We were both worried. This wasn't just a ride anymore. It was everything Ran had left after the last few days of chaos.

The grandstand was full. Jake sat in the front row with Angie and Colley, all wearing cowboy hats and shades, looking like they'd bought half the merch tent. Tara sat beside them, chewing her thumbnail, her eyes locked on her brother.

Rita sat beside her, hands clasped tightly in her lap. Lily was there too, out of the hospital and wrapped in a bright woven shawl, her silver hair shining in the sun. She gave me a knowing nod across the arena, as if she already knew how this story ended. Anna and Elena were in the stands somewhere, though I hadn't spotted them yet. Only Randle was missing.

The announcer's voice boomed over the speakers, calling the next rider. Ran's name crackled out. He swallowed hard, stepped up to the chute, and started climbing. That's when I saw him. Randle came limping through the gate on his bad leg, moving faster than I'd ever seen him move.

His face was set, jaw tight, but there was something different in his eyes—something clear and steady that hadn't been there before. Dusty and I both froze. Ran looked up from the chute rail, his face going from pale to shocked.

Randle stopped right in front of his son, breathing hard from the walk. For a second, nobody said anything. Dusty and I braced ourselves, waiting for the lecture, the anger, the same old speech about broken bones and ruined lives. Instead, Randle put both hands on Ran's shoulders and looked him dead in the eye.

"I'm proud of you, son," he said, voice rough but clear. "Prouder than I've ever been in my life."

Ran blinked, stunned. "Dad," he said.

Randle leaned in closer, voice dropping low so only the three of us could hear.

"I got one bronc-busting secret I never told anybody. Not your mother. Not Lily. Definitely not another bronc rider."

He cupped his hand to Ran's ear and whispered something I

couldn't catch. Ran's eyes widened, then something clicked behind them—some old, buried instinct waking up.

Ran grinned and said, "Thanks, Dad."

Randle stepped back, clapped his son once on the shoulder, and gave him a nod.

"Now go ride that son of a bitch like you mean it."

Ran climbed into the chute. The gate man looked at him, waiting. Ran gave one sharp nod. The chute flew open. Diablo exploded out like a demon set loose from hell—twisting, kicking, sunfishing so hard the crowd let out a collective moan.

Everyone in the stands was already leaning forward, expecting the kid to eat dirt in the first two seconds. Ran's body whipped back and forth, but he stayed centered, his free hand high, his spurs working in perfect rhythm.

The horse bucked harder, trying to fling him into the sky, but Ran rode the storm like he'd been born inside it.

The eight-second horn blew.

Ran didn't just ride it out—he waited a full two beats after the whistle, sitting tall, then launched himself off Diablo's back in a clean dismount. He hit the dirt running, hat still on, and jogged toward the fence while the pickup men moved in.

The crowd lost its mind. People shot to their feet, screaming, stomping, waving hats. The announcer was hollering something about the ride of the day, but nobody could hear him over the roar.

Randle burst out of the gate faster than a man with a bad leg had any right to move. He was laughing—actually laughing—his face split wide open with joy as he met Ran halfway.

He grabbed his son in a crushing hug, both of them falling over in the dirt while the stands kept cheering like the roof was about to come off.

Dusty and I stood there, stunned, watching father and son hold on to each other like they'd both just won the world.

Tara was already climbing down from the stands, tears in her eyes, Rita and Lily right behind her. Jake and Colley were on their feet, hollering and clapping as if they'd just watched the final scene of the best movie ever made.

I felt something loosen in my chest, I hadn't even known was tied up tight. The loose ends weren't all tied yet—the Harmony Generator, the Resonator, the fracture still hanging over everything—but right here, right now, under that bright Santa Fe sun, one family had found its way back together.

And that felt like enough to start with. Randle looked over Ran's shoulder, caught my eye across the arena, and gave me the smallest nod. I nodded back.

Randle wasn't done, shouting to the crowd. "Did you folks just see what my son did? We're heading to the nearest bar where all the drinks are on me for the rest of the day, and everyone's invited."

Ran broke free from his father's bear hug, kissed his mom and grandma, and then climbed over the fence to find Dusty. He didn't have to go far.

The rodeo wasn't over, but for the first time in a long while, it felt like the ride might just turn out all right.

EPILOG

The bar was called The Rusty Spur, a massive open-air cantina on the edge of Santa Fe that looked as if someone had taken an old warehouse, a rodeo arena, and a honky-tonk and smashed them together under strings of colorful lights.

The night after the rodeo, it was packed wall-to-wall with winners, losers, cowboys, tourists, and everyone in between. Music thumped from a live band on a raised stage, boots stomped on the wide wooden dance floor, and the smell of spilled beer, mesquite ribs, and green chile hung thick in the warm desert air.

I sat at a long table near the edge of the chaos, nursing a cold Coors and watching Ran make the rounds with his shiny new championship belt buckled proudly over his Wranglers.

He was grinning ear to ear, still riding the high of that impossible eight-second ride. Dusty was right beside him, laughing loudly and showing off the buckle to anyone who'd look.

Jake and Colley were holding court at the far end of the table, spinning exaggerated tales about rougarous and chupacabras. Angie had to be in Tulsa and left town after the rodeo. Jake motioned for me.

"Everything okay?" I asked.

"Couldn't be better

"I thought you might be interested in the rest of the Cryptid Hunter shoot," he said.

"It crossed my mind," I said. "What next?"

"Hell, Buck, with all the atmospheric scenery footage and our interviews with Randle, Kermit, and Lily, we have more than enough for a dynamite episode. I'm calling it a wrap and sending the footage to editing."

"Where to next?" I asked.

"Don't know yet. Colley and I are heading for New Orleans tomorrow. Angie and Bradley kissed and made up, and she's coming with us."

"She's a keeper, but I guess you already know that," I said.

He grinned. "Without her, you, Colley, and Mama, I'd be a derelict on a Camp Street sidewalk."

"I don't think so," I said, "Seen Tara?"

I didn't know what it meant, but I didn't miss the knowing glance exchanged by Jake and Colley.

"She's here somewhere," he said.

Tara had been avoiding me all night—laughing with friends, dancing with strangers, always managing to stay on the opposite side of the room whenever I glanced her way. Every time our eyes met, she'd flash a quick smile and find somewhere else to be.

I was halfway through my second beer when Kermit Sanderson and Janelle Delgado walked in arm-in-arm, as if they'd been doing it their whole lives. Kermit looked ten years younger, his silver braid neat, an easy smile on his face.

Janelle was radiant beside him, her dark auburn hair loose for once, wearing a simple turquoise blouse and jeans. They hadn't stopped holding hands since they walked through the door. Kermit spotted us and steered Janelle over. The table quieted a little as they pulled up chairs.

"We did it," he said, voice low enough to stay under the music but loud enough for us to hear. "The Harmony Generator is online. We shut down the burn and reversed the worst of the damage. The fractures are sealing. Yuri's already gone back to wherever he usually lives—in secrecy, of course."

Jake leaned in, eyes sharp. "And the bad actors?"

"The Qataris were funding the operation," Kermit said, "but the radical German group—the Iron Order—was the real brains and the real threat. They wanted the Resonator for themselves. They're finished. Your pull with the F.B.I. worked, Jake. Most of them are already in custody or running for the hills. Major prison time coming their way."

Colley raised his glass. "To loose ends getting tied up tight."

We drank to that. Kermit and Janelle still hadn't let go of each other's hands. I watched them for a moment, the easy way they leaned into one another, and felt something loosen in my chest I hadn't realized was still knotted.

I must have been staring because Janelle noticed. She reached into her pocket, pulled out a worn business card, and slid it across the table to me. I turned it over. On the back, in Kermit's precise handwriting, were his phone number and the words: I love you, Janelle. Call me. You need your memories.

I looked up at her. "And?"

She smiled, soft and sure, the kind of smile that comes after you've made peace with the past.

"Kermit didn't leave me dangling."

Kermit squeezed her hand, and they both laughed quietly, the sound warm and private amid the noise of the bar.

The party rolled on around us—Ran showing off his belt again, Dusty dragging him onto the dance floor, Jake and Colley arguing over who told the better version of the chopper rescue story. Laughter, music, the clink of glasses.

For the first time in days, it felt like we could breathe. Then a big cowboy—about Tara's age, blond, broad as a barn door—came out of nowhere. He didn't say a word. He just hauled back and sucker-punched me square in the jaw.

I hit the floor hard, stars exploding behind my eyes. The guy straddled me before I could get my bearings, his finger jabbing down into my face.

"Tara's my girl," he said. "Got that?"

The bar noise dimmed for a second. Then Tara stepped out of the crowd. She didn't look angry. She looked… relieved. She stepped forward and planted a deliberate kiss on the big blond cowboy's mouth.

When she pulled back, she glanced down at me—still flat on the floor, rubbing my jaw—and mouthed one silent word

"Sorry."

Then she took the cowboy's hand, and they walked off together into the crowd.

Ran appeared a second later, offering me a hand up. I took it, wincing as I got to my feet.

"Sam Barnett," he said, clapping me on the back. "Tara's squeeze since they were in high school. Looks like the flame's still burning."

I worked my jaw, tasting blood, and managed a crooked grin. "Figures."

The party kept rolling. A few minutes later, someone tapped my shoulder. I turned, ready for round two, but it was Anna Luna standing there, chestnut hair loose, those big brown eyes sparkling with amusement.

"Sore jaw?" she asked.

"Something like that," I said, still rubbing it.

"She was too young for you, Cowboy," Anna said, tilting her head toward where Tara had disappeared with Sam.

"Exactly what I was going to tell her," I said.

"Liar," she said, but she was laughing.

I grinned, the pain in my jaw already fading. "I'm not lying when I say you're the prettiest woman in Santa Fe. Buy you a beer?"

Anna's smile widened. She looped her arm through mine without hesitation.

"Thought you'd never ask, cowboy."

We walked toward the bar together, the music swelling around us, the lights bright, the night young. Behind us, the celebration rolled on—Ran showing off his belt, Dusty whooping on the dance floor, Jake and Colley still telling tales, and Kermit and Janelle holding hands as if they'd never let go.

The Resonator was silenced. The bleed was closing. The bad actors were finished. Yuri was safe. Lily was recovering. And Tara… well, Tara had found her own way forward.

As for me? I looked down at Anna's arm linked with mine and felt something settle into place that had been loose for a long time.

The rodeo was over, the ride wild, dangerous, and more than a little impossible. But damn if it hadn't ended exactly as it was supposed to.

I tipped my hat to the bartender and ordered two cold ones. "Make 'em tall," I said. "We've earned it."

Anna laughed, leaned her head against my shoulder, and the night kept spinning—bright, loud, and full of promise.

End

BOOK NOTES

Adobe Moon is the fifth book in my Paranormal Cowboy Series, featuring Buck McDivit, a soldier of fortune turned Cryptid Hunter. The high plains of New Mexico served as an ideal setting for this fusion of science fiction, the supernatural, and Buck's brand of rugged adventure. I hope you found as much thrill in reading it as I did in writing it.

Fans of the *Paranormal Cowboy Series* might also enjoy my *French Quarter Mystery Series* and the moody, haunted streets of New Orleans, where my primary character, Wyatt Thomas, reigns as a private investigator, and my *Oyster Bay Mystery Series* featuring a cast of interesting characters who live on a supernatural Louisiana island located about fifty miles from New Orleans.

To my readers, thank you. Your support breathes life into my stories, keeping them from fading like morning fog over a forgotten lawn. Without you, my words would vanish into the Great Unknown. Here's to shared adventures and the stories yet to come.

ABOUT THE AUTHOR

Eric Wilder is an American author known for his gripping mystery novels set in New Orleans. He was born and raised in Louisiana, where he discovered his love for storytelling at a young age. After completing his education, Wilder spent several years in the oil and gas industry before pursuing a career as a writer.

Wilder's breakthrough came with the publication of Big Easy, which introduced readers to his signature blend of suspense, action, and local color. The book instantly succeeded, drawing critical acclaim and a devoted following. Wilder followed up with a collection of thrillers set in the heart of New Orleans.

Wilder's writing is characterized by his deep knowledge of the city and its unique culture and his skillful use of suspense and plot twists to keep readers on the edge of their seats. His books have been praised for their authenticity, vivid descriptions, and compelling characters.

Today, Eric Wilder is a respected author with a loyal fan base and a reputation for delivering top-notch thrillers that transport readers to the heart of New Orleans.

Wilder is the author of twenty-eight novels, several cookbooks, many short stories, and Murder Etouffee, a book that defies classification. His series features characters who often find themselves involved in the paranormal.

Eric Wilder lives in Oklahoma near historic Route 66 with his two dogs, Moe and Buddy.

OTHER BOOKS BY ERIC WILDER

Of Love and Magic
Diamonds in the Rough
Ben's Magical Midnight Garden

Anthologies and Cookbooks

Murder Etouffée – out of print
Over the Rainbow – out of print
Lily's Little Cajun Cookbook

ERIC'S LINKS

Twitter: EricWilderOk
Blog: Murky Bayou Blogspot
Blog: Eric Wilder Blogspot
Facebook: Louisiana Mystery Writer
Instagram: Louisiana Mystery Writer
Website: Eric Wilder Books

www.ingramcontent.com/pod-product-compliance
Lightning Source LLC
LaVergne TN
LVHW030918080826
845145LV00013B/2945

* 9 7 8 1 9 4 6 5 7 6 2 9 3 *